T0385306

Once Was Willem

ONCE WAS WILLEM

M.R. CAREY

orbit

orbit-books.co.uk

ORBIT

First published in hardback in Great Britain in 2025 by Orbit
1 3 5 7 9 10 8 6 4 2

A CIP catalogue record for this book is available from the British Library.

HB 978-0-356-51944-9
C format 978-0-356-51945-6

Typeset in Bembo 11.25/15 pt by Palimpsest Book Production Limited,
Falkirk, Stirlingshire
Printed and bound in Great Britain by Clays Ltd, Elcograf, S.p.A.

Papers used by Orbit are from well-managed forests and other responsible sources.

Orbit	The authorised representative
An imprint of	in the EEA is
Little, Brown Book Group	Hachette Ireland
Carmelite House	8 Castlecourt Centre
50 Victoria Embankment	Dublin 15, D15 XTP3, Ireland
London EC4Y 0DZ	(email: info@hbgi.ie)

An Hachette UK Company
www.hachette.co.uk

orbit-books.co.uk

For Pauline, my big sister, remembered with love

A Prologue or Prefatory Declaration by me, Once-Was-Willem

ell a day!

My fingers are black with ink and my head aches as if it is about to burst at the seams like an over-stuffed flour sack, but this treatise at last is ended. I lean back from my labour and I draw breath, as God Himself did on the seventh day. His work was great and mine is small, but all makings of the mind and heart are sacred and this that you hold – good or bad as you may account it – is no exception.

The words that follow are true. I set my hand to them. I would have set my seal too except I do not have one. You will find in these pages a full and circumstantial account of all the things that passed in Cosham village and in the fiefdom of Pennick in the year of our Lord 1152. A word of warning: these events were monstrous and terrible and I have not shrunk from any part of them. The horror, the foulness, the pain and the pity: all are here without varnish. I felt I owed it to the dead, and to those for whom the blessing of death will never come, to chronicle as plainly as I could their doings and their undoings.

Ah, you will say, Pennick! It is like enough for dread things to come out of that quarter. And it is true that the land I call my

1

home, for all its beauty, was ever a place with a grim reputation. The forests of the Chase are said to be home to nixies and boggarts. On the road that leads under Great Chell, benighted wayfarers claim to have heard bears and wolves address each other in human speech. There is a common belief, passed down through many generations, that Pennick Castle houses an unquiet ghost of terrible and malign power. These rumours I can attest are not unfounded; indeed, as you will see, they fall short of the truth by a long way.

As for what came to be called the curse of Cosham, that was a later thing. It did not come until the summer of my twelfth year. Still, I can and do confirm the particulars of it. The villagers of Cosham failed in their duty to God and man, and a great evil fell on them thereafter. Perhaps those two things were not enchained one to another, but were entirely separate. It was a dark time. Unnatural things walked the land (you may trust me on this, for I was one of them). There was enough misfortune abroad for all to take their share.

You might think me a doubtful witness of things that passed when I was still a child, but I assure you again that my word is good. Since I died and then was dug up out of the ground to live again (which I will come to in its place) my mind has had a clarity it never knew erewhile. Every moment I have lived stands before me now, as soldiers stand when their captain bids them rise and rally, ready to answer whatever they are tasked withal.

Gird yourself, therefore. I speak of monsters and magic, battle and bloodletting, and the crimes of desperate men. I speak also of secret things, of that which lies beneath us and that which impends above. By the time you come to the end of this account you will know the truth of your own life and death, the path laid out for your immortal soul, your origin and your inevitable end.

You will not thank me.

I

Which tells of the fall of Robert Carne and the sacking of Pennick

leven hundred and some years after the death of Christ, in the kingdom that had but recently begun to call itself England, there was a time of great disorder and misrule. Old king Henry, the first of that name, had died. The throne stood empty, and half a dozen powers had declared an interest in it. Invading armies trudged hither and thither across the land, pillaging as they went.

In Cosham, north of Trent, where I dwelled at that time along with my mother and my father, we understood very little of the causes of these things, though we surely felt their effects. The laws broke down in those years. Christ and His saints, it was said, had all fallen asleep. Many battles were fought, many towns and villages burned; the peasants that fled from the towns and villages had nowhere now to dwell and no way of earning their keep. The greatest number of them starved, but there were some – and not a few – that turned thief or cut-throat. They had a simple choice, after all: if they could not earn an honest living, they must either surrender up their lives or set aside their honesty.

This was already a bad thing. With thieves abroad the bands of amity begin to fray, setting neighbour against neighbour. People were afraid now to stir from their houses lest they be set upon by footpads, and none dared to take the public roads after dark. But worse was to come. The thieves began to find each other and to league together. You can lock your door against a robber, but not against an army.

Cosham village was part of the fiefdom of Pennick, which belonged to the baron Robert Carne. Pennick in those days stretched from Cauldon almost to Thorn's Dyke. It was goodly land too, blessed by the Trent and Erren rivers with such bounty as you cannot imagine. Upwards and eastwards from the Erren rose the forests and hills of Pennick Chase, where the baron had leave from the king to hunt deer and draw timber from October to February. But in the time of which I speak this royal lease was not worth a fart in a cupped hand. The forests of the Chase had filled up with brigands, who slaughtered and cooked what meat they liked.

These rogues were all of one household, and they had a leader whose name was Maglan Horvath. Nobody seemed to know where this man had come from. Neither his given nor his family name rang like English coin. It was said that he had come into the realm as the captain of a Norman raiding party, but then had been stripped of his position and cut loose on account of some egregious misdeed.

At any event Horvath was a bold-faced villain and a scourge on the public weal. He made the woods of Pennick his home and his fastness, but from there he went where he liked. Some forty of his followers had raided the town of Burslem in search of food and treasure and left the place as bare as a plucked chicken. They had even emptied out the kitchen and pantry at the abbey and haled six basket-loads of fish from the father abbot's trout pond, for these scofflaws saw all the world as their banquet and ate with an indiscriminate appetite.

Such offences could not go unchallenged. Robert Carne rode out from his hold at Pennick to clear the fiefdom of all that unruly company. At first they could not even find Horvath, the woods of the Chase being both deep and wide. Then they came across a dozen ragged men dressing a freshly slain deer – all brazen, full

4

on the forest road. The brigands dropped their prey and ran head-long into the trees. Robert gave chase, hallooing his men through denser and denser thickets until finally they came into a clearing of wide extent.

It was an ambush. As soon as Robert and his followers broke from cover they were assailed with arrows and slingshot stones from all sides. The rogues they had been pursuing now turned in their tracks, took out knives and cudgels and engaged with them, while others harried them from behind.

The knives and cudgels were no great matter, but the bowmen in the trees were altogether more concerning. Robert saw at once that he and his cohort stood in great peril. He led a retreat, turning in his tracks and carving his way through the brigands who had hoped to pen him in. Still he lost full two-and-twenty of his tally and was himself bloodied. He limped back to Pennick Castle on the arm of his eldest son, Geoffrey, defeated and shamed.

This Pennick Castle was not the stone keep that stands now. It was a much simpler thing. The fortifying wall was really no more than a stout wooden fence with a single gate. A tall mound or motte stood within, that touched against the part of the fence furthest from the gate. Robert Carne and his family lived in a donjon built on top of the mound, while his soldiery and servants for the most part were accommodated in longhouses or smaller buildings of wood and roughcast stone in the bailey yard at the mound's foot. More than a hundred souls resided there – though that number was now considerably reduced.

Robert felt the sting of this rout very keenly. He was meant to keep the law within his own fief, and he had been humbled by a common rabble. Perhaps he felt the loss of his men, too. I cannot tell. Nobles are wont to look at such things differently than most, and I would not presume to sound their consciences.

At any rate, Robert decided to raise a general levy, that the Normans call *arrière-ban*. Such a levy would bring under his flag all the men of the fief old enough to have beards on their faces – a formidable force, at least in numbers. True, they would not know how to fight and would surely take much harm, but Robert had good hope that the sight of such a host would be enough to persuade Maglan Horvath to quit the woods and find himself a quieter place to bide in.

Acting on this plan, Robert sent messengers that same day to all the settlements within his fief to bid their menfolk equip and ready themselves. He would ride through the farms and villages himself on the morrow morn and gather the muster, then forthwith back to the woods to bring Maglan Horvath to a reckoning.

Robert retired early to his chamber that night, tired out by his labours but greatly solaced by the quick and bold decision he had made. His lady, Isobel, went with him, but his son Geoffrey was taken by the day's events in quite another way. He found he could not sleep at all, and so stayed up gaming and drinking, at first with his brothers Hal and Martin and then with some among the men-at-arms. He was still awake at the second change of the watch, when a great commotion was heard at the gate. Someone was hammering on it from the outside, and the blows were hard enough to make it shake and lean in on its hinges.

Geoffrey ordered those on watch to sound the tocsin and to man the standfasts on either side of the gate. Whoever was down there needed to be repulsed before they broke the gate open. The rest of the guard came stumbling from their beds, some with boots and some without, strapping on their swords as they came. The first to arrive hurried up onto the standfasts, while the rest lined up in front of the gate to be ready if it fell.

As they stood there rubbing their eyes and girding up their spirits, Maglan Horvath attacked – but not through the gate. Instead a volley of arrows was launched at the men-at-arms from the very quarter from which they had just come. Six or seven went down before they even knew they were imperilled. They turned to find an armed host coming on them from behind, from within the keep. It was the self-same host they had met in the woods the day before, and the memory of that first encounter, still all fresh and sore, gravelled their spirits.

Horvath had not taken Robert Carne's invasion of his woodland court well, even though he had come out best in the encounter. He feared a renewed assault – rightly, as things fell out – and had decided not to wait for it. But he was not so foolish as to attack a fortress at its best defended point. All the noise and banging at the gate was partly to bring the defenders together in the wrong place and partly to mask the sound of his real efforts.

Horvath had suborned a man, one Hugh Catspole, who had been cashiered out of Carne's household for being drunk when he was needed sober. Catspole told Horvath of a failed assault on Pennick Castle shortly after it was built. The Danes were come to beard Bastard William in the north, and since Pennick lay full in their way they had tried their best to burn it down. They had not managed it, but there was a place at the rear of the stockade wall that had been first torched and then breached. When the time came to repair the ruined part, new posts were driven in all along that length. The posts were sturdy enough, but the holes in which they sat had not been dug deep enough. Robert Carne's father, also named Robert, had decided to buttress the weakened stretch, but the buttresses were placed to counter an enemy pushing inwards.

Horvath had his men throw weighted ropes up onto the top of the fence and – once they caught and held – had used harnessed oxen to pull the posts out of true. At length the stockade had sagged outwards far enough at that one point to allow Horvath's brigands to squeeze through the gap.

So now they were come upon the castle's defenders from within their own walls, surprising them before they were yet ready for the fight.

The front ranks of the raiding party were composed only of longbowmen, who loosed their shafts as they advanced. At such a distance the arrows bedded themselves in the flesh of the startled men-at-arms so deeply that the fletches barely stood proud. Then the archers retreated quickly to either side and drew again, aiming now at the men up on the standfasts, what time their comrades with swords and axes ran upon the startled defenders on the ground.

7

After that all plans were moot and all was blood and chaos. The raiders seemed to have the advantage in number but Robert's men-at-arms were more seasoned and better trained. They recovered quickly from their shock and went at the invading brigands with a will. Their intention was to carve a way through to the donjon, where they expected their lord to appear at the head of his own retinue.

But Robert did not appear – and something else stepped into their path. The something else stood on two legs like a man, but it was bigger than any man that ever walked. It was an *ulfeðnar*, a wolf-brother, though this one seemed much more bear than wolf. He had a bear's pelt, long and shaggy and of so light a brown that it seemed in the dim and uncertain light to shine like gold. His arms were as thick as tree trunks, and at the end of each arm was a clutch of claws curved like reapers' sickles. With those claws the beast-man proceeded to do the thing that reapers do.

Seeing this awful apparition, the men-at-arms were unmanned. Some few fought still with courage and discipline, engaging the *ulfeðnar* and forcing him back with their swords. But the greater part of the cohort fled across the bailey yard to the steps that led up the side of the mound to the donjon's door. This was just as Horvath had hoped, and indeed was the main reason he had sent his bear-man into the fray. The steps being long and the mound steep, the men as they climbed were an easy target for Horvath's archers, who had hung back all this time and waited for their moment. Only a few defenders reached the top of the mound and the donjon's door.

They found the door barred against them. Robert Carne's spirits had been sapped by the previous day's failures, and he had no stomach to fight. He hoped to weather the raid within the donjon's walls, and then emerge again once Horvath had taken such grain and cattle and vengeance as he desired.

Exposed on the mound's flat top, the few men-at-arms that were left saw their friends below eviscerated by the beast-man, while they themselves were picked off one by one by Horvath's longbowmen. They would have fought bravely, but there was nobody to fight. They fell and died with their backs against their master's barred and bolted portal.

Horvath had now the run of the whole castle, barring only the donjon itself. He called his beast-man to him. The *ulfeðnar* was all over bloody, but most of the blood was not his own. His appearance was so frightening that the fighters who engaged him had fought with only half their hearts and swung with less than half their strength. The few cuts he had received were shallow.

The *ulfeðnar*'s name was Kel, and he had come into England with the Danes when Swein Astridsson pressed his claim against William of Normandy. He was (as his two-footed stance and slope-shouldered shape bore witness) a bear-man rather than a wolf-man, but there was no name for such a thing. We will have much to do with him later in our story, and with his sister Anna, who was stranger still than him.

For now it is enough to say that Kel allied with Maglan Horvath not out of any great liking or loyalty towards the man but out of a sense of what was needful and good. He was of the woods and hills, and Pennick's woods and hills in particular he had loved from the first moment he came into them. He had heard strange silences there, and he had observed how even when the wind was high the trees sometimes stood still as if it had not touched them. He approved of Horvath only because Horvath's coming into the margins of the woods had deterred anyone else from passing through into their deepest heart. Then too, Horvath had flattered Kel with gifts and with respect, treating him as an equal when most men treated him as a monster.

Now Horvath did so again, offering Kel first pick from the spoils of the dead and asking his advice on how the donjon might be taken. He hoped that Kel might know a trick or two from his days as a Danish reaver.

"Look," Kel said, pointing. "Yonder is the castle's well. The sweetest water for ten leagues, or so I've heard."

"And what of that?" asked Horvath.

9

"Why, it's out here," Kel said, "in the open yard, where Carne and his men can't get at it. They won't last out any kind of a siege without good water to drink, be their storehouses never so full."

"Aye," Horvath said, "but there might be a second well inside the donjon walls, might there not?"

"Aye, but there isn't."

"You know this for a truth?"

Kel shrugged his massive shoulders. "When Bastard William built these fortresses he built them quickly — to hold the north against my old master, Swein, and Greybeard Harald, and any Saxons hereabouts who were emboldened by them. The case was somewhat urgent, and more times than not they decided that digging one well was labour enough.

"But this time the decision was made for them. That mound the donjon stands on, full forty ells high, is not piled and packed earth but rock as firm as granite, with a great cavern underneath it. My life as gage, master, there's no well in that donjon. You may wait them out. Three days will see an end of the matter."

Horvath considered this plan, and though it seemed sound enough he decided against it. "I like not to sit here so long," he said. "Anyone might come on us while we wait. It's best to settle this suddenly."

"Well then," Kel said, "if suddenness is your aim, do you take up one of those great posts where we came in through the stockade wall. They're set shallow, as you found, so it won't take long to dig one out. Carry it up to the top of the mound and use it as a ram to break open the gates of the donjon. They'll give way, late or soon, if you keep at it. You'll lose a fair few men doing it, though, for there'll be archers at those embrasures firing down on you the while. If you had a mage in your company, you could raise a great wind and blow their arrows off their course, but you've none so you'll have to abide the insult."

The arrows did not trouble Horvath a whit, since he had no intention of coming himself within their reach. As for the loss of a few men, well, he knew his followers to be for the most part the vilest of rogues. Come feast or famine, rogues are never in short supply.

He gave order, and the thing was done. It took the best part of three hours' hammering, but the defenders' arrows ran out after the first hour and after that it went easier. At the last moment, when the gates were already hanging off their hinges and must surely fall at the next blow or the one after that, Robert Carne offered surrender. He was prepared, he said, to give order that his men-at-arms should lay down their swords and spare further blood-shed. In exchange for this promise he asked for assurances that the men would be allowed safe passage out of the castle, and that whatever befell his own person, his wife and sons would be allowed to go forth without hurt.

Horvath gave his word freely – and kept it partially. He had no need or desire to slaughter the men-at-arms. He offered any that wished to stay a place in his company, and there were more than a few that took that offer. But to Robert and his family he showed no mercy. The baron, his three sons and the Lady Isobel were put to the sword. The bloodletting was swift and merciless, and the bodies afterwards were cast onto the midden behind the donjon wall to stink in the open air.

It was not that Horvath loved killing for its own sake. It was rather the opposite. He preferred when he could to get his way through indirection and to maintain his place through judicious threat. But he knew in this case that if he gave the baron leave to pass he would only have to deal with him all over again a few months down the road when he had resupplied. The same argument went for the sons, who were bound to make every kind of nuisance of themselves when they were come of age. The lady's death he did not directly order, but he did not forbid it and was not surprised when he learned that it had come to pass. Taking all things into account he thought it was probably for the best.

Now we come to the nub of it, and the seed of all that passed later. Horvath had no reason to linger in the castle, his purpose there being won, but he did not leave. Even in that short tarrying he had found there were many easements to be had in Pennick's walls whose absence he had long missed. The barrack room and sundry other outbuildings provided space for all his men to sleep under a roof, which with winter coming on was no small thing. He himself could now remove to the donjon, which offered even greater comfort. There were besides two dozen pigs and more than a hundred chickens, fifty sacks of flour fresh from the mill along with eighty sacks of wheat not yet ground. There was also the stockade wall, for all that it was in need of repair: a wall like that would fend off a great many vexations.

Horvath had only come to Pennick Castle to remove a thorn from his side, but now that he was here it seemed to him that only an idiot would leave again.

And what was a man who lived in a castle? Why, he was a lord. True, the king had not sworn and sealed him such, but the king was far away and had other matters on his mind. Things being as they were, it was like to be a long time before anyone came from London to see what was tiding up north of the Trent river.

Horvath made up his mind to it, and was well content. He had been a soldier, then a robber. Now he would be a baron, and let any man who said he was none come armed for a sharp answer.

II

Which explains the curse of Cosham and whence it came

have run ahead of myself and must now turn and go back. I have told you that Robert Carne, after his first clash with Horvath in Pennick woods, had decided to raise a levy. I have said too that he dispatched a messenger to tell his tenants in the villages round about what he required of them. The messenger set out in the late afternoon of that day, when the men of the baron's household were binding their wounds up in the castle and Horvath's brigands were moving all unseen towards them.

I remember his coming into Cosham village, which was the first stop along his way. He was a sallow-faced, ill-humoured man, wearing a tabard of green and yellow – Robert's colours – over a tunic and breeches of coarse grey wool. His name was Joseph Payne, and he was himself a man of Cosham but preferred to forget that fact now he was somewhat risen in the world. He stood in our main street and rang his bell until the people of the village – myself the least among them – paused from their labours and gathered to hear him.

Payne told them that his master was calling on them under *arrière-ban*. All men between the ages of fifteen and fifty were to present themselves at the door of the kirk the morrow morn and

13

wait on Lord Carne's arriving there with his company. Thereupon they would swear allegiance and be impressed, or else stand proscribed traitors and be sent from the land. Oyez, all oyez, for such was the lord's declaring.

There was a great clamour raised, with many begging to know what this levy was for, but Payne had a long way to go before dark. He did not linger to explain himself. With a final adjuration to the men of Cosham to be no strangers to their duty, he took himself away to the next village.

My mother wept that night, and my father did his best to smile past his sickened heart and comfort her. The great wars that had already been fought in the north, going back past the memory of any wight living, had grazed Cosham in passing as an arrow's head might graze a leaf on its way to the stag's heart that is its target. The very flimsiness of the leaf makes it bend out of an arrow's path, and so it had been with Cosham up to now. It was too small and weak for anyone to covet it, too far from a main road to be useful as a base, too poor and bald to merit an army's sacking it. A few had perished here and there, but mostly by the accidents of lawlessness I have already mentioned.

Now it seemed a war of sorts had come to Cosham, and those who lived there found they had but little stomach for it. My father, Jon Turling, was a farmer born of farmers. He had never hefted any weapon more formidable than a mattock, and his only enemies were the crows that ate his seedlings. He could not imagine himself making mêlée. In truth, when he tried to imagine a battlefield, he only saw one of his own fields with angry men standing in its neat furrows. No matter what enemy this levy was raised against, he saw but little chance that he would prove a brave or competent soldier. More likely he would die and his farm would go to his sister Mary's husband, leaving his wife and son to walk the roads.

But the bloody battle that haunted Jon's sleep that night never came to pass. When the sun raised its head over the horizon he climbed all unwilling from his bed, kissed my mother goodbye and went to join the men and boys gathered in a sullen group at the kirk's door, waiting to add themselves to Lord Carne's column when it passed through the village.

Matthew Theakston, as the foremost man in the village, took his place at the head of this company. Theakston called himself bailiff after the Norman fashion but was in plain fact a farmer like anyone else, only with leave to speak to the castle on the village's behalf. Parson Lebone came out to bless them all, asperging them with holy water – a blessing that was not entirely welcome in the chill dawn air.

Just as they were about to set out on their journey, one of the youngest boys present cried out and pointed. Another man was come into the village, covered all over with mud, staggering and stumbling like one in the very last of his strength. They thought at first that this must be another messenger. Then when he was closer they realised from the richness of his dress that he was something more. Finally the parson recognised him. He called out, "Good my lord, what has happened to you?" and ran to give the man succour.

He was not quick enough. The newcomer swooned and fell, pitching face forward into the filth of the street.

"It's Geoffrey!" Parson Lebone declared to the men who were watching all astonished. "It's Lord Carne's firstborn, Geoffrey. He's taken hurt!" They all hastened then to help, carrying the insensate young man into the kirk where they laid him down on a bench. My father, at the parson's hest, ran to fetch water. The rest stood back but did not leave. They wanted to know what this meant.

Geoffrey Carne was in no wise able to tell them. He was wounded, as Parson Lebone had said. The broken shaft of an arrow was in his shoulder, and his pate had been laid open at the crown. How he had stayed upright so long with such injuries it was impossible to tell. Alan the sexton, the oldest man there, gave as his opinion that only God's grace could explain it. But now, being here, Geoffrey was fallen into a sleep so deep it was like the sleep of the grave.

"Well," Matthew Theakston said, "leave him lie. Someone fetch

Marlie Scour to tend to him. I'll to the castle and tell Lord Robert his son is hurt, belike by vagabond men who overtook him on the road."

"And stole his horse," another man added. "For surely he didn't mean to come all the way to Cosham on his two feet."

Parson Lebone was pondering all this while. "Go lightly, Matthew," he advised. "I like not the look of this. After the message that came last night, it makes a man wonder what might be towards."

"How does the one thing bear on the other?" Theakston asked, annoyed as he oftentimes was when some other wight seemed to be thinking quicker than him or talking louder.

"Belike it doesn't," Lebone said mildly. "But if it does, there may be more to this story than footpads. If I were you, I'd not venture all the way to the castle alone. I'd take some stout souls with you."

Theakston did not like to be advised, any more than he liked to be gainsaid, but he saw the sense of this and yielded with as much grace as he could. In the end five men went – that was Theakston himself, Jem Makepeace and my father that were the only other yardlanders in the village, along with Saul Randel the blacksmith and his brother Brian who were as big as two houses with muscles like marrows thrust into a sack.

They made their way to Pennick, taking narrow paths and bridleways in case there were robbers on the high road. When they got there they saw no sign at first of anything amiss, but then Saul noticed that there was a great seethe of crows circling and settling where the rear of the stockade wall met the base of the castle's motte.

Had Parson Lebone not spoken up with his warning they might have gone straightway to the gate and sued to be admitted. As it was, and with growing presentiments, they went to see what those crows were about. They found a great horror. The bodies of the castle's defenders and of the lord and his family had all been thrown in a heap, after first being stripped of anything about them that might have value. The men-at-arms had no boots, no helms, no weapons or tackle. The lord had no cloak, his lady no jewels. They

16

none of them had any eyes either, for the crows had already been at table.

Shouts and laughter from within the stockade made it clear that the castle was occupied. The goodmen of Cosham had no great desire to meet the new residents, so they took themselves away with all haste.

On the road they met with small groups of men, one after another. These were the musters from the further villages, coming to the castle to answer Lord Carne's call since he had not come to them as was promised. On being told by my father and his companions what awaited them, these men without exception turned around and went quickly home again, convinced with good reason that the action they had been summoned to join had already been fought and lost.

Back in Cosham, Matthew and his companions found the whole village gathered at the church door waiting anxiously for news. When they learned that the castle had fallen they were filled with dismay. They did not dream that Maglan Horvath, for all his evil reputation, could have done such a thing. Robbers took purses, not castles! The general opinion was that Empress Matilda's armies, long abroad in the south, had come northward at long last, though some thought it might be the Danes returned for more spoils.

Whoever it might be, they all agreed that they wanted not the smallest part of it. Though Lord Robert's edict of *arrière-ban* was still in force, and obliged them by direct effect to defend the fief against attack, they did not see what they could be expected to do against a force large enough and fierce enough to take a well-defended fortress.

"Belike if it's Empress Matilda she won't stay long," Saul Randel ventured. "She would only have sacked the castle if she was going further north and didn't want enemies standing at her back. There's nothing weighty enough in Pennick to make her tarry."

"And if it's Danes," said his brother, "they'll go away again out of the country as soon as someone pays them to do it. We need to keep our heads down or else it's us that will abide the payment!"

17

"What of Geoffrey, though?" my father asked.

Geoffrey Carne was then in the rectory, a single room behind the kirk which Parson Lebone shared with a cat named Origen and seventeen books that he said were Scripture. In case a cat and seventeen books seems less than enough to fill a house, he had thereunto a table no bigger than a lady's kerchief, a joint stool with three uneven legs and a bed box with its own mattress. Geoffrey had been laid out on the latter and a woman named Marlie Scour had been sent in to tend to him. Marlie was Cosham's burg-rune, which is to say she knew how to clean and set a wound, how to bind a flux or allay a fever. She was Cosham's midwife, and also its healer, and as is ever the way with such women, whenever she was not being desperately sought after for her skills she was being whispered against as a witch.

At all roads, Marlie had done her best to tend to the young lord's hurts and make him comfortable. He still had not recovered from his faint, so not a word had come from his mouth about what he had seen and suffered in the castle's sacking. Matthew Theakston was all for waking him and questioning him, but the parson would not have it. "Those are not trivial wounds he's taken," he pointed out. "And he'll go hard to mend if we don't let his body knit itself together again. Sleep is the first thing needful for that, Matthew."

So they left Geoffrey sleeping, and since their lives allowed but little room for leisure they went back to their work.

Nothing more was done or decided that day. Not much was said, even, for everyone's heart was so full of apprehension that their words were stopped in their throats. Their fear had transformed them into superstitious children of them: they did not want to make some dreadful thing come to pass by speaking of it.

But the morning brought a fresh wonder. Four men came down from the castle, grim and rough in their aspect, in search of beans and potatoes for a pottage. They did not offer to pay for these things. They claimed them in the name of Pennick's new lord, their master, Maglan Horvath.

"Horvath?" Brian Randel said. "Horvath the outlaw?"

One of the four men struck him a buffet across his pate that near to knocked him off his feet. "Are you deaf?" the rogue demanded. "I said he's Lord Horvath now!"

Brian was a big man and a strong one besides, as I told you erewhile, but these men had an evil look to them and their very arrogance was a warning – as were the swords at their waists. If they were not afraid to come into the village and make such demands, it was because they were part of the company that had just taken the castle and routed or slaughtered its defenders.

Brian bowed his head. "Aye," he muttered, "so I meant to say."

"Lord Horvath," his tormentor pressed him. "Say it."

"Lord Horvath."

"And bend your knee to him, like the churl you are."

Brian went down on one knee, all in the mud of the street.

"Well then," said another of the four. "Three sacks of beans, and two of potatoes. Yarely, you dogs. Now you know who it is that's asking, and I promise you you'll not want to stand in his displeasure."

Cosham had already given its yearling dues to the castle. There was no one in the village who could spare so much. For a long time nothing was said. Then my father ventured a suggestion. "It will take us some while to gather the beans and potatoes and stow them in sacks," he said. "We could give you some now, and some later. Or if it were not irksome to your master – that is, to your lord, or . . . or to *our* lord, as I meant to say, then we could bring the whole load up to the castle this afternoon in a single journey."

"Aye," said the foremost brigand. "Do that, then." And they went their ways.

No sooner were they gone than all the men and all the good-wives with them fell to arguing about who should provide the beans and potatoes, or if no one could do so what answer might be given.

"We'll all starve, is the bloody answer!" shouted Sarah Theakston that was Matthew's wife.

"Aye," said my mother bitterly. "When did we not? Carne always

19

took what he wanted, and didn't even have the name of robber. Why should this Maglan all-and-someone be any different?"

But then came Alan the sexton running from the kirk with news that master Geoffrey was awake, and every man jack of them went running off thither, with the beans and potatoes for the moment forgotten.

Geoffrey Carne was standing at the rectory door. His face was as pale as milk and he had to lean on the parson's shoulder for his own legs would not carry him.

"It's good to see you well, young lordship," Matthew Theakston ventured.

"Well?" Geoffrey repeated, as if the word was a curse. "Who said I'm well? My father's castle is whelmed by knaves and cut-throats. My father and mother I hear are killed, and my two brothers likewise. I will not be well until I see Maglan Horvath's head on the end of a pike, and the road to Pennick lined with gibbets with Horvath's men swinging from them."

There was a cheer at this, for everyone present approved of the sentiment. But Geoffrey was looking for more than applause. In sobs and broken fragments he told the villagers how he had survived the slaughter at the castle gate by feigning to fall and lying still among the dead. Then he had chosen his moment and slipped away when the fighting went hand to hand and all the raiders were busily engaged. He told this tale as if it was a miracle – as if God in His infinite mercy had chosen him out of all those in the bailey yard to be gathered up in His hands and swaddled against danger. In Geoffrey's mind this was firm proof that he was meant both to revenge and to rule.

"I'll remind you you're all under *arrière-ban*," he told the men of Cosham. "I want you to send messengers to the other villages in the fief. Tell them to muster here. Tomorrow we'll retake Pennick and put Maglan Horvath to the sword."

"The men will have no weapons, my lord," Saul Randel pointed out mildly.

"They'll have shovels, hoes, mattocks, knives, stout sticks,"

Geoffrey answered him. "And they'll have right on their side, which is more than all. Offer me no excuses, for I'll listen to none. Every moment we do nothing is a moment that virtue lies bleeding and evil triumphs over it. Send out the messengers. Tell them I am lord now, and tell them the fight is towards. Tell them to come."

By this point he was so weakened, what with his injuries and his great passion, that he could scarcely keep his feet. The parson and the sexton carried him back indoors, after which a meeting took place in the kirk itself.

I say *it took place* rather than *it was called* because none remembered afterwards whose idea the gathering was. It was felt by all that these momentous events needed to be discussed. Those who hadn't heard Geoffrey's exhortations or met with Horvath's brigands were sent for so they could be told. Theakston waited until all were in and then closed and bolted the doors. Only Marlie Scour and Parson Lebone were absent, for Marlie was tending to her patient and the parson was helping her.

There were many who spoke up, but little that was said. They rehearsed the same few arguments over and again. Was Geoffrey now their lord, or was Horvath? The law said the eldest son must inherit, but it was not inheritance that had put the Carnes in Pennick. It was the Norman writ, casting out the Farleys who had chosen the wrong side at Hastings field.

Horvath was a thief and a cut-throat, to be sure. He deserved to be put out, and all would cheer him on his way. "But to be clear," Jem Makepeace said, "he triumphed over twice thirty men-at-arms who knew their weapons. I like not to go and wave my sickle at him – or my Fleur's paring knife. We thought to muster alongside proper soldiers, but there'll be none. It will just be us."

"And them being inside the castle and all," Thomas Seaver said in a kind of sad wonder. "Whelming a castle's no fit work for the likes of us."

"The men of the other villages will be with us though," said someone.

21

"They're the same as us – or worse. The men of Hareton can't find their arses to wipe them."

"And what will Horvath do to pay us out if we gather under Geoffrey Carne's banner?" Brian Randel demanded. "He won't leave stick on stick or stone on stone. God help our womenfolk, is all I say, for we'll be dead and they'll be out on the road!"

And back and forth, and forth and back until at last the thing was decided. Again, I do not say by who. There was no vote. They scarcely admitted to themselves what it was they meant to do.

These were farmers and the wives of farmers, craftsmen and labourers with their hands. The wars that had raged on and off through their entire lives had now become a constant drumbeat of terror and despair. Some of them were old enough to remember the harrying, when William the Bastard decided he preferred a wasteland to an insurrection and gave order to scourge the north of England until there was nothing left there to bleed. If they had learned one thing through the trials of the last few decades it was this: that it is better to bend than to break.

I do not know for a certainty who it was that went to the castle. I supposed for a long time that it must have been Theakston: in normal times it was a distinction he coveted to be the conduit between the village and its lord. But then again, Theakston was ever a slippery one, adept at claiming privileges and ducking burdens. I would be surprised, frankly, if he did not find a way to pass this off onto someone else – the parson, perhaps, or one of the other yardlanders. Nobody, not even my father and mother within doors at night, ever spoke of this again, so it is a secret I'm not privy to.

A man – it would certainly have been a man – went up to Pennick and presented himself at its gates. If Horvath had set guards on the standfasts the man would have hallooed them and asked leave to deliver his message: if not, he would have knocked timidly and waited.

He would have come before Horvath in the donjon's hall. Or perhaps Horvath would have come down and met him in the yard

22

in the midst of all his reavers. Either way the new lord would have asked where his beans and potatoes were.

And the man would have abased himself, pleading the poor harvest and the old lord's intransigence. So much had already been taken! If they gave any more they would not survive the coming winter.

But we have something else to offer, if it please your lordship. We have your enemy's son, who is trying to raise up a host against you. Is it not better to have your hands on him and eat thin pottage than to feast and have him still at large? We offer him freely, in the hope you'll forgive us the rest.

Horvath's men came for Geoffrey Carne that same night. They hammered on the door of the rectory to be admitted, and when Parson Lebone wasn't quick enough in answering they kicked the door off its latch and went inside.

Geoffrey was asleep in the room's one bed and he did not rouse. Marlie Scour had dosed him with poppy for his body's hurts – and perhaps out of mercy, knowing what was like to come. Parson Lebone had been sitting in a chair next to the bed writing his sermon for the next Sunday's mass. He stood and interposed himself between Geoffrey and the reavers. "This room is part of the kirk," he told them. "You may not come here. You have no lease here."

One of the brigands struck the parson a blow that laid him on the floor. When Lebone still tried to forestall them, fastening his grip on the nearest man's leg, he was kicked and pummelled until he was still. The reavers dragged Geoffrey from thence into the street, threw him down in the mud and killed him there, hacking him with their blades until there was but little left of him. My father said Geoffrey did not wake, and my father was not given to lying so it may well have been so. He was not present though, so he was only repeating what he had been told.

The body was buried in the cemetery ground behind the kirk, but no stone was set over it. Maglan Horvath had given out word that he would not have any monument to the Carnes in his demesne.

23

Cosham got all that it had wished for. Its menfolk did not have to fight and die, and the tithing of their beans and potatoes was forgotten.

In later times, though, when foul fortune descended on them and their days became a diet of disasters, the villagers were wont to say this. That there was a curse on Cosham, and that Cosham could thank its own self for that. For they had purchased every inch and ounce of their misfortunes with Geoffrey Carne's blood.

III

Which treats of my death

Now I come to my own part in this story, and I see that it will not do. I had meant to tell it as though the events of my life lay all in a straight line, but they do not. How could they? My death comes in the middle, when for most people it is wont to mark the end – and the manner of my going away and coming back bent all things out of true.

I cannot even say *I* and mean one thing by it, for I am two things at least and the second stands all askew on top of the first. I make mention of my mother and my father, but the words do not have the heft and weight for me that they should have for I am speaking of the father and mother I had when I was first alive. Since my resurrection I have none and do not much miss them. This is not cursedness on my part, only the acknowledging of a truth: I did not come out of my grave the same as I went into it.

I will lay these matters out for you as best I can, but I will not pretend any more that I am Willem Turling. It angers me when others do it, for its laziness and its making the wish become the word, so it is bad faith in me to do the same thing myself. I'm only a thing that bears Willem Turling's face, and carries inside him (the way coins are carried in a purse) the memories of what Willem

25

Turling did and said and saw. What I am now you will learn when I am come to telling you.

Willem Turling was born in the year of the long rain. His father was Jon Turling, a yardlander in the fiefdom of Baron Robert Carne, some six or seven miles north of the river called Trent. In case you don't know what a yardlander is, the word signifies a farmer whose land, sometimes called a gyrd or a virgate, is of such a size that it needs two oxen yoked in a team to plough it. Jon Turling farmed full thirty acres, and it was goodly land that gave a proper yield. Wheat was what he mostly sowed and harvested there, enough for his family and his yearling debt, along with peas and beans, barley and carrots. There was also a patch nearest to the house where Margaret, Jon's wife, grew sage and hyssop and dill for her cooking pot, leaving a corner full of wildflowers for her heart's good.

The Turlings, you will have seen, were favoured by fortune. In all of Cosham village, where they lived, there were few more prosperous and I dare say none happier. They had but the one sorrow, which was that Margaret for a very long time could not bear a child. Her womb quickened thrice in three years, but none of the babies that grew in her stayed the course.

"Is it sin in us, do you think?" Jon asked his wife after the third time. "Would confession save us, Meg?"

Margaret knew of no great sin on her own head, and had seen none in her husband, but in the absence of great sins small ones will do. "Were you not of envious heart," Margaret's friend Alice Randel asked her, "when Judith Post walked before you in the blessing of the river? Perhaps it's that."

So Margaret took herself off to the kirk and laid out her soul before Parson Lebone, who did his best to sift it. He gave her meagre penance for her meagre trespasses, and was chagrined when she demanded more. A few paternosters, she told him, would not answer her need.

So he bid her fast a seven-day, and walk to the river and back holding a great stone in her hands. These expiations were not from any canon but from the parson's own wit, designed to satisfy Margaret's need for atonement without doing her any serious harm. He was not a man that held the mortification of the body to be a holy or a needful thing.

Jon made his confession too, and was given the same answer, so he fasted along with his wife and carried his own boulder to the river's bank. Their neighbours watched them there and back, some offering up prayers for their wellbeing while others speculated on what grave fault might merit so heavy a penance. Fornication, Jem Makepeace declared with confidence. It must needs be that they had had to do with each other on a Sunday, or else in Lent. And that, likewise, was why Margaret Turling's womb had been made barren.

But whether God was watching or whether it was only chance, Margaret was got with child again only three months after she dropped that rock into the rushing Erren. And this time she dropped the baby too, as easily and as gratefully as she had let go of that heavy stone.

It was Willem that she bore: a boy with skin as pale as a lily's flower and a head of hair that was as light a brown as ground-up flax seeds. Jon being dark and Margaret being blonde, they joked that the boy was a jug into which they'd poured equal halves of themselves. Whatever qualities he showed as he grew, good or bad, they fitted them all to this same tune: he had Jon's stubbornness but Margaret's gentle heart, Jon's piety but Margaret's mischievous humour. They saw in their son their union writ large and prolonged into the uncertain future. They loved him so much they came close to suffocating him.

Life was as hard in those times as it is now. Harder even. I would not have you think the boy grew up untouched by pain. He had his share of bumps and falls, of fears and fevers, even of tragedy. The time of his growing up was the Anarchy, the time when the laws slept. There were trials enough for all that lived through those years. Yet Jon and Margaret contrived to shield their beloved Willem from the worst of it. Always they found some way to cheer or

27

console him, to soothe his sorrows and still his fright. They made of him their heart's heart, a precious cargo for them to carry with watchful care through the thorny thickets and winding ways of the world.

And their labour was not in vain. With such cossetting Willem might have grown up selfish and wilful, but he did not. Perhaps I who am so close to him should not say this, but he had both a sweet nature and a forward wit. Almost as soon as he could walk he was carrying water to his father in the fields, shelling peas for his mother, milking the family's goat, Ermint, and watching so she didn't stray. Then when he was older he became Jon's second self, ploughing and planting beside him, tending the gyrd like a yeoman born.

But then, in his twelfth year, Willem fell ill. It was only a dry cough at first, but it worsened day by day. A fever grew inside him, and the heat seemed to shrivel him and wear him away as if he were a plant left without water in the heat of August. At length, almost in despair, Jon and Margaret decided to consult a doctor. Unusually for peasant farmers in Cosham they had a little money of their own, given to them when Baron Carne had needed to build a new barn and had asked Jon to give him seven weeks' more labour than his vassalage required. To be paid in coin was a strange thing and Jon had not liked it much, but now he had nine shillings to his name. He asked Parson Lebone whether this would be enough, and where a physician might be found.

The parson had no idea as to the first, and for the second could only say that a town such as Burslem or Wolstanton would be large enough to provide a good living for a doctor and therefore ought logically to have one. Each was at least a day's journey away from Cosham by foot, the first to the north and east, the second to the south and west.

"But how will we go, when Willem can't walk?" Margaret lamented.

"I'll go myself," Jon said, "and bring a doctor back."

He walked to Burslem. The village had an ox-cart that was

owned in common, but it was needed elsewhere so there was no help for it. As you have already heard, the roads at that time were a-crawl with bandits and desperate men: it was no small risk Jon took, but he met with no miscarriage and arrived in the town towards evening. On being directed to a doctor's house he did not wait until morning but hammered on the man's door and importuned him to come at once. The leech, a man named Holt, gave him a flat refusal. He saw no point in setting out so late and being benighted on some desolate heath. No, he would come to Cosham the next day, and in the meantime he would accept four shillings against his fee.

Jon slept in a doorway and headed back to Cosham with the first light. Doctor Holt had said he would follow by horse, so Jon hoped he would be overtaken on the road. He was not.

As soon as he reached the bounds of the village he knew something was amiss. The bell up at the kirk was ringing a dirge, and the wind carried the wailing of women to him. He ran at once to his own house where all his fears were realised. The boy Willem had come to his crisis in the night. His breath had come shallower and shallower, Margaret told Jon in a voice that cracked with grief, until finally it did not come at all.

The two held each other, heartbroken. Each longed to comfort the other, as they had through many lesser ordeals, but in this time of greatest need their sorrow struck them dumb. Parson Lebone offered some words of consolation, but it's far from certain my parents heard them.

Doctor Holt, I mention for the sake of completeness, arrived at last in the middle of the afternoon, riding a fine chestnut trotting horse with a saddle of yellow leather. When he found his intended patient already passed beyond his care, he demanded another four shillings for his wasted journey. It was well for him that he made this request of the parson, out of the hearing of Jon and Margaret and the neighbours who had come to mourn with them. Lebone gave the man a blessing and advised him to begone before anyone thought to take issue with his tardiness.

29

It being then summer, the funeral followed hard upon the death. Perhaps that was one reason why Jon and Margaret continued so very unhappy afterwards: they scarce had time to realise their son was gone before he was put in the ground. But given how much they had doted on him, it's not needful to look for further explanation. If Willem had been their heart's heart, they were as bereft now as if their hearts had been cut out while they yet lived. They still went about the business of their day – farming is a labour that permits no interruption – but they were like two unhoused souls, speaking never a word, scarcely aware of the tasks their bodies were performing.

And so they might have continued, if it had not been for the magician.

Almost a year to the day after Willem Turling was laid in the ground, the rumour ran through Cosham that a sorcerer had come to live in the deep forests on the far side of Great Chell. He had cleared a circle of ground near the Wolstanton road and built his house there. Demons or damned spirits must have helped him for he had done all this in the space of a single night. He was never seen to cut timber, yet smoke rose straight and black from his chimney. He did not hunt, for he did not need to: game of all kinds came willingly to his door, where he chose what meat he had a mind to. He was green of eye and white of hair, as tall and thin as a yew branch, and his name was Cain Caradoc.

Nine tenths of all of this, Jon and Margaret thought sure, was only story – and story grows fat by feeding on itself. They did not set any store by it. But then after some little time had passed they heard more. The mage had helped this one to mend a plough that was broken beyond a smith's skill; he had cleared that one's field of rocks in a single day, and for yet another he had made a crop of corn that was pale and stunted with mildew to grow hale and whole again.

Jon and Margaret were fearful of hoping, but the despair that had sat in their souls since their son died was like a hot stone that they swallowed afresh every day. Their guts were wrung out with it and their hearts exhausted.

"Where is the harm," Margaret asked after sundry such tales had reached their ears, "in going and talking to the man? If he's a worker of miracles, it may be that he can work one for us. If he's none he'll bid us begone and there's an end of it."

"Isn't magic the Devil's work, though?" Jon asked her – but in truth he only asked in order to be argued out of it, and Margaret was more than ready to oblige him. "If Caradoc's magic is of that damned sort," she said, "why have so many of our neighbours seen fit to sue to him? It's only us that's stood here wringing our hands, when it may be there's help to be had."

Help to be had, she said. She meant the raising of the dead, a thing that reeked of blasphemy and mortal sin. But Margaret had an answer for that too. "It was well enough for Jesus," she said. "I don't see how it can be a trespass, if He that's as white as the lamb rolled away the stone from His own grave!"

Jon was almost certain there was a flaw in this argument, but he did not care to go digging for it. This is how he reasoned with himself: say we do sin, Meg and me. That's on our head, not on Willem's. We'll go about to shrive ourselves after, and haply find mercy. Or if we don't, still our boy will be in the world again and that's a good that outweighs any harm.

So they took themselves away to the sorcerer's house. It was a long journey, a great deal further from Cosham than they had ever been. Night overtook them still on the road, not even halfway yet to the wooded slopes of Great Chell, and they were obliged to seek shelter in the trees.

They would have been happy enough on a bed of moss, but there were only brambles as thick as rope knouts. And then a cold rain began to fall.

"I'm chilled to the bone," Margaret lamented. "Better to keep on walking than to suffer this."

"And turn our ankles in the ruts, or break our pates by tripping over stones?" Jon said. "Nay, Meg, it won't do. But see, yonder is a light. It might be some shepherd's bothy, and the shepherd might give us leave to sleep on his floor."

31

The light he spoke of was a good way off among the trees, but the trees seemed to part before them as they walked towards it. In less time than it takes to tell the thing, they were there.

It was no shepherd's hut that greeted them, nor a charcoal burner's cottage. It was smaller than either, no more than a lattice of woven branches with a door that was more of the same and a roof of poorly banded thatch. It did not look as though it would keep the rain out but it was the only shelter offered, and the light that shone through the only window shifted in a way that suggested a fire was burning within.

With the rain drenching them and a rising wind buffeting their shoulders, Jon and Margaret did not hesitate long. They went to the door and Jon made to knock. Before he could, a voice called out to them from inside. "Come in," it said. It was a thin, high voice that somehow could have been either an old man's or a child's. It was impossible to tell.

Jon and Margaret opened the door and entered. The room in which they found themselves was very different from what they had expected. To be short, it was not a place that sorted in any way at all with the hut's exterior. It seemed to have walls of stone, which was impossible, and it was far greater in extent than the narrow sides of the hut could have compassed. Not only was there a fire but there was a fireplace, wide enough to accommodate an ingle-seat beside the embers. There were niches in the walls where tallow candles burned. On a broad oaken table were piled up a great number of books (Jon and Margaret had only ever seen a single book in their whole lives, which was the parson's Bible). On the floor, animal skins were strewn instead of rushes. More skins had been spread across a bed in the far corner of the room.

"Well, close the door," said that high voice, "ere the wind puts out my candles!"

There arose from the ingle-seat a strange figure. If the inside of the hut did not match its outside, so this man did not match his voice. Despite his white hair, which reached to his shoulders, he was young. His pale face boasted no beard. He had the slender frame of a stripling boy. Only his eyes betrayed him. They were the wrong eyes to be looking out of that youthful face, and their green, ageless gaze made the face seem a mask put up hastily to hide something unseemly.

This was the sorcerer Cain Caradoc, who I may rightly call my second father.

IV

Which recounts my resurrection

"You're late," Cain Caradoc said. "I expected you here before nightfall. It sits ill with me, being made to wait."

Jon and Margaret were all outfaced. They guessed easily enough who it was they were speaking to, for they had gone to seek a magician and this man could be nothing else. But they could not for their souls' salvation make sense of the rest. What was this place? And how could they be expected here when they had found their way by merest chance?

"So please you, sir," Jon ventured, "my name is Jon Turling, a yardlander of Cosham village, and this is my wife, Margaret. If you're the mage Cain Caradoc, we looked to find you on Great Chell, many miles hence. But . . . but we did not imagine that we were expected! Perhaps we should have thought that a man such as you would know a great many hidden things. But for you to extend your hospitality to us is more than we ever . . ." His store of words failed him and he ended by ducking his head in a bow.

"You were best sit," Cain Caradoc told him. He pointed, and the Turlings saw there were chairs set at the table now that had not been there when they entered. They went and sat down. Their wits were in such a pother that they would have sat on the floor

34

if the mage had told them to. He came and joined them, taking his place at the head of the table in a carver chair whose high back was wrought with intricate designs of birds looking out from under leaves. The wood was darker than oak and had such a high lustre it looked as if it had been dipped in oil.

"You are in the right of it," Cain Caradoc said. "My house is on the slopes of Chell. But at the same time it is anywhere else I wish it to be. And seeing how slow a progress you were making I became tired of waiting and decided to meet you on the road. Even so you were tardy. You must have taken many rests on the way, which speaks no great urgency in your suit to me."

Jon and Margaret were distracted while the magician spoke by the carvings on his chair. Were those birds that were peering from between the leaves, or some other kind of creature? Whatever they were, they seemed to move whenever the eye was not upon them.

Margaret gathered her courage and spoke up. She swore on the four gospels and the gospel saints that she and her husband were no frivolous suitors, that their errand was a solemn one and close to their hearts. Jon showed his purse, in which sat the five shillings they still had to their name. He put the coins on the table and spread them out so that Cain Caradoc could count them. Together both husband and wife told him of their son Willem's death, how heavy it was on their hearts, how much they longed to have him back. "And you being a man of such art and such power," Jon finished, "we thought it might lie within your skill to help us."

"To help you?" Cain Caradoc leaned forward and rested his chin on his fist. "Help you how? Speak plainly."

"To bring back our son."

"From his grave?"

"Aye."

"For five shillings?"

"Aye." Jon's heart sank, and so did his wife's. The mage had made no move to take their coin, and his voice dripped with disdain.

But his next words astonished them. "I will consider what may be done. And whiles I think on it, you must break bread with me."

He reached out and took up a glass decanter, pouring three stoups of dark red wine. Worked glass was a thing my parents had never seen outside of a church, so that was a marvel in itself, but more marvellous still was the fact that neither the decanter nor the cups had been there a moment before. Nor had the repast of roast meats and black bread that was now of a sudden set before them. The table had been stacked with books, now it was full of good things to eat – such bounty as these simple people had never imagined.

They ate and drank, and by and by they dared to hope again. Why would Cain Caradoc have put himself in their way if he meant to deny them? And what could his kindness portend except more kindness to come? These expectations, along with the wine and the warmth of the room, loosened their tongues. They talked at length about their home and the recent doings there. They were ashamed to confess what had befallen Geoffrey Carne when he came to Cosham, but everything else they unpacked, from the coming of Maglan Horvath through the fall of Pennick Castle to the present moment. And the mage listened with great interest.

Cain Caradoc was then two hundred years old. If he seemed younger it was because he had found ways of gleaning youth from the places where it was most readily to be found, which is to say the young. All his care was to prolong his life for as long as might be managed, and so to put off indefinitely a conversation with his maker that he feared might be irksome and unpleasant. A dead child was a piece of business Cain Caradoc could turn to profit, and all this show of hospitality was a way of wooing Jon and Margaret to his purpose.

But there was more besides. As part of his striving to ensure his own immortality, the sorcerer was wont to scry his future and find what opportunities and obstacles might lie in his path. The magics he bent to this purpose were volatile and the insights thus gained were of necessity oblique and obscure. Still, he had been brought to know through conversations with unhoused spirits that the lands around Trent were important to him – which indeed was why he had come there. Furthermore, the spirits had promised that he would reach the height of his art and attain his dearest wish in

36

the service of a foreign lord lately raised to power and eminence in this northern clime.

So when these two guileless peasants told him of Maglan Horvath's coming into the fiefdom of Pennick, Cain Caradoc felt the satisfaction of a knot pulling tight or a circle drawn to its full round. He had ventured forth this night only looking to conclude a bargain; it pleased him greatly that he had gained such useful intelligence besides.

All three of them had supped and drunk. The man and the woman were drowsy with wine and wearied from their journeying. It was time to bring the matter to a conclusion. "You may keep your shillings," Cain Caradoc said, pushing them back across the table. "I have no use for wealth. I am a scholar, and my needs are few. For God's grace and my soul's weal I will answer your plea and give you back your child."

Hearing this, Jon and Margaret could not contain their joy. They fell to their knees and thanked the sorcerer, taking hold of his two hands and kissing them ever and again. They swore themselves to his service, pledged to pray for him and to light candles for him at Cosham kirk, and much more to the same purpose.

"There is yet one other thing, though," Cain Caradoc told them, enduring their excessive gratitude with scant patience. "Take your seats again and listen to me. The spell that will bring your son Willem back from his grave is not a simple one. It will take a great toll of me. It might even kill me if I am not fortified against its effects. So I ask you this. Let me take a tithing from Willem's soul. The thinnest wafer, so small it will never be missed. And I will use it to replace the vital energies that I will lose in casting the spell."

The Turlings were somewhat dismayed at this proposal, but the sorcerer assured them Willem would take no hurt from it, and was adamant besides that there was no other way the thing could be achieved. It was this, he said, or else it was nothing. Still, Jon and Margaret hesitated. To be dealing in souls — and their own son's soul, no less — seemed no Christian business, and for all their grief and longing they could not quite bring themselves to agree to it.

"Well then, go your ways," Cain Caradoc said with asperity.

37

"You've eaten my bread and drunk my wine, but I make no charge for that. Only I could wish that you had not wasted my time, when you do not love your boy enough to see the matter through."

"It's not love that's wanting." Margaret wept. "Only how can we give what's not ours in the first place?"

"You may give it freely. The two of you are the two halves of Willem, are you not? The authors both of his spirit and of his flesh. None else besides you could do it, and neither of you could do it without the other, but if you both agree then the bargain will have force."

"Surely, master," Jon pleaded, "there's some other payment you'd take!"

"I told you," said the magician, "it's not payment. It's a needful thing for the spell to be performed. But hey ho, I am done. I have told you what I can do for you and what it will require. If you won't give what I ask freely, I'll not beg for it. Please to go out by the door whereby you entered."

Jon and Margaret stood, trembling as if an ague had seized them both. They looked each to other, and each saw their own face reflected in the other's tears. They had come so close to their heart's desire, and now must they go out again into the rain and the cold and the emptiness of a life without their boy?

That dread prospect helped them, in the end, to find their resolution.

They said yes. They swore to it.

"You have made the right choice," Cain Caradoc applauded them. "Go home now and wait. When the thing is done, which will be soon, you will know it."

And this at least was no lie.

Six feet under Cosham kirkyard, without a coffin but wrapped in cerements of lead, Willem Turling had lain now for a year. The cerements were to keep his flesh from insult, and they had done their job well. No worms or flies had found their way to Willem's body. No rats or dogs had got the scent of him. If death is a sleep, his sleep had gone undisturbed.

38

But a body carries its own corruption within it, and you cannot keep out what was inside all along. Have you ever known any meat to keep fresh for a year? Within the leaden shroud Willem's flesh and sinews had putrefied, unlacing themselves from his bones and then rendering down and down until at length the greater part of him had been distilled to a liquor. The bones were still whole, though they had separated each from other and lay all tangled at the bottom of the fleshy broth.

It is said by some that when a caterpillar spins a cocoon its body within that envelope becomes just such a liquid before taking on the winged form in which it will finally burst forth. However that may be, Cain Caradoc's spell began now to work on what was left of Willem and transform it.

The sorcerer's command was that Willem should rise up out of his grave and stand again in his own likeness. That likeness being lost, the liquid mass within the cerements did what it could. It congealed into a kind of semblance of a body, picking up in the process such of Willem's bones as seemed to fit. It was not an hour's work, or even a day's. On the one hand the cerements being moulded to the outline of Willem's body gave the liquor some hints to start with as to the general shape towards which it should tend. But this was of no great use when it came to the fine detail. As for the bones, they were more of a hindrance than a help, for they were embedded in the quickening flesh every which way, and stuck out at unavailing angles.

What clawed its way up to the surface at last, having cast off the heavy cerements and burrowed upwards through the earth as blind as any mole, did not look much like Willem. It did not look much like any child ever born of woman.

Then again, it was not. *I* was not. I was born from death. Cain Caradoc conceived me and the cold grave bore me. It's a miracle I'm not more thwart than I am.

But it's not a miracle that Jon and Margaret Turling were thankful for, when at last I came stumbling home.

39

V

In which Cain Caradoc offers his services to Maglan Horvath

And what benefit did the sorcerer Cain Caradoc derive from the atrocious business of my second birth?

That is not easily explained, for it is a thing that defies nature. He had asked my parents for a tithing of my soul, but my soul and my flesh had by this time gone their separate ways. In bringing them together again, he did not simply pour the one into what was left of the other. There were many other manipulations he performed first, the effect of which was to take some of what had once been Willem Turling and wind it into his own being, as a weaver winds the fibres of flax into a coil of yarn.

This was how Cain Caradoc had lived so long. He made use of other people's lives, snipping or scraping away a little here and a little there and adding them to his own store of years. He worked with life, carded and spun and wove it with his busy hands and his subtle wit. Children's lives were the materials he liked best of all, because in a child the life is so strong and so vivid that it overflows like honey from the cells in a beehive – which meant that Caradoc could gather the most with the least effort.

But he always needed more. Drawing off a year from a child's allotted store and taking it into himself did not give Cain Caradoc an extra year to live. Life finds its level, just as water does, and a man of two hundred years is like a cistern all rusted and shot with holes. The most part of anything you pour into it will drain away again forthwith. What the sorcerer wanted – what he had wandered far and wide to find – was a way to seal the cistern all at once and for ever, so that his body would become immune to the ravages of time. He wanted to have an angel's body, renewed from moment to moment by the fervid and unceasing torrent of his power.

Such was his hope. And he had come to believe that the water-lands of the Trent were the place where this hope would be fulfilled. So as soon as his business with my parents was concluded, before ever I broke out of my cerements and walked again on the earth, Cain Caradoc presented himself at the gates of Pennick Castle and sued for an audience with its new master.

"Bid him go away," said Maglan Horvath when he was told that a magician wanted to do with him. "And if he does not go at once, empty a privy or two on his head. I've no time for such wastrel buggery."

The man who had brought the news was Walter Scold, one of the worst of Horvath's brigands. He went away to do as he was bid, enjoying in his mind's eye the prospect of the so-called sorcerer being roundly cursed, covered in piss and sent on his way.

When he got back to the gate he found Cain Caradoc standing on the inside of it. "I would have waited," Caradoc said, "but you were as slow as a snail. All you want is the shell on your back."

Baffled and incensed, Scold stepped forward to apprehend the magician and put him out of doors again. But Caradoc was not where he appeared to be. Somehow he moved around Scold, tapping the man smartly between the shoulder blades as he passed by. Scold gasped at that touch. He felt as though he had been stung. Moreover, as he turned, a strange weariness fell on him so that it seemed almost too great an effort to move.

At any rate he was too slow. In the space of a breath, Caradoc had crossed the bailey yard, three hundred paces from end to end, and now was climbing the steps to the donjon above. A few men

41

tried to intercept his progress but ever and anon they found that when they reached the place where the magician seemed to be he was somewhere else again.

When Caradoc came to the donjon's door he stopped and made a gesture with his hands, touching them together and then making them part again with the fingers spread. The door flew wide and he entered.

He came before Maglan Horvath in the great hall. You might imagine that Horvath was sitting in state on a throne, surrounded by his vassals and his supplicants, but in truth he was only feeding his dogs. There were ten or twelve of them, strays from the parishes all around that had gathered at the edge of his forest camp, encouraged and partially tamed by thrown scraps, and now had removed with him to the castle. There were no guards or men-at-arms in the room. Horvath had not yet got into the habit of having attendants round him to enact his whims and wishes.

He was surprised to see the man he had ordered to be sent away now standing in front of him. He did not stand up, but only carried on feeding his mongrel pack with the lungs and lights and gnawed bones of hares. "What in Satan's name are you, then?" he demanded.

Cain Caradoc did not immediately make answer. A strange sense had fallen on him all at once, both pervasive and utterly stupefying. This donjon was the seat of a colossal power, a force of magic greater than anything he had ever felt or heard of! It was as though a giant had turned over in its sleep and now was lying so close to him that its spent breath enveloped him like a cloud.

In truth, Caradoc was astonished. All his life he had worked in magics. He had bent his every effort on acquiring arcane knowledge and putting it to use for his own profit. Being now in his two hundredth year he felt himself much more master than journeyman. But whatever power it was that sat in this keep it was as far beyond him as a waterfall on a high fell is beyond a drop of dew falling from a leaf. It had nothing to do with the man in front

42

of him. If he was sure of anything, he was sure that this power was older by far than the castle or anyone in it.

With some effort he collected his thoughts. "My name is Cain Caradoc," he said. "I am a master of hidden arts. If you have need of such, I'm willing to enter into your service in exchange for sundry considerations and rewards, most of them too trivial to be worthy of mention."

Maglan Horvath felt that there were far too many words in that sentence. He picked out one of the early ones and ignored most of the rest. "You're called Cain, are you?" he said. "Belike you should have a mark on your brow, then, but I don't see one. Why did your father christen you after a murderer? Is murder so much prized where you come from?"

Cain Caradoc strove for a calm and indifferent tone, though the presence that abided in this castle – whatever it might be – still sat across his shoulders like a yoke. He had said that he was willing to enter Horvath's service. The truth was that he would have begged to stay if he had thought that begging would avail. He needed to find the source of this vast power and take it for his own use. So he put on a bland and pleasing manner, determined to ingratiate himself with the castle's master.

"Cain is not my given name, my lord," he said evenly, "but one that I took upon myself when I was come of age. And it was not Cain's mark that guided me in that choice. It was his immortality I had in mind. God cast Adam from Eden for fear he would eat of the tree of life eternal – yet we are meant to believe he gave that immortality to Cain as punishment for murder. I think it was rather a reward for Cain's triumphing over his brother when they fought, as the strong must ever prevail against the weak."

Horvath said nothing to this. He only ruffled the hair of Lightning, the mastiff bitch that was his favourite among the dogs, and whispered in her ear to lay on.

Lightning turned at once and sprang. She went for Cain Caradoc's throat, but her teeth did not close in his flesh. Instead she seemed to pass right through him, and fell dead on the far side. She had

43

been cut in pieces, as neatly as if she had been laid out on a butcher's slab and the butcher had gone about with his sharpest knife to disassemble her. The slices of dog flesh lay where they had fallen. No blood spread out from them to stain the stone flags. Blood is the stuff of life and the sorcerer had taken it, even in that briefest of encounters, to add some odd minutes to his own tally.

Horvath loved that dog and felt the loss. He felt too the danger of being face-to-face with a man who could perform such feats. For the space of a moment he considered trying what his sword might do, but he had no great desire to end up in thin parings on the floor of his own hall.

He was afraid, but to be afraid is not the same as being a coward. He turned his back on Caradoc and walked to the door, where he called on one of his men to come and clean up the mess. Then he sat himself down on a stone bench under the window embrasure, resting his hand on his raised knee. "Well that's a fine earnest of your service," he said, "to kill my dog."

"After you had set the dog on to bite me."

Horvath waved the point away, as being true but not to the purpose. "What would you do for me if I employed you?" he asked Caradoc.

"Whatever you ask. My power is considerable, as you have seen."

"And what would you ask in return? I've no great store of gold, if that's what you're thinking. It might be you should go and offer your services to some foreign potentate who can reward you proportionately to your worth."

Cain Caradoc looked about him. "I like it here," he said. "I have heard a prophecy that Pennick's lord will do great things and rise to glory. I should like to be a part of that rise, and share in that glory."

Horvath did not trouble to hide his disbelief. "You've very modest ambitions," was all he said.

"No," said Caradoc, "very wide ones. But so long as they tangle not with your own, we may do each other good."

Horvath tapped the tips of his fingers against his knee one by

44

one, like a man counting on his hands. "That is what I do not see," he said. "If you've other tricks besides the carving up of dogs, I apprehend well enough what your magics could do for me. The other side of the bargain – the advantage you seek here – is not so clear to me."

Cain Caradoc, being tired of standing when his host was seated, raised up his feet one after the other, tucked them in and sat cross-legged on the empty air. "Well," he said, "I grant you, there is more to my being here than my desire to advance you, Maglan Josip Horvath."

If Horvath was surprised that the sorcerer knew his name, he did not show it. "I should have thought so," he said. "Go on."

"I need raw materials for my conjurings. Stuff that is sometimes hard to come by when a man works alone and has little commerce with the wider world."

"What stuff do you mean?"

"The kind that cries out loudest when you gather it."

Horvath was puzzled. "You need slaves?"

"No. As I said, materials. I could explain further, but it would profit neither of us. Are you a Christian man?"

Horvath frowned. "More than any on these islands. I cleave to the *Srpska Pravoslavska* of my native Serbia. It is the only church that holds true to Christ's teachings. The pope of Rome is a whore who preaches to whores."

"That's nothing to me, either way," Caradoc said.

"Then why did you ask?"

"Only to know if you're wont to shrive your soul. Because the less you know of my labours the less you will have to confess."

"I like not the sound of that," Horvath declared.

"Perhaps not. But I warrant you, you'll like the work itself. I didn't lie when I said you would rise to greatness. I mean to do wonders here that were never seen on earth before. I dare say you'd prefer I did them for you than for someone else."

And that was a proposition Horvath could not deny. He still did not trust the sorcerer. He preferred always to work with people

45

who were less clever than himself, and he had a shrewd suspicion that Caradoc had the advantage of him in that respect. But to send the man away would be to make an enemy of him. To kill him where he stood, on the other hand, would be a fine thing – but he was doubtful of success and feared the outcome if he failed.

The best option, therefore, must be to make use of the sorcerer now while learning as much as possible about his weaknesses.

Horvath spat into his hand and held it out. "We've a bargain, then," he said. "And if your performance goes half as high as your promising, I'll not be sorry."

Caradoc took the hand and shook it, doing his best to hide his distaste. This Horvath was an oaf, he thought, and might be troublesome to govern, but as a means to an end he could be tolerated. The invisible power still pressed on him all this time, saturated his being, teased and tormented him. He felt as if his nerves were plucked strings, resonating in a key he could not hear.

But once he had made himself at home here he would seek it out and take possession of it. He would graft the power onto himself and become immortal. And thus, he thought with great glee, would the prophecy be fulfilled.

VI

Which brings me home again to Cosham village

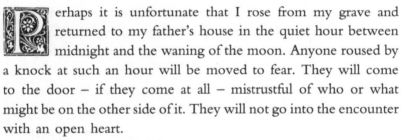erhaps it is unfortunate that I rose from my grave and returned to my father's house in the quiet hour between midnight and the waning of the moon. Anyone roused by a knock at such an hour will be moved to fear. They will come to the door – if they come at all – mistrustful of who or what might be on the other side of it. They will not go into the encounter with an open heart.

Then again, would full daylight have been better? The hideousness of my form is extreme, and with no night to hide it the effect comes on the beholder all at once. Some have wept. Some have fainted. Many have run away, and as many more emptied their gorge.

My father merely stared, wide-eyed and open-mouthed. Behind him, my mother stood on tiptoe to peer over his shoulder, but I do not think she saw me. The moon was still up but it was only in its first quarter and did not shed much light upon the scene.

I tried to form words: *Father, it's me, Willem! Please to let me in!* But the muscles in my throat were woven all askew. All that came forth from my mouth was a bubbling sound like that made by water in a bog when gases are stirred up from its bed and break the surface.

Then my father fell to his knees. He knew, I think, what it was he was looking at. He knew, and it unmanned him. He bowed his head as if to a yoke – and I suppose that was how it must have felt to him when all at once the enormity of what he and my mother had done was made clear.

Margaret, all anxious, stepped forward to help him, crying out his name. I did the same. Our two faces came within a hand's span of each other, our gaze fixing each on each.

In my mother's scream was more of pain and more of misery than I had ever heard before, or ever want to hear again. There was fear there too, of course, but less than you would think. Like my father she had seen through my awful transfiguration and recognised my face. She knew that this monster standing at the threshold was her son.

What happened then was a portent of what was to come. My parents spoke my name a great many times, in hoarse and broken tones. They reached out their hands to touch me but could not bring themselves to do it. They fell on each other's shoulders and wept.

At last my father led me to the small shed that served us as a barn. He rousted out the chickens that were roosting there and cleared a space for me in the hay. "We can't . . ." he said. "In the house . . . your mother . . . In the morning we will see what must be done." These halting words were the best he could muster. He turned and fled.

I lay me down in the hay and tried to sleep, but that was a thing my reshaped body found hard to do. I could not find any comfort at first. The bones that stuck out at strange angles from my flesh forced me to twist myself awkwardly and were pushed deeper into me when I chanced to settle on them.

At length, though, I realised that merely by thinking about it I could make the bones shift into new positions. You must remember that I had been liquid; now I was solid again, but only up to a point. My body seemed firm enough to the touch but I could thin out that firmness with an effort of will, becoming in places

48

and for a few seconds something more like a jelly. I rearranged myself and was able at last to lie at peace.

My thoughts, though, were far from peaceful. I had yet to understand what I was. My mind was full of Willem Turling's memories just as my corporal form was full of Willem Turling's bones, but the memories (again like the bones) were jumbled and misplaced. I could not understand how I had come to be there. I remembered rising up out of the ground but not going down into it. It baffled and distressed me that my mother and father had not embraced me and taken me in.

I believe now that this confusion was not so much because of the manner of my return as because I had died of a fever. The last days of my life had been nothing but confusion and suffering: I had come adrift as it were, like a boat badly tethered, and had floated away into spaces where nothing was real and nothing could be relied on. In trying to make sense of my current situation, therefore, what I lacked was precisely the knowledge that would have been of most use to me – the knowledge of my having died and been buried.

This must sound strange. How could any man – or boy, rather – claw his way out of lead cerements and dig his way up from a grave in the middle of a country cemetery behind a goodly kirk and not think, *Ho then, I am come back from the dead!* Perhaps I'm just slow of wit. All I can say is that the understanding did not come to me all at once, and when it came it made me at first very miserable indeed. I had been a boy. What was I now?

The night passed in these thoughts, exceeding slowly. When at last morning was come my mother and father ventured into the barn to broach me and ask me the self-same question I had been asking myself. What manner of thing was I? They had wished for their child to be returned to them, and they were not so foolish that the connection between their wish and my arrival escaped them. But their resolve had hardened in the course of the night and they now rejected with great force the most obvious explanation – the one that had occurred to them almost at once when they met me at the door. I could not be Willem – but obviously I must be something accidentally raised up by the sorcerer in Willem's place. Now how might I be persuaded to go away again so that their son could come home?

I tried my best to explain that I *was* their son. Forcing the words from my twisted gullet and lopsided lips was a struggle, but that was not the hardest part. I needed in addition to the words a belief in the truth of them, and it would not come. I remembered Willem, but the memories came all jumbled together like a fever dream, and with a fever dream's exaggerations and elisions. It seemed to me as though some of what had formerly been Willem was now some of me, but I could not tell how much, or what the rest of me might be.

And since I could not make myself believe, no more could I convince my mother and father. I have said that both of them when they met me at the door saw Willem's face in mine. Yet now they fought against that seeing, for it was the dashing of all their hopes and at the same time a thing for which they were themselves terribly to blame. Easier to believe that this was some ploy of the sorcerer's to cheat them out of their bargain – to promise one thing but then play hey-pass re-pass and give them something different.

You may wonder why I am so certain they were wrong. Cain Caradoc was enough of a rogue to have played such a trick, and he would not have thought twice about it. But the bargain mattered because it was through the bargain that he obtained the tithing of Willem's soul for his own use. If he had cheated, then all was null and void and he could not come by his payment.

But this was nothing to Jon and Margaret. They worked themselves into a rage at the way they had been treated, and the rage protected them from any shame or sorrow they felt when they looked at me. If I was only a counterfeit passed off on them in bad faith then I was not a thing that needed to be cared about or accommodated. Most definitely I was not a thing that needed to be loved.

"You must go back to the sorcerer's house," Margaret instructed

50

her husband, turning her face from me, "and tell him forthwith that we will not be cozened. If he will not do as he promised we will bring him to Wolstanton assizes and swear against him."

Jon was dismayed at this declaration. "Swear against a magician for not performing the magic we bargained for? Belike we'll be hanged ourselves for making the bargain in the first place. And what of this thing?" He looked sidelong at me. "What are we to do with it?"

Thing was a fine word to choose. It widened even further the chasm in my parents' minds that separated me from the child they had lost, making of me no more than the tangible evidence of their grievance. They had been cheated, lied to, taken for fools, and look what had been wished upon them!

"Turn it out of doors," said Margaret. "It's nothing of ours."

Jon went to the house and returned a few moments later with a pitchfork. He did not wound me, but roused me up out of the hay with brisk prods of the fork's tines against my shoulders and back. Once I was on my feet he threw down in front of me a long tunic made of grey wool. It was an old one of his own, not one that had belonged to Willem. He bid me put it on and hide my nakedness, which I had scarcely noticed until then. I had not been put naked into the grave, of course, but the clothes in which I had been buried had rotted away before I rose again.

"Begone," Jon told me when once I had shrugged on the tunic. "Begone now, and trouble someone else. It will be the worse for you if we see you here again."

Miserable and fearful, and propelled by a few more violent thrusts of the pitchfork, I stumbled out of the barn into the daylight. It lacked only three days of midwinter, so the light was not much to speak of, but still I flinched from it. It made my skin prickle and my sight grow dim. My new-made body, it seemed, was more at home in the dark.

"If I could stay a few hours longer . . ." I begged.

My father brandished the pitchfork fiercely and my mother spat on the ground at my feet. I went my ways.

But in truth I had not a single idea in my head about where I should go. My steps took me first into the village, because it was a way I knew and I wasn't thinking. The shrieks and shouts that met me there soon made me flee again.

A numb sorrow had settled on my soul. I knew not what I did. A night came and then a day, and on its heels a second night. When I grew hungry I ate whatever came first to my hand; birds' eggs from a bush, berries from a hedgerow, the remains of a hare with wagon ruts across its burst belly. I drank from a mill-race, a pond, a puddle. Sometimes on my knees I sucked dew from morning grass.

I walked a great distance but went nowhere. Around and around the fields and farmsteads I trudged, never more than a few miles from Cosham and from my parents' farm.

Wherever I was seen, I was chased away. This happened often for I did not have wit enough to hide. On the contrary, I was drawn to human things and human places. In my heart I felt as though I belonged there, and despite the curses and cudgels that came my way so often, my heart would not learn its lesson.

Nor my body neither, come to that. When the villagers beat me with sticks my flesh forgot its bruises in the space of a breath. A knife or a billhook would tear me, but the rents healed over so readily there were only a few drops of blood squeezed out. And if I were not in the mood to be so provoked, a sweep of my arm would lay my tormentor on the sod. I did not know where my strength came from, but certes it was not a child's strength.

All this time I was still struggling with the riddle of who I was. Willem's memories, which at first had been all a-churn, were now settled enough that I could hold them up to my mind's eye and see them more clearly. This gave me both solace and distress. On the one hand it comforted me to remember a time when I had been the apple of my father's eye, the all and only of my mother's care. But the more I remembered, the more keenly I felt the difference between what I had been and what I was now become.

I could not give a name to that difference, but I knew it was more than mere flesh and blood could account for. When Cain Caradoc's spell had found me it had done whatever was needed to hale me back from the cold earth into the open air, but that had been a much more exacting task than if I had been newly dead. What ingredients had the spell had to work with, after all? A few pints of broth, some bones, and whatever of Willem Turling's soul had not been pared away by Caradoc for his own ends. Such items were clearly a fit recipe for something, but not for a boy. I was the best the spell could do with what it had, and as far as I knew there was no name for such a thing. Certainly I could not lay claim to the name of Willem Turling.

Once I had reached that conclusion and accepted it, I found a little peace to leaven my loneliness and sorrow. It did not matter so much that my parents had cast me out, for they were not my parents. If none of Cosham could abide me, well, none of Cosham had ever known me. Yes, I was alone, but I had never been anything else: I had never been anything at all before now.

This may seem like threadbare consolation, but it was more than Jon and Margaret had been able to find. Jon went back to the place where he and his wife had met with Cain Caradoc, but Cain Caradoc's house was gone. There was only a blackened patch of earth to show where it had been, and some footprints besides that Jon thought must be his own and his wife's, but of the man and his dwelling place there was no sign.

Had Jon known it, Caradoc was very close at hand – but knowing it would have been no help. My father could not force admittance at the castle or even convey a message there. He would not have dared to try.

As it was, he returned to his house and admitted to Margaret that he had failed. He tried in some sort to comfort her, saying that if they were no better off than before they met the sorcerer then at least they were no worse. Caradoc had not taken their money when he might have done it, so all they had lost was their peace of mind. There was now a monster abroad that wore their son's face, and wore it somewhat askew. That was a terrible thing, but with God's grace they need never meet the creature or think on it again.

Life is not so simple though. The villagers of Cosham and the other yardlanders and smallholders round about had by this time had many unpleasant encounters with me. When they came against me to drive me away I sometimes fought back and broke limbs and pates, but even without meaning to I vexed and terrified many. A woman at Fenchley Holt had miscarried when she saw me, her guts clenching so violently that she lost her child. A drunk man at Addlestane had been in such dread of me that he had run into Erren river, and the river being in spate had straightway drowned.

Now the villagers all came in a great pother to my parents' gyrd and delivered themselves of their grievance. The likeness I bore to Willem Turling had not escaped them. They could not tell what I was but they knew to whom I belonged and they declared that it would not do. Clearly I was a penance that had been visited on Jon and Margaret for some misdeed, and since the sin was theirs the remedy must needs be theirs too.

"Send it away," Jem Makepeace said. "Or if you can't then take yourselves away and pray it follows you. Before God you'll answer if that thing is not gone from here before the bells ring on Sabbath morning."

My parents protested that they were not in any wise kin to me, but they could not explain my being there without revealing that they had consorted with a magician. People have been hanged for lighter sins than that, and there was nothing in their neighbours' faces that made them hopeful of a fair hearing.

"I'll seek it out," Jon said when the deputation was gone away again. "It may be I can drive it off, or kill it."

Margaret liked this plan not at all. "We've lost our boy," she said weeping, "and now we've lost a great deal more in trying to get him back. The only thing left to me to lose is you, Jon, and I don't think I'd abide it." But she knew too that if they left Cosham they would be in a sad state indeed, turned out into such violent and lawless times with only five shillings to their name.

54

So Jon went off to find the monster and put an end to it, hoping thereby to win back what little corner of his and Margaret's former life they had left to them.

Finding me was not hard. I was tied to Cosham as by a tether, and in all my wanderings never went more than five miles from the kirkyard where I had my second birth. Withal I moved very slowly, and the sight of me was a thing not easily forgotten. All Jon had to do was to follow the chain of reports and pointing fingers until he found me at the end of it.

I was in a pasture behind a farm, watching a calf being born. I was fascinated to see it and had lingered there a long time. The calf emerged at first inside a gossamer curtain of flesh, its front hooves pushed out in front of its head as if it meant to come into the world in a headlong charge. Its snout ranged this way and that looking for its mother's teat. *Well, you are wise, little one*, I thought, *for you know already what life requires of you and what you yourself require.* And the beast got what it demanded, though the cow had first to lick that fleshy envelope away from its mouth, from its eyes.

A voice called from behind me. "You. Creature!"

I turned to find my father approaching at a rapid stride. My heart swelled with joy to see him. I still crept often to the Turlings' house by night and sat at their threshold a while to play at being home again. It had been a great comfort to me in the first few weeks of my second life. "Father," I said. I threw open my arms to him.

He had brought an axe and he went to it with a will, cursing me in anguished tones as he hewed and hacked my limbs. I did not try to defend myself. I was too surprised at the suddenness and wildness of the attack. A dozen blows he landed on me, and most bit deep. The pain of the strokes, if I am honest, was not much. The greater pain was the discovery – or the reminder, for he had shown it before but I had made myself forget – that my father hated me.

He hewed until he was exhausted. I had fallen by then and lay stretched out in the long grass. Then, as Jon watched in horror, my sundered flesh knitted itself again together. The wounds (that had scarcely bled) pursed and closed themselves like the lips of mouths that are determined to keep a secret.

A low moan came from my father's throat. He sank to his knees. The handle of the axe slipped from his hand.

"Why, Father?" I demanded of him when the great wound in the centre of my face had closed and my mouth was whole again. "Why do you wish me dead?"

"I'm not your father!" he protested. "I'm nothing to you!"

I did not answer – or at least not in words. I sat up in the grass, got my knees under me and brought my face close to his. He made to pull away, but I clapped my hands down on his shoulders and held him in place. I was a great deal stronger than him, it seemed. We knelt like that for the space of a dozen breaths.

A change came over my father very slowly. At first his face was twisted in disgust. Then as his eyes peered into mine, his grimace loosened, much as a slipping knot loosens from a rope when you tug on it. Tears ran down his cheeks. He began to sob.

"Willem," he said at last. There was no breath behind the word. It barely stirred the air.

I saw his despair, how hard and heavy it sat on him. If I was Willem then what had he done to his beloved son? How was his soul stained? What was left of his hope, whether of joy in this world or of Heaven after? I could not blame him then for having seen me as something alien and loathly. The other way led only to despair.

And through thinking on that I came to a truth, all unexpected, as one digging up stubborn roots may come upon the crown of a long-dead king buried in the earth an age ago. It was this: we are the sum of all that has befallen us, and therefore every great event, every great pain sunders us. We jump over the gap and come down on the other side – assuming we did not fall – changed for ever.

"No," I said. "No, Jon Turling, I am not Willem. Not any longer. You were in the right of it when you disowned me. Whatsoever

56

I have been before is gone now, and this that's left is its own separate self."

I took my hands from his shoulders and placed them on either side of his head. I turned him, perhaps ungently, to face the cow and the new-delivered calf. "That is me," I said. "That is the image of me, a thing newborn. And you and your lady Margaret must study to be the same. You must forgive yourselves, if you can find a way to it. Be midwives to your own souls, and deliver yourselves into another life."

I let go my hold on him and stood, but he stayed kneeling. He looked at me now in confusion, but some of his grief had lifted. "You have my son's face," he said at last. "But my son could never have spoken such words."

"No more he could," I agreed. Perhaps I should have reached this conclusion before, but I had spent the time since my rebirth not in thinking but in brute sensation. Now my mind quickened, and knew itself. I had been a child when I died, but I was not risen as one. I think it is a wonder similar in sort to the way I heal so quickly when I am hurt. My reknitted flesh is all of a piece. I cannot be wounded to the heart for all of me is heart. All of me is liver, lights and lungs. And by the same token all of me is mind. I think with the whole of my being, which is a powerful thing.

"I do not blame you, Jon Turling," I said to my father, "though I might. You committed a weighty sin, but you have suffered greatly for it and I think you will go on suffering. You should not stay here. The sight of me will torment you past what you can bear. Go your ways. Cleave to my mother. Help her, and take the help she offers you. It may be you can find some good thing to do that will balance the harm you have done erewhile. Certainly you will know your own heart better, going forward."

He rose up at last. He tried to embrace me but the great ugliness of my person at such close quarters defied his efforts. He placed a hand on my chest, and I put my own hand over his. He swallowed once, and once again, and at last spoke.

"I loved him," he said.

57

"Aye." I nodded. "He loved you too."

"I meant no harm. I meant no harm to him. I only wanted to see him again."

"I do not blame you," I told him again. He stood a while longer but said no more. At last he went away.

When next I passed by the Turlings' house I found it empty and the door standing open. I went inside and walked from room to room, remembering. Jon and Margaret could not have taken very much, for all looked the same as it had when I lived there with them.

I left Cosham too, on the self-same day. I cannot tell you where my mother and my father went, but I betook me to the deep woods beyond Pennick Chase and the mountain that stands above them. I knew now that I was not in the count of humankind and had no wish to be among them any longer. In truth, I was done with them for ever.

Or so I thought.

VII

Which treats of the chamber under the motte

eing now in Maglan Horvath's good graces, or at least under his roof, Cain Caradoc the sorcerer bent his efforts to the task of making himself indispensable.

He did this with spells that astonished and awed the onlooker but cost him little. Most of them were simple glamours. He decorated Horvath's hall with cloth of gold and cloth of arras so that its splendour rivalled that of King Stephen's hall in London town. He made Horvath's coat of arms (a horse rampant, gules, on a field sable) fly above the donjon on a banner as big as the sail of a ship that hung unsupported in the air. He caused Horvath's armour, which was black iron and dinged from many a fight, to gleam with the yellow lustre of untarnishable gold. All these things were nothing but illusions, but Caradoc knew well that when a man's eye speaks to his heart his wit mostly stays out of the matter. Lord Horvath, being well pleased with what he saw, did not question it.

In more practical matters too the magician was not found wanting. When Horvath's foragers went hunting, he charmed beasts of all kinds to run onto their spears or into their nets, so the lord's table was never bare. He put a spell on Horvath's sword so the merest cut from its blade would be fatal to any foe. He raised the ghost of Robert Carne, which had not wandered far, so that Horvath could question his predecessor on the running of the castle and the proper disposition of its defences.

All these things Cain Caradoc did in much the same manner as a nursemaid might quiet a fretful child with a rattle or a kick-shaw. The most of his thought, as you might well imagine, was on the great store of power he had sensed as soon as he set foot within the donjon's walls.

He had not yet come to any understanding of what the power was, but he felt that his first perception – that of a sleeping giant – was close to the mark. The power was not being *used* at all. It was quiescent and still, a reservoir from which nobody was drawing.

Caradoc searched for the source of the power with the greatest diligence. Horvath had given him a room within the donjon, only one level lower than his own chambers but on the opposite side, its windows looking eastward across the moors towards Wetley. This was a far drearier prospect than the Chase and the adjoining mountain on which Horvath looked each morning as he rose, but the sorcerer did not mind this in the least. Being apart from his master, or from the man who thought himself his master, gave him the more freedom to pursue his explorations.

He rose each night when the household was all abed and wandered each level of the donjon in turn, feeling the ebb and flow of that strange energy and trying to trace it to its wellspring. He thought there must be some mystical artifact, a charm or totem, buried under a floorboard or mured up behind a wall, but he found none.

He realised, though, that the lower he descended through the donjon's levels the stronger his sense of the hidden power became. Into the cellars and storerooms he went, where indeed it seemed all-pervading, but still he could not tell whence it flowed.

In the lowest cellar at last he found a trapdoor of solid oak. It led not to another room but to a flight of stone steps going down and down into the dark. There was a cave under the donjon, of enormous extent. The entire mound was hollow, and all of it was a single chamber. The steps, which were almost too narrow for

Caradoc's feet, wound around its walls to deposit him at last on a floor of packed earth. In the centre of the floor there was a table carved out of what he took at first to be white marble.

It was a curious thing, this table. It was roughly circular, but to one side of it there were rounded projections that deformed its outline, as if its maker had lost interest before he could realise its final, perfect shape. Its sides did not taper at all but were of uniform width. It had been embedded deeply in the hard dirt of the floor, but not deeply enough: it still stood a little too tall for any man of normal stature to sit at comfortably. And it was not marble, as Caradoc had thought at first, but the purest ivory.

All of this, though, was of little immediate interest. Caradoc realised, as he descended and made a circuit of the huge cavern, that he had come at last to the seat or source of the power he had been sensing all this while. Whatever it was, this cave was where it made its home.

"What are you?" he said aloud. "Speak to me." And then when no answer came, "By what title shall I address you? I charge you to reveal and name yourself."

Still nothing. The silence was unbroken. Just as he had first thought, whatever dwelled in this place was profoundly asleep. It did not know itself, therefore it could not defend itself. What could a man not achieve if he could but put such a force in harness?

Caradoc tried to do it there and then, reaching out with the invisible tendrils of his art to make contact with the alien sleeper and draw its essence down into himself. He was cautious, knowing so little about what he was dealing with: he went slowly, ready to retreat at once if he met with any resistance or reversal.

He came to his senses again some hours later to find himself lying on his side on the cold earth. Drool had flowed thickly from his mouth to soak the shoulder of his robe. His whole body throbbed like a single bruise, not with pain but with power. Even in that fleeting contact he had taken so much magic, so much shaping and binding and hectoring *force* into himself that he could scarcely contain it. He felt as though it must spill out from him

61

with every gesture. And yet the power he sensed all around him was not changed or diminished by the smallest iota! This bounteous harvest that Caradoc had reaped with a momentary, glancing touch was nothing to what slept here.

It was a long while before he could get his legs back under him and stand. The atmosphere in the room had not changed. Caradoc sensed no anger or hostility. It was not as if the sleeper had noticed what he was doing and struck out at him in despite. There was just too much of power here, too much of the might of magic which is to bend the world around the user's will. Touching it even so briefly and so slightly had brought it fully and instantly to bear on Caradoc. The flood of it had drowned his senses.

And in addition to the power, it had left him with memories that were not his own, memories of the gulfs between the stars and the *Tohu Va-Vohu* that boiled endlessly before the waters above were separated from the waters below.

He went to the centre of the chamber, where the ivory table stood. He knelt and dug into the loamy earth beside it, scooping out a hollow. He worked with vigour, but however deep he dug he did not find the base of the pedestal. Instead he found an inpouching in its sides, as if it tapered to a point. He laboured on, and a few feet further down encountered an outgrowth as the tapering reversed itself.

Stepping back he surveyed what he had uncovered and knew it for what it was. The table was no table but the topmost vertebra of a colossal backbone, buried in the earth. By the same token the chamber he stood in — the interior of the mound on which the donjon stood — was the hollow of a skull, the jawbone having rolled away or perhaps been removed. Some titanic being had laid itself down here to die, and now he stood in its remains.

But it had not died. Perhaps it could not die. It had decayed indeed, and to some extent discorporated, yet still its power was shored up here in a vast reservoir, and the lingering imprint of its mind coloured the air.

Caradoc did not need to be told what manner of thing this

being was. The memories that had torn free from the sleeper's mind and lodged in his own now quickened there. They told him the sleeper's name, and as a consequence revealed to him the true story of the making of the world.

The Elohim who rebelled against God fashioned the earth from the stuff of the firmament, and made men and women to people it. That making was the all and sum of their rebellion: there had been no war in Heaven, only the Elohim deciding that the universe was worth nothing if there were none to see and love it. This vast body in whose brainpan Cain Caradoc now stood was Samael, also called הֵילֵל, Haylale or Yaldabaoth, the general of the rebel angels. He had expended the greater part of himself in the making of the world, and finally laid himself down in this place and given himself over to something like death. Something like death, yes, but also something like sleep. Yaldabaoth's essence, only a little less than divine, was not yet extinguished.

This was the first-born of God, or what was left of him.

And for a man who wished to be immortal it was the perfect, the only needful ingredient. To harvest this power was to ascend as near to godhead as made no practical difference.

The sorcerer made his way on shaking limbs back up the precarious steps, shut and bolted the trapdoor and sealed it with a spell for good measure. The spell made it invisible to any eye and immovable to any hand save only his own. He would once have had to labour for hours to fashion such a charm, but now he had merely to imagine the outline of it and the thing was done.

Away to his own bed Cain Caradoc went, his body bruised and his head all a-clamour both with pain and with excitement. He had been right to come here – and the prophesying spirits had been right to send him. He would enact his destiny in this place. He would become immortal and remove himself from death's reach for ever. Furthermore, he would become – as Yaldabaoth had been – the god and prince and master of this world.

As he lay and turned in the dark, his mind quickened with dark purpose. On the morrow he would birth atrocities.

VIII

In which (for well or ill, who can say?) I
make new acquaintance

hen I forsook Cosham and the homes of men it was
not without misgiving. I feared that life in the forest
would be hard and bleak and that I would be lonely
there.

Nothing could have been further from the truth. Among human
settlements and homesteads I had been an outcast to be driven
away with curses and cudgels, but that was because they saw in
me a human shape hideously bent from the true. In Pennick woods
and on the nameless mountain that stood behind them I was only
an animal among other animals. I hunted when I was hungry,
drank from a pool or a freshet when I was a-thirst, and at all times
went where I would. I found me a cave on a cliff's side three times
as deep as my stretched length, its floor angled upwards so the rain
would not come in. I made myself a bed of gathered ferns that
were as soft as any rushes. The nights being chill I crawled in
among the leaves and piled them again on top of me. I was never
cold for long. My body burned with a furnace heat, it seemed, so
I was my own warming pan.

Surrounded by nothing but beasts and birds, I all but forgot
human speech. I went on four legs more often than on two, and

when at length the woollen tunic that Jon and Margaret had given me became so torn and rotted that it fell off my frame, my nakedness did not trouble me much at all. Eve and Adam had worn never a stitch until they were cast out of the garden. I had found my way to a second Eden, for such it seemed to me. I had no more need of being covered over than they did.

I had much to learn, though, about my new home – and some of the lessons came hard. I had not been in Pennick three weeks when, the moon being full, I stayed out hunting too late and lost my way. My cave being high on the mountain's side I thought I had only to keep going up, but I found myself on the wrong side of a ravine and was forced to retrace my steps.

Coming to the edge of a clearing I stopped of a sudden, for something very large was moving in front of me. The moon lit up the space almost as bright as day, but still I could not tell clearly what it was I was seeing. It was a beast of some kind. Beyond that, though, my words falter. It had tusks like a boar's, except that they were longer than the span of a man's arms. It had besides great taloned forepaws, wings like an eagle, a furred coat that here in one place was white, in another black, and in a third all tawny stripes. But this was the thing I could not fathom. It was dancing in the moonlight, and as it danced its outline seemed to shift and remake itself ever and again. Now it rashed the earth with its claws. Now it dug into the ground like a mole, its pads all broad and flattened. Now it raised a horned head and bayed to the sky, rearing up on back legs that were grey stumps as wide as the bole of a tree. Its wings spread wide – but now they were leather wings instead of plumed ones, as if a bat had grown to the size of a shire horse.

Anna is my good friend now, but this was the first time I ever saw her and my heart misgave at the sight. She was at once so fierce and so strange, her aspect so fluid, her shifting flesh so monstrous that I was terrified to behold her. I watched her wild cavorting for a full minute, but only because I could not marshal my legs to take on the task of turning around and fleeing. At last

65

I backed away, stumbling over rocks and tree roots, tangling myself in hanging branches. I must have made a great noise but if she heard she took no heed of it. She was lost in the joy of her dance, a gift she gave back to the moon that gave to her this gift of change.

I did not stop running until I was back at my cave, and I did not venture out again before morning.

Another time, and this by day, I came into a part of the forest that was all grey and sickened. Where I had stumbled upon Anna all at once, this was a thing that crept on me by inches and ounces. Each tree I passed had fewer leaves than the one before. The grass and weeds at my feet became ever sparser, their green bleaching and blotching into yellow or spotted with black rot. Even the sun seemed paler here, and the air was heavier. I do not mean it was heavy with scents. It seemed heavier in itself, as though it carried some invisible freight. It was with effort that I heaved it in and out of my lungs.

I had been hunting. It was some days since I had eaten, and though my body's needs are not so great now as they were when I was alive, it still tells me when it hungers and protests if I ignore it. I kept on walking, sure that whatever this sick place was it must be small in extent and I would soon reach the other side of it.

Instead I came to a hollow in the ground that was both deep and wide. The floor of this hollow and the steep slope that led down into it were devoid of any growing thing, but three great grey stones stood together at its centre. Two of the stones had been set upright, with the third laid across them to make a kind of gate or doorway. I had heard of such things, as places where people used to go to pray and to sing the sun home before the word of Christ came to these islands, but I had never seen one with my own eyes.

Curious, I clambered down into the hollow and approached it. The closer I came, the more that heaviness of the air oppressed me. It was cold withal, and deathly quiet. I could not remember when I had last seen a bird, or heard one sing. Certes there were none here.

Being now very close to the stones I could see that they were not altogether grey. There was a blackness at the base of the two standing stones all blotched and uneven like a stain. Something about this place made me uneasy, and I meant to pass on by.

But as I came level with the stones, I saw a thing that had been hid from me until then. There was a rose bush that had grown up there in the space under the arch. Very stunted and sparse it looked, but at least it was alive in this place where everything else was dead. It bore a single flower, a rose of a very deep and beautiful red.

"What are you doing in this harsh place?" I said to the rose. "I think you were better come with me and cheer me in my cave, the whiles you live." And I went to pluck it.

I stopped with my hand on the rose's stem. A thorn had pierced my finger, but that was not why I paused. A rhyme that I had heard erewhile came back to me all unbidden.

> If e'er you walk on Pennick Hill
> Be wise and close. She bides there still.
> Walk through her gate or speak her name
> Or pluck her flower, 'tis all the same.
> Be you under a roof or under the sky
> She'll hale you to Hell with her blood-red eye.

It was a childish rhyme my mother had taught me, as she had learned it from her mother or father when she was a child herself. There was a story that came with it. The story told of a traveller who lost his way, plucked a red rose that grew in a sad, bare place and earned the anger of the one who tended it, the hellish sprite whose name could never be spoken without summoning her. That was why Jill of the Wastes was also called Unsung Jill. It was dangerous even to think of her, but whether I wished it or not I could not then forbear from doing so.

"Who comes into my circle?" said a voice right at my ear. It was the voice of an old woman, but so very low and with such a rolling growl in it that it made my teeth ache in my jaw and my eyes in their orbits.

"Nobody, beldam," I said in a faltering voice. "Nobody that matters. I came here without meaning it, and away I will again."

"Where are your manners, child? Turn and look at me when I speak to you."

"So please you, I'd as lief not."

"Do as you're bid, or I'll beat you with this willow switch. Do you see it in my hand?"

She meant to make me turn, but I did not. I ducked my head under my shoulders and closed my eyes tight.

"Or will I skin you with this paring knife?" the voice said. "This wicked little knife I have here, with an edge as sharp as a viper's tooth?"

Still I did not look. I felt her closeness, like a great boulder about to fall on me. I smelled her breath like the foulness of a bog into which many things have sunk and died and rotted. You may think I did not need to fear such a monster, being monster enough myself already, but I remembered the words of the rhyme – *she'll hale you to Hell* – and though the dead ground was flat under my two feet I felt as if I stood on the edge of a great precipice.

"I . . . I beg your pardon," I stammered. "I meant no offence to you, or to this pretty flower of yours."

"If you mean not to offend, look me in the eye."

"I will not!"

"Then you're foresworn."

Still her breath huffed against my cheek, and I knew that if I opened my eyes, even by the smallest crack, I would see her. Falling to my hands and knees I crawled across the hollow to its further edge. The sharp edges of rocks cut my skin, but that was not so much.

"I have not given you leave to depart," Unsung Jill said, still from right beside me.

"I mean to do it nonetheless, beldam," I said, mumbling the

words. "And hope you will abide here when I do. Pray pardon my transgressing, which was done from ignorance and not despite."

She said nothing to that. I crawled on until my searching hands found an upward slope. Out of the hollow I climbed, and still did not dare to open my eyes. I scrambled on through gorse and bramble thickets, tearing my flesh, bumping ever and anon into rocks and trees and finally splashing across a stream. I felt myself safe then, since most bogies and creatures of the night will not willingly cross running water.

Ah, but what about your own self, Once-Was-Willem?

There are exceptions, it seems, to every rule.

IX

How Cain Caradoc searched for a maid unblemished

here are exceptions, it seems, to every rule.

Maglan Horvath's belief – that to take a castle was to become its lord – was badly mistaken. There is in any fief a great web of oaths and obligations, traditions and understandings which binds servants to their masters, leaseholders to their liege and each and all to the Crown. In ordinary times, Horvath's tenure in Pennick would have been brief. The kith and kindred of the Carne family and all those bound to it by licence and precedent would have petitioned the king to honour their allegiance and deliver retribution. And the king, knowing that order must be maintained, would have assented.

But these were not ordinary times. The broils between King Stephen and Empress Matilda were still towards, and the king did not sit easy on his throne. He was unlikely to intervene in any purely local dispute, especially one that was taking place so very far from London.

And precedent is a horse that any man may ride if he can sit it long enough to tame it. Horvath wrote to the king's chancellor, Robert of Ghent, pledging his absolute loyalty to the throne and to the king's person. At the same time he sent criers to all the villages and townships of the fief to assure the reeves and bailiffs and landlords that their positions were safe. So long as they paid their tithes and taxes, as they had in Robert Carne's day, they would continue to enjoy the protection of the castle and the support of its master. If any defied him . . . *but my lord does not imagine that any will be so wicked and lost as to test his mercy in such a wise.*

There was some dragging of heels at first. Each landowner looked to his neighbour to see what he would do, determined not to be taken for a fool. Judging his moment carefully, Horvath hanged two men in Adderley and one in Burslem, declaring that their tithes had fallen due and they had made no effort to pay. *For open breach and public despite*, the proclamation said, *their lives and goods are forfeit.*

The lesson was well taken. The normal business of tax collection resumed, and commerce with the castle went on as if Carnes had never been.

All this was greatly satisfying to Horvath, but it brought Cain Caradoc's ambitions no further along. He had gone back to the chamber under the donjon many times, and had tried by all the tricks and stratagems he knew to draw off the entirety of Yaldabaoth's simmering power for his own use. He could not do it. The momentary contact was all he could manage before his wind and will and spirit were overwhelmed. These fleeting touches brought a bounteous harvest, increasing his store of magic beyond anything he had known before, but they would not make him immortal. Each time he had limped back up the narrow steps, drained and aching, slammed the trapdoor on his hopes and gone back to minding Baron Pennick's business (this being how Maglan Horvath now styled himself).

But now a new plan had come to the magician. When you need to pick up a hot coal you use tongs of iron, and so should he. His error had been to try to touch Yaldabaoth's sleeping might with his own bare hand when what was needed (as it were) was a kind of glove or gauntlet to go between.

71

In furtherance of this end he began by hints and indirections to work on his master's thoughts. "Have you considered, good my lord, how easily the castle fell to you? Now that you have declared your loyalty to King Stephen, it might be that the empress will turn her eye towards you. How long will Pennick stand if she brings her armies here?"

This conversation took place not in the great hall but in Horvath's privy chambers, which Caradoc had bedecked in silk and gems and cloth of gold (or the likenesses of such) until it outshone the divan of a heathen prince. A woman of unearthly beauty danced before them, and though she too was nought but illusion, the perfection of her movements entranced the eye and enslaved the mind.

"So what of it?" Horvath grunted, unwilling to be distracted from the lady's performance by mere matters of state. "I had to declare for someone, and Stephen has the upper hand right now. If that changes, so will I."

"But what if Matilda forestalls you? Haply the king will come to your aid, but that will hardly help if the castle has fallen before he can arrive. Now is the time, I think, to tear down that wooden stockade and raise up a wall of good dressed stone – and to turn this donjon into a proper keep that will not fall open at the first knock."

Horvath scowled. The castle's vulnerability was not an idea on which he liked to dwell. "But your spells will protect me, Caradoc. Isn't that why I keep you?"

"My lord, all my sorceries are at your command. But just as a good meal needs bread and wine as well as meat, a good defence needs stone as well as magic. And there's wisdom, besides, in giving employment to the masons and carpenters of Trent. They will bless you for it, and when they come home with full purses their wives and children will bless you too. You rule by fear now, and fear does well enough, but love is a stronger bond and this will make them love you."

It was not the work of a day to make Horvath yield, but yield he did. Before the year was out the stockade was torn down and work began on a stone wall to replace it. The stone was limestone from the quarry at Cauldon, which being within the fief was cheap and easy to bring. An army of stonemasons, smiths, carpenters and joiners descended on Pennick, and the din of their labours could be heard both night and day.

The other part of the plan, which Horvath now believed was his own, was to rear up a stone keep to replace the donjon, and this was where Caradoc had been aiming all along. So now he came at the baron again, choosing a moment at the end of a meal when Horvath had eaten and drunk his fill and could scarce rise from his place. "I believe there is a custom, good my lord," he remarked with seeming carelessness, "in the region where you were born. A rite to entreat the favour of what the pagans call the *genius loci*, and thus ensure that a castle once built can never be breached."

"What are you talking about?" Horvath demanded. "What custom? I know of no such custom."

The baron was lying. He knew well what Cain Caradoc meant, but did not wish to consider it.

"The tradition as I understand it," said the magician, "is to find a child of maiden years, whether boy or girl, and immure them in a hollow under the foundation stone of the castle's keep. That would be here." Instead of touching his finger to the plans he gestured and made the image of the stone keep erect itself in the air before them. A place under the entrance gate glowed red as if a fire had been set there.

"That's barbarism," Horvath said. "I'll have none of that."

Caradoc affected surprise. "Did not your lordship kill the children of Robert Carne when you took the castle? I've heard it said so. And I do not see where this is any different."

Horvath grimaced. He put his hand on his sword's hilt as if in warning. "It feels different to me," he said. "I killed Carne's sons because when their beards had grown in they would have challenged me. It was for a purpose."

"And so would this be," Caradoc persisted, "I'd have you consider it. Blood magic is strong. The child's death by itself secures nothing, but with my spells and wards woven in withal the benefit would be great. You'd never need to fear siege engines or fire. With the right enchantment I could make it impossible for anyone of harmful intent even to enter your keep."

"But then they would not need to," Horvath said grimly. "The harmful intent being already all within."

Seeing that the baron would not be moved, Caradoc let the matter drop. He was both annoyed and surprised to receive this response. He had not expected to find Horvath's conscience so tender. But there's many a one that will slit his neighbour's throat in a quarrel over a pennyworth of flour, and then forbear from kicking a starveling dog out of his path. That is to say, every man has his maggots and his sticking points – and once you know where they are you can oftentimes find a way to go around them.

Caradoc went forth from the castle that evening and walked the three miles to Cosham. Once there he sat himself down on a piece of common land that fronted the church, rested his back against an oak, closed his eyes and listened. Among his other skills both natural and otherwise he commanded the mystery of sending his spirit abroad from his body. Though it seemed he did not remove from the common, in fact he wandered in and out through all the houses of the village. He was seeking a particular thing, and he was prepared to keep on seeking until he found it, whether in Cosham or in one of the other villages of the fief.

But he was fortunate, if such a word can be used for good success in a bad cause. He began his search in the nearest house, which was also the largest. It was the house of Matthew Theakston, whose name I have already mentioned to you, a yardlander of Cosham and the village's self-appointed bailiff. And in Theakston's house he found straightway the thing he had come looking for.

Theakston had a wife, Sarah, and between them they had made a daughter, Betheli, that had then eleven years on her back. They had three sons besides, who were hale as horses. Betheli was not. She had a phthisis, a cough that was consuming her slowly. She had always been sickly but now was wasting away, and all her parents could do was to make her comfortable.

Caradoc's spirit hovered over the girl and over the rest of the family. He observed how they had already bid farewell to the girl in their hearts; how they crossed themselves when they spoke her name, as you would if you named a saint; how her mother had already sewn the dress of pure white linen in which the girl would be buried, for status and precedence could not be set aside even in a time of tragedy.

Caradoc was well pleased. Rising from his rest, which was no rest at all but only its semblance, he went back to the castle and presented himself again to Baron Horvath. He told the baron that in Cosham village there was a maiden who was so close to death that if death was a suitor you would say he was overly familiar.

"Why are you telling me this?" Horvath asked. "I thought I had already made clear to you—"

"What you said to me," Caradoc said, boldly breaking in, "was that you would not brook the thought of a sacrifice. But how if a sick child were laid in a hollow place under that foundation stone and in due course she died of the sickness that already wracks her? With the stone once laid over her I could still make the magic I described to you, without blame or reproach or harm to any."

Horvath approached this idea as a rat approaches a trap, all wariness and mistrust. "And you have not already spelled this girl," he asked, "to make her sick?"

Caradoc raised an eyebrow. "Do you think I'd waste my talents on such a thing, my lord? Truly? Are ailing children such a rarity?"

"I suppose not," Horvath conceded. "So we'd do nothing to hasten her death? Only let the sickness run its course?"

Caradoc shrugged. "That's for you to choose, my lord. I'm as happy one way as the other, so long as she dies and the spell is made."

Horvath pondered a while longer but at last assented. He saw the benefit of making his new stone keep impregnable from the outset, and although he was sure Caradoc's frank manner concealed

75

some ulterior purpose, he was unable to see how he could lose by this. He summoned his messenger. It was that same Joseph Payne that had been in Robert Carne's employ. He had contrived to survive the sacking of the castle and offered his services to its new master. "Go you into Cosham," Horvath ordered Payne now. "Inform the bailiff, Matthew Theakston, that he is to present himself here with his daughter tomorrow morn."

Payne went at once to complete his errand, the quicker because Theakston had given him a drubbing once when they both were children and he had never forgotten it.

"But my daughter is too ill to walk," Theakston told Payne when he came and announced the summons.

"Let her ride, then."

"On what? We've no horse."

It was not in Payne's nature to show either sympathy or hesitation. "Put her in a cart's bed, for all I care. She's to come, man. That's all there is to it."

"But what does his lordship want with our Betheli?" Sarah Theakston wailed when her husband relayed the news to her. "Can she not die in peace?"

"It doesn't matter a fart what he wants," her husband said, his helplessness in the face of this absurd demand making him quick to anger. "We must do as we're bid. I'll go now and be back before night."

With some difficulty Betheli was removed to the village ox-cart the next morning on the mattress of thin ticking on which she lay. She was in one of her fainting spells and could scarcely raise her head.

"Where are we going?" she asked her father.

"To Pennick Castle, my dear one. Baron Horvath wants to see us."

"Why? Why does he want to? Who are we to be looked at?"

"I cannot say."

The road was rough and the wagon in poor repair. Betheli winced at every jolt and jar, but she did her best not to cry out because she hated – as only those with a lingering sickness can hate – to appear weak. At length she was eased by the rocking of the cart into a shallow sleep.

When Theakston came at last to the castle he was met by men-at-arms who took charge of the cart, bidding him leave it – and his daughter – in their safekeeping. He was loath to do so. These men were rough in their manner and he did not trust them. But seeing he had no choice he let himself be led away to one of the longhouses, where the baron was residing while the donjon was levelled and the new stone keep built up.

The baron sat at a great oaken table with a stoup of wine at his elbow and Cain Caradoc hovering close at hand. Horvath still had not entirely made his peace with what he was doing, but he put the best face on it he could. He told Theakston he had heard of Betheli's sickness and meant to ease her last days, giving her such comforts as the castle could offer. He threw down a purse of silver, which he said was not in exchange for the girl – he was not buying her, by any means! – but only meant to console Theakston and his lady for the loss of their child.

Theakston was sorely confused. It seemed a great thing for the baron to give him such a mark of favour. But he had not brought any of Betheli's clothes with him, having no notice that he would be leaving her behind at the castle when he left it. And what would he say to his wife? And how would they go about visiting Betheli if she was mured up in Pennick? He was not used to come to the castle except when he was summoned, and his wife never came there at all. She would be outfaced to walk among so many rough men.

Theakston began in a halting way to explain all this to the baron, but it was Caradoc who answered him. "These matters would be somewhat of a problem," he said, "if the girl were likely to live much longer. As it is, you may say your farewell to her today. There's no necessity for you to return."

"But . . ." Theakston tried again. "My wife . . ."

"I'm sure she said farewell to your daughter back in Cosham,"

77

said Caradoc with the same cold indifference. "What's gained by doing so again?" He held Theakston's stare until at length the other man was compelled to look away.

"Aye," he said weakly. "Only, we had thought . . ."

"There's ten shillings in that purse," Baron Horvath offered. Theakston's dismay shamed him, but he hardened his heart. A man should show more fortitude at a child's dying, he thought, given how very prone to death children seemed to be. He had none of his own, unless there was a by-blow somewhere he had not been told about. His soldiering and then his brigandry had been at the expense of any other kind of life or expectation.

Theakston was still struggling with himself. A man did not say no to his lord, but to say yes to this was more than he could manage. His daughter! The least and yet the most of his four children!

It seemed, though, that his agreement was now being assumed. Baron Horvath had already turned away. Caradoc gave signal to the men-at-arms who stood at the door. They came forward to lead Theakston away, one of them putting an ungentle hand on his shoulder.

"My lord!" Theakston bleated at the last, as Horvath reached the door. "What of the funeral? Can I come to claim my daughter's body to be dressed for burial?"

"There is no need," said Caradoc. "She will be buried here."

Theakston took this fresh blow with as much fortitude as he could muster. "But . . . we will be called? The parson will tell us when . . . When Betheli . . .?"

"We don't require the parson. We'll conduct our own service. If time allows, you and your wife will be brought for it. If not, you may light a candle for her in Cosham kirk. Your prayers will still reach her."

Theakston made one final effort. "But my wife has sewn a dress for her laying out!"

"You may bring it and leave it at the gate."

No more words were spoken. Theakston was taken from the

room back out into the yard, where the cart he had come in stood empty. What had become of his daughter he could not tell. The gates were already held open for him and the soldiery stood all around him, as grim of mien as if some fight were towards.

"Off you go now," said the captain. "Be swift."

Theakston looked from one face to another. He saw no mercy or patience in any. He wept as he climbed up into the cart's seat, and he wept as he drove it away.

And all the way home to Cosham, where Sarah would ask him where their daughter was and he would have no answer to give.

X

Of Betheli, the manner of her life and death

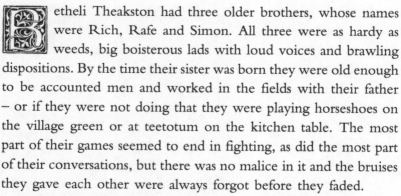etheli Theakston had three older brothers, whose names were Rich, Rafe and Simon. All three were as hardy as weeds, big boisterous lads with loud voices and brawling dispositions. By the time their sister was born they were old enough to be accounted men and worked in the fields with their father – or if they were not doing that they were playing horseshoes on the village green or at teetotum on the kitchen table. The most part of their games seemed to end in fighting, as did the most part of their conversations, but there was no malice in it and the bruises they gave each other were always forgot before they faded.

A girl growing up in such circumstances must perforce be robust or she will be pummelled out of existence. But Betheli was a tiny thing, as pale as a tallow candle and as thin as a stripped lath. Her brothers knew not what to make of her, or how to show their love for her without shouts and buffets and wrestlings. Lacking any other ideas as to how to pursue the matter, they withdrew from her.

But Betheli would have none of that. She toddled after her brothers at their work and at their play, and would not leave them alone for so much as a moment. She walked under their legs when they were ploughing, danced between them when they were at football where even the burliest of lads might be trampled. If they wrestled she threw herself pell-mell into the fight. If they punched each other, her weightless fists rained down as many blows as the best of them, even if they were not generally noticed.

And since the boys could scarcely touch this scrap of humanity without knocking her down, they surrendered at last and reconfigured themselves so they faced outwards with Betheli in the middle, defending her against the world which she greeted both with the pugnacity that was native to her and with what she had learned from them.

And so she grew, at the centre of a great infolded knot of speechless love and kindness, feeling that the world's countless cruelties could not touch her. They could, of course, and in due course they did, but even as her sickness gained on her she took comfort in her brothers' devotion to her. She had besides every indulgence her parents could provide. Being unable to work she had little to do but to keep her bed and to dream waking dreams. She lived a life inside her own thoughts.

But her own thoughts were not a calm place. The more her body wasted, the further did her spirit roam and the more elaborately did her fancy build. She kept court over phantoms of her own creation and went on journeys to inner landscapes of vast extent. Her brothers, who she loved best, were ever her companions in these imagined excursions and achieved great feats of arms in her service. She rewarded them for their valour with lands and titles. Her demesnes growing ever wider, she could well afford it.

This was the girl on whom Cain Caradoc had settled for the realisation of his plans, and it is needful now to reveal what those plans were. The magician had promised Baron Horvath that a sacrifice carried out upon the cornerstone of the new keep would make that keep invulnerable to assault. This was, as he had said, a widespread practice in the Frankish kingdoms where Horvath had spent much of his youth. The magic was of the kind called *imitatio* or effigy, in which a desired property is borrowed from one thing so that it may be applied to another. A maiden's body has never been penetrated, so when she dies either on the cornerstone or under it that inviolability is passed to the stone.

It must be said that Caradoc did not care a fart whether the keep stood or fell. He did not mean to bide there for a single hour longer than he needed to. Once he had taken Yaldabaoth's power into himself and become immortal, he would be away and gone before the next cock-crow. But every time he tried to touch that power directly it shook him off like a flea. When next he coped it, he must of necessity put something in between, a barricade or prophylaxis, so that he might finish his spell before he was rendered insensible. A child's soul would do very well for this, he surmised.

The spell of *imitatio* would depend on and make use of Betheli's body. It would also leave her spirit immured in the stone. Caradoc believed he could hold that little imprisoned soul before himself like a shield to keep back the hurtful force of Yaldabaoth's raw power the while he tapped it and drew it off into himself.

With suchlike thoughts in mind, he took charge of the affair. He was somewhat afraid of the baron's interfering, but the baron left him to it, making no secret of his distaste for the whole proceeding. The men-at-arms too were fearful of sorceries and devilments: they had been instructed to assist Caradoc but were clearly very desirous of going away again as soon as ever they were allowed to. Wherefore once Caradoc had ordered the girl removed to the summit of the motte and laid out upon the limestone slab that would become the new keep's cornerstone, he was very soon left alone with her.

Betheli had realised long ere this that she had not been brought into the castle for any good purpose. Though she was tender in years and had had but little commerce with the world, she could read men's faces well enough, and what she saw in Cain Caradoc's gave her to fear. She wondered indeed why her father had left her with such a man, but she did not doubt that the sorcerer's intention was to hurt her, and she did not deceive herself that she had any means of defending herself against him. She could not even run away, though she had been left unbound: her sickness made her too weak.

So she did what seemed wisest, which was to learn as much as she could and see whether anything she learned might change the situation. "What are you?" she asked Caradoc.

He answered never a word, but took from the belt at his waist a slender, long-bladed dagger.

"You mean to murder me then," Betheli said.

"Say sacrifice, rather," Caradoc said, standing over her. He began to mutter charms over the dagger, preparing it for its unholy purpose.

"How is that different?" Betheli asked him.

"The one is a crime, the other a sacrament. Be silent now, and let me work."

"The sacrament is bread and wine, or else it's giving a babe its name."

"It's whatsoe'er it needs to be," Caradoc snapped, "and here and now it needs to be your blood. If you speak again I'll bind your mouth with a cloth."

"What cloth? You have no cloth."

Caradoc swore a terrible oath. He had lost his place in his conjuring and now must begin again. He warned the girl that he would stifle her into silence if she spoke another word.

"Go to," Betheli invited him. "If you bring your hand in reach of my teeth, I'll give you some blood for your sacrament."

Caradoc, still weaving his charm over the knife, raised his voice to drown out the girl's words, but this only gave Betheli the more encouragement for she saw that she had vexed him. She began to sing.

She sang the song that is sometimes called "I Will Tell You One-oh". The Jews sing it, and the Christians likewise, and each believes they invented it. It is taught to children to make them remember their numbers, and the theme is call and answer.

I will tell you one-oh.

What is your one-oh?

One is God in Heaven-oh, in grace and good for aye.

I will tell you two-oh.

What is your two-oh?

Two is the blameless babes, one is God in Heaven-oh, in grace
and good for aye.

I will tell you three-oh.

What is your three-oh?

Three went in the furnace, two is the blameless babes, one is God
in Heaven-oh, in grace and good for aye.

I will tell you four-oh.

What is your four-oh?

Four the gospel creatures, three went in the furnace, two is the
blameless babes and one is God in Heaven-oh in grace and
good for aye.

And so on, for as long as you can count. Betheli knew it all the
way up to thirteen.

Caradoc would have beaten her into silence, but he was afraid
of stumbling once more in his spellcraft. There is a balance in such
things that is both nice and exacting. He could not afford to hack
and hew it too much, or it would work against him or else not
work at all. He spoke louder still, and Betheli shouted ever the
more. "I will tell you seven-oh! What is your seven-oh?" It became
a race between them, yet with only one of the two wishing to
reach the finishing tree.

Caradoc finished first, bellowing the final words of his conjuration ". . . *quemadmodum carnem decerpo!*" and turning on his heel
to plunge the dagger into Betheli's chest.

She perished at once, but the song echoed on in Caradoc's ears.
Betheli had carried it over death's threshold with her, and (though
she had now no breath left to sing with) she finished three more
verses while the wizard listened in consternation. It was unlikely
anyone else could hear. Only the bond between their two spirits

84

allowed him to eavesdrop on the thoughts that still crawled in her cooling brain, and they dwindled soon enough into silence.

Still he was shaken and angry. The girl had defied him! A peasant slattern with no more wit than a hen in a yard, and she had dared to raise her voice to him. Almost, she had made him stumble in his spellcraft. The worthless chit! He wished that he had twisted the knife a little, to vex her the more in her passing.

In all, the rite had had more of crude farce to it than of solemn dread. Caradoc had meant to push on straight away and see what he might achieve with the girl's soul now cemented in place, but his concentration was gone and his calm all shattered. Perhaps it would be better to turn to matters of housekeeping instead.

He called the men-at-arms back up from the yard. They balked a little when they saw what had become of the girl, but they saw in Caradoc's face that it would not go well with them if they spoke of it. Under his direction they removed the body and laid it down in a shallow pit that had been dug nearby, to the exact measurements of the cornerstone. With the aid of a block and tackle they lifted the great slab, moved it by the width of some four or five paces and set it down again atop Betheli's corpse.

Good enough for now, Caradoc decided. Tomorrow the masons would begin to build and this place would seethe like a bees' nest. But at night he would come again and try his mettle.

The girl might have slighted him in life, but being dead he dared swear he would make her dance.

XI

Which mostly treats of the changers
that lived on the mountain

Being yet unused to my new state that was not dead nor properly alive, it still surprised me when I met others who were the same. Not that anyone was quite like me, with my limbs askew and my bones all jumbled like spillikins. But there were others in Pennick Chase besides myself that were in a like state of death-in-life or life-in-death.

There was Unsung Jill, for one. I had thought her nought but a story until I came upon her hollow in the hills and almost looked into her eye. Now I thought all stories might well be true and swore to keep my wits about me when I walked abroad in case there were more bogies and hobgads lurking in my way.

But despite my wariness I was still deceived when one morning I came to a spring or freshet where I was wont to drink and found a woman there dressed only in a shift of grey hessian, washing her clothes in the running water. I stopped at the edge of the trees, thinking to withdraw before she saw me and was affrighted. But even as this thought came into my mind she turned as if at some sound – though I had made none – and saw me.

She smiled.

"Ah, so it's you," she said. "I wondered when we would meet

again." Her voice was strangely accented, the tones harsh and halting but with a pitch and pull to them like the rhythm of half-heard music. She beckoned to me to join her. "Come sit with me, and tell me who you are. When last we met you did not linger, and I did not have a chance to ask. You must have a name, I'm thinking, and most likely a story to go with it. I'm Anna, in case you wished to ask me. Anna Kjetil's Daughter."

I ventured forth from hiding and sat me down on the rocks some little way from her. I was all amazed. It seemed this woman was not abashed by my hideous appearance nor by meeting a monster such as me in so remote a place. Her beauty made me tongue-tied, too. Her hair, which was as yellow as flax, fell halfway down her back. She was as broad across the shoulders as my father had been, and though she was then kneeling it seemed to me that when she stood she would be taller than him too. Her eyes were blue, a hue so bright and sharp they reminded me of the stones set for decoration around the outside of Parson Lebone's communion cup. There was a calmness and a grace about her that I cannot give words to, and I was sure that I had never met her before that day. There was no way I could have forgotten the sight.

I said as much, and she laughed. "But yes, you saw me at my steps the other night." She raised an eyebrow. "I was naked. You should be shent to spy upon a maiden so."

My mouth fell open, which could not have been a pleasant sight. The strange beast that I had seen dancing with only the full moon as her lantern, this was her! "But . . . but how can that be?" I stammered.

"I'm a skin-changer," the woman said, as bluntly as if she had said *I come from Adderley* or *it's like to rain*. "It runs in my family. My brother Kel has it too, but in a different way than me." She saw in my face that I was still confused. "We are *ulfeðnar*. You've heard of *ulfeðnar*?"

I had, of course. Everyone knew there were beasts whose hair was hid on the inside of their skin, until the moon turned them the other way out and showed the truth of them. "But *ulfeðnar* turn into wolves," I said. "And you . . . the thing that you became . . . if I were asked to name it . . ."

She only laughed again. She seemed to be taking a great pleasure in this conversation, as if we were two old friends that had met again after a long parting and were overjoyed to renew the acquaintance. "When I dance in the moon, there are no names. You still have not told me yours, by the way."

"I'm Willem," I said, but then I bethought me. "At least, I was, once. Now I suppose I'm something different."

"Well, Once-Was-Willem, you should beware of putting too much trust in the words and wisdom of men. Oftentimes they tell as solemn truth what's nought but guessing – or wishing, which is worse. We changers are no two of us alike. Why should we be, when change is all our being? My brother turns bear when the moon kisses him – as big and beautiful a bear as you ever saw, that can swim quicker than an eel and topple a tree by scratching his arse on it.

"And you saw what I become. I am all things and nothing, a fountain that runs with shapes instead of water. I am the memory of all flesh that was and all that will be. And am I not beautiful?"

"You are," I said truthfully. "I never saw anything to equal it."

"Well then, go to. *Ulfeðnar* is a cloth that fools drape over their ignorance. I wager they call you revenant, and think they have then explained you."

I had not thought until then that there might be a name for me. In some small way it comforted me – not because I thought a name could tell me what I was but because it meant I was not completely unexampled and therefore not completely alone.

We talked a little longer, the while Anna washed her clothes and wrung them dry. Then she bade me farewell, promising the next time we met to introduce me to her brother.

That next time was not long in coming. After our first meeting (or our second, I should say) I saw Anna many times, both at the spring and in the woods, and Kel was with her more often than not. He was as huge as her and with the same mane of blond hair, though he had a great beard thereunto and tufts of coarse hair up his arms that were all the same bright gold.

He told me he had come into England with Swein Astridsson of Denmark, to whom his father owed allegiance. Anna came with him as a camp follower, because they loved each other dearly and did not wish to be parted. Kel fought at Fulford, where the Norse won the day and all men present thought that the road to London and the throne must now lie open. But then when Hardrada was slain at Stamford's Bridge that great enterprise all came to nothing. Brother and sister had decided then to linger on in England, whose woods and hills they had come to love.

Kel told me too of his time with Maglan Horvath, from whom he had but recently parted. "He's a good master after his fashion. Fairer than most, I'd say, unless you slight him to his face. But now he's taken up with this sorcerer, Cain Caradoc, a cunten bastard if ever there was one."

"Cain Caradoc was the one that haled me back from the grave," I said. "He owns a tithing of my soul."

"Is it so?" Kel made a sour face. "Well I pity you for it, for I wouldn't trust that whoreson more than a sparrow's weight."

"Tell him why you left Horvath's service," Anna urged him.

"There was a girl brought up to the castle. A sickly one. Betheli, her name was."

"Belike that is Matthew Theakston's daughter, of Cosham village where I was wont to live. She's Betheli."

"Better to say *was* than is, for Caradoc made an end of her. It was a rite of some kind. Necromancy. I know not. But I spoke with the men who saw the child's body afterwards and they said he had stabbed her through the heart with a dagger. And when I went to Horvath to tell him what was done, he told me it was no man's affair but his. He had given order for it, he said, and there was an end of it. If I liked it not I could go to the Devil.

"'I think if I go to the Devil,' I said, 'I'll find you there before me. God bye you, Maglan Horvath,' I said. 'God bless you and God bye you. You'll weep for this day's work but I'll not be standing close enough to wipe your eye.'

"And so I went. Horvath was furious that I had bearded him to his own face. He gave order that I should be held and chained to a stake like the bear I was. Well, I said, I make this promise to the man that tries it, that I'll hold no grudge against him but still I'll give his head to his best friend as a joint stool. And I walked out of gates, with none offering to stop me."

Anna put her hand on her brother's shoulder. "I'm glad to have him here with me again," she said. "The children of Eve and Adam are all very well, and it's a fine thing to talk and drink with them from time to time, but it's best not to stay close to them for long. Our mother used to say that when men were not our meat they were our tormentors, and nothing in between."

"There are some of them that have goodness in them," Kel said.

"I don't say there aren't. Only that it's best for our kind to have no truck with them. Look what they did to Peter Floodfoot."

Peter Floodfoot was another one like us that lived in Pennick Chase, not on the mountain's side like me nor in the deep woods like Kel and Anna but in Erren river, which rushes down to feed the Trent at Kinsley. That's a misspeaking, but I do not know how to say it better. Peter does not live in the water, he is of the water and the water is of him. And when the people of Kinsley made a bridge over his stream they hurt him sorely. He would have turned the river another way but there was a man of learning in the town who bound him with a spell to make him stay. He was now somewhat a slave, with the river tied to its course and him tied to the river. He hated them for it, as well he might, and would drown any of Kinsley that fell into his waters. Children of Cosham were taught to say their names when they swam in the Erren or drank from it. "So please you, Peter Floodfoot, I am so-and-so of Cosham village, not of Kinsley." I cannot say whether or not this appeased him, but he never harmed any of us.

So now I was less lonely than I was before. I had been wont sometimes, when a sad mood was on me, to creep down into

Cosham at night and sit with my back to a house's wall, listening at the window for the sounds of human speech within. Most often I would choose my mother and father's house – or what used to be their house, though now my father's sister Mary lived there with her husband Kenneth and some of my cousins that had been my playmates. Hearing the clatter of trenchers, the scuffling of feet on the rushes within and my aunt's shrill voice bidding the children say their prayers I would close my eyes and pretend I was back with my family again.

But now that I had friends that were closer to my own spirit and suasion, I found my longing for Cosham lessened. The pretence had been a hard one to keep up, for I knew that the smallest glimpse of me would have had my little cousins shrieking and wailing and their parents praying God to save their souls. But Anna always smiled when she saw me. "Ho and hey to you, Once-Was-Willem," she would say. "What news?"

"There is a skein of starlings over the woods," I would tell her, or "The big yew by the torrent is down in last night's storm," for the woods were alive as a bustling market town is alive and there was always news to tell. And then Anna would reward me for my intelligencing with a trout or a salmon she had caught or with the haunch of a hare.

Kel was slower to trust me, for whenever I was by him he could smell the magic that had made me and it made his hackles to stir and raise themselves. Cain Caradoc having been the cause of Kel's removing from the castle and his friends there, he hated everything that reminded him of the sorcerer, which meant that for some little while he could not unbend to me. But when he had heard the whole of my story he was moved from his despite, seeing well that I was no ally or tool of Caradoc's but one that had suffered as he had at the sorcerer's hands.

It was then full summer. Half a year had passed since my resurrection, and I had seen more changes in that time than I can easily number. The biggest change came first of course, which was from death to life. Then from my home to a kind of exile, when I lived wild in the fields and tithings around Cosham. From there to the woods and the mountain, and a new life for the most part out of the way of humankind. And now from solitariness to the care and comfort of my friends, which made me happier than I had ever been.

Dying is a sorry thing, I thought, but it was worth going through death to come finally to this. Nothing I had lost could be half so dear or half so sweet as what I had found.

And so I might have lived to this day, and known no sorrow deserving of the name. But humankind was not done with me yet. Great sorrow, great travail, great loss and perturbation were in store, for me and all of us. There is a saying: call no man fortunate until he is dead.

Wait a little longer, is all I would say.

XII

Of Peter Floodfoot, and the flute that made no music

ut wait, here is one other thing — a small one in its way, and yet a great deal came to depend on it.

I was used in this time to spend the most part of my days in long, rambling walks through the woods and across the mountain's face. I was hungry to know every inch of the land that was now my home, so that I could say I loved it with no word of a lie and nothing omitted. Both the paths and the pathless places, the caves from which the freshets sprang, the sheer cliffs where the wild goats ambled so carelessly, the groves so thick that light never came there: my care was to them all, and I paid court to them like the most besotted swain that ever was.

One day, having been lost for some hours in thickets of oak and alder, I came out on the Erren's bank in a place I had never visited before. A turn of the river, where it went of a sudden from a rush to a trickle, had left behind a bank of sand in which a few curious things lay half-buried. Here was a brooch of silver which must once have held a precious stone of some kind, the setting now hanging open like a mouth with half its teeth missing. Here again was the broken blade of an oar from some boat that had braved Erren's waters and come to grief (perhaps, I thought, there had been men of Kinsley in it).

And what was this now? Ankle-deep in the wet and sucking sand, I leaned forward and fished out something from the shallows that gleamed as white as bone.

It *was* bone, though from what part of what creature I could not tell. Whatever it had been to begin with, it had been worked on and shaped. The main part of it was a rod or tube a little longer than my thumb and twice as thick, that branched out at one end into three narrower tubes like the pipes of a pan flute. It had been hollowed out, and holes had been let into these narrow pipes all along their length. The other end had a wider opening.

I had seen whistles made of tin, flutes of carved and polished wood, and once a set of border pipes that a minstrel carried when he came to Cosham for our Easter festival. This did not look exactly like any of them, but it called them all to mind.

I brought what I thought was the mouthpiece to my mouth and blew, with all the holes open. Not a sound came from the other, three-forked end: the whistle remained silent. I tried again, stopping first this hole and then that one, but never a note came out of the thing.

"What are you, then?" I asked it.

"It doesn't play." The voice came from behind me. "I never knew it to make a sound."

I turned and saw a boy all water, rising out of the river into the air as if a waterfall had been turned on its head. The water as it rose made the shape of the boy's body, his limbs, his face – then when that was done it fell again into the Erren and became one with the water all around. The boy's features wavered from one second to the next but he was not hard to see because the Erren had enough of mud and grit and sand to give some weight and colour to him. He was not formed all of water, in other words, but also of the things that were in the water. He was very tall and very thin, with dark green weeds for his hair. His eyes were all one with his face and had no colour of their own at all.

"Are you Peter Floodfoot?" I asked him.

"Of course I am. Who else would I be? And you're Willem Turling of Cosham village."

"I used to be, yes. How did you know that?"

"You told me many times, whenever you bathed or swam in Erren or crossed over it."

I nodded. "I wanted you to know I was not of Kinsley. Do you know where this came from, then?"

"No, boy of Cosham. I don't. But it's lain on my banks these many years and I've seen what happens when people pick it up. They all try to play it. Then just as quickly they throw it down again, looking fearful or angry, and wipe their hands. One or two have tried to break it, but it's stronger than it looks. None has ever taken it away with them."

"What were they afraid of?"

Peter shook his head, which wobbled all out of shape for a moment and then remade itself. "I cannot say. Perhaps it made them afraid on purpose, so they would not take it. Perhaps it has been waiting for you all this time."

I thought about this. There was nothing about the bone-flute that frightened me. If anything it drew me. I liked its shape, and its feel in my hands. Withal I was pleased to have met Peter at last, and to find him so much more companionable than he was fearsome. Without a thought I held out the flute for him to take. "Here," I said. "I found this in your waters, so by rights it's yours."

He made no move to take it. In fact he drew away from it a little, the base of his water jet dancing on the river in tiny circles as he moved. "Not I!" he exclaimed. "I've no breath to play it with. And I like not to have a piece of someone else's magic within me. Not when it's as strong as this is."

I looked at the flute again, with more of respect and perhaps more of caution than before. "There's such great power in this?"

"Oh yes."

"Is it dangerous, then?" I was thinking of Unsung Jill and how close I had come to disaster when I met her up in the hills. I had no great desire to repeat that experience with another bogey – one that was looking for the missing piece of one of its bones.

"It might be," Peter admitted. "But I don't think so. There was no evil intent in the carving of it. I'd know if there was. I'm not saying you should keep it. Do as you will. Only don't throw it back into my river, for it troubles me like an itch."

"I'll take it then," I said, "and leave it on the side of the mountain somewhere, where haply the winds will play on it. It was good to meet you, Peter Floodfoot."

He bowed. "Likewise, Willem Turling."

"I'm not him any more. Anna calls me Once-Was-Willem. I think that fits me better."

"Then that's what I'll call you. Farewell for now – but come and drink from my springs whenever you like. Only there'll be no need now to say your name each time. Only if you decide to change it again!"

He was gone in an instant, his water spout falling apart all at once into drops and spray that splashed down into the river or were carried away on the wind. A few drops touched my cheek, where they felt like kisses. I went away from that place in good spirits, feeling that I had made another friend.

I was not mistaken in that. Ever and again, when I came to a stream or a pool to drink, Peter would rise up and greet me. He was chained to Erren's waters, but a river is a thing that goes in and out of many places: all the streams that fed the river were playgrounds to Peter. And he was indeed of a playful nature – a thing that surprised me because of the war he waged on the villagers of Kinsley. When I asked him about this he laughed. "I never warred on them," he said. "They needed someone to blame when their boats overturned or the fish spurned their hooks. I do drench them from time to time. I like that they make me such a fearsome creature in their stories, and I'd think it shame to let them forget me."

That was Peter's way. He loved riddles and songs and stories of every kind. "Every tale I'm told," he said, "I take them all down to the sea and throw them in, and the sea carries them to other rivers that are far distant. That's what the sea is for, Once-Was-Willem. We'd never keep such a big, untidy thing if it didn't serve some purpose."

One of the stories he told was about Unsung Jill, the most fearsome and forbidding of his neighbours. He told me she had been a kind of fairy once, a sylph that had her house inside a tree and was the tree's cousin. But then she saw a thing she was not meant to see, and this sight was so terrible that she could not afterwards be free of it. She rubbed her eye raw and red, but still the thing she saw stayed lodged there. And that was why she was of such a cursed disposition, and preyed on those that came within her circle. For whenever her red eye was open she was seeing the same awful sight.

"Was it Hell she saw?" I asked him. "For that's where her eye is said to send people if you look into it."

"That must be it then," Peter said. "Unless it's just the hay fever that makes the eye so red and a headache that makes her surly. But that would be a poor story, so I'll have none of it."

I was glad that I had met him, for I loved his company. But I never did throw away the bone-flute, as I had told him I would. When I thought about it, it seemed wrong and disrespectful to whoever it had been a part of. And also, if I could not sleep at night for sorrow or cold or restlessness, I found that tapping my thumb gently against the side of the flute was enough to make a sort of listening silence spill out from it and fill my little cave. It did not make me any warmer, but still it was something like a blanket that spread itself over me.

So I kept it with me, tied around my neck with a rope of plaited flax I made for it with my own hands. I grew used to having it there, the only thing that made me less naked than the animals. Later, when I went to Hell, I learned from the Elohim themselves whose instrument it was.

And who I was carrying it for, which was not the same.

97

XIII

Of the fight within the cornerstone

Betheli Theakston, once she realised she was dead, wasted no time in grief or fearfulness.

Grief? Grieving is what the living do. They say it's for the dead but it's mostly their own full hearts they're mindful of. And fear? What should she be frightened of when the worst had already happened? She gave herself instead to rage. Cain Caradoc the sorcerer had done this to her, when she had offered him no harm or insult. True, she had sung while he was spelling, but that was not so much. A man who could not take a little mockery of his seriousness was not a man at all but a puling babe. Betheli swore she would work him ill for this injury. Come hap or harm, she would pay it back on him.

The worst of her situation, she quickly discovered, was the straitness of it. Cain Caradoc's spell bound her to the cornerstone, a block of cut and dressed limestone five feet long, a yard wide and two spans thick. Her body lay in the hollow beneath the block; her spirit was tethered within it. It was a reliquary for her soul, holding her penned until the passing of ages should finally reduce the stone to dust — at which time perhaps the dust would carry her away, broken into countless pieces and lost for ever.

But that would only happen if she allowed it, and she was determined that she would not. The wizard had set her there for a purpose. She needs must study to thwart that purpose, and haply break his power so that she could then win her way free of it.

These cogitations and decisions all took place within the first few minutes after the stone was set over her body and her spirit was drawn into it. Then to her horror she found that Caradoc's spell had not yet taken its full effect but was still working on her. A torpor was spreading through her. The insensibility of the stone was infusing itself by the magic of *imitatio* into the spirit of the girl. This indeed was the most part of Caradoc's purpose, to effect a bridge between the one and the other – between the human soul and the *genius loci*, whatever it might be, whose power and presence were so strong here.

Betheli felt herself falling into sleep as if into a pit that had no bottom, and then at last she felt afraid. How could she escape, or even defend herself, if she had no sense of what was happening to her? Nobody who loved her knew that she was here, so any rescue could only come from herself. If she slept she would lose everything. Yet still she could not keep herself awake, and do what she might the darkness reached out to take her into its heart.

She sang. She could think of nothing else.

I will tell you one-oh, she shouted silently in the dark. And then: *What is your one-oh?* The song goes all the way to thirteen, which is God's thirteen virtues, and so did she. Then she began again at one. The song was a tiny thing indeed, but she clung to its rhythms furiously.

I will tell you one.

Two.

Three.

Four.

Five.

Six.

Seven.

Eight.

Nine.

Ten.

Eleven.

Twelve.

Thirteen.

One.

Two.

Three . . .

The night was long, but it was not everlasting. The sun rose again, as it has since God first taught it how to climb the sky. The masons came and went about their work. Now that the cornerstone was laid they could begin to build up the walls of the new keep and they went at it with a will, knowing they would not be paid if they were judged to be slack. Through all the day the top of the mound rang with their hammering and was raucous with their song. Betheli was cheered by it. She added her own voice to theirs, though none heard it.

Then when night came again and all was still, Cain Caradoc returned. There was never a time when all the castle slept, but this was an hour when the only men awake would be those on watch at the gate and on the walls. He went to the cornerstone, which now had other stones cemented in beside it and on top of it. He knelt and touched his hand to the side of the block. It was warm to the touch, whether because it still held some of the heat of the day or because the maiden's spirit warmed it from within.

Caradoc began to speak under his breath the words of an incantation that he had already devised and practised. It was a spell that would gather Betheli's spirit and send it before him like a thread into the cave below the mound. As light as thistledown, as thin as cobweb, the thread would seek out and touch the spirit of the sleeper who lay there in the dark. Like the cunning thief in the story, with the thread Caradoc would haul up the twine and with the twine the rope and with the rope the anchor chain. The first contact would make all the rest possible. He could draw up Yaldabaoth's power from the mound as water can be made to climb

100

a wick, and take it into himself. What would happen in the process to the girl's captive soul Caradoc neither knew nor cared. Either she would remain immured in the stone or else she would be consumed and cease to be. He could not be expected to trouble himself about such trifles.

He completed his conjuration with a fiercely whispered "*surgat, surgat mihi!*" then waited, tense and rigid, for his apotheosis. But it did not come.

Chagrined and angry, he felt around the edges of the stone. His wards still held. The girl's spirit was trapped in the spell-cage he had made for it. The stone was perfectly positioned with its corners to the four cardinal points and his own sigil discreetly cut into its two exposed faces. Everything was as it should be, yet no power had flowed.

Caradoc tried again, repeating the words of the spell with less haste and greater care. Perhaps he had elided a syllable or mispronounced a word. But the outcome was the same. Despite his meticulous preparations and careful execution, nothing at all happened.

Actually, a great deal had happened, but none of it was visible to Caradoc. He could not see inside the block, where Betheli wrestled with his spells as Jacob wrestled with the angel in the Bible story. She felt the magics wrapping themselves around her, tightening, binding, shaping. She could not escape by running, and she knew she could not fight.

In her desperate need, responding to some instinct deeper even than her fear, she cried out for a protector and a protector came – then a second, and in due course a third. They did not come from outside but from within her, for she had brought them with her when first she came into the stone. They were the champions she had crafted in her imaginings when she lay on her sick-bed. They wore the faces of her three brothers, but they shone as bright as candle flames in the darkness.

But those were only dreams, you might protest. And so they were. But Betheli herself was dream-stuff now – or soul-stuff,

101

which is every bit as fine and every bit as light. And Caradoc's spells were a more tenuous substance still, the essence of his will distilled into words and then translated into insidious force. When they came, they came on spidery legs, weaving threads of gossamer that drifted in from all sides towards their prey. *Surgat*, they whispered, *surgat mihi*.

But the three bright boys came between. They swung their swords with a steady rhythmic motion, across their bodies, waist-high and then up, as Betheli's brothers when she watched them in the fields had swung their sickles. At the touch of their shining swords the threads of Caradoc's magic withered and burned away. Not a one touched Betheli where she crouched behind her champions.

Unknowingly and without being taught, the girl had woven her own counterspell to Caradoc's conjuration. His magic could not take hold of her, and so could not reach through her to the power that lay down in the cavern below.

The sorcerer's chagrin was great. He had laboured hard to get to this point. For this he had set in motion the immense enterprise that was the rebuilding of the castle, and gone to so much trouble with the preparing of his materials (the chief one being Betheli), and now all his schemes were wrecked on this inexplicable, invisible reef.

He cursed bitterly and went away to take counsel with himself what might be done. He had no idea that the ghost in the stone had set her will against his. He only knew the spell had failed, and he would have to devise some other conjuration in its place.

Betheli sensed Caradoc's going or the fading of his spell, perceiving it as a weight lifting from her back or a miasmic fog dispersing from the air. Perhaps she smiled, if it means anything to say that a spirit smiles. She bade her brothers stand down. They clapped each other on the shoulders, uttered such salutes to each other as young men are wont to and vanished like snuffed flames. But Betheli knew that they would come again when they were needed.

And she knew that would be soon.

XIV

Of Drede Ich Nawhit, how he came to be and why he did not last

thing came to pass at this time that is needful to be told because of its later import.

Among Baron Horvath's meinie there was a man named Walter Scold. I have mentioned him before, but you may not remember. It was Scold who tried to bar Cain Caradoc's way when first he came to Pennick Castle to meet with the baron. Caradoc dodged him smartly with the aid of a spell, and touched him in passing with another.

"You were as slow as a snail," he told the man. "All you want is the shell on your back." And he tapped with the top of his finger a place on Scold's back between his shoulder blades.

In the days that followed, Scold found that the place on his back where the wizard had touched him began to itch. It was only a little at first, but it worsened day by day. Then the itch became a chafing, the discomfort growing until it became a drumming ache that could not be ignored. Scold could not sleep for it. He must needs lie on his side to keep from pressing on the sore place. If he dozed off and chanced to roll over onto his back he woke in agony, crying out so loud that his comrades who shared a room with him cursed him for a dog and said they would beat him if he did not stop.

The place that hurt was high up on his back and hard for him to reach, but by wresting his arm almost out of its socket he could touch the very edge of it. The skin there seemed to be thickening, becoming smooth and hard.

Day by day, week by week, the sore spot spread. The pain did not grow any greater – if it had, Scold would have run mad. Rather it eased as his hard skin toughened further. It was no spot by this time: it was as big as a trencher or a shield. His friend Cullen told him it looked somewhat like a shield too, being as shiny as metal. "It's not silver, though. It's brindled brown and black like the pelt of a cat."

The sore spot wasn't flat like a shield either, but flared outwards like a bell. It was hard for Scold to throw on a jerkin over it. The upper part of it, having a sharp edge that dug into his neck, forced him to bend into a kind of crouch when he walked. With his head down and the growth thrust upwards he looked like a hunchback.

The other men of the garrison had noticed his affliction by this time – as how could they not? Their response was to shun him, afraid that whatever contagion had taken hold of him would pass to them too. He no longer slept in one of the bailey's longhouses but out in the open under an overhang of the wall. He did well enough so long as the nights stayed dry, but when it stormed the wind would bite his flesh and blow the rain in to drench him. At such times he found that it helped a little to roll onto his stomach and crouch down, letting the spreading growth on his back keep off the worst of the weather.

In the mornings when he rose, he would discover that a kind of jellied broth had oozed from his body during the night, staining his jerkin and breeks as if he had lain in a mire. His back ached all the time now, and his posture was like that of an old man bent almost into a hoop by arthritis. His skin had paled to the yellow of turning milk, and it glistened with an unhealthy sheen.

Scold was not ignorant, of course, as to how all this had come to pass. He knew who had done it to him, and why. Cain Caradoc's touch had brought down a curse on him, for no other reason than

104

that he had refused to open the gate when the sorcerer demanded an audience. The curse was to make him resemble more and more the snail to which Caradoc had compared him. He laboured now under this heavy case because of Caradoc's hurt pride, and for no other reason. He felt he must find a way to pay Caradoc out for the insult and thereby balance the scales.

But it was not easy for Scold even to come close to the sorcerer, let alone to strike at him. By this time building had begun on the new stone keep. Cain Caradoc was closeted with the baron for most of the day examining plans, instructing masons and carpenters, and therefore surrounded by armed men. Scold watched his comings and goings closely but somehow, no matter where he went or what he essayed, he could never close the distance at a time when there were no others by to see and stay him.

There was but one time and but one place when Caradoc was alone. At day's end, he always climbed the stairs to the top of the mound and did not come down again until just before the dawn watch came on. What he did up there Scold did not know and did not care to guess. Belike it was some devilry no Christian man would touch with the toe of his shoe. But tide what might, he determined to avail himself of the opportunity.

It would not do to seem to be following the man, so Scold ascended the motte at the end of a drowsy afternoon when the masons were finished for the day and his own duties were done. He kept his head down and did his best to look like a man on an urgent errand, but when he reached the top of the mound and found none there to challenge him he dropped all pretence and straightway looked for a good place to hide. After some hesitation he chose the angle of a wall, where piles of dressed stone and cut timber made a perfect barricade from which he could look out without being seen.

The afternoon wore on into evening. The builders packed up their tools and went down into the bailey to find their dinner and perhaps a cup or two of mead. Still Scold kept his place and his silence.

The hours passed slowly. At first he was afraid of dozing, but the chill air that came with the fall of darkness made that much less likely. At last he heard footsteps nearby, and peering out he saw the sorcerer ascending the steps. Caradoc walked right by Scold without seeing him, and stepped across the shallow ditch marking the line of the wall still to be built.

As stealthy as any cat, Scold crept out from his hiding place and followed close behind. One quick thrust with his knife, he thought, and the deed would be accomplished. Let Caradoc magic that away!

But as he went to straddle the ditch that Caradoc had just jumped with ease, it seemed that he ran up against a wall he could not even see. It was so sudden and so surprising a check that he almost went sprawling on his back, which would certainly have alerted the sorcerer to his presence. As it was, though he staggered, he managed to keep his footing.

He tried again, this time with his hands held out in front of him. The effect was subtle at first, a slow shivering and thickening of the air, but the harder he pushed the more sternly the unseen barrier resisted him. He could not go a step further, because of the spell that Caradoc had woven with Betheli Theakston's flesh and blood. Even though the building of the keep had barely begun, the magical shield protected its perimeter against any who came there with harmful intent.

Scold knew nothing of this, but he needed none to tell him that this was magic he faced. Frustrated and angry, he scurried along the line of the ditch with his head ducked low. He was trying to keep the sorcerer in sight, but lost him quickly in the darkness.

A moment later a glimmer of light flashed out. Caradoc had lit a candle, or else had been carrying a dark lantern with him this while. Scold advanced as far as he could, pressing up against the congealed air to see what his enemy and tormentor was doing.

Caradoc had crouched down and was peering at the ground. Then of a sudden he seemed to shrink and diminish, taking the

106

light with him. In the space of a few breaths he was gone and the top of the mound was dark again.

There must be a hole in the ground, Scold realised – a hole, or else a tunnel. Caradoc had not melted away to nothing but had gone down into the mound's interior. Perhaps he had hidden some treasure here in a secret storehouse. If only there were some way of coming at it!

Indeed Scold was not wrong. With the dismantling of the old donjon, the trapdoor that led down into the chamber under the mound was now open to the sky. Caradoc had hidden it with a spell so that none but he could see it, but he lived ever in fear that one of the builders would come upon it by accident – wherefore he came every night to make certain it was still secure, and to try his subtle skills yet again against the power that slept there.

Having no other option, Scold chose a new place of concealment, this time in a clump of gorse that was growing near the top of the steps. He would waylay the sorcerer as he started back down into the bailey yard.

But the hours went by and the sorcerer did not re-emerge. And now despite the chill – or perhaps because of it – a great weariness grew on Scold. Ever and again he drowsed and almost slept, until he was obliged to raise his head and let the sharp edge of the growth between his shoulders grind against his raw and reddened flesh. This at least had the additional effect of keeping his hatred and determination keen.

At last he heard the creak and slam of the trapdoor, muffled a little by distance but still unmistakeable. Caradoc was returned. The sound of his unhurried tread across the sward and the swinging light from his lantern announced that he was approaching the steps. Scold crouched low behind the gorse bushes, preparing to spring out and drive his blade home. The sound of approaching footsteps grew ever louder, until of a sudden it ceased. The sorcerer had reached the top of the stair but had not begun to descend.

Scold felt that he could afford to wait no longer. He tensed himself to spring – only to discover that he could not do it. A strange paralysis had seized him. He stood like a statue, one hand spread to part the bushes and the other tight on his dagger's hilt. He rocked slightly on his feet because he had begun to lean forward in the precise moment that he froze. Every muscle and sinew in his body had now rebelled against his will. He could not even draw breath.

Without undue haste, Caradoc parted the gorse and peered through at his would-be attacker. He examined Scold with the very mildest curiosity. "If you meant to take me unawares," he said, "you would have done better to come at me out of a crowd. Up here it's just the two of us, and I knew you were there from the moment I came. I heard your heartbeat, and smelled your fear. You're one of Horvath's men, aren't you? Who set you on to kill me? I give you leave to speak."

Scold felt the paralysis recede from his mouth and throat. He sucked in a breath, and then another. Any words he might have spoken scattered from his head. He could not even beg for his life. Heartily he wished that in spite of his suffering and the wrong that had been done to him he had left the wizard to his own devices.

"Who sent you?" Caradoc repeated. "I promise you, I'll squeeze it out of you drop by drop if you don't tell me freely."

"Nobody sent me!" Scold cried out at last. "I came of my own purposing, to pay you back for what you did to me!"

"What I did?" Caradoc seemed surprised. Then he bethought him, noticing at last the rounded hump that grew between Scold's shoulders. "Ah! Of course. Yes, I know who you are now. You're the slow one."

"I'm a man for all that!" Scold snarled. Cold terror had gripped him. If it were not for the spell that held him he would be shaking like a spider-web in a gale – but he was angry too, and the fierceness of his fright fed through into his rage. "I did nothing to deserve this curse, and you're a bitch's bastard for putting it on me! Let fall your magic and you'll see what sort I am, for I'll beat you into a blood-pudding and fling you down the hill so your neck breaks!"

Cain Caradoc made a mime of great terror, but could not keep it up for long. He gave in to his amusement and laughed a goodly while. In truth he had been troubled by the thought that some unknown enemy had managed to place an assassin so close to him. But finding it was only some truckle-witted soldier with a private grievance he was much relieved.

He was also, when he saw what the grievance was, somewhat impressed. The spell he had cast on Scold had come of a moment's irritation, but he had wrought well. With a flick of his fingers he charmed away Scold's jerkin and examined by the light of his lantern the spreading mass of horn on the man's back. He ran his hand across its surface, fascinated, then tapped it with his fist. "It's like armour," he said. "I should think it would be an advantage in your line of work."

"I can barely walk for it," Scold said bitterly. Now he could move again, but only in obedience to Caradoc's commands. He longed to strike the man's smile off his face, yet he could do nothing. He was like a poppet in a mummers' show that dances when it's jerked up and down. "It chafes and tortures me when I move. It keeps me awake at night, for there's no way I can lie that doesn't press on it. And each day when I rise out of my cot I find it's spread a little further. You've killed me, you whoreson, only the death comes on me like sand through a glass, a little more and a little more. Either free me or take me all at once, I care not which!"

"Oh, you care not?" Cain Caradoc said. He was still staring at the shell on the man's back with its swirled patterns of green and brown and black. "Well then, I will choose for myself."

He gathered his power and sent it forth, waking the spell that was already there and whipping it along as a man whips his horse or a child a top. The shell spread this way and that, and at the same time it reshaped itself. It covered Scold's body, then his limbs and last his startled, fearful face. It became what Caradoc had said it resembled, a suit of armour, with plates that parted and flexed to let the man's joints move freely but hid him altogether from the world's view. There were not even holes through

109

which his eyes could peep out, but only a smooth and featureless mask.

"Now there is a soldier!" Caradoc said, laughing in pure delight. "And such a one as will daunt any foe. You shall stand at my side, master Scold, and any of bad intent who comes my way must needs cope you before they get to me."

Scold tried to speak, but found he could only grunt. The shell that had grown over his face gripped his jaws so tight that they would scarcely part. He raised his hands to try to prise it off, but found that his fingers were fused together. Though he could not see it, his left hand was now become a rounded mass like the head of a mace or club, fit for battering a foe to the ground but for nothing else. His right hand and forearm, meanwhile, had stretched and flattened themselves out into something like the blade of a sword.

Cain Caradoc was well pleased with his work, but he perceived that some small refinements were still needed. A soldier who could not see would fight at a disadvantage – so with a gesture he made the shell in front of Scold's eyes as clear as glass, but only from the inside looking out. To any that fronted him his face would still be hidden.

Last of all, and most delicate and difficult, Caradoc decanted a darkness into Scold's thoughts. Hopes, memories, intentions, reasons, plans, all were painted over with featureless black. It was as if Scold was newborn in that moment. Nothing henceforth would be real to him except his master. And knowing nothing else he would cleave to Caradoc as the only thing of light and colour in all his world.

This was a great magic. Caradoc had not set out to do so much, but he was carried away by his own cleverness – a thing that had happened to him more than once before. Nothing else would do but that he enact his will and see the thing through, though it used such a great deal of magic that he would once have quailed at the thought.

"Kneel," he said when he was done.

The man who had been Scold went down on one knee. Then on both.

"You are not Walter Scold," Caradoc told him. "Your name is Drede Ich Nawhit, which is to say 'I fear nothing'. You will go always beside me, to keep me safe against the wiles of the world. He who hates me will be hateful unto you. My command will be your joy and my word your gospel. What say you?"

The man who had been Scold said nothing. He pitched forward and lay lifeless on the ground. The terror and the pain of these transformations had been too much for him. His heart had given out.

Caradoc was filled with chagrin. He had spent a great deal of skill and effort on this conjuration, only to see it brought down because the man that was its focus was too weak to bear it. But he consoled himself with the thought that the shell of Drede Ich Nawhit could be quickened again with another soul whenever he should chance to have one at his disposal. He could even, if he wished it, transmigrate into the shell himself if any great danger threatened, and become at once a warrior buttressed with sorcery to the point where no foe could stand against him.

In the meantime, he made the empty shell stand, make obeisance to him, and place itself to the left of what would become the keep's entrance gate. Let it rest there as a marker, and as a symbol of his mastery. True, the keep was Horvath's to command, but Caradoc would not need Horvath much longer. As soon as he solved his present conundrum and came at Yaldabaoth's power, he would be lord of a much greater fiefdom than Pennick!

You may wonder why I have told you of this thing, since it had no outcome. Wait, and you will see. However much we might wish it, we are not done with Drede Ich Nawhit yet.

XV

Of Morjune, how she would not go to Hell when she was sent

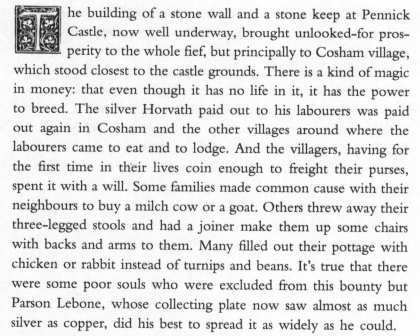he building of a stone wall and a stone keep at Pennick Castle, now well underway, brought unlooked-for prosperity to the whole fief, but principally to Cosham village, which stood closest to the castle grounds. There is a kind of magic in money: that even though it has no life in it, it has the power to breed. The silver Horvath paid out to his labourers was paid out again in Cosham and the other villages around where the labourers came to eat and to lodge. And the villagers, having for the first time in their lives coin enough to freight their purses, spent it with a will. Some families made common cause with their neighbours to buy a milch cow or a goat. Others threw away their three-legged stools and had a joiner make them up some chairs with backs and arms to them. Many filled out their pottage with chicken or rabbit instead of turnips and beans. It's true that there were some poor souls who were excluded from this bounty but Parson Lebone, whose collecting plate now saw almost as much silver as copper, did his best to spread it as widely as he could.

Amid these great transformations, one smaller change passed almost without notice. Marlie Scour died, and her daughter Morjune took her place as Cosham's burg-rune and healer.

Now here is a fact unknown to any. Marlie Scour, when she lived, was a witch. Many wise women are so, but the wisest do not speak of it; Marlie knew her neighbours well enough to hide her powers. If someone came to her with a burn or a bruise she would fix a poultice on it, and at the same time bespeak it with magic. When the burn healed, she swore it was all thanks to the poultice. If someone had a flux or a fever she would bleed them and give them broth made from woundwort that is also called heal-all, or else with sage and goldenseal – but she would weave a small enchantment too, in case the herbs were not enough on their own.

Marlie had taught all these skills to her daughter, seeing that Morjune had the spark of magic just as she did – and along with the teaching she had exhorted Morjune to be as secret as she could. "Mark me, girl," she said. "Cosham folk are as good as any, but they love best what they know best and they fear what they don't. If they come to learn the power that's in you, they'll turn on you like dogs. It won't matter that you only ever used the power to help them."

Morjune took these lessons to heart, or at least tried to – but heart was all her problem. She was too tender, and could never bear to see any suffer if she thought she could ease them. Her cures came to be talked about; how she knitted the bones in Piers Goode's foot after it fell under his own ploughshare and was crushed, or how Ellen Shaw was given up for lost when pox sores blossomed on her face, but Morjune anointed her skin with spring water and the sores were all washed away.

Holy mother Church was arguing with itself in that time about what witches were and were not and what should be done about them. It was not so very long since Pope Gregory had forbidden the hanging or burning of women for witchcraft, saying in so many words that women had not the power to make crops fail or summon storms. But the hangings and the burnings went on, and the authority of Christ was still adduced to justify them.

Parson Lebone had thought deeply on this and often preached

about it. The burning of witches depended for its biblical authority on a single verse from the book of Exodus: *maleficos non patieris vivere*, you must not leave a witch alive. But *maleficos* meant no more than evildoers. It translated a word that in Greek could just as easily have signified a poisoner, and in Aramaic a slanderer. It had no direct or provable link to witchcraft, if such a thing even existed. But the parson felt that his exhortations did little good. The fear of necromancy was a thing that came and went across the Christian world like the seasons, and always it left dead women in its wake.

Morjune's fatal error came when Brian Randel's wife, Alice, was in childbed. Like her mother, Morjune was a skilled midwife. She needed no magic for this, only common sense and good patience, and the deftness and gentleness of her hands. She came at a run when Alice's waters broke, shooed her husband out of doors and tended her through the griping of her belly as the child within her began to clamour to be delivered.

In the normal run of things this clamouring becomes greater and greater, the gripes and strainings both fiercer and closer together until at length the baby is brought forth into the world. In Alice's case, the straining went on and on, hour after hour, but the baby did not come.

Morjune could feel it struggling, its spirit as bright and sharp as a tiny star, vivid and ravenous in its eagerness to be born. It was as if it hurled itself at the world but could not break through.

Alice was in great pain, and little by little the pain was consuming the energy she needed to push out her child. Though Morjune exhorted her on the crest of each wave of effort to give everything of herself she could summon, that everything was now becoming less and less when it needed to be more and more.

Brian Randel was praying at the house's threshold, or at least was trying to, but the words escaped his wits and most of what he said apart from God and Christ was purely nonsense. Alice herself had torn her throat so raw with shrieking that she could only moan. And now at last the baby was coming – but at the same time it was going away. Its spark was fading, the light draining out of it as it lost its hold on life before ever it found life's nearer shore.

In this moment of crisis Morjune did not think but only acted. She reached out with her own spirit to cup and keep the child's from draining away. It was like trying to draw up water in a rush basket. Spirit is so fine, so subtle, it is the hardest thing in all the world to hold on to. For a moment Morjune thought she had managed the thing. She touched the little life that was there, and it touched her back. But when she reached for it, it drew away. It was already retreating from the world and the flesh, from the frail body that even now Alice Randel was finally – all too late – pushing out of herself.

Leaving her own body behind and above her, Morjune plunged down and down beside the little soul. She was trying to get beneath it, to pen it in and push it back, up and up, until spirit met flesh again and each cleaved to the other. But the child went around her and through her and was gone. It was nothing loath; it was only going back to the great repository of spirit from which it had momentarily broken away. All things that rise fall again, and all things that fall rise. To the spirit, naked and endless, the difference is not more than drawing in a breath and letting it out.

So now Morjune realised she had no choice but to let it go. But she herself had gone too far. She had launched herself a great long way from the world of solid things in her striving, and now she could not find her way back to it. She was lost in a realm where she had no good reason to be, a realm with no signposts and no landmarks.

She had thought of herself as heading *down*, but once she slowed she had no sense of where *up* might be. All directions looked and felt exactly alike. She cast about, now this way, now that, but she could not tell if she was drawing closer to the living world or falling further from it.

Well then, she thought at last, if I'm not to go where that baby went, I must perforce hang out a lantern that will light my way

115

home. She thought of a spell, one that would have been the very simplest of charms if she had had a voice to speak it into words or hands to play it into gestures. She thought and thought the spell instead, trying to give the magic a solid enough shape inside her mind to connect her back to the world she had left.

Back in the Randels' hovel, a light shone out in the middle of the room. It was made from a great many smaller lights, like the *ignis fatuus* that shines over a marsh in the deadest hours of night. Morjune's purposing, as clever as it was desperate, was to bespeak each mote of dust in the room and tell it that it was no mote but a spark of fire struck from a blacksmith's forge. *Burn, little suns*, she told them, *and light me home.*

In the dark of the other world she saw the sudden light shine out and turned herself to face it. Up again through the gulf of being she rose, even as Brian Randel came stumbling in through the door to gawp in amazement at the blazing sun that shone in the middle of his house.

In the living world, all this had played out in the space of a heartbeat. Morjune still knelt beside Alice's bed with the dead child in her arms. Its cord was not cut but the awful pallor of the baby's skin, more grey than white, was proof enough that all was not well – as also was its silence, and its lying so still.

"What has she done?" Alice moaned in her pain and panic. "Husband, what has she done to me?"

This was the moment when Morjune returned into the tabernacle of her own flesh, and snuffed out the light with a movement of her hand. Brian Randel, his thoughts all in a jumble because of the urgency of the moment and the wonder he had just seen, tried his best to join all these things together in a way that made sense. There had been a light, but now the light was gone. The light was gone and the child just dropped from his wife's womb was dead.

Morjune raised her head. She opened her mouth to speak, to say she was sorry she had not been able to save the child though she had done all she could. Before she uttered a word Brian Randel

116

felled her with a blow that knocked out two of her teeth and sent her sprawling, the back of her head coming up hard against a wooden beam. She fell unconscious and knew no more.

What bad begins must often come to worse, they say, and so it was here. Alice's contractions had all but stopped, and her husband had just brained her midwife. She was obliged to pluck out her afterbirth herself, hauling it up hand over hand. She did but a poor job of it. Within minutes she had begun to bleed – a trickle that grew by degrees into a torrent. Before the hour was up she was dead.

By that time Morjune had been haled away by Brian Randel's brother, Saul, who took her to the shed behind his smithy and bound her to a stake there with a chain of his own forging. The parson was called, and the matter set before him – not by Brian, who was too overcome with grief to speak, but by Saul and his wife, Harriet, and Alice Randel's sisters, Agnes and Osyth.

The facts could admit of only one explanation, they said, shouting each over other to get the story out. Left alone with Alice – may Christ and His angels bring her to Heaven-gate! – Morjune Scour had sacrificed Alice's newborn baby to the powers of Hell. A devil had come from the abyss to claim the baby's spirit. Hell being a furnace, this devil had shown itself as a great flame which Brian Randel had witnessed.

Parson Lebone listened to all this with sick dismay, though he tried to keep a calmness and a soberness in his face. I have spoken of the priest before, but I did not explain what he was. He was a man of learning trapped in a role that was for the most part repugnant to him. He came from a wealthy family but had four older brothers, wherefore he had no expectation of inheritance. He had chosen to enter the Church because the only thing that interested him was study. Books held all the learning of the world, especially the Classical world, and the Church (it sometimes seemed) held all the books.

Lebone had hoped to go to Paris and study at the university there, but the wars had rendered that impossible. He went instead to the town of Oxford, where the scholars of England were attempting to build a university of their own. It was not much as yet, but it had a library of enormous extent – almost four hundred books, with more being added all the time.

Lebone had found there the sustenance his spirit craved. He was especially drawn to the philosophy and learning of the ancients, though it survived only in fragments. He had no Greek, of course – there were few who did – but he read Apuleius's translation of the *Phaedo*, in which Plato considered the possibility that history might move in vast, slow cycles; the *Meno*, which argues that human souls exist *ab aeterno* and learn by remembering what they knew in past lives; the *Timaeus*, where the creation of the world is ascribed to a being called the Demiurgos who is separate from any God or gods. He read what he could find of Aristotle, Plotinus, Porphyry, Heraclitus.

And the more he read, the more his faith was tested. It had not been robust to begin with, and had ever been outweighed by his eager curiosity. At Oxford it died away altogether. He became a philosopher, which was not the same thing at all as a divine. By the time he took his orders he no longer believed in God. He believed in the spirit of man and in the cosmos itself as an ordered system – an ineffable and beautiful interconnectedness, vast to be sure but yet within the scope and apprehension of the human mind.

He had hidden his loss of faith from everyone. He strove still to follow the teachings of Christ because even in the absence of belief his reason found them to be sound. He tried to live a useful and a virtuous life, augmenting the harmonies of the universe rather than degrading or running against them. His perpetual dread was that he would be exposed as a nullifidian, a heretic, in which case he would lose his benefice, his home and most likely his life.

So now, faced with this tale of witchcraft, Lebone was sure he was hearing only baseless superstition. I should mention that he had never seen me since I was reborn. He had found my empty

118

grave but thought wolves had despoiled it. The stories of my return he ascribed to credulousness and rumour. He had taken his watchword from Saint Thomas: *nisi videri, non credam.*

So now he tried gently to pick apart the strands of the Randels' account. Had any besides Brian seen this fiery demon? How had it gone about to burn in a house of wooden beams and make no charring on them? Was it possible that Brian, coming into a lit room from the dark outside, had been dazzled by a simple lantern and imagined what he saw?

The parson went down on his knees to be on the same level as Morjune, who had been present for all this discourse but had spoken never a word. He asked her to give her own account, to the Randels' huge indignation. "What passed inside the house, Morjune? Tell me, if you can."

Morjune could hardly speak. She was terrified and miserable, still grieving the baby's death but wishing with all her heart she had not gone so far in trying to save it. She had ignored her mother's advice and this was now the issue of it: she was bound and tormented by those she had sought to help.

"I tried to deliver Alice Randel of her child," she mumbled. "I could not do it."

"And are you a witch? Speak truth, and save your soul."

Morjune did not for a moment consider the option of speaking truth. If lies would save her she was prepared to lie the sun out of the sky. "I'm none," she said. "I know nothing of a witch. I'm a good Christian girl and will say any prayer you ask me to."

"Say the Lord's prayer, then."

"Our father in Heaven," Morjune recited, "may your name be held holy and your kingdom come to pass. Your holy spirit come upon us and cleanse us. Give us each day that day's bread and forgive our sins as we forgive them that sin against us . . ."

"That will do well," Lebone said. "Be brave, child, and no harm will come to you."

He straightened again. "You must let her go," he told the Randels. "I mourn for Alice, and for the baby, but the Holy See tells us

119

there are no witches. And even if there were, you heard her pray to Heaven which should tell you there's no devil in her."

"Aye, but there is!" Saul Randel bellowed. "My brother saw it with his own eyes!"

"A man can be mistaken. Let her go, I say. She's not a dog, to be bound at a stake."

"No, she's a witch, to be burned at one!"

The parson pleaded and commanded in vain. The Randels took their plaint to Theakston the bailiff. Theakston was at pains to point out that he had no authority to put Morjune to question or to pronounce any kind of sentence on her. In the days when the Carne family ruled the fiefdom it would have been logical to appeal to the castle, and there was nothing to stop them doing so now. But all was changed since Baron Horvath laid claim to Theakston's ailing daughter Betheli, who had not been seen again. In his bitterness and grief he refused to venture near the castle unless he was expressly summoned. What had once been his proudest boast, that he spoke for Pennick to Cosham and for Cosham to Pennick, was now a bitter reproach to him.

Parson Lebone reminded them all again that the Church saw witchcraft as superstition and condemned burnings. The matter might have passed off with no further harm, but Jem Makepeace spoke up then and put the weight of his words in the other scale.

"There's witches in the Bible," he said. "We all know it, father, saving your presence. Haply Morjune Scour is innocent, but if she's not we've clasped a viper to us all this time. The thing needs to be known."

"How can it be?" Lebone asked, throwing out his hands. "We've only Brian Randel's word – that a fire burned hurtlessly in a wooden hut, and the fire took the shape of a demon."

"Well then we must wait for a justice to come to Burslem or Wolstanton under the articles of eyre," Makepeace said. "They hold assizes at least twice a year at Wolstanton. We'll ask for a special assize to be held here, and try the matter properly. God forbid we let it slide without first probing all the way to the heart of it."

120

I have wondered often what was passing in Makepeace's mind when he said these things. Was it pure mischief or malevolence? It might have been, but I do not think so. I think he was only puffed up with his own importance, and excited to have the drear routine of village life interrupted by such a sensational crisis. He was loath to let it go too soon, and therefore did what he could to keep it at a boil.

In any case, his word carried. Morjune was removed from the smithy to her own house, which now became her prison. The windows were nailed shut and the door fitted with a bolt that sat on its outer side.

For five months Morjune lived in the dark. The villagers took turns to bring her food, and they gave her a bucket to use as a privy which they sometimes remembered to empty. That was as much kindness as anyone thought was due to her, since in their hearts she was already condemned.

You might ask why she did not use magic to leave. The plain answer is that she could not. The only charms she had were to take away pain, close wounds, knit bone and cool fevers. Besides, Cosham was all she knew. She could not get so far as to plan an escape because she could not think of a place where she could go. So she waited, hoping against all hope that kindness would win out over fear.

Then the justice came. He was a coroner, which meant he was licensed to hear Crown cases, and that was the most part of his work. After all, the courts of eyre were set in the first place to make sure taxes and coronal debts were paid when they were due.

So when Theakston and the parson journeyed to Wolstanton to ask this itinerant justice to sit on a case of witchcraft he was not much disposed to oblige them. His name was Simnal and he was the younger brother of a lord, the Baron Amesbury. He set much store by his name and the dignity that attached to it, and he did not greatly care to stir from a comfortable room in a market town to venture into the mud and mire of a village that did not even boast an abbey or a priory where he could spend the night in

121

comfort. The villagers were obliged to pay him for his pains, and to walk beside him back to Cosham while he rode on his horse, a grey palfrey, complaining the while about how many potholes there were in the road and how deep were the puddles.

Nothing about the village dispelled Simnal's prejudices about country folk and country life. As soon as he saw how poor and bare the place was, he called for the accused to be brought before him without delay. He wished to proceed to judgement and be gone as soon as ever he could manage it.

He had set up his bench in the kirk, though it was no bench at all but only the bed box from the rectory set on its side with a blanket draped over it. It was not much of pomp, and Simnal was afraid lest it lessen him in front of all the villagers who had come to see the trial. He was used to sit at a solid wooden table on which he could pound when necessary with a slug of lead stamped with King Stephen's seal. If he pounded on this flimsy frame he was afraid it would fall apart.

Morjune was brought from her dark house, blinking and cringing in the light. She was led along the aisle past the pews that were crowded until they groaned, past the faces of everyone she knew in this world. Not a single one looked kindly on her. She stood at last before the bench, where a stranger sat in judgement over her. In that moment the fact that he was a stranger gave her the more of hope.

"What is your name?" Simnal asked Morjune.

She could scarcely answer. After so long indoors with no light, no exercise and only so much food as her gaolers were prepared to spare, she was hard put to it even to stand on her own feet. She stammered out her name, and her slurred voice (not to mention her knotted hair, slack face and shitten smock) at once convinced Simnal that he had to do with one that was touched or simple.

But as Brian Randel gave his evidence, and as his brother and sister-in-law attested that they had seen the strange light Morjune made glowing through the very walls of Randel's house, he changed his opinion. He had never heard a case like this before, and the facts of the matter made a deep impression on him. The death of a child by supernatural means, and the death of the mother soon after! If true, it was a crime whose barbarousness cried out for the gravest penalty.

This in turn made him suspicious of what he thought of as Morjune's dullness. A shrewd witch might well wish to escape her exposure and punishment by acting in such a wise. He questioned her closely. And Morjune, judging him a man of both intellect and learning, answered as fully and plainly as she could. She swore again she was a good Christian and stood ready to recite from memory whatsoever prayer he asked her to.

She could not have done worse. Parson Lebone had given her water to drink, and she was now grown more accustomed to the light. In her hope and in her trust of the justice's wit and conscience she spoke now much more clearly than before. Seeing this change, Simnal thought she must have been trying to cozen him earlier when her words seemed to come so haltingly. If that were so then all she said now must be lies.

Simnal called more witnesses, people who had seen Morjune effect cures that went against nature – and now were prepared to swear they had seen Morjune's mother Marlie do the same. Morjune protested in vain. All the good she had ever done now stood against her. There was nothing she could say that would sway the argument.

So she fell silent at last, and this again was a mistake. Simnal took her speechlessness for a surrender to the case that was being built against her. By then he needed but little convincing.

The last to speak was Parson Lebone, who had asked leave to address the court and refused to be gainsaid. He had not been a witness to these events, he freely admitted, but again he was obliged to remind all present – but especially Simnal himself – of Pope Gregory's letter to the king of Denmark stating that there were no witches. He trusted that the honourable justice would take this into account when he gave his verdict.

Simnal did not at all appreciate being lectured by a country priest. He had learning enough of his own to bring to the table,

123

and he would not be gainsaid by the Pope's letter. A letter was not a decree. The book of Exodus warned against witches, he pointed out coldly, and so did the most holy abbot Regino of Prüm in his *Canon Episcopi*, a calf-bound copy of which was one of Simnal's most treasured possessions.

He adduced it now, reciting aloud from memory: "*illud etiam non omittendum, quod quaedam sceleratae mulieres, retro post Satanam conversae daemonum illusionibus et phantasmatibus seductae, credunt se et profitentur nocturnis horis cum Diana paganorum dea et innumera multitudine mulierum equitare super quasdam bestias, et multa terrarum spatia intempestate noctis silentio pertransire, eiusque iussionibus velut dominae obedire, et certis noctibus ad eius servitium evocari.*" (It is also not to be omitted that some wicked women, who have given themselves over to Satan and been seduced by illusions and phantasms of demons, believe and openly profess that, in the hours of night, they ride upon certain beasts with Diana, the goddess of pagans, and an innumerable multitude of women, and in the silence of the dead of the night do fly over vast spaces of earth, and obey her commands as of their lady, and are summoned to her service on certain nights.)

True, having written this testimony Regino inexplicably sought to distance himself from it, claiming that the women who made such assertions were oftentimes deceived and then deceived others into believing they saw magic done. This seemed to Simnal to be the height of perversity. If the Devil's servants saw fit to declare their own allegiance, why should any man of faith or conscience seek to cast doubt on what they said? In their arrogance and depravity, witches ever and again allowed themselves to be seen for what they were. All that was left after was to decide what to do with them.

The judge pronounced his *verum dictum*, that Morjune Scour was guilty on the heads of charge as a witch, a necromancer and a trafficker with devils. At these words the church rang to its rafters with the villagers' cheers. Seeing justice done right there in front of their eyes lifted up their spirits remarkably. It was like the harrowing of Hell in miniature. Jem Makepeace came to his feet, his hands clasped in an attitude of worship and a wide smile spreading across his face.

"So now it falls to me to pass sentence," Simnal said. "Morjune Scour, you will be burned to death in a fire. The fire will be set no sooner than tomorrow week, to give you time to confess your sins before you perish."

Morjune sank to her knees, struck dumb by this calamity. Bitter sobs were wrung out of her. Matthew Theakston seemed scarcely less dismayed. "We had thought to cast her out," he said, "not to kill her."

Simnal turned up his lip at this suggestion. "That will hardly answer, goodman. A witch is perforce a heretic, and therefore no common criminal. Burning is the punishment prescribed in law, and practised across the whole of Europe."

"I denounce this court," Parson Lebone said. "And this judgement."

Simnal only shrugged. He had no wish to argue the point further and risk his dignity. His job done, he took his payment and departed at once, convinced that he could make his way back to Wolstanton before the light failed.

Morjune was taken back to her house and locked in again. They had nowhere else to put her, and of a sudden there were very few who were keen to look her in the face.

Parson Lebone visited her three times to take her confession. Three times she met him with silence and a stony face. Perchance she did have sins to her name, but since burning folk alive was not among them she felt her soul spotless compared to those of her neighbours.

As for the people of Cosham, having got what they thought they wanted many now found they did not greatly like the taste of it. They would not admit that what they were feeling was either shame or uncertainty, but the silence that settled on the village was an unhappy one. People when their paths crossed in the street would not meet each other's eyes – and they stayed as clear of the dark house where Morjune was penned as they well could in a village so small.

The same doubts could be seen in the building of the pyre. The villagers did not set it on the green but out in the furthest corner of the commons. Half a yard more and it would have been Adderley's weald they were building on.

It was a thin company that went with Morjune from the house where she had spent most of her time on earth to the fire that would take her out of it. All had said they would come; most found a reason not to. The yardlanders were obliged to attend and bear witness, and the Randels came all together to see justice done for Alice and her babe. There were not many others, although Jem Makepeace marched at the head of the procession and seemed well content to be there.

Once Morjune was tied to the upright stake, Parson Lebone made one last attempt to coax confession and repentance out of her. For his own part he was convinced of her innocence, but he thought it might comfort the girl to feel that she had put herself right with Heaven. "Will you not pray with me," he asked gently, "for Christ's forgiveness?"

Morjune peered at him, blinking. The months in the dark had weakened her sight, so he was only a blur of black with a blur of white above it. The shadows under her eyes made it seem as though she was regarding him from the depths of a cave. "No, father," she said. "I think I won't."

The priest had no answer to make to this. The girl's calm shamed and outfaced him. If he were a stronger man he would not countenance this. He would go against the law and the village and all. But he had not that fortitude, and he did not know how to set about such a thing. He said nothing more, but drew back to let Makepeace – who had volunteered for the office – come through with the lit torch that would ignite the blaze.

The torch went out before ever it touched the kindling. Makepeace was obliged to take it aside and spark it back to life with the striker from his tinder box. Then when he thrust it into the pyre it straightway went out again.

This happened three more times, and the consternation of the villagers could not be imagined. They swore the Devil was in it, but feared in their hearts that God was. In fact it was neither one, but only Morjune herself. She was speaking under her breath to the flame and sending it to sleep. The charm was one she mostly used to quiet a fever: it seemed to work on fire as well as flesh if she set her will to it.

But she could not keep it up for ever. Magic is like any labour, except it wearies the mind rather than the body. At last Makepeace got the torch well alight and Morjune could not bespeak it out again. With the last of her strength she did the opposite. It's a hard thing to make a fire not burn, since it goes against the grain of the thing. It's easier far to push it where it already wants to go.

"Hold you, James," she said in a hoarse voice as Makepeace approached with the torch. "You've had no great luck with that spillikin so far. Let me help you."

She stared hard at the torch, and the fire leapt out from it like a trout climbing a mill-race. Again and again it jumped, touching the loose straw and oil-soaked punk around the base of the pyre so that it lit up all at once with a great roar and a great billowing of smoke.

The villagers cried out and fled. Knowing now that they were in the presence of a true witch they did not stay to see justice done on her, but ran. Most did not stop running until they came to their own houses. Parson Lebone went the least distance, for he tripped in a ditch and broke his leg high up near the hip – an injury that would plague him from then until the day he died.

It is a hard thing to be burned. I will say no more than that. It is a hard thing and a bitter thing to be burned by those you thought of as your friends and neighbours, those to whom you gave the care of your heart and the cunning of your hands.

When the fire burned out at last, what was left? The hardness, and the bitterness, and one thing more.

Three days after the burning Elswyth Tait noticed there was a lamp lit in the Scours' house, which with Morjune's death should

127

by rights be empty. She hurried home and told Drustan, her husband, who went to the house to see for himself what was what.

The windows of the cottage were still nailed tight, but there was a crack where a board had split. Drustan Tait set his eye to the crack and peered in.

There was no lamp. Morjune was there, and she was still on fire. It was not a blameful fire, though. It ran across the floor of the old house, and climbed the walls, and licked at the table and chairs, but none of those things were consumed. Morjune sat in the kitchen corner at her ease, and did not look up when Drustan's gaze fell on her. She seemed half in a dream, he said later, when he was able once again to frame speech. He did not think she had noticed his being there at all.

Most of those he told thought it was Drustan himself that had been dreaming. He was known to be a sot, and the liquor he favoured was not small beer but a strong mead he brewed himself. Nothing seemed more likely than that the ghost he had seen was only in the bottom of his cup.

But the next night and the night after that, the light shone out again. And those who were bold enough to go and see for themselves found that Drustan Tait had spoken true. There was Morjune in the nook of the fireplace, staring into cold ashes that were many months old. She did indeed look as if she dreamed. The walls and the furniture around her were all ablaze, and so was she, but she did not seem to mind it.

There was little that could be done until Parson Lebone was recovered from his fall. Every night the abandoned cottage was a blaze of light. The villagers went far about to avoid walking past its door, and crossed themselves and prayed whenever by accident or fearful curiosity their glance fell on it.

At last Lebone was able to walk again, though with a heavy limp. He came to the cottage in the middle of the day, summoned thither with some urgency by Jem Makepeace. Makepeace had been very much perturbed by Morjune's return and wanted her gone again with as much expedition as could be managed. Saul

Randel struck the bolt from off the door and the parson went inside. There was no sign of the ghost, but then she had never been seen when the sun was up.

The priest went all around the cottage's single room, sprinkling it with holy water. He said a prayer besides, *hinc removere*, for the daunting and expulsion of evil spirits. His voice rang out loud and strong, and those who listened were greatly comforted. If that did not send Morjune to Hell then nothing would.

Lebone himself was a great deal less certain. He had never believed in magic until he saw Morjune bespeak the flame at her own burning. Now he must perforce accept what his own eyes had witnessed. But he did not believe that Morjune, who as far as he knew had done nothing but good in the world, could be a servant of Hell. And he could not muster any belief in his own powers as the agent of a God he did not credit. He did not even want to succeed. He only went through the motions.

When night fell the light poured forth again – this time through the cottage's door, which stood now ajar, as well as through the chinks in the windows.

Well, I am glad, the parson thought. If she takes some comfort in being in that house, though we made it her prison at the end, she has more right to be there than we have to chase her forth.

Notwithstanding which he went back to the haunted house and made a second essay, again at Makepeace's insistence. This time he went at night, with bell and book and candle and the Saint Michael prayer, the whole ritual of expulsion. He paused at the door. The light was shining through the chinks in the wood and around the edges of the jamb.

Lebone thought it shame to walk into Morjune's house without Morjune's invitation. He knocked instead. There was only silence from inside.

"Morjune?" the parson called. No answer. He knocked again.

Come in, a voice said at last – such a voice as did not stir the air at all. *And close the door behind you. It's letting in a whoreson draught.*

129

His heart all a-hammer, Lebone opened the door fully and went inside. This was the first time he had seen Morjune since her death. He was not one of those who had crept by night to the chink in the shutters and looked in on her, and therefore he did not know what to expect.

She sat in the chimney corner with one leg crossed over the other. The ashes were piled high in the grate, but they were very old and had naught to do with the fire that surrounded her. Morjune did not seem to know that she was ablaze. Her face was calm and somewhat lost in thought. She looked up at the parson for a small moment, then down at the ashes again.

What do you want, father? That quiet voice came again. *It's late to be about.*

Lebone tried three times to speak, and at last managed it. "I wanted to speak with you, Morjune. May I sit?"

You should. That leg of yours won't take much more standing on. Morjune nodded towards a stool that sat across the fireplace from her. Lebone had not looked to come so close, but now he saw there was no other chair. Summoning his courage he hobbled over to the ingle and sat him down.

Did you knock more than once? Morjune asked.

"I did."

Ah. I was asleep, I think, when first you came. I have been all a-doze, since my mother died. How long ago is that? A week?

"It is more than two years."

Hah! Then whose death am I remembering? Did someone die, a sennight ago or a little longer?

"Your own death was the most recent. That was near three months ago."

My death? Morjune looked up at last and fixed Lebone with a stare. *How did I die? No, wait.* She raised her hand and turned it, watching the play of flames across her palm, her fingers, the back of her wrist. *I remember now. It was the fire that took me. Her gaze went back to his face. The fire you set, father.*

"I . . . I did not set it," Lebone stammered, dread now making

130

his whole body shake. "James Makepeace set it. But I stood by and let you burn. I'm sorry for it now. I was mostly there in case you wanted to pray with me, but . . . but I should have stopped them. Or tried to."

All this while the ghost's face had worn that same softness, as of one that dreamed or else tried to lay hold on a dream that was drifting away. Now it sharpened, as if one memory at least had come clear. *In case I wanted to pray. Yes. For my sins' forgiveness, I think it was? But I did not, and so we parted. Are you come now to ask me if I've changed my mind?*

"I'm come to ask if you'd be willing to go away from here, Morjune."

Go away? From my own house, that was my mother's house erewhile and before that my grandmother's?

"It . . . I . . . yes." The parson nodded. "I'm supposed to compel you, in Christ's name, but I like not to do that. I'd rather you made your mind up to it with no forcing from me or any wight else."

The ghost smiled, but it was a sour smile that was more than halfway to a grimace. *How now? You were happy enough burning me, but now you remember your manners? It doesn't matter, father. Compelling won't answer and entreating is no better. I didn't choose to come back here, so how should I go about leaving? I don't know my way to any other place.*

So be off with you now. A fuck and a fart on you, and two of each upon your Christ. This was where I lived, when life was mine. This is where I'll bide still, until a better place offers. A place in Heaven, haply, for I died blameless. I tried my best to save Alice Randel's babe, and I would have saved Alice if her dolt of a husband hadn't dashed half my brains out before I could summon a spell.

Lebone stood. "Try to forgive them," he said. "For the most part they did what they did out of fear."

For the most part, the ghost echoed him. *Oh yes. Doubtless they did.*

As she spoke, the flames began to spread out from her in all directions to engulf the room. The parson cried aloud as they

131

spilled over him and climbed his body, but when he realised there was no heat to them his fears were calmed.

"I'll leave you then," he said at last.

You can try your bell and book and candle first, if you've a mind to.

"I think I will not. Good night to you, Morjune."

God bye you, father.

The parson left the house, closing the door softly behind him. On the doorstep he deliberated. It seemed to him that he had reached the end of a road, and he was greatly surprised to see where it had brought him. He had come to the cottage to perform the ritual of exorcism as Makepeace and the other yardlanders had bid him, but now his gorge rose at the thought of such a insult. If he even tried, he would be acquiescing in the evil thing that they (all of them, himself included) had done.

He stood irresolute for the space of some breaths. Then he went back to the rectory, where he burned the candle for a short while to make it look as though it had been used and poured the holy water out of window.

The next day he told Matthew Theakston that he had done the best he could and now could do no more. He said it with frank face and untroubled heart because it was no word of a lie.

Cosham lay stunned under this blow. They met in Theakston's kitchen and talked in hushed tones about what might be done. The parson was absent from this meeting. He had been invited, of course, but said he had a sermon to write. Its theme would be drawn from the gospel of John: Let him that is without sin cast the first stone.

"We should burn the house down," Jem Makepeace offered fiercely. "When it's gone, she'll be gone too for she'll have nowhere to lay her head."

"But fire's her element," Osyth Chapman snapped. "How big a fool would you be to carry more flame to her? She'll come and visit it back on us, and we'll all burn in our beds!"

"Tear it down, then," Makepeace said, nothing daunted. "Take every plank and carry it away. Put them in different places, maybe, or break them up. Can the bitch haunt splinters?"

"And will you set your hand to it?" Theakston asked him. "If you will, James, go to. Nothing stays you."

Makepeace blushed furiously and did not remove from his seat. He cast his eyes down at the rushes on the floor. "Well if any here's got a better argument," he muttered, "I'll hear it gladly."

"How if we made pilgrimage?" Mary Turling, that was my father's sister, spoke up. "We could take the cross from out the kirk and carry it to Wolstanton Abbey. The friars there will give us blessing, and haply pray with us."

"Only if we pay them," said her husband. "And what will the friars' prayers do that Parson Lebone's didn't?"

"We should make a candle from the fat of a calf that was born dead, and light it in the cottage. The ghost will follow the smoke, and so be gone."

"We must beg Saint Aidan's ankle bone from the great church at Burslem and let it sit in the cottage for the space of a week."

"There's a maid lives in Stoke that saw holy Mary and the angel of the annunciation when she was tending sheep on Sneyd Hill. If she spend but a night in that house, her saintliness will send Morjune helter-skelter back to the Devil her master!"

All these things and more were proposed and debated, but the villagers reached no resolution and at length they disbanded, greatly cast down.

There was one more attempt made to remove the dead witch. Makepeace came by day, when Morjune was not to be seen, and started to tear down the cottage as he had said he would. He was struck with terror and wonder to discover that it made no difference. When he prised the door off its hinges, another door stood in its place. This second door, that looked in all ways like the first, had as little substance as smoke. Makepeace's hand went hurtlessly through it. He tore down a shutter, and there again was a second shutter that the eye could see but the hand could not touch.

Being only the ghost of a witch, it seemed Morjune had dreamed herself up a ghost cottage to live in, that stood in the exact same place as the real one. Makepeace cursed bitterly, for he saw well enough that his efforts were hopeless. Moreover a strange chill was creeping now into his hands where he had touched the ghost wood of the door and the ghost iron of its hinges. He could see the white of frost shining on his fingers' tips.

It was not just fire, then, that danced to the witch's bidding.

Makepeace retreated with his head hunched under his shoulders, hoping that none had seen his failure and his humiliation. But someone must have seen, for whenever the story of Morjune was told this detail was always its capstone – that the house of the ghost-witch was itself a ghost, and would cast a blighting curse on any who tried to take it down.

But the story was not told in Cosham. In Cosham Morjune's name was not spoken at all, and the villagers became so used to looking the other way when they passed her door that they almost came to forget that she was there at all.

I tell you truly, they would remember by and by.

XVI

And what of me, this while?

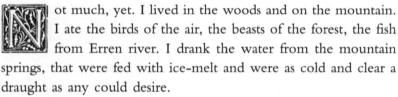ot much, yet. I lived in the woods and on the mountain. I ate the birds of the air, the beasts of the forest, the fish from Erren river. I drank the water from the mountain springs, that were fed with ice-melt and were as cold and clear a draught as any could desire.

I had so little to do with men and women that I all but forgot I was ever of their number. When I happened across Kel or Anna in my hunting I grunted at them, they growled companionably back at me and that was all our conversation. Human speech had not altogether deserted me, but I had no use for it. When I dreamed, I did not dream of my life as a boy in Cosham village but of the silence of the heights and the whispering of the trees. When I went, I went on all fours like any other beast.

Was I happy? I have said that I was, and I believe it to be true. But also I was waiting, though I could not have told you what for. I think for all the joys of my new life there was yet a small part of me that could not forbear from thinking of itself as Willem Turling. I think that small part of me stood empty, as a barrel with a hole in it remains empty no matter how much of rain it swallows. Days and months and years . . . just rain, flowing in and flowing out. Until humankind came seeking me again and filled my mind with thoughts and feelings all unbidden.

But I draw ahead of my own story, for Caradoc comes first. Caradoc and his hunger that moved so many things out of their courses. You may wonder, knowing the harm he had wrought already, that he was not done withal.

He was barely begun.

XVII

How Cain Caradoc made a poppet

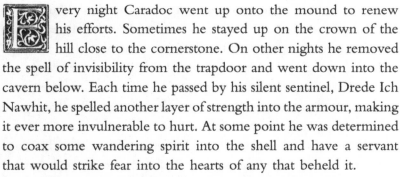 very night Caradoc went up onto the mound to renew his efforts. Sometimes he stayed up on the crown of the hill close to the cornerstone. On other nights he removed the spell of invisibility from the trapdoor and went down into the cavern below. Each time he passed by his silent sentinel, Drede Ich Nawhit, he spelled another layer of strength into the armour, making it ever more invulnerable to hurt. At some point he was determined to coax some wandering spirit into the shell and have a servant that would strike fear into the hearts of any that beheld it.

In the meantime he had loftier goals. Night after night he bent his every effort to make a conduit that would lead from the great reservoir of Yaldabaoth's pent and sleeping power, through the ghost trapped in the cornerstone and so into his own soul. And night after night he failed.

That the power was so close, that it was as limitless as ever, that it seemed to lie undefended all ready and open for his use, these things tormented him past bearing. He flung his will against it, a furious tide that should have thrust through or pushed aside every obstacle. It did not avail him. It seemed to have no effect at all.

If he could have looked inside the cornerstone though, he would have seen a different story entirely. There in the darkness and straitness of Betheli's blind prison, Caradoc's nightly invasions were a crisis that never ended. On the first night she had shaped in her fancy three guardians that wore the faces of her brothers. They had stood between her and the questing tendrils of Caradoc's spell. They had made sure nothing touched her.

On the second night those three were not enough. They fought with might and main but they were overcome. Feeling the peril in which she stood, but now with a slightly better idea of how to counter it, Betheli dreamed up a fortress wall so high it had no top, so wide it had no edges. By the time her champions fell, the wall was strong enough to stand. Caradoc's spell failed again.

On the third night she dreamed both champions and wall, but the contest was almost lost when Caradoc's casting became a dank fog that drifted in from everywhere at once. The fog was like every winter there had ever been all compacted together. It froze the three champions where they stood. It cracked the stone, so the wall began to crumble in a hundred places at once.

Betheli imagined a dragon, Heart of the Sun, whose breath was as the furnace in which the swords of angels were cast when wars were towards in Heaven. When a portion of the wall fell away the dragon stood in the breach and belched out such fire as was never seen. The fog tried to pour through the breach but met the dragon's breath and could not sustain. It faded into air and was no more.

None of these things were really happening. What was happening was this: a bound and shackled child felt herself assailed and made desperate shift to shake off the spells that were being laid on her. There were no soldiers, no tendrils, no walls or dragons or cold fogs.

And yet, and at the same time, there were. I did not know then, but have learned since, that the one world we know sits mid-way in a great tower of worlds that stretch away for ever above and below us. These worlds reflect each other, you might say; more truly, they are like bells all hung in a frame. When one bell is struck it rings out with its note, and that note hits all the others so that they sing to themselves, very softly, the note of the bell that sounded first. You will not always hear it, it may be too subtle for your ears to make it out, but still all the bells are singing, each to each.

Betheli had no light to see by, but in her imaginings the magics of Cain Caradoc were like a freezing fog or a sea of clutching tentacles. In her imaginings there were three great champions, there was a wall, there was a dragon. We may not ever come upon the world where those things were true and could be seen with the eyes of the body, but only a fool believes that truth ends all on a sudden at the point where his own sight fails him.

What matters is that Caradoc strove and strained, fashioned and fought night after night, but did not come at his goal. He could not tell why he failed. Sometimes he felt himself to be close, standing at the very brink of success, only to be repulsed again. He knew the deficiency lay not in himself but in the cornerstone and the little ghost he had trapped there. The girl's spirit, Betheli Theakston's spirit, was not doing what he had meant it to do. It was not sufficient to the task, which was to open a channel between him and Yaldabaoth, the sleeper under the mound, so that he could take into himself the huge store of magical force that still clung to the rebel angel's remains.

He was certain that his overall plan was sound. Spirit was the medium through which the power that people call magic moved, and therefore spirit was the best and only way to come at the treasure he sought. But it seemed that one spirit was not enough.

What happened next was inevitable.

Caradoc went to Baron Horvath, not by night but in the balm and brightness of noon-day, and accosted him thus. "Good my lord, you know that your safety and your comfort are foremost in my thoughts."

"I do believe it," said Horvath, who did not. He was these days subdued in his spirits. He was discovering that ruling a fiefdom is not the same as leading a band of outlaws. There are more parts and parcels of it, more decisions to be made, taxes to be collected and disbursed, messages to send and to reply to, factions to be appeased or coerced, laws to be made and applied, from sun-up to the third watch of the night. At the same time the noise and bustle of the building works, the hammering of the masons and the sawing of the carpenters, distracted and displeased him. With the stone keep still very far from finished he kept court in a long-house in the castle's bailey. The air was full of sawdust and the stink of busy forges. There was no peace to be had.

Wherefore he said no more but went back to the letter he was writing to Earl Roger of Montgomery, to whom he had now (as lord of Pennick) made himself vassal. He was accounting for some eighty-seven pounds in tax revenues and explaining from which landholdings they had come. His head was full of these things and had no room to spare for Caradoc and his schemes.

"As part of my service to you," Caradoc went on, "I've fenced you round with spells to keep you from any surprise or insult from your enemies. But my lord, I'm dismayed to find one of my spells failing. It's no imperfection in the magic itself, only an insufficiency in one of the ingredients. I beg your leave to gather more."

"Aye," said Horvath without looking up again. "Go to."

But some second thought forewarned him as Caradoc turned on his heel to leave. "Wait," he said. "What ingredient?"

Caradoc had hoped to avoid that question, but since he was brought to it he smiled and put on an air of innocence as if he had meant to say it all along but had forgot, it being a thing of so little moment. "The girl, my lord," he said. "The child I killed upon the cornerstone."

"The child you *killed*?" The baron's voice was tight with displeasure. "You said you would only let her die of her disease. Was she murdered, then? I forbade she should be murdered, Caradoc."

Caradoc affected astonishment and hurt. "Good my lord, all I do is for your benefit, and that remains my only yardstick. The child's death was required. You assented to it. The means and the manner I no longer fully recall."

Horvath's face twisted with distaste. "You don't remember

140

whether or not you killed a child? I would think even you might be struck by such a thing, no matter how—" A thought occurred to the baron and stopped the flow of his words. "A moment," he said. "This ingredient you want to gather. Is it some herb or powder you're speaking of? Or a cat's liver, or a horse's stale, something of that nature?"

Caradoc shrugged. "I think your lordship has already divined what I mean."

"God shrive me!"

"I don't ask it lightly."

"Christ and all his—" Horvath came to his feet. "Are we to fucking bathe in the blood of children? Are we to walk to the privy and back on their broken bones?"

Caradoc clasped his hands behind his back and waited out the storm. "My lord is pleased to jest," was all he said.

"No. No, he is not." Horvath came around the table. He gripped Caradoc by the throat. "I would to God that I had never seen you," he said. "You whoreson, you have a heart as cold as yesternight's ashes. For that one girl I'll answer. I should have told you no and I let you sway me. I'll burst and bleed before you sway me again."

So saying, he dragged Caradoc towards the door of the long-house. He purposed to throw the man out into the yard on his arse. After that, he thought, let fall what might but he and the sorcerer would no longer keep company.

With Horvath's grip so tight upon his throat, Caradoc was unable to speak any words of power, but since magic is of the will words are not always needful to bring it to bear. He gestured instead, his fingers drawing the shape of three potent runes upon the air. Horvath felt the strength leak from his arms like water from a cracked jug. He let go of Caradoc perforce and staggered back.

Still, he had fifty men-at-arms within the bailey yard, ready to come at his bidding. He opened his mouth to call them. Caradoc made another gesture and the air was sucked away from the baron's throat, leaving him no breath to speak. He spelled Horvath still, and he spelled him silent.

What now, though? He needed the baron's patronage in order to stay on at the castle, which was the core of all his plans. He could not fight the entire household if they came against him, and he knew he was neither liked nor trusted by Horvath's meinie. They would put him out of gates, and he could not by any means allow that to happen.

Frozen in place, the baron glared at him with eyes that all but bulged out of his head. It was clear that Caradoc could look for no truce or reconciliation.

He cudgelled his brains. The baron must now be disposed of, and yet it was only by the baron's good graces that he was able to stay here. The only solution he could see was to make a new baron closer to his desires. It would not be easy, and it would not be cheap. It had ever been his care to husband the greatest part of his magic so that he could maintain his youth and vigour and keep death ever at a pike's length away from him. Of late, though, both in his nightly forays against the cornerstone and in the making of Drede Ich Nawhit, he had spent magic as carelessly as a sot spills beer. It was Yaldabaoth's power, though he had barely broached it, which allowed him to do these things – and now he knew he must expend a little more in order to win all. He stifled his qualms and went to.

He hollowed out the baron as a man might hollow out a turnip to make it into a jack-o'-lantern. His dark art was a keener blade than any knife yet fashioned by cutler and he made quick progress. He made an incision in the baron's stomach, and through it he drew out all that was within. The baron suffered greatly as his internal organs were scraped and scooped away, but he could not move and the only sound he made was a soft sighing. The pile of innards grew, wet and foul. Something would have to be done with them, but that was a problem for later. With yet more words of art Caradoc dried and salted and tanned the inner surface of the baron's flesh so that it would not stink, and stiffened it so it would stand without bones or sinews to prop it up.

So now he had a poppet baron that was answerable to his commands. But in his haste he had forgotten about the eyes. They were now two very unsettling holes in the baron's skull, through which an onlooker could peer and see plainly that the man was hollow. A substitute would have to be found, but for the moment Caradoc was moderately content with his efforts and their outcome.

"Give you good evening, baron," he said.

He made the baron's mouth to open, and charmed a few words from out of it. "God bless you, my faithful servant." There was a distinct suggestion of an echo, but the voice was like enough. It was unpleasant to look into the baron's mouth, though. Where there should have been tongue and teeth and tonsils there was only blackness. Still, who looked long or hard into another man's mouth? It would do. It could be made to do.

Caradoc rounded the table and settled himself in the baron's chair. He gave the unfinished letter a single glance. Taxes. Smallholdings. He could not keep up his interest long enough to finish the first paragraph. Let the fiefdom go to Hell or wherever else it would. He needed the baron for other things.

He practised making the poppet move. Its arms, its legs, its head and neck. The movements were jerky and absurd. The limbs had a tendency to sag in on themselves, hinting at the emptiness inside them. A spell here, a charm or a bespeaking there . . . Little by little the baron became more like himself. Caradoc had him stride up and down, strike the board as if in a rage (his hollow hand made a soft smack there – that would need work), strut and point and gesture. Finally he made the baron dance, bent over with his elbows thrust out and his feet scuffling like a chicken scratching at the dirt. The sight was so ridiculous the sorcerer laughed uproariously, in the process losing control of his poppet. The baron folded at the waist, his legs remaining upright while his upper body heeled all the way over until his head rested on the floor.

It was altogether an unfortunate moment for the captain of the guard to come into the longhouse to consult with his master. He stared in open-mouthed horror at the grotesque figure before him, that looked like the most ill-made of scarecrows.

Caradoc pointed his finger. The poppet baron straightened up, so that the captain was now staring into its empty eyes. A small moan escaped the man, giving voice to his terror and confusion. The baron drew his sword and thrust it forward, quick and true. Pierced through the throat, the captain fell dead before he could utter another sound.

Ignoring the sprawled corpse, Caradoc made the baron straighten up and walk around the room. Again and again he put Horvath through his paces, honing and refining his movements until he looked more and more like his living self.

Having stepped in the pooling blood of the dead captain, the hollowed-out baron left red footprints where he walked. If Caradoc noticed he did not care.

When at last he was certain that he had got the trick of it, he had the baron leave the longhouse and walk to the pigsty. Caradoc himself walked along behind, carrying the mess of viscera wrapped in the captain's cloak. He dumped the foul lading into the sty, and – killing two birds with one stone – deftly removed with one last spell the eyes of one of the pigs that had just farrowed. The pig squealed and squirmed in its sudden blindness, but Caradoc quickly charmed it silent. He slipped the pig's eyes into the baron's head. They did not look altogether at home there, since they had no whites, but they would do better than nothing.

Leaning against the side of the pen, Caradoc recovered his strength after this mighty effort and considered his position. Killing the baron had been an act of last and desperate resort, but for so long as he could conceal what he had done he had the baron's authority and the might of his household to call on. He would need to move quickly and decisively now, applying all his wit and all his resources to the problem at hand.

If one trapped ghost had not sufficed to access Yaldabaoth's power, the answer was surely to try with more than one. He would slaughter the children of Cosham and walk to immortality and omnipotence over their tortured souls.

XVIII

Which treats of the children's crusade

o Cosham the next Sunday morning came Baron Horvath's messenger, Payne. Sunday was the perfect time to address the whole village, since they would reliably be at church. Payne had aimed to arrive before the service began, but heavy rains had left the roads a slough of mud. He heard the kirk's single bell calling the people to worship when he was yet a mile out. Riding at last into the marketplace he found the church doors closed.

He tethered his horse to an upright post beside the well and went to the kirk's door where he stood a while, listening to the voices within singing a ragged hymn. If he waited until the mass was over, he thought, he might bide here for hours. Better to get this filthy errand over with quickly. Bracing himself for what was to come, he threw open the doors. He strode into the kirk and walked up the aisle past rows of questioning and fearful eyes to the pulpit.

Parson Lebone had just commenced a sermon that took as its theme a verse from St James's gospel: "Resist the Devil, and he will flee from you." He faltered into silence as the messenger approached. Payne was not a subtle man, nor a mannerly one. He

145

indicated with his thumb that the parson should descend, then took his place at the pulpit as soon as it was vacated.

"Render unto Caesar," he said gruffly. "Christ's words, not mine. But I'm come today to tell you Christ was right. It's always wisest to give Caesar his due when he asks for it. Baron Horvath, my master and yours, bids me tell you that he is determined to raise a host a hundred strong, and to that end he has imposed a levy."

A murmur of dismay went around the room. Neighbour looked at neighbour. They knew the baron had promised aid to King Stephen in return for the recognition of his title, but they had hoped and prayed the war would not come their way. Evidently they had not prayed hard enough. Who would be taken, they wondered, and how would the choosing be done?

"You may have heard," Payne went on, "of Étienne the shepherd of Cloyes, who raised up an army of children to free the Holy Land from the Saracens' yoke. My master was much inspired by that story, and he wishes to emulate it. He is therefore asking each village in the fief to give up twenty of its children to the noble cause – and the honour falls first to you. Your children will travel with my master into Jerusalem, which they will wrest from the pagans' hands with God's help and in despite of Hell. The levy will be made up as follows: ten boys and ten girls, between the ages of five and twelve, whole in body and sound in mind, with no limbs missing nor no visible disfigurements. You need not think to palm off on his lordship your idiots and your cripples. He wants your best, and he will not be taking any bruised fruit. Bring them now, and say your goodbyes along the way. They must follow me straightway up to the castle."

Bluntness was ever Payne's way, but even for him this bluntness was extreme. The truth was that he disliked this commission, and he disliked even more the baron's manner when he gave it to him. He had only been in Horvath's service a short while, but he had thought he knew all the man's moods. He had been mistaken. He had never seen Horvath as he had appeared today, his eyes all a-squint and his voice hollow, his body twitching ever and again

146

as if a hundred tics and itches plagued him. "Ask for ten," he had said, and then "No, ask for twenty. Ten of each, boys and girls. With a goodly mix of ages. Who is to say what will make the difference?"

"The difference in what, lordship?" Payne had asked. He had not meant to be impertinent, he was only trying to reach an understanding of what was needful so he could explain it to the villagers when they tasked him – as they surely would – with their questions.

But Horvath had raised his voice in a thin shriek, like the yowl of a drowning kitten. "Don't think to measure lengths with me, you cunten cur! By God, if you don't go from me now I'll beat you down to blood and bone. See you come back at once with the children. All of them. Every last one. I'll offer no stay or exemption. Go! Go, you bitch's bastard!"

Payne threw out his hands, pleading. He knew he risked a blow on the pate, but better that than to go off on an errand that couldn't be filled and take the brunt of the baron's wrath later. "How if they will not come with me? Lordship, you know how chary people are of their sons and daughters! It's not as if I were to beg a loan of a shovel or a bite out of an apple. I'm ever your vaunt-courier. Only tell me what to say!"

Horvath had fallen silent a while. His face had seemed empty, as though all thought had left it. Then he had told Payne about Étienne of Cloyes and the children that went on crusade. He had said it in a way that left no doubt at all it was a lie.

Payne had bowed and taken his leave, with a heavy heart and a churning stomach. The story of what Cain Caradoc, the baron's wizard, had done to the sick girl that came in the wagon had by now made its way around every man of the household. The thought of more such slaughter made the bile rise in Payne's throat, though he was not usually a man that flinched from brutal deeds. On top of that, there was the strangeness that had come over the baron himself. He seemed changed in some wise. A distemper or else a rheum had filmed his eyes so it was pity to look at them, and turned his voice into that braying squeal.

147

And the wizard himself, Cain fucking Caradoc! He had stood the whole while at the baron's shoulder, saying never a word but watching all with a face like a starving man come to the buttery bar. Payne was in no doubt at all that the children were sent for to serve Caradoc's turn, not the baron's.

Now as the villagers all cried out in consternation and distress he affected such coolness as he could, but wished that he were anywhere else or had any other message to bring than this. "Come!" he cried out. "It's a godly work your sons and daughters will do. You should be proud!"

"But to ask such a thing of us!" Matthew Theakston shouted, his voice rising over the general hue. "It's all our lives, and all our hopes. The baron cannot mean it. He cannot!"

"Can't we offer up prayers instead?" another voice – Payne did not see whose – called out. "If we made a . . . a mass for the freeing of Jerusalem, and raised a collection, and all the other villages did the same . . ."

"A mass will not serve," Payne said. "Nothing will serve but only this. Make your peace with it."

But that was what the people of Cosham could not do. They had risen up from their seats to throng around the pulpit, making it impossible for Payne to step down. All around him were upturned faces, red with shouting. The noise was now so great that no single voice could be heard any longer. The congregation's misery was curdling quickly into anger. Payne expected at any moment to be plucked down and trampled on. He wished that he had stayed at the back of the kirk by the doors, where he might have reached his horse before the villagers overtook him. He wished he had not come at all. He could have turned east instead of west when he left the castle and ridden halfway to Oulton by now. Nobody knew him in Oulton.

Out of the ocean of baying peasantry, Parson Lebone waded forward and placed himself at the bottom of the pulpit steps. He raised his hands for quiet, which after some little while the villagers accorded him. Payne hoped the parson might finish his sermon, dropping his former theme in favour of *thou shalt not kill*.

148

But Lebone did not address the villagers at all. Instead he turned to Payne. "You must give them time," he said. "You can't expect them to hand over their sons and daughters so suddenly. There's work to be done first. If the children are to go to Jerusalem they'll need clothes for the journey. They'll want to pray and to be shriven here at my kirk. I think it were best you accord us some days' grace. And then when all is done we'll bring the children to you. I'll walk them up to the castle myself."

His gaze met Payne's squarely. They understood each other. The matter stood, as it were, balanced on a hair. A breath would topple it, whether this way or that way. If Payne wanted to leave the kirk alive and whole he were best mind what words he gave breath to.

"Aye," he said. "That's . . . that's a reasonable request. Most reasonable and natural. Three . . ."

"Seven," said the parson.

". . . seven days to choose the children, outfit them and shrive their souls. And on the seventh day to come to Pennick gates and be taken in. I'll allow it, so you swear you will not be late."

"Seven days or seventy, what matter?" someone shouted.

"It will matter a great deal to the children," Parson Lebone said mildly. "Draw off now, and let this man go back to his master. He's delivered his message and no doubt has other errands to run."

The villagers did not draw off far, but a narrow channel opened in the crowd. Payne did not wait but plunged into it. He tried to walk with the same arrogance and authority he'd worn when first he entered, but it quickly deserted him. Though no violence was offered him he cringed and scuttled his way to the door, and so departed in haste.

He rode back to the castle in a daze of unhappiness and trepidation. What would the baron say when he heard of the seven days' grace? What would he do? The day was bad begun, but Payne knew well it had kept its worst for last.

XIX

Of silver and sell-swords, but not much of either

hut the doors, and lock them," Parson Lebone said as soon as Payne had made his exit. "We have much to talk about and much to do."

The villagers were still all but stunned by the calamity that had fallen on them, but someone – one of the children – ran to obey. Then Lebone bade them all take their seats again, the while he climbed back up into his pulpit. They thought for a moment that he meant to resume the interrupted sermon, but that impression was dispelled as soon as he spoke.

"I am a sinner," he said, "and I must make all of you my confessors. When I said I'd walk with the children to the castle, I told a flat lie before God and man. I will not do it. I'd rather walk on hot coals to Hell's hob."

A cheer met these words – a ragged one, to be sure, for all were afraid and all were lost as to what they might do, but Lebone's defiance heartened them all the same. "I lied," he repeated, "but the messenger lied first, so some of the sin is his. Maglan Horvath does not mean to go to Jerusalem. He took Matthew and Sarah Theakston's daughter Betheli and they never saw her again. What colour did he give it that time, Matthew?"

It was not the bailiff that answered but his wife, her voice thick with grief. "That her last days might be brightened," she said, and spat. "That he might give her comfort. The devils in Hell know what he gave her, but I am sure in my heart it was not comfort." She broke off, sobbing. When Matthew tried to embrace her she pulled away from him. She had not forgiven him for being the one that took Betheli away and did not bring her back.

"And that was an argument that held for one child," Lebone went on. "Now Horvath needs an argument that will hold for twenty. Is there any here who believes it? That an outlaw ruffian only lately turned lord, with foreign powers in the land and the Crown itself threatened, should of a sudden decide he wants to go crusading? And with an army of children?"

"He thinks us fools!" cried Saul Randel. "But he'll find we're none!"

"But how are we to defy him?" Mary Turling asked. "He's got a hundred men-at-arms. More than a hundred."

"I know not how," Lebone said. "I only know we must do it."

"How if we were to send the children away?" piped up Osyth Cole. "To Stoke, perhaps, or Audley. Somewhere that's far enough away, and big enough, that Horvath won't be able to find them. We can raise a little money, between us, for their upkeep. And at the same time we send a letter to the king, telling him what's towards and begging his intervention."

The suggestion was met with silence.

"But Horvath is the king's man," Jem Makepeace said at last. "Why would he listen to us against our own lord?"

"Because the king is wise, and has wise counsellors. Because we would set out our reasons so exactly and make our case with such circumspection that he could not deny us."

The silence took hold again. "I think we were better defend ourselves than ask the king in London town to defend us," said Parson Lebone. "London's two weeks away. Horvath could spirit all your children away before ever a letter got there."

"Or after," Sarah Theakston moaned. She was rocking back and

151

forth in her seat with her arms wrapped around her body. "Oh, my boys! My sweet boys! To be dragged from my arms and haled away to Jerusalem!"

"They won't come within a cunten mile of Jerusalem," someone else growled.

Matthew Theakston stood, but at first he did not speak. He was, as I have said, a man very fond of his own voice and his own dignity. When he set himself to spend a word or two it was not often he found his pockets empty. But now he was diffident, and seemed to be consulting with himself what he should say.

"Speak, Matthew," Jem Makepeace said at last. "We want wisdom."

Theakston shook his head. "I'm not sure I've any to offer. Only, an idea came to me just now, as I sat and listened. Most like it's nonsense, but I'd as lief lay it out and see if anyone can build something better on it. What was this Horvath before he was our lord?"

"A bandit in the woods," said Makepeace.

"And before that?"

"A soldier in Matilda's army, they say."

"But a mercenary soldier. A sell-sword. That was why King Stephen was ready to take his apology and his oath and give him the mastery over Pennick when he asked for it. It was only for hire that he fought for the empress against the king, and everyone knows a sell-sword takes his hire from any that pays him."

He swallowed, squeezing his one hand with the other in his nervousness. "But see now, he's not the only one, is he? There's many a man came out of Normandy or France or Denmark, or . . ." He shrugged helplessly: he did not know the names of any other countries. ". . . Or further away than that even, to take Matilda's coin and fight against the king. And there's many a one that dropped out of the fight and stayed in the land, just as Horvath did.

He was come to the point at last, and he blurted it out all at once. "So suppose we found some of them, and put them into our own hire?"

He had expected uproar, but there was only doubtful silence. "Matthew," Parson Lebone said, "we cannot afford mercenaries. Their pay is great enough to task kings and great lords. It's too much by far for the likes of us."

"Nay, but listen," Matthew said. "We're richer than we were — because of the building work, because of the markets, because of all the strangers coming by us. There's few of us don't have a coin or two put away, and fewer still that have got anything to spend it on."

"What's a soldier's hire?" asked Agnes Makepeace. "Start there. What's a soldier's hire, and who here can sum on his hands?"

They all looked to the parson, as the one among them who had most knowledge of the world. "It cannot be less than sixpence a day," he said. Faces fell at that. It was as much as a mason or a carpenter earned, or a little more. It seemed to most of them that killing needed less of skill and less of learning. Why, they themselves had done it when they burned Morjune, and they had not found it hard until afterwards.

"Sixpence for the best of them, certes," Theakston said, rallying a little. "But there must be others that will do it for less. And we wouldn't need to buy an army, only a few stout men that have their own swords and bows. Belike when the baron sees we mean to make a fight of it he'll go to one of the other villages and take their children instead of ours."

"It were a terrible thing if he take any!" his wife cried.

"Well so it would, Sal, but our first care is our own. There's nothing to stop them of Adderley and Kinsley from doing what we do. We all must make what shift we can. Doesn't the Bible say, parson, that God gives most help to them that strive the hardest?"

"To those that put their own talents to best use," Lebone amended scrupulously. "But that parable teaches us—"

"How much can we scrape up between us?" Sarah Theakston broke in. She was in no good mood for parables. "If we know what we've got we'll know what we can buy."

There were nods all round at this. Matthew's idea had found

approval with most that were there – and not least with his wife. Nobody wanted to give up their children without a fight, but they knew that if they fought themselves they were unlikely to fare well. They agreed with few words to go home and bring back each of them such money as they had managed to save.

The count came to five pounds and some odd shillings, which was more than anyone had expected. "That's enough for a whole army!" Jem Makepeace said. "If it's sixpence a man, and there's twenty shillings in a pound . . ."

He could not make the calculation in his head, but Parson Lebone supplied the answer for him. "Five lots of twenty is a hundred. But see you, James, that's if we pay them all for a single day. If we need them for two days it halves to fifty. After ten days it's gone down to ten, and so on. And no matter how we go about, we'll never get a hundred men to come here all on the same day. They'll come by ones and twos, and once they're here we must both fee them and feed them. Our five pounds are not like to go very far, when that is all counted in."

"Still, father, as soon as the fighting's all done with . . ."

"How will it be done with?" Agnes Makepeace snapped. "If the baron comes against us and he's rebuffed, there's nothing to keep him from coming again the next day, and the day after. It's not like a game of horseshoes. There's no rule saying he only gets the one throw!"

That cast them down afresh, but after much more discussion in the same wise they were forced at last to admit they had no better stratagem to pursue. They agreed among them that two men of the village would go together into Wolstanton and ask there after mercenaries for hire. Why two? So that each could be the conscience of the other and neither would be tempted to abscond with the purse of money.

Straws were brought from a nearby barn and the two were chosen by lot from among the men there present. The short straws were drawn by Saul Randel and by Hapless John who was a simpleton. John stood there with the straw in his hand, smiling all

154

around, as if he had won a prize in a race. "Well, we will draw again for that one," Matthew Theakston said. This time the straw went to a stout carl by the name of Ort Woodley who had no land of his own but laboured on Theakston's and Makepeace's plots turn and turn about. So now all were satisfied, for there were not in Cosham two more formidable men of their hands than Saul Randel and Woodley.

They would not do it that same day, not so much because it was the Sabbath as because they would need to make an early start to walk the eighteen miles to Wolstanton and not be benighted on the way. The roads were not safe at night, and it would be pure calamity if they were to be robbed. They would start the morrow morn, taking all the hopes of the village with them.

XX

What passed at the Bell

olstanton is not like London. It is not even like Burslem, which has a wall and a town watch. What made it fit for the villagers' choosing was that there was a butchers' shambles there on a Tuesday that brought buyers from all the corners of the fiefdom and even from outside. Butchers are not soldiers, for all that their skills somewhat overlap, but in such a great press of people Saul and Woodley felt they could not fail to find some sell-swords in search of hire.

Arriving late on the Monday afternoon they cast around for somewhere to stay the night, intending to wait until the next day to broach their purpose. A friendly soul directed them to an inn, the Bell, which did not let rooms but had a fire in the main parlour that was kept fed through the night. Visitors could sleep in a chair there if they paid a penny. Two pennies would buy them a stoup of ale or cider to keep them company.

Being strangers, Saul and Woodley were noticed. More than a few asked them what business brought them to Wolstanton. They kept their own counsel at first, but the ale was so good and the company so hearty that at length Woodley declared their purpose. "We've come to hire soldiers," he said, slopping his beer on the

156

floor as he gestured broadly with his two hands. "A whole company, to keep our village safe from harm."

"A company!" said a pock-faced man with a stained jerkin. "Why, belike you must have a purse bigger than your balls!"

"It's big enough, I warrant you!" Woodley chuckled, laying his finger aside his nose. In fact he carried no money at all. The purse was with Saul, and there was ample opportunity for all present to assess its size when he took it out to pay for their drinks.

The night wore on, and their new friends mostly departed. The pock-faced man was one of the last to leave, in company with two or three others, all of whom had seemed very mindful of the purse whenever it appeared.

Some little while later, Saul inquired of the host where the privy was to be found. "It's out in the yard," the man said, pointing. "You'll see a dry wall, and then you'll see a ditch."

Saul staggered out. While he stood over the ditch with his pizzle out and his thoughts mostly idle, someone came up behind him and hit him such a blow on the head with a cudgel as might have killed him outright. He woke to find himself lying in his own piss with his purse-string cut and his boots gone from off his feet.

He had not yet paid for their place at the fire, so he and Woodley were thrown out of the inn with little ceremony. They passed that night in a hedgerow, cold and shivering. The next morning they wandered around the shambles in hopes of encountering again the pock-marked man or one of his comrades, but having no luck they gave it up at last and turned for home.

They arrived back in Cosham long after nightfall. Saul was in a very bad way, both because of the blow to his head and because the stones on the road had cut his naked feet deeply. When at last he came in sight of the village he sank to his knees and could go no further. He had to be carried to the green and laid down on the kirk steps, what time Woodley stood by and wrung his hands.

Randel wept as he told his neighbours what had befallen. "I've ruined all!" he said, ever and again. "I'm sorry! I'm sorry! Whip me for a sot, I've ruined all!"

157

"Any of us might have done the same," Matthew Theakston said. He wanted to kick Randel down the steps and all across the commons, but he knew he would feel no better after.

"We must flee away," Sarah Theakston said. "And take the children with us!"

"What," Matthew cried, "keep them from being stolen by dragging them away instead to starve in a ditch? There's nobody can help us now."

"There is one," Parson Lebone said. "There might be one."

All heads turned to stare at him.

"There is the monster."

XXI

How the people of Cosham made their petition

he men and women of Cosham village knew well where I had gone after they cast me out. The mountain is large but there are roads across it, and paths that lead even through the deepest parts of the forest. I had been sighted often by travellers, by hunters and poachers, even by ecstatics seeking a vision of truth up on the mountain's peak. All had brought their stories back with them, and their stricken faces gave their stumbling words the more credence. That there was a monster in Pennick fief was a fact nobody contested. Even Parson Lebone, after his encounters with Morjune, no longer doubted it.

Still, it must have taken the villagers a goodly while to find me. I know not how many hours they wandered, sometimes calling my name, sometimes oppressed into silence by the great silences that surrounded them.

They came on me at last as I was eating, which was perhaps not the best time. I had found a dead bird, an eagle or large hawk, on a high rock where it had fallen. I had plucked out most of the feathers, but left the bones in to give it some crunch. I didn't really taste things any more, but when I ate carrion the jagged ends of bones would sometimes cut into my cheeks and the roof of my mouth, which was almost the same as eating something with spice to it.

There were three of them, two men and one woman. Matthew Theakston and Parson Lebone I well remembered: the woman stood back with her head bowed so I could not see her face.

"Go away," I told them, speaking around a spiky mouthful of flesh and bone. Seeing them there in my new home, my sanctuary, brought back painful memories and a sour sadness that turned quickly to anger. "Run, run, run back down the mountain. If you get to the bottom before I count to a hundred, I will not come after you. Run! Now!"

To tell you truth, I think they came very close to doing it. All three were terrified. The parson was seeing me for the first time since my rebirth, and the other two had most likely forgotten how ugly and ungainly I was. I had changed further on the mountain. Finding it more convenient most of the time to go on all fours I had let my arms extend and thicken, my hands spread like shovels. Some of the bones that had been stuck in me all a-thwart now made a ruff or crest across my shoulders, and two stuck out at my elbows like spurs. I was a hideous sight even to my own self, when I chanced to see my reflection in Peter Floodfoot's spring.

"Please, Willem Turling," the priest said, when he could bring himself to speak. "We are come a great long way, both to entreat your pardon and to ask a boon of you. Will you do us such grace as to hear us out?"

I spat out some feathers. "Not Willem Turling, but Once-Was-Willem. Give me my proper name, or I'll slap the face from off your skull."

Lebone bowed his head. "I beg your pardon. We have not been kind to you, Once-Was-Willem. We know it, and we ask – in all humility – that you forgive us. You left Cosham because you did not feel welcome there, is that not true?"

"Yes, very true. Pitchforks were stuck in me. Mattocks were swung at my head. Was I wrong, father? Was I welcome after all?"

Lebone shook his head for no. Whatever else he was, he was

160

no hypocrite — at least not in this. Another time I might have warmed to him for that honesty, but I was still angry. "Look not for the sheep to be clean if the shepherd's all shitten," I said, quoting the proverb.

"You'd be welcome now though," Matthew Theakston said, twisting his cap in his hands as if it were a chicken and he meant to wring its neck. "We want you to come back."

I will admit the words surprised me, and took a little of the edge from off my despite. It was long since I had stopped thinking of myself as a man, but some nights I still dreamed of being a child again: of being lifted in my father's arms, or of my mother singing me to sleep. Those dreams were like a hot coal inside me that kept its heat after I woke. Sometimes the burning was a comfort, sometimes a gall, but it could never be ignored.

"Come back?" I repeated doubtfully. "To my father's house?"

"No," said the woman. She raised her head and I saw at last who she was. She was Mary Turling, my father's sister. The villagers must have thought the sight of one of my own kin might move me. "I live in your father's house now, with my husband Arthur and our children. That's Luce and Arran, that you knew in former days, and Eda, that's our newborn. Now we're five instead of four we could not readily move back into our old house. It would be too strait for us. But . . ." She swallowed her disgust bravely but could not hide it. "But you might bide in the barn, so long as you came not near the house."

"There's many a place," Theakston said hastily. "We might build a hut for you on the far side of the fallow."

"This welcome is cooling already," I said.

"Please, Once-Was-Willem," Theakston said, "don't be angry with us. We're afraid of you, and well we might be. We've never seen anything like you before."

"I doubt there is anything like me."

"Why then, go to. But if you came to live once more among us, belike in time we'd grow used to you and our fear of you would lessen. And you . . . you could sleep in a bed again, warm

161

your hands at your own hearth." He groped for more words, and found some inspiration in the bird's half-eaten carcase. "You could have fresh bread and good pottage for your dinner, and wash it down with a jug of ale." He spread out his hands to show the hugeness of all that was on offer. "You wouldn't need to be alone any more, out here on the mountain's face."

That last was enough to bring a smile to my face, at the which all three of them stepped back hastily. My smile is a hard thing to bear. "Well," I said, "if I was alone I might be the more swayed by that. But I have friends enough, by God's grace. If you keep not your wits about you as you go back down the mountain, you may be unlucky enough to meet some of them." This was only said to affright them. Kel and Anna do their hunting in the full moon when their changes come easily and naturally to them. To change at other times is cutting against the grain for them, and it leaves them ragged.

"May I tell you at least why we've come?" Parson Lebone pleaded.

"I thought you had told me already. What was all this other pother, then?"

"We've tendered apology, and made what we thought was a fair offer." The priest came closer, one faltering step at a time, until he stood right before me and my breath was in his face. "But we didn't tell you what our need was, that brought us. Baron Horvath, who rules now in place of Robert Carne, has commanded that Cosham village hand over its children to him. He already took Matthew's daughter, and – saving your presence, Matthew – none knows what became of her. We mean to defy Horvath, but we've no way of defending ourselves if he sends his soldiers to take the children from us."

Kel had told me that the baron had taken a sick girl into the castle, and I had thought then it must be Betheli Theakston. I was sorry for it, but I hardened my heart. "Well there's scripture for that," I said. "Render unto Caesar that which is Caesar's." I did not know that I was echoing the words of Horvath's messenger, and at that time I would not have cared.

"You're not so cruel," Lebone said. "You cannot be. I knew you as a child, Once-Was-Willem. Or I knew the child you were. I baptised you. I gave you communion. I know there's grace in you yet."

I only laughed at that.

Theakston went at it another way. "Your cousins," he said. "Arran, Luce and Eda. One of them is sure to be among those taken. Will you not stir for them at least?"

"I told you I was not Willem Turling," I said. "Yet you go on talking to him. I've no kin in Cosham. I've no kin under the sun." I reached out with my broad, bulging hand, picked up a rock as big as a man's head and flung it at a tree that stood nearby. The rock went through the tree's bole as if it had been sent from a catapult, shattering it into splinters. The three staggered back, Theakston falling on his arse in his haste.

But the heat of my words and the violence of my hands sprang from the same cause, which was not anger but dismay.

I remembered Arran, and Luce. Not Eda, for she was yet unborn when Willem caught his fever and died – but the other two had been his playmates. Arran was Willem's own age, Luce a year younger. Because she was smaller and weaker than the two of them, with a club foot that made her too slow to join in racing and running, they had invented a game where she was a dragon and they were knights that had come to try their courage against her. The gaiety of the entertainment came from Luce being so small and yet so fierce. The knights were arrogant, certain sure that they would win. The tiny girl breathed fire and burned them, caught them in her claws and crushed them, ate their hearts out of their chests. It was a grand game.

I was squarely caught, in other words. They had given me at last a reason to care what became of Cosham, for all that I hated them. They did not know this though, and so fell to pleading again. I left them to it, the whiles I finished my meal. But the dead bird had no savour now. It seemed to me that the mountain had tilted. If I did not dig in my heels I might tumble down, pell-mell and heels-over-head, until I came to rest once more in the world of living men and women.

"Enough with your noise," I said at last, loud enough to make them quail into silence. "I'll think on what you've said, but only if you stop saying it now and go away."

But as they made to leave I called after them to hold. They stopped in their tracks and turned again to face me. "How many men-at-arms has Horvath?"

"We don't know," Theakston said. "He had a large company when he was in the woods, and he kept some of Carne's men when he took the castle. We think it must be more than a hundred."

Too many for me to fight, in other words. But that would have been true even if the number had been much smaller. I could not be everywhere all at once. Having an army of one man – or one monster – is like having a fence with only the one post. It won't keep the cows out of the corn for very long.

Parson Lebone, who was the sharpest of the three, saw from my face that these or suchlike thoughts were passing through my mind. "You'll help us then, Once-Was-Willem?" he asked.

I shrugged. "I said I'd think on it. But yea or nay, you'll need more help than me. A force of a hundred or more will flow around me and not even slow, though I kill every man that comes within my reach."

"We have no money," Theakston said. "All we had was lost at Wolstanton town in the jakes of an inn. We can't afford the hire of a single man."

"But if you know of any that might help us out of Christian goodness," Lebone came in quickly, "we'd not say no to your bringing them along."

"We who live up here on the mountain have little store of Christian goodness," I said. "Perhaps even as little as you who live in Cosham. Go now. If I come at all, I'll come tomorrow. And it may be that I'll bring some friends with me. But don't build your hope on it for I make no promises."

They went away at last, no doubt in as much perturbation of spirit as I was myself.

XXII

In which I begin to make a daisy-bracelet

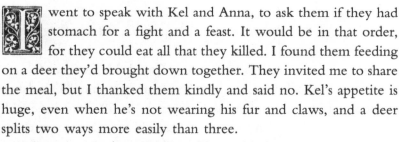went to speak with Kel and Anna, to ask them if they had stomach for a fight and a feast. It would be in that order, for they could eat all that they killed. I found them feeding on a deer they'd brought down together. They invited me to share the meal, but I thanked them kindly and said no. Kel's appetite is huge, even when he's not wearing his fur and claws, and a deer splits two ways more easily than three.

When they had eaten their fill, I told them about the baron demanding Cosham's children be delivered up to him.

Kel shook his head, his mouth set in a grimace. "It's not Horvath that's doing this, Once-Was-Willem. It's Caradoc."

"Aye," I said, "belike it is. I know he took a sliver of me for his payment when he brought me out of the grave – and he took Betheli Theakston whole, as you yourself told me. Now it seems his hunger has grown greater."

Kel looked to his sister. "I like this not at all," he said.

Anna sat back, her hands pressed to her taut and bulging belly. "No more do I. But when the Aesir made the world they didn't build for our sole pleasure. It's not our fight, *min bror*."

"I think it might be mine," Kel said quietly. "I was in Horvath's muster when he played robber king and kept his court in the woods. I helped him take the castle, which gave him dominion over these people. If he's using that power to claim a tithe of souls for Caradoc, I have to take my share of the blame."

"Take it, then. But make sure you take only your share. There were a hundred others beside you, I think."

"I don't keep their consciences, Annika."

"No. Nor mine, neither."

Kel threw his huge arms wide. "When have I ever dragged you into my brawls? When I enlisted with Swein Astridsson you followed me, out of love. And you stayed on when I made pact with Horvath. But you never fought, either as a woman or as an *ulfeðnar*, and I never asked it. I'd cut off my hand, rather."

Anna reached out with her foot and prodded his thigh. "Don't," she said. "You need both hands to scratch that great fat arse of yours."

Kel sighed. "It's my own sister who says this. Blood of my blood, and she says it."

But their teasing words came mostly from habit: neither of them, I saw, was in much mood to jest. Anna turned to me. "This daisy-bracelet you're making troubles me, Once-Was-Willem," she said. "You're tied to Cosham by your family's history. Now you come and tie Kel up by his conscience, and I'm tied in my turn by the love I bear him. I wonder where it will end."

"I should not have asked," I said, meaning it. "I'll fight alone, for I'm sure this body of mine can take no harm. I wouldn't for anything put either of you in the way of danger."

"If you think Caradoc can't hurt you," Kel said with a stern frown, "you're deceiving yourself. That man is compacted with every devil in Hell, and they've all dropped their gifts in his lap. Think on it, Once-Was-Willem. He made you. Would he have done that if he did not have a way to break you again afterwards? No, I'll join you in this endeavour, at least until I see where it's tending. Anna, you'll stay here on the mountain."

"I'll go where I please," Anna said. "As I always do."

I went to Peter next. He mourned the children's plight, but said there was not much he could do to help me.

"You can't leave the water, even for a little while?"

"The water is my being, Once-Was-Willem. I can no more leave it than a tune can leave a song."

"A tune can leave a song quick enough if I'm the one that's singing it."

Peter laughed at that, but he sobered quickly. "Are you sure you want to go among them again," he asked me, "the kith and kin of Adam? All they know is each hurting other, in a great round that never ends. That was why you went from them the last time."

"I'm changed since then, Peter."

And that was true, but it was not a truth that had any great weight to it. We're ever changing, those of us who are alive — whether for the first or the second time. But it does not follow that we're getting wiser or stronger.

"I'll do what I can," Peter promised, "though it may not be much. I won't be of any great use in a fight, unless Caradoc decides to take ship and come at Cosham by the river. But I'll scout for you and give you such aid as I can. Water's a changeable element, but I warrant you my word is good."

He tumbled back into the spring and was gone. He had said he could not fight with us, yet still I felt that my daisy-bracelet had another link in it. I was happy withal.

But there was yet one more wight I had to cope. I went around the flank of the mountain to that blasted hollow where the three stones stood. I did not go in this time, but knelt at the rim of it and bowed my head.

"Beldam," I said. "Will it please you to speak with me?"

Not the smallest sound came back to me, but I waited. I waited long. At last I felt her presence again; the sense of a great weight pressing on me and on the air and the earth all around me.

"Well now." The dead, still voice sounded from right beside my ear, like a rustling in dry leaves. "The boy. The insolent boy who came and went with such scant courtesy."

167

"I'm sorry if I gave insult. I meant none, and mean none now."

"No?" Unsung Jill rumbled. "What do you mean then?"

"To entreat your help, if you'll give it. For I've work towards that I think might be too much for me."

Silence, for a long time. Then, when I'd given up hope of any answer: "What sort of work?"

"A fight. A great broil between men – the stronger coming against the weaker. But none as strong as you. All that saw you would be fearful of you, and the word would spread. None would dare to come into your hollow or try to pluck your flower. Not for a generation."

The wind sighed. And there was another sound, as of something hard grinding against something heavy, though there was nothing I could see that would make it.

"That's an empty promise," Unsung Jill said. "Night and day I watch here. None that comes gets by me. Why should I stir abroad to make men fear, when they already foul themselves at the sound of my name?"

I thought about this. "For the sport of it, perhaps," I said at length, but I knew that was not quite right. I tried again. "To have a change from this drear place, and from the endlessness of your guarding it."

This time the silence had a different heft to it. The sense of her, the sense of her closeness and her circling me all about grew stronger. I was careful not to look up.

"Change is for flibbertigibbets," Jill said, "and careless children."

It may sound strange but I took heart from this. Though she swatted my words away like flies, she still saw fit to answer – and she still lingered near. "I know you're none of that, beldam," I said. "I only thought, you've lived a long time in the one self place. A very long time. Some say you were never born at all."

"They say true. When God said *yehi* and *or*, and so made the light to be, I slipped between the first word and the second. That is how old I am. There are not many things older – although that bone you carry is one."

168

I had forgot the carved flute I had found. It was long since I had given up trying to play it. I held it up on its flaxen string. "Will you help me if I give you this?" I asked her.

Unsung Jill laughed. The sound of it was so terrible that I will not try to tell you how it was. I put the flute away again with hands that shook. "I want no part of that," she said, "for it reminds me of things that cannot now be helped. If you were wise you'd put it back where you found it. But then if you were wise you would not have come here. Do you know what I am, stripling boy?"

"No," I admitted. "Only that you're mighty. How is it that you came to live here on this mountain, beldam? And how is it that your gaze sends men to Hell?"

I put as much of innocence and of courtesy into my voice as I could. The longer she talked to me, I thought, the greater the chance that I might come upon a way of making her say yes.

I felt a tickling on my cheek as something sharp — I think it was Jill's long fingernail — touched me there. "You ask me to tell you my story?"

"I do, yes."

"Why? What will it avail you?"

Her closeness pressed on me like a weight, and made it hard for me to think. "I . . . I know not," I stammered. "But . . . but if you gave me such grace as to tell it, I would like to hear. Since you are so old. And so wise."

"Oh, I am both. But when I was young I was brash and foolish, just as you are now. Do you know of the Elohim, boy?"

"Not by that name."

"They made the world."

"Please you, beldam, I was taught that God did that."

"You were taught lies then. God made the universe, but He took the project no further. The angels that made this good earth called themselves the god-like ones, the Elohim, because they continued God's great project without God's blessing. You might say that they were brash and foolish too, for all their might and majesty."

169

Her voice softened as she spoke. It seemed to me that a kind of sorrow or wistfulness crept into it. "That was a fine work they did," she said. "A fine making. It gave me joy to see it. But afterwards there was tumult and reproach. God had thought to stop at the angels, it seemed, and saw no need for lesser things. Perhaps He was envious that His playthings had made playthings of their own. Or perhaps it was only that they did not ask Him first. In any case, that was when Hell came to be."

It was dizzying to hear such things, and to know that they were true – for I did not doubt Jill's words for a moment. There was too much of weight and too much of sorrow in the way she spoke them. "How?" I asked, greatly daring. "How did it come to be?"

"I know not. It was just there, between one moment and the next. Whether the Elohim made it as a redoubt or God as a punishment, I cannot say. But I saw it. I saw it, and the seeing lodged in my eye like a mote. My left eye, it was. And ever since then, that eye sees nothing else. Only Hell. Except if someone meets my gaze. Then I am blessedly blinded for a moment. The window becomes a door, swinging open, and I am given some respite."

The tickling at my cheek went away. Her hand now rested on my head. It rested lightly, but I could feel the iron heft of all that strength held back. "For the sport of it, you said. Well now, revenant child, how would this be for sport? Look me in the eye, like one that's civil, and I'll be one of your seven."

"My seven?" I thought I must have misheard her. "We're only three, beldam. Me, and the two changers. Peter Floodfoot says he will help us, but he cannot fight."

"However you count it," Jill said, "I'll make one with you if you hold my stare, let us say for the space of three breaths."

I had not begun to hope, so I will not say my heart sank. "Will no other challenge do?" I asked her.

"None. Only that."

"I cannot do it."

"You have not tried."

I backed away from the hollow, still with my gaze fixed on the ground.

"God bye you, child," Jill called after me. "Until next we meet."

That would be long, I thought. I had come twice to that dreadful place, and I wished it had been two times fewer. I promised myself there would not be a third.

XXIII

In which I come back down from the mountain

ur coming into Cosham was a great wonder. Labourers in the fields and farmers grazing their cows on the commons saw us first. They pointed and cried out. Many of them followed us into town, though they kept their distance.

In the main street (which was really the only street, with a few stubby lanes leading off it) people came to the doors of their houses or peered at us out of windows. The procession behind us got bigger.

When we came onto the green, in the shadow of Cosham kirk, we stopped at last. Kel settled himself on the coping of the well, while Anna and I sat cross-legged on the grass. Rumour must have run its round that these were Cosham's champions, wherefore Cosham's people ventured closer at last to see us what we were. This being noon-day, neither Kel nor Anna were in their beast-shapes. The change came easier to them by night than by day, and easiest of all at the full of the moon. So what the villagers saw was a monster, a hairy man and a tall, broad woman.

The parson came out to us, and Theakston and Makepeace not long after. Theakston's gaze flicked back and forth between us, no doubt wondering what sort of folk would see fit to consort with a thing like me. "Are these your friends that you spoke of?" he asked me at last.

"I'm Anna," Anna said. "This is my brother Kel."

Theakston nodded. "We're grateful that you've come. We hoped for more but still, we're grateful. We should withdraw to my house and sift what should be done next."

"No," said Kel. Of the three of us he was the only one that knew anything of war, so we had agreed before we came that he would be our general and decide on all things that bore on the fight.

"No?" Theakston seemed all astonished to be gainsaid.

"I think not." Kel nodded his head at the crowd all around us. "Aren't these the mothers and fathers of the children that are to be taken?"

"They are."

"Then they must be party to this conference. All of you must. For we'll need all of you if we're not to miscarry."

"We can't fight," Saul Randel said. He still bore the marks of the beating he'd received in Wolstanton. The left side of his face was all one bruise. "We're only what we are, and none of us are soldiers."

"Any fool can see you're not soldiers," Kel agreed. "But the fight's coming to you, will you or nill you. You won't get to send it back when it arrives because it's not to your liking." To the crowd at large he cried out, "All of you come closer. Bring your children out too. Bring every beldam from the kitchen nook and every shepherd from the pastures. There's no time to be wasted in saying things twice."

There was such command in Kel's voice that all hurried to do as he had told them. Theakston bridled a little to have someone else sit down at the head of the table, as it were, but there was little he could do about it. "I like not to bring the children into our counsel," was all he said. Kel did not trouble to answer.

The people began to gather. I drew myself off a little way, to the kirk steps. Anna glanced curiously after me, then came to stand beside me. "Don't you want to hear?" she demanded.

173

"They're afraid to get too close to me. If I stay by the well they'll all linger at the edge of the green and the most of Kel's words will be lost."

Anna huffed out an angry breath. "How do you bear them? How can you look in their faces, that are all full of stupid hate and fear, and still abide them?"

"I remember what it was like, I suppose. The world has given them enough that's worth their hate. And their fear."

"You could say the same of any rabbit."

I turned to look at her. Her gaze was all on Kel. It was because of the danger to him that she had come – and it was for the same reason that she was angry. I remembered then that she had followed him all the way from Denmark into England. Her words were fierce, but it was not cruelty that spoke. It was only her great love for her brother.

When at length all were come, Kel stood up on the well's coping so he could be seen, and spoke as follows. "Men and women of Cosham, I am Kel the changer. Anna my sister stands on yonder steps, and by her is Once-Was-Willem who you know. Haply you think we're come to save you and be a bulwark for you to hide behind, but hear me now: there is no hiding from this.

"You've set yourself against your rightful lord. He's got men-at-arms to enforce his will. He's got money to buy more if he needs them. And what's worse than all, he's got a whoreson magician.

"What you've got is the three of us, and we won't be enough. Late or soon you'll need to pick up the fight yourselves. All of you."

"I'm no coward!" a man called out. "Put a sword in my hand and I'll fight."

And a woman, close on his heels: "We'll all take up swords, for our babes' sake. Never doubt us!"

"Well I've no swords to give you," Kel said. "And I mean no blame to you but soldiering is a mystery like farming is, or like smithing or shepherding. You can't hope to learn it in a day. A trained soldier will go through any and all of you without knowing you're there. So we must find other ways for you to fight."

174

He began to set it out, and such authority was in his bearing that all listened. But it was not just that. He gave each one a role, a place in the plan, and made them feel how the whole of it depended on the parts. When he was done at last and asked if any had a question to put to him, there was silence across the green.

"Go to, then," he said. "Make the most of the time, for it stands not on our convenience. Let's try what happens when the mouse beards the lion."

"The lion treads him under," Anna muttered, "and wipes his paw clean later when he's had time to notice."

Kel's plan was very simple, but it was not the less clever for that. He proposed to turn the whole of Cosham into a trap, or a series of traps, for Baron Horvath's men-at-arms. That is how a weaker force can get the advantage of a greater one, he said, especially when the weaklings know the ground better.

There were only so many ways of coming into Cosham, after all. The trick was to salt those ways with as much mischief as we could manage. And firstly he set the people of Cosham to the digging of holes. Two ells wide and two ells deep these holes were to be, and all across the width of the street at its eastern end, which was where anyone coming from the castle would have to pass. "And the whiles some of you dig," Kel said, "the rest of you can go up to the Chase and collect me some branches of elm and hornbeam and holm oak. The straighter the better, and as long as your arm or longer."

When this was done, and the first of the ditches dug out, Kel showed the villagers how to sharpen the wood from the branches into stakes and set them in the bottom of the ditch, bedding them deep and packing the earth tight around them so they would stand with their sharp ends pointing upwards.

Parson Lebone shuddered when he saw what was taking shape in front of him. "This is a wicked thing!" he said.

"For wicked men," Kel reminded him.

"Or just misguided ones."

175

"You'd be the one to guide them, father. All I'm come to do is kill them."

Kel went away to set some other of his plans in train, while I stayed behind to help with the digging – a thing to which I was well suited on account of my great strength. When I started I was in the midst of a crowd, but by degrees the other men and women that were working drifted away from me until I was digging my own ditch and they were digging theirs. This cast me down a little, but it was not a whit surprising. In full daylight I am a thing that would inspire dread in any.

After some little while, though, I noticed that I was being watched by two children, a boy and a girl. Both had the same red hair and the same stocky build. The boy was almost come to manhood, the girl perhaps a year younger. They took great interest in me, and if they were fearful of coming closer at least they did not bolt.

Then I saw that the girl had a club foot, and I knew who they were.

"How now, Luce Turling," I said. "How now, Arran Turling."

Their eyes went wide to hear their names spoken by such an uncouth creature as I. "Are you . . . are you our cousin?" Luce asked me. She spoke the last word with a heavy and serious emphasis, and the boy shaped it with his lips even as she said it. This must have been a question that was turning in their minds since they first saw me, and it had brought them close in spite of their fear.

I could have said yes, or even no, but a lie told to a child is a weightier thing than one told to a grown man or woman. Children haven't come to an understanding of the world, and they may build your lies into their believing in ways that will come to hurt them.

"Well that's a hard question," I said. "Have you not asked your father and mother?"

"We asked," Arran said, "but they wouldn't answer. They said it was a great shame and a great sin and not to be talked about. Father said he'd beat us if we gave word to it again."

"But some of our friends said you're Willem that was our uncle

176

Jon's son," Luce took up. "But we played with Willem oftentimes, and he was no taller than my brother." She nudged Arran with her elbow to show he was who she meant. "And you're bigger than our father, or any man in Cosham."

I reached up out of my ditch and took two shovels that were lying in the road. I held them out to the boy and girl, holding on to the blades so they could take them by the handles. "Help me with my digging," I said. "Scoop the earth I throw up away from the lip of the hole so I can work the faster, and I will tell you how I came to be."

After some hesitation they took the shovels and set to. Ever and again they glanced at me out of the corners of their eyes. It took courage for them to stay by me. I smiled at them. Then I remembered what I look like when I smile, and stopped.

"Your cousin Willem died," I said. "Of a fever. His father, your uncle Jon, buried him in the kirkyard, as he might have been expected to do. But when he and his wife, your aunt Meg, went home, their grief did not abate. Instead it grew stronger and stronger. People who are sorrowing do foolish things, sometimes. My mother and father did something very stupid indeed. They went to a wise man, a sorcerer named Cain Caradoc, and asked him to bring their son back."

"But he lied?" Arran said.

"Another hard question. The spell was made, and what came up out of the grave was me. Some of me is, or was, some of Willem Turling. But I'm not him, and I don't answer to his name."

"What's your name then?" Luce asked.

"Once-Was-Willem."

She laughed at that. "I was called Goosey or Goosey-Lucy when I was small. I might say I'm Once-Was-Goosey if I wanted to. It's like a riddle, where you hint at what something is without saying it."

"Very like," I agreed. "And I am something of a riddle even to myself, Luce. I remember games of hide-you-seek-you and jacks and chivvy chase with you and Arran, but I remember them as

177

things I saw through Willem's eyes rather than as things I did. Then too, there was a piece of Willem that Cain Caradoc took away and kept for himself – so no matter what I might imagine I am changed, inside as well as out, from the boy that did those things."

Luce looked up into my face. She did not flinch at all, or only a very little. "You're not altogether changed," she said. "I think I hear Willem when you talk, even though your voice is very different."

"That's a kind thing to say," I said. "I too like to think a part of Willem lives on inside me. Everything we remember changes us, or adds itself to us. By that token, he's not gone yet."

"We missed him very much after he died," Arran offered, a little timidly. "We live in his house now, did you know? Our mother being uncle Jon's only blood kin, she claimed the longhouse when they went away. Willem had a whipping top and a hobby horse that we kept. But . . . but we could give them back to you if you want them."

I shook my head. "I'd rather you kept them," I said. "I'm too big to ride a hobby horse now." They laughed at that, as I had hoped they would. "You'll be too big yourselves soon," I added. "But haply you'll give them to your own children when you have some. Luce, I give unto you Willem's top, and Arran, I vouchsafe you Willem's hobby horse."

"I'd rather the horse," Luce said.

"That way, then."

"But how if the wizard takes us? What will become of us after that?"

"He won't take you," I said. "You see how big and strong I am. And my friends, too. We are sworn to keep you safe."

"Against magic?" Arran asked.

"Against anything." But I remembered Kel's words to the crowd on the green and I did not stop there. "We'll do whatsoever we can, come Hell or hap, but you're right to squint your eye at such a promise. When the time comes, it may be that you'll need to make shift for yourselves. Don't wait for others to come and save you, in such a case, but try what can be done with your own hands and your own cunning."

They nodded solemnly, the boy and the girl together. My heart ached as it had not done for a very long time, for I remembered the time when they were Willem's closest friends and companions, and when he had had no better wish in all the world than to while away a summer day with them until it became a summer eve. Like everyone, I contemplated the mystery of how my past had become my present, and like everyone I could find no way to parse it.

We said no more then, for Mary Turling came at a run to tell her children they were needed elsewhere. She gave me a fearful look as she said it — as if she thought I might harbour some grudge against her and her husband for taking the house I had used to live in and making it their own.

"We were only talking about times gone," I told her, hoping to disarm her fears.

"I see no use in that," she said, putting her hands on the children's shoulders to hasten them away. "It's only idleness."

For once I let my anger show. "It's idleness to look outside the present moment? How else are we to understand it then?" But Mary was already hurrying away. Her back was turned and she did not answer.

It was a foolish question in any case. For the most part when we think on the past it's not understanding that we're looking for, but only the reassurance that we were in the right course all along. If understanding means touching on a sore place, we will go a different way.

XXIV

Of words and water

hen Joseph Payne came back to Pennick, bringing the news that he had given the villagers seven days of grace, Cain Caradoc was not well pleased. He had the baron, his poppet, order the man soundly beaten as a warning against his presuming to exercise such initiative again in the future.

While this order was being carried out, Caradoc considered with himself whether to keep Payne's promise or to break it. He itched to have the children in his hands and to be about his spell-casting, so any delay was hard to bear. But if he pushed too hard and the villagers took it into their heads to resist him he might find himself in an invidious position.

He still must needs hide behind the baron, in order to command the obedience of the baron's men. But there was a limit to how far the poppet would hold. Even emptied of its viscera and tanned like a calf's hide, the corpse had begun to stink and the jellied orbs that were its eyes to thicken and discolour. There was fraying at neck and knee and elbow caused by the bending of the baron's head and limbs, which could be hidden for now but would lead sooner or later to tearing. Caradoc was reluctant to expend further magic in repairs at a time when he might need it for other things.

This was a crucial juncture in his plans: he could not risk any miscarrying.

All in all, then, he felt it would be far preferable to have the villagers hand him their children of their own free will. If he were obliged to enforce the edict through Horvath he feared his poppet might not be up to the task. He decided to wait, though it went hard against his nature.

But he could not, in the end, bring himself to wait the full seven days. On the fourth day – the day when Kel and Anna and I came down into Cosham to offer our help – he gave in at last to his impatience and decided to act. He had the hollow baron summon his guard captain – in a dark room, to conceal the signs of his deterioration. This captain was one Giles Fisher, a man of Horvath's forest cohort who had only recently been promoted to replace the man Caradoc himself had despatched. He was keen to make his mark, but wary of going the same way as his predecessor, whose sudden disappearance had not gone unnoticed.

Horvath – or rather Caradoc speaking through Horvath – charged Fisher to ride into the village at sun-up on the following morning and collect the children. A dozen men-at-arms should be more than enough for the task. Fisher should give no warning and brook no argument.

Fisher made obeisance and went to choose his cohort. He had them line up in the bailey yard and gave them their orders for the next day. At his right hand stood the well that served the whole castle.

The water in the well was still the while he talked. Then it roiled and splashed of a sudden as Peter Floodfoot took his leave.

From the castle he went by streams that ran beneath the ground and by great reservoirs hid from men's sight, until he came at last to Cosham village. I was sitting on the well's coping with my legs dangling down when he surged up and drenched me.

"How now, madcap boy!" I said, shaking the water out of my eyes.

"I'm none of that," Peter gave answer. "For I'm ever sober, even when I'm drunk. You've less time than you thought, Once-Was-

Willem. The baron's men will come the morrow morn, with no message sent nor warning given."

I thanked him with all my heart and ran to bring the news to Kel and Anna. I found Kel in earnest conversation with Saul Randel, to whom he was trying to explain what a caltrop was and how to fashion one by welding one iron nail to another and twisting their ends. Anna was nearby with a group of women who were breaking up pieces of slate and scraping them on whetstones to put a fine edge on them.

"Dawn," Anna muttered in disgust when I told them. "The worst hour of all for Kel and me. And two weeks out from the full moon, besides."

"You'll be able to change, though?" I asked, for the grim look on her face troubled me.

"We'll be able to change," Kel assured me. "It will just tire us more quickly. This is good news, Anna. Since we know they're coming we can make it work for us. We're not like to get another chance like this, when they send a small force that thinks it's not expected." He smiled, but it was a cold smile with no trace of good humour in it. "We should meet them on the road," he said, "and save them some of their journey."

Anna nodded. "There'll be a dozen of them, Peter said?"

"Aye."

"Well we can muster twice that many to answer them."

Kel scratched his chin. "I think we should try what the three of us can do alone."

"Why?" Anna looked bewildered. "Aren't we training these people to fight?"

"We're training them to defend the village – and they'll need to do it soon enough. This is their home: they'll have advantage here because they know the ground. Take them out into the field and they'll only find ways to kill themselves, most likely tripping us up in the process."

"I'd rather a few peasants die than you, *min bror*," Anna said. "Or every fucking peasant there ever was, if I'm honest."

182

Kel tilted his head as if to let the words go by him. "Think of the peasants as coins we've got to spend. There's no point in emptying our pockets before we've even come to market."

They could not agree on it. I saw them take it all the way to the edge of a falling out, then carefully pull back again, a step at a time. Kel's plan carried in the end, but it was not because Anna thought he was right: it was because she loved him too much to quarrel with him.

"We should go to our beds before the sun sets," she said at last, bringing the matter to rest. "It seems we'll be up betimes."

The villagers had given no thought at all to the question of where to bestow us. Parson Lebone offered his rectory, but any one out of the three of us would have filled it by ourselves. "There's the kirk," he said doubtfully. "But there are no rushes on the floor there, and . . . and some might be dismayed to learn that you . . ." He balked at saying it, but he did not need to. I was a revenant, raised by necromancy, and a changer is a creature of pagan magic. We were all three of us unholy, and people might think the kirk tainted if we came there.

In the end the Theakstons gave us their barn to sleep in, which served us well enough. Anna took the hayloft, while Kel and I kept the family's three cows company down on the floor. That was what we purposed, anyway. In the event we found we could not sleep, so we only sat and talked.

"Where did you live," I asked Kel and Anna, "before you came here?"

"We were born in Tønsberg," Kel said. "It's a very old town in the country of Norway. Vikings built it."

"And was the change a thing that came from your mother's blood or your father's?"

"We have it from our mother, Berit," Anna told me. "She was full *ulfeðnar*. When the moon waxed she was a wolf, and did not come near the haunts of men. When it waned she was a woman – and a lusty and a wild one. She fucked her way through half the men of the town, dropped her babies wherever she happened

183

to be and walked away from them without a thought. Our father, Kjetil the thatcher, brought us up. He was much in love with Berit, and she favoured him enough to visit him often. But she stopped coming as soon as our change came on us. She didn't like that it took us so very differently."

"Kel is a bear, when he changes," I said, choosing my words with care. "Would it offend you, Anna, if I asked what you are?"

Anna only laughed. "Well that depends. Are you paying court to me, Once-Was-Willem? Because there are some things a maid will only tell to the man she means to marry."

I had not been a man when I died, but a boy of twelve. People forget that because in my risen body I'm so much bigger and stronger. I blushed at Anna's words and stumbled over my own until Kel clapped me on the shoulder. "She's joking with you, lad!"

"I am," Anna said, "and I should not. Forgive me. I'm everything, Once-Was-Willem. I used to think it was only things I'd eaten that I could become, but it's not. It's all the things that ever were. Do you know what a homuncule is?"

I said I did not.

"How can a woman's womb give forth a baby? The baby must needs be in her already, but very small, and it commences to grow when its time is come. But what about the baby's mother, then? Was she not a homuncule herself once, wrapped in her own mother's body? And when she was, was her daughter not inside her then? Small within small within small, all the way back to Eve that was our grandam.

"In just such a way, all the things that changers can become are locked in me, all together. You've seen me under the moon. You know I don't change into one fixed form, but that all forms flow through me as waves flow through the sea. That's my glory. I'm the one whose changes have no boundary-stone, the dancer who becomes the dance."

"Mother hated her for it," Kel said. "She said it was ugly, that Anna had no shape of her own – and warned her that she would have less and less as she grew older."

"'You'll end up a puddle on the floor,' she told me, 'howling out of a hundred mouths.' It was the last time I talked to her."

Anna grinned as she said this, but her tone was bleak. Kel laid his hand on her arm, offering comfort. "The last time either of us talked to her. I left for the war soon after, and you came with me."

"Aye. I did."

So that was how it was, I thought. And I marvelled (not for the first time) at the twists and turns that people take in their lives and in themselves, only for love – whether it's the love of a child or a sister's love for a brother or whatsoever it might be. We're all of us changers, and love is oftentimes what changes us. Although I would imagine that hate and fear and greed and wrath can do it too.

Enough of this. If we cannot fathom the water then we should not wade there.

XXV

Which treats of the fight on the Cosham road

The next morning a small column left Pennick Castle and made its way westward towards Cosham – which at a steady march, for men both young and strong, was less than an hour's journey. They brought two wagons with them, pulled not by oxen but by horses, so that the children once collected could be brought back to the castle the more expeditiously. Their captain, Fisher, rode in one of these wagons at the head of the column. His men marched after, and a carter led the second wagon at the rear.

The road led mostly through fields and pastures, and at one point across a stretch of land that we were used to call the Wider Fallow. Makepeace and Theakston both laid claim to this acreage, and since the dispute had never been settled the land was never sown. At the time I speak of it was less fallow than wilderness, covered in brambles as thick around as a man's fist. The hedgerows there were likewise overgrown because nobody had tended them for some years. The hawthorns leaned over the road and spilled out into it, with the brambles threaded through them. The wagons were obliged to slow as the way before them narrowed. The men-at-arms closed their ranks, pulling into the centre of the road.

That was when we took them.

The hawthorns and brambles were no barrier to Kel and Anna. They charged from both sides at once, crashing through the thick screen of branches and into the midst of the column of soldiers, rending and tearing as they went. Both were in their change-shapes, and they were terrifying – Kel a honey-gold bear that stood taller at the shoulder than the top of a tall man's head, Anna a whirlwind of flesh and fang.

The men knew not what was upon them, but they kept discipline and fought back. Some of them had pikes which they dropped into the position called the tarry, holding the two changers at a distance the whiles their comrades strung and launched as many arrows as they could. Kel could not charge the pikes, but Anna clambered over them, between them, through them, taking some wounds along the way but not slowing until she came among the pikemen and cut loose with tooth and claw.

Since they had struck the column in the middle, Captain Fisher had not been engaged. Seeing what was happening he called out to the nearest men to jump into the foremost wagon, where he sat, and took off at the gallop.

I saw them coming. We had expected that some of the soldiers would try to break away from the fray towards the village, and it fell to me to stop them, but I had not expected a wagon. If I had I might have chosen a better place to hide.

I was lying full in the road a hundred strides ahead, buried in a shallow ditch. A pile of leaves and branches hid my head, which was the only part of me that stood proud of the road's surface. It was Kel's contrivance of the ditches in Cosham that had put the idea in my head. I thought I could spring up in the midst of the cohort and take them by surprise.

I had only a moment to think what to do. As the wagon passed over me, I sat up and thrust both my arms through one of its foremost wheels. I was hoisted up at once out of my hide and hauled along the road, my limbs turning and twisting as my body was dragged up into the axle shaft and bent around it.

The wheel locked and the wagon slowed. My arms had been pulled almost out of their sockets, but with a desperate force I pulled back. The wheel parted from the axle, the wagon tipped and slewed around and I was sent sprawling down onto the hard ground.

Fisher had been thrown out of his seat in the crash and was stretched out full length in the road. The soldiers had fared better, and though they must have been harrowed by the sight of me they rallied quickly. They swarmed down from the wrecked wagon and began to set about me with their swords, hacking and stabbing with a will. I could not defend myself, for my arms were still wound around the spokes of the wheel so tightly it was as if I were wearing gyves.

The sword-strokes did not trouble me overmuch at first. My flesh flowed over and around my wounds, beginning at once to heal itself. One of the men-at-arms, quicker than the rest, saw this and went about a different way to kill me. He set his sword against my neck and sawed it back and forth, aiming to bring my head from off my body. His comrades, once they realised what he was doing, helped by kneeling on my chest and legs so I could not move.

I struggled mightily, but the wheel hampered me so much I could not get any purchase. I could feel the blade biting deep into my throat. But Anna came then, grappling onto the man who was beheading me and scattering the others with a scything sweep of some part of her that was snake-like but covered in roundels like the bosses on a shield. The swordsman struggled in her grip as she raised him up to her face. Her mouth gaped until it was almost as wide as a well. She put his head inside, bit it off and spat it out.

She finished his two fellows while I freed my mangled arms from the wheel. The muscles in them were too broken for the nonce to obey me, so I had to pound the wheel against the ground until it shattered.

Kel came limping back to join us. He was in human form now, and boltered all over with blood. He had a deep gash in his thigh, from which blood had poured freely and was still running in a sluggish stream. He favoured that leg as he walked. Leaning against the side of the wagon, he bowed his head and took his breath in gasps.

"You've taken hurt," Anna lamented, resting one of her many hands on his shoulder. Unlike her brother she could speak in her change-form: she did it by growing a human mouth in whatever place was most convenient to her needs. "Why did you change back, brother? You can abide the wound better as a bear!"

"The carter ran away and hid," Kel growled through bared teeth. "It took me some while to find him, and by the time I was done with killing him I had lost the change."

I was struck with dismay to hear this. I struggled to speak. The torn muscles in my throat made my voice even harsher and more hideous than it was wont to be. "Kel, the carter was no man-at-arms. He could not have hurt us. And he only did what he was told to do."

Kel pointed at the bodies on the ground, grimacing in pain as he did so. His shoulder had taken a wound too, though it was not so deep as the gash in his thigh. "These men would have hid behind the same argument," he said, "if you had asked them. 'Oh spare us, for we did nothing but what we were bid!' It was needful that none lived to tell their master what passed here, Once-Was-Willem. This way Horvath will be in doubt. Is there an army in the fief? If there is, whose might it be? Might some host be even now marching towards his gates? Uncertainty will slow him, and haply drain some of the courage from his men. We're not so many that we can squander an advantage."

I knew he was right, but still I mourned for it. I saw perhaps for the first time that any fight, whether you be in the right or the wrong of it, makes ripples of misery and misfortune spread out across the world. The greater the struggle, the wider the ripples. Our war was barely begun, and already we were killing innocents.

"Enough of this, Kel," Anna said. "Your hurt must be tended. But I can do nothing until you turn bear once more." She was

189

hurt too, I saw. There were arrows in her, two in her shoulder and one low down on her side, but she did not seem to have noticed.

"I'm too weak, Anna," Kel said, his eyes shut tightly. "I can't do it."

"You must. Is the second wagon whole?"

"It was whole when last I saw it. But the horses bolted. It's likely a good way up the road."

"Once-Was-Willem, go and find it. We'll take Kel back to Cosham in its bed."

I ran to do it, spurred on by the urgency in her voice, but it took some time to find the wagon, almost a mile up the road. Then I had to gentle the horses, that reared up when I drew near and would have bolted again, either from the smell of blood that was on me or just from the dread sight of me.

By the time I returned, Anna had hauled all the bodies off the road and killed one of the two horses from the lead wagon, that had broken its leg when I toppled it. The other horse had pulled itself free from its traces and was nowhere to be seen. The arrows that had been in Anna's flesh were now on the ground, broken, and the holes they had made in her were already closing. Kel was sitting in the grass at the road's side, his head bowed almost to his waist.

"At last!" Anna said, seeing me come. "Did you walk all the way to Adderley? Help me get him up."

Between the two of us we lifted Kel into the wagon. He hung on our arms like a sack.

"Now put on your fur coat again, brother," Anna said. "Do it now."

"I don't need any of this," Kel said hoarsely. "The wound will heal by and by."

"You'll be dead by and by. You've bled too much already. Do as you're bid."

Kel uttered a fierce oath that turned into a snarl as his mouth became once more a muzzle. The change came over him as a wave washes over a beach, beginning at his head and spreading in a ragged line until at last it reached his feet.

190

Anna shrugged one shoulder and then the other, stretching back her head. Her neck extended, and her muzzle grew longer and narrower. She leaned down and bit a great chunk from her own forearm. She chewed it twice or thrice, then lowered her head and spat the wad of flesh into the wound in Kel's thigh. Once there the bloody, half-mashed gobbet seemed to move of its own will, spreading itself to cover as much of the wound as it could.

"That will slow the bleeding," Anna said. "And knit the muscle together where it's torn."

Kel could say nothing, being now full bear again, but he licked her hand.

"You can control the meat of your body even after it leaves you?" I asked Anna, all amazed.

She gave me a warning look. "The change isn't a thing that unpacks itself easily in words. My flesh has quickening power – it makes itself at home wherever it finds itself. But that's a perilous thing, in most cases. It might seal a cut, but then grow into a chancre – or something worse still. Kel being blood of my blood can endure it better than most, especially when he's changed, but still I would not risk this if his hurt were less. We must bring him back to Cosham now so he can rest. That will do more good than anything."

She went back through the hawthorn hedge, where she had left her clothes before she changed, and came back shrugging into her smock. We both climbed up into the wagon and she took the reins, urging the horses at once into a canter.

"Well that's first blood to us," I said to Anna, meaning to raise her spirits for the look on her face was grim.

She gave me a cold look. "Aye, we did wonderfully well! Against a dozen men, whom we surprised – and with both the baron and his magic-user far away from the scene. And still Kel has taken a wound that stands in hard cure. If this makes you hopeful, Once-Was-Willem, go to. Hope your heart out of your chest. I'm afraid I see it differently. The real fray will not play so much in our favour."

191

The real fray. Until she said it I had not seen it in such a wise, but of course she was right. Horvath's soldiery knew their work and they had done it well, the pikemen holding Kel and Anna off, the whiles the archers fired on them, and the ones who coped me quickly finding a weak spot in my hurtless flesh. A few more men-at-arms, a braver or more resourceful captain, a single stumble or mischance on our part and all might have been different. When Anna said those three words, *the real fray*, I saw at last how daunting the challenge was that faced us, how great our peril.

XXVI

Our need for medicine, and how it was answered

e made a great stir when we rode into the village, the two of us all splashed with gore and with a great bear in the bed of the wagon behind us. A crowd ran to meet us and to question us on how our ambush had gone forward. Anna waved them out of our path and did not slow until we reached Theakston's barn. Both Matthew and Sarah came out to us, with all three of their sons following after. They gasped and backed away when they saw the bear lying wounded and bloodied in the wagon bed.

"It's only my brother," Anna said. "He won't bite unless you give him cause."

All five Theakstons looked stricken at this. Sarah crossed herself. Matthew tried many times to speak and at last managed "But . . . but God save us, that is a bear!"

"Aye," Anna agreed. "Sometimes." The events of the morning had left her in no mood to be patient. I saw her forearms thicken and the lower half of her face thrust itself forward as she began to go into her change. Then she thought better of it, perhaps because she would ruin a good smock. She led the horses on into the barn instead.

"You asked me to help you," I reminded Matthew Theakston, whose eyes were as round as saucers. "And I said I would seek out others. Did you think I meant others like you?"

"I think . . ." Matthew said. "I think this thing goes against nature. It cannot be Christian!"

"But Christ was a changer too, Matthew. Did he not change from god to man, and then back again?"

"That's blasphemy!" Sarah cried out.

"Very well. Then think of how the world changes, when it passes out of summer into winter. Or think of worms and caterpils, how they knit themselves a velvet coat and come out of it with wings on their backs. You cannot say change is unnatural when all of nature bends to it."

I went inside to see to my friend. I am not much for words at the best of times, and this had exhausted my store.

We managed with some difficulty to lower Kel from the wagon into the straw. He lay there in his change-form for some hours. Ever and anon, low growls were forced from him as the pain of his wound wracked him. Anna lay beside him and talked to him the while, reminding him of things they had done and seen together and all the foreign places they had visited. My job was to keep the wound clean with water from a bucket. The plug of Anna's flesh had closed it, but it had swollen up all around its edges and was now an angry red shot through with purple veins.

Kel fell gradually into a shallow sleep, and as he did so he changed by degrees back into his human shape. The wound looked much worse now: the swelling and discoloration seemed to gain ground in the transformation until it extended from his crotch almost to his knee.

"We need to summon a doctor," Anna said at last. "Bring me that idiot Theakston."

I ran to fetch Matthew from the house. He shook his head when Anna told him what she wanted. "I'm sorry for it, mistress," he said. "But there's neither doctor not apothecary closer than Burslem."

"Send to Burslem then," Anna told him. "Here. You can take one of our horses." She freed both the beasts from their traces and put the reins of the closer one in Matthew's hand.

"I cannot ride a horse," Matthew said.

"Then find some whoreson who can!" Anna shouted in his face.

Matthew offered no more argument but led the horse away.

The day wore on and nobody came. We knew it would be long ere they did, even if Theakston fared well in his errand.

By the time darkness fell, Kel was burning with fever and very sick indeed. Anna was beside herself. If there were only a moon, she said, he might have drawn some strength from it once it rose. But the sky was black, pinpricked with a million stars that shone as bright as jewels but offered no help to us.

We did what we could, Anna washing down Kel's face and arms and chest with a cloth soaked in cold water from the well and I giving him to drink from a pewter tankard whenever he roused enough to take it. His breathing had been shallow all day. Now it seemed to halt and start again as the wind rose and fell. We sat on either side of him, straining to listen, fearful of the moment when the silence between breaths would stretch out too long to ever resume.

Still nobody came from Burslem. Theakston ventured fearfully into the barn to tell us that he had given the horse to Ort Woodley who said he had ridden before and was keen to wipe out the shame of his misadventure at the Bell in Wolstanton. A blanket had been thrown over the horse's back to make a sort of saddle, buckled on with a cincture of black iron that Saul Randel had to hand. Woodley had left at the gallop without looking back. Later we would discover that the doctor in Burslem, the same Holt who had come too late to save Willem Turling, had made him wait three hours on the doorstep and then – with a great deal of spiteful pleasure – had declared he would not come. He had had enough of Cosham village, he said, and a little more besides. He would be damned if he came there again, unless it were the king himself that summoned. Woodley was obliged to come back empty-handed.

195

An hour after midnight or a little later, Anna and I both fell into a doze. It was the light that woke me – the shifting, flickering glare of a fire. I opened my eyes to see the whole barn alight. I yelled and scrambled up, looking around for Anna to help me move Kel out of danger. But Anna only sat and stared at the back of the barn where the fire was fiercest.

Three things I realised, each hard on the heels of the last. The first was that the fire brought no heat with it. The straw around us, the wooden beams above our heads, all had been swallowed up by the blaze, but the night's chill was not lessened by the smallest degree.

The second was that there was a girl standing in the heart of the fire. She was slight of stature, so thin that her knees and elbows stood out like knots in a cord. Her head was bowed as if she was too shy to meet our gaze.

The third was that I knew her.

"Morjune?" I said in wonder. "Morjune Scour?"

Aye, she said. *Give you good even, Willem Turling. It's long since I saw you in Cosham village.*

"It's long since I was here. But Morjune, are you . . . are you dead?"

She nodded. *Aye, I am. We can gossip later though. I think I can help your friend, if you'll let me.*

XXVII

In which Cain Caradoc seeks intelligence about his foes, and Betheli about her situation

In our haste to tend to Kel's wound, and then to bring him back to Cosham where he might rest, we forgot a thing of great moment. We did not count the dead. If we had, we would have noticed that at the end of our fight there were not twelve bodies on the ground but only eleven.

Hid in the bushes and shaking like a man with a quartan ague, Captain Fisher watched us depart. That meant he saw Peter's change, and Anna's too. He marked all three of us and heard the words that passed between us. When we were gone, he retraced his steps to the castle and hammered on the gates to be let in.

The sentinels were astonished to see him back again so soon. That he came alone, with his pate all bloodied and his shirt and breeks spattered with the mud of the road only added to their wonder. Ignoring the men's stares and their questions he went straight to the longhouse and presented himself to his master – or rather to the poppet that wore his master's face.

He told the baron all that had passed, sparing no detail. "This was not a thing that happened to us by chance, my lord," he said, "it was an ambush! The monsters were in the service of the villagers of Cosham, and put themselves in our way to keep us from coming there."

Standing behind Baron Horvath with his arms folded, Cain Caradoc swallowed this bitter news in grim silence. You must remember that he had never seen me since I came back up out of the ground. He had had no interest in doing so: the bargain he struck for a tithing of my soul was all that had mattered to him at that time. So it did not occur to him that one of these monsters was of his own making. He went immediately to a different conclusion – that the villagers had found themselves a magician of their own to set against him, and that this magician had shaped some servants for the task.

Who could this upstart be, he wondered, and how had they contrived to hide themselves from his sight? Great conjurations perturb the air and the earth. You cannot perform them in secret, not when another spellcaster is near. Besides, Caradoc knew most of the magic-users in England and its sister isles. He had contrived ways to spy on the ones he considered his rivals, so that they could not move without his knowing it. This must be some newcomer then, and one that was skilled enough to work in covert.

In his great rage at being so forestalled, his first thought was to have the baron order up the garrison and fling it at Cosham forthwith. It mattered not how many men died so long as the insult was answered.

A second thought checked him. The insult was nothing when it was weighed against his wider goal of coming at Yaldabaoth's power. It was vital that he keep his eye on that great endeavour, no matter what else should pass.

Were the children essential to that endeavour? Not really. It would be possible to build the conduit he needed using the baron's men-at-arms, or anyone else for that matter. But children's souls were the material he knew best. And besides, Cosham had defied him. It would please him to heap ruin on them for doing it.

All these deliberations passed through the sorcerer's mind while Fisher was still talking. Now with a twitch of his smallest finger he had the baron rise from table and with a peremptory sweep of his arm silence the captain in his endless self-exculpations. "Tell me of the monsters," he made Horvath say. "What were they?"

Fisher grimaced and wrung his hands. "My lord, everything passed so quickly. And in the turmoil of a fight, nothing is clear. I can't swear to what I saw."

"I don't ask you to swear to it. Only to be as particular as you can."

The captain tried his best. "There was one that was like a bear."

"How like?"

"Very like, my lord. Very like indeed."

"*Was* it a bear?"

"Haply it was. But the biggest I ever saw! I'd have had to reach up on my toes' tips to tap it on the shoulder."

"Well that's one, then. Go on. What of the other two."

"There was one . . . It was—" Fisher made shapes with his hands. "It seemed all beasts at once. I could not tell you how many legs it went on, or what face it wore. It changed as it moved. And probably it did the most harm to us out of the three of them. It seemed to be everywhere at once. Teeth and claws and tail and . . . I cannot say!"

The description was absurd. It seemed most likely that the man had been frighted by a pack of hounds and mistook it somehow for a single animal, but Caradoc said nothing. He had already decided that he would need to verify the captain's account through other sources. "How for the third?" he made Horvath ask.

Here Fisher hesitated and looked at the ground. "That was the one that came up under our wagon," he said, "and toppled it. I saw it only for a moment as it burst up out of the ground ahead of us. I think it took hurt as we rolled over it. I could see one of its bones poking out of its skin. It squirmed like a snake, it seemed to me. Or like an eel."

Caradoc ignored these comparisons. Three enemies of very different kinds, it seemed. Their nature was a mystery, and mysteries were not a thing he was minded to accept. Also, he would not be so foolish as to assume without evidence that these three champions were all the village had to boast. They might be the vaunt-couriers of a larger force – though where the abject simpletons of Cosham had found them and how they paid their hire beggared his imagining.

He had Horvath dismiss the captain. It might have afforded some amusement to have him flogged, but he remained one of the more capable men in the garrison and there were much better ways to chastise him for his failure once his usefulness was at an end.

The most needful thing at the moment, Caradoc decided, was intelligence. He needed to know what was passing at the village, the full tally of its defenders and as much as could be discerned about their plans. When next he moved against them it would not be a column but a full cohort that he sent – and they would be bolstered besides with weapons both magical and otherwise that would decide the outcome beyond any possibility of a doubt.

But it would be foolish to send anyone without knowing more about what it was they would be facing – and Caradoc was grimly determined not to be anyone's fool twice. He would perform a divination first and make his plans after.

He went to the sty and chose one of the pigs, the biggest of the lot. He led it off to the base of the mound, into a narrow space between the piles of dressed and uncut stone brought there to progress the building of the keep. He hobbled it with his knife and drew a circle around it with its own blood. Circle was too grand a word, really, for the wavering line of smeared gore, but it went around the beast and met itself again at its start, which was all that was required.

The invocation, likewise, was a snake that ate its own tail, being a *palindromos* spoken between two mirrors. Caradoc used two discs of highly polished copper which he held up on either side of his head as he intoned.

The air above the pig thickened and grew darker. A vague shape appeared there, made up of smaller shapes that turned around each other in tight arcs. It reminded Caradoc of a writhing mass of maggots. It hung still in the air for some little while, then descended slowly towards the pig.

Caradoc intoned the summoning again very softly, under his breath. Until it took the bait the boaganach was dangerous. It had smelled the blood and was clearly hungry, but it still might choose him over the pig.

At last, though, the roiling mass stretched itself out into a long filament and threaded itself into the pig's mouth. The pig stiffened and then sagged as the boaganach began to feed.

"*Clausa est ianua,*" Caradoc announced briskly. "*Stare in loco.*"

He stepped back with distaste as the pig convulsed, spraying the area around with blood and gobbets of flesh as the boaganach pounded and pummelled it from the inside. *No!* it roared. *No no no! Let me out, you cozening bastard! Set me free, you dog, or I'll rip out your heart and piss on it!*

"Keep a civil tongue," Caradoc advised it, "or you'll stay in there until the pig rots, and then its death will become yours."

Silence fell. Caradoc folded his arms and waited.

What do you want? The boaganach demanded at last.

"To know what my enemies are."

Better men than you, belike. I wish them well!

"Vouchsafe me answers to my questions, and I'll set you free as soon as I'm done with you."

The sprite was not so foolish as to assent to such an open-ended bargain. *And the questions will be about your enemies?* it demanded slyly.

"Yes."

Those who waylaid your men upon the road?

"Just so."

And they will touch on no other matter?

"Agreed."

Ah, but swear it.

"I do so swear, on my soul's weal."

For my part I have no soul, but I swear on my true name.

Caradoc was cautious too, bargains of this kind being notoriously slippery and perilous. "Say what you're swearing to."

To speak only truth. But no more truth than I'm asked for.

"And not to seek to harm me after you're freed."

The boaganach laughed – an ugly, grating sound, but Caradoc knew that none but he could hear it. The sprite was speaking in the way of its kind, a speech that did not stir the air or enter through the ears. *Yes! Very well! You were wise to stipulate so, for I'd have unseamed you like a fish if you'd not thought to bind me.*

"You would have tried. And I'd have had the tedious task of destroying you."

Perhaps one day we can resolve that question between the two of us. But we'll not settle it by flyting. Question me and be done.

"The first of my foes is a bear that walks on its hind legs and stands taller than a man. What is his name, and what his nature?"

His name is Kel Kjetilson and his nature is ulfeðnar. *He is a changer. He was of this very company before you came here, but the two of you did not overlap for long.*

"What's the best way to counter him?"

Why, to stop the change and kill him as a man – since a man is weaker than a bear.

"And what will achieve that?"

Command his blood, which is where the change resides.

"How do I go about to command?"

Use a nail. And his name. And the rune gyfu, which is shaped like a cross.

"Good enough. Now for the second. The man who saw it said it was compounded out of parts from many different beasts. What was that one?"

Ulfeðnar *again. But she's of the pure blood – a queen of her kind. Her name is Anna.*

"The same remedy then?"

By no means. She has no true shape, and so can't be bound in such a way. All shapes belong to her. If I were you I would not cope her at all. But if you must, do not seek to bind her. Loose her instead.

"Speak more plainly."

Listen more carefully, you preening cur. I mean you must attack her where she is weakest. Being all things at once, a true ulfeðnar, *one such as she that has no dilution, is not one thing more than another. The hardest part is the choosing, and then the holding still in the form that was chosen. If you fog her mind she is like to lose her shape entirely and become unavailing flesh.*

"Very well, I understand you. That's two of my foes then, but how for the third? My man said its bones stood proud of its skin, and it wriggled like a snake."

Your man is a fool.

"Belike he is. But tell me what he saw."

One that lay in his grave a while, but now walks abroad again.

"A revenant? A lych? No more than that?"

All men are more and all men are less, so how should I answer you? This one is the one that brings all the others. You should be mindful of him.

Caradoc pricked up his ears at this. "The others? You mean the changers?"

Not just the changers.

"There are more? Tell me their names and natures."

The boaganach was silent.

"Tell me!" Caradoc ordered it again.

I will not. Our converse is finished.

To his chagrin the sorcerer realised that he had overstepped. The bargain stipulated that as soon as he asked about anything other than the three on the road he must set the boaganach free. It had set a trap for him with its teasing mention of these other enemies, and he had fallen into it.

With an irritable gesture Caradoc dismissed it. The boaganach laughed mockingly as it departed. Nor did it forget to feed. It left nothing of the pig's carcase save gleaming white bone.

It moved quickly away from Caradoc, but it did not at once leave the castle. It was still angry at how the sorcerer had trapped and used it, and it hoped to work him ill. But it judged that Caradoc's power might be equal to any insult or mischief it could contrive, and quickly gave up any thoughts along those lines. Sullen and disgruntled it lingered in the air, looking for someone else on whom it could vent its spite.

All of this had taken place in the shadow of the castle's mound, and now the boaganach chanced to hear a ditty being sung from somewhere up above. The singer's voice was somewhat like its own, in that it did not stir the air but addressed itself directly to the spirit. *I will tell you one-oh*, it sang, and then *What is your one-oh?*

Curious, the boaganach followed the sound all the way to the cornerstone of the half-finished keep. The singing was coming from inside the cornerstone. The creature made to enter the stone, but paused. It sensed a barrier there, a spell that made the keep (and therefore the stone itself, as part of the keep) inviolable. Being spirit rather than flesh, the boaganach could have made itself tenuous enough to slip past the barrier and penetrate the stone, but the spell felt like the workmanship of the self-same wizard that had just caught it and coerced it so easily. It was understandably cautious.

What are you? it asked the voice inside the stone.

Betheli had spoken to nobody since her death except the dream friends she fashioned for herself, but she had not forgotten how – and her joy at hearing another voice cannot be imagined. *I'm Betheli*, she said. *What's your name? Can you help me? The wizard killed me, then locked me up in the dark! Will you to my mother and father and tell them where I am?*

No, the boaganach said, *I will not. Nor will I tell you my name and give you power over me. What's a Betheli?*

The girl did not hold back. She could not have done so if she had wished it. Her story poured out of her, what time the boaganach tested the efficacy of the spells that bound her and sniffed out their nature.

You're part of a spell-weave, it told her when she was finally done with her tale. *The sorcerer used you to build a wall around this place that none save its defenders can cross. But he's run another strand through the spell – a binding, it seems.*

To hold me inside the stone? Betheli asked.

204

Not just that – although that's a part of it. You're bound to something else besides the stone. The other presence that's here.

Betheli knew full well what the boaganach meant by the other presence. She had become aware long since that she was not alone. *The one that's asleep,* she said.

Aye.

What is it?

A very old power. Much older than me, and I was here when the giants yet lived – Magog and Azagog and their kindred. If your sleeper has a name, I don't know it.

It's bigger than me, Betheli said.

Bigger than your wizard, too. And you're like a tiny burr stuck in its skin. Best hope it stays asleep and stays in place, for if it should wake and move it's like to hale you with it. Or it will try to – only the stone will keep you where you bide. I know not how that will fall out, but I think it will go ill with you. God bye you now, little ghost.

Wait! Betheli wailed. *Don't leave me! I've got nobody to talk to here! I've been alone for so long, and it's so dark here!*

The boaganach was not by nature kindly or compassionate. It cared nothing that the girl was trapped in the stone, or that she stood in such peril. But it was still angry at being cozened and would willingly have worked some harm on Caradoc if it could think of a way to do it. These spells were strong and had been worked with care. It followed that they were important to the wizard and had been put there as part of some larger plan.

If you can't get out, go further in, it told Betheli. *The spells are part of your being. Embrace them. Learn where they touch you, and where they shape themselves to your touch. Spread yourself across them and into them, like water soaking into cloth.*

What good will that do? Betheli asked.

I cannot say. None, perhaps. But there's a great deal that rests on a cornerstone, little ghost – and on this cornerstone more than most. It might be a fine thing to make it shake.

Whereupon the boaganach departed, having no desire to stay long enough in Cain Caradoc's presence to be noticed. It never came near Pennick after that, and never thought again of this conversation. But it's said, great trees may often grow from the smallest seeds.

Trees, and other things.

XXVIII

The fashioning of a homuncule

aradoc was irked. He was not more than half done with his questions and the boaganach had slipped from his grasp with insulting ease. He could begin again with another pig, but there was now a miasmic residue of rage and hatred in the air that would likely alert any wandering spirits to his trap. Besides, he saw that there was a need to go himself to Cosham, since the confounding of his foes would require that he lay hands on certain ingredients.

He wasted no time, but straightway knelt down beside the carcase and scooped up a handful of earth. Raising it close to his face he bent his will upon it and at the same time shaped it with his hands.

The power in magic, I can attest, is a thing that is most like water. It can be made to flow readily from one vessel to another, and it transports along with it anything with which it has been mixed. Caradoc shaped the moist earth into what Anna when we talked erewhile had called a homuncule, a tiny copy of himself, perfectly like except that it had wings. And he allowed a little of himself to flow into the thing – enough to give it life.

"Eyes will not see you," he chanted, cupping the diminutive creature in his two hands. "Ears will not hear you. But you will see and hear all. Go now to Cosham. See what is there, and let me see it too."

You may wonder why he took so much trouble, when he could merely have sent his spirit forth from his body, as he did at Cosham when he sought for and found Betheli Theakston. He might well have done so, except that he did not require the homuncule merely to gather intelligence for him. He was also desirous of obtaining a drop of Kel's blood for the spell the boaganach had described, and therefore it needed not just eyes to see but hands to grasp with.

He released the homuncule and it shot up into the air like an arrow sent from a bow. It winged its way westwards from the castle until the belltower of the kirk came into view. Then it swooped down again like an eagle stooping on its prey and alighted on the branch of an oak that grew full in the middle of the village green.

It cast its eyes this way and that. There was little to see. On the common land three cows were grazing. Two women were busy at the well, one of them letting down the bucket while the both of them talked each to other. A man sat on his own doorstep repairing a torn jerkin with the heel of a sack.

These things were of no interest to Caradoc at all. The homuncule sniffed the air, sifting it for a sense of hidden strangeness and occulted power. It found nothing at first, but it persisted – and was rewarded all at once with the pungent whiff of magic. There was someone or something here that was far more than flesh and blood.

And here she came. A woman, to look at her; but just as a crack willow will show green and then suddenly silver when the wind changes quarter, so this woman was only one face of a many-faced thing that yearned to shift and show itself.

She was carrying a coil of rope in one hand. Behind her, in the other hand, she hauled a man who was weeping. She walked directly to the tree in which the homuncule had roosted. For a moment it thought she must have seen it there, but no, she had chosen the tree for a different reason.

She flung the man face-down in the grass and set her foot on his back. She was a big woman, and strong withal. Though the man tried to rise he had not the might to do it. He babbled words that the wind took away.

Others were coming now, running out from their houses to see what was toward. The woman ignored them. She slung the rope up over a branch, caught the free end of it and fixed it with a running knot. That done, she made a noose at the other end and leaned down to slip it over the man's head, securing it at his neck.

A hanging, then. Caradoc was intrigued. If the monsters that Captain Fisher and the boaganach had described were indeed Cosham's champions, then Cosham was at war with itself. That could only be good news. The homuncule crawled down the bole of the tree to a lower branch, where it set itself to watch and listen. At Pennick Castle, three miles away, Cain Caradoc watched and listened too, with the growing conviction that his work was being done for him.

You will see from this that the two parts of my story have come unseamed, one from the other. Events in Cosham had moved on from when I brought you there last, and now I must go back and expound them for you.

XXIX

Which treats of a hanging

ying had not lessened Morjune's skill as a healer. It had only stripped away the need for subterfuge. Being a ghost she was able to work inside Kel's body as well as outside it. I have said that magic is like water, and like water she flowed into his wound. She knitted flesh and sinew where it was broken, chilled the swelling until it subsided, rebuked the poison that was beginning to take root and bade it leave. Within the space of a few hours Kel went from a sweating, groaning fever to a deep and natural sleep. By the time the first light of the new day found its way down to us from the barn's one small window, nothing remained of the wound but a puckered seam that ran up the inside of Kel's thigh. The dead girl had saved him.

But by her coming and her telling us her story she broke past any mending the strained trust there had been between us and Cosham. When Anna heard of Morjune's burning she began to shake, not so much with rage as with the effort of holding her rage back.

She would not leave Kel until she knew he was safe. She knelt beside him through the night and did not so much as blink. But as soon as morning came and he opened his eyes she snatched up a coil of rope that was hung over a hook on one of the beams and was gone. Up to the house first where she marched in on the Theakstons at their breakfast – which was late because they had not slept much knowing there was a wounded bear in their barn. "Where does this James Makepeace bide?" she demanded of Matthew. "Bring me to his house."

"It's the longhouse at the other end of the street, nearest the green," Matthew told her. "If you'll wait until I've——"

Anna upended the board, tipping all that was on it (which was only bread and cheese, and a slice of beetroot each for the three boys) into the rushes on the floor. Sarah wailed in protest, for they could scarce afford the loss, but Anna paid her no heed. "Makepeace!" she yelled. "Bring me to him, sot, or I'll beat you into a wicker bottle!"

She was wearing then her human shape, not the dancing flesh that was her glory, but as I have said she was a woman that stood taller than most men. Withal her manner was so fierce that Matthew made no further argument, but rose and brought her where she asked. At the very least it took her away from his wife and children.

When they came to the Makepeaces' house he pointed. The door was closed and locked but Anna kicked it so hard that the bolt broke away and straightway walked inside. Jem Makepeace and Fleur that was his wife came running to see what was towards. When Jem saw that it was one of the two strangers that had come into the village along with the monster, and that she was standing in his hall, he did not hesitate but strode at her all at once to put her out again.

Anna's first blow broke his jaw. Her second laid him low. Fleur jumped on her shoulders but with a shrug Anna threw her off again. She picked Makepeace up by the scruff of his neck, dragged him back out of doors and flung him pell-mell down in the dirt of the street.

By this time I was come running, and I was not alone. From every house around the villagers emerged into the daylight, roused by all this noise and pother. With her foot on Makepeace's neck

Anna addressed them all. "You whoresons!" she shouted. "You lying curs and worthless bitches! You called on us to keep your children safe from harm, and what did you do to one of your own? For the spark of magic that was in her you burned her alive, and this cunten bastard lit the fire!"

It took the villagers some little while to realise that it was Morjune that Anna meant. When they did, a man at the front of the crowd shouted "Morjune was a witch!" thinking that such explanation would be enough. Anna walked across to him, felled him with an open-handed slap, then went back to Makepeace. He had rolled over onto his stomach and was trying to crawl away. Anna set her foot upon him once again and pressed him down hard into the dirt.

"This is only my fight because it's my brother's," she said, glaring into each and every face she saw before her. "A peck of shit for all the rest of you, for your families, for your cattle and for your whole pustulent village. But when you go about to burn children, and then come puling and begging because your own are threatened . . ." In her great passion the words fled from her. In truth, I had never seen Anna so greatly moved about anything excepting only her brother's welfare. I wondered what she herself might have suffered as a girl that made her feel Morjune's suffering so deeply. As a monster myself, that had been shunned and driven off on the wrong end of a pitchfork, I thought I might venture a guess.

"Fuck you all," Anna finished. "I'll stay as long as Kel stays, but any of you that dares to speak to me will take a blow on the pate for every word – and this one hangs." She gripped Makepeace by the scruff of his neck and set off towards the green, haling him behind her like a sack of meal. There was a great oak that stood full in the middle of the green. When Anna was come to it she slung the rope up over one of its branches, made it secure, and set about to tie a noose in the end of it.

I had no love for Jem Makepeace, and like Anna I was angry at what he had done to Morjune, but I could not see any good coming out of his being hanged. We could not protect the children of Cosham without Cosham fighting beside us, and this would make them afraid to come near us. "Anna," I said, "haply we should wait until all is done to settle scores."

"The rest of the scores, by all means," Anna said, dropping the noose around Makepeace's neck. "This count I'll answer now."

By this time Parson Lebone was come. He had been slower than most because of the injury to his leg, but seeing at once what was happening he took hold of the rope just above the noose and wound it quickly around his own hand while it was yet slack.

"You'll lose that hand, father," Anna warned him, hauling on the rope to make it taut. Lebone was drawn up onto his toes' tips, but he did not try to pull free.

"You mustn't do this, Anna Kjetil's daughter," he said. "You must hear me out first."

Anna brought her face down to his and spoke with terrible calm. "Be careful with that word. What I *must* or *must not*, that's mine to say."

"I only meant," Lebone said, "it's not your choice to make."

"No? Whose, then?"

"Hers," Lebone said. He pointed to where Morjune was walking through the crowd towards them. I say she walked through the crowd and I mean exactly that. The ghost did not mark who was in her path. Her substance was as hurtless as the air, and she went where she chose. The women and men whose bodies she glided through cried out or fell to the ground in terror. Though she was yet aflame, Morjune's touch was as cold as ice. She did not stop until she was come up beside Anna and the parson – and Makepeace too, although he had his eyes tight shut and had not yet seen her.

Thank you, she said to Anna, *for wanting justice for me. It's kind of you. But I've always held that mercy mattered more.*

Makepeace opened his eyes when he heard Morjune's voice. He stared at her in misery and dread – the ghost not just of the girl but of his guilt, for he could not deny that he had been foremost in murdering her.

"Mercy's wasted on offal like this," Anna said, giving him a look of fierce despite.

No, Morjune said. *It's never wasted.*

Anna bared her teeth. "You think he should come away unpunished then? For such a foul thing?"

No. But I've no great appetite for answering one murder with another. I mislike this man enough that I don't want to keep him company in his folly and his cruelty. He lit that flame with all the village looking on. He only performed what was in all their hearts, and hanging him won't take away from that. She looked around as she spoke at all the frightened faces round about, and then down at Makepeace's again. He worked to speak, but his broken jaw would not let him. Only a sort of moan came from his mouth. *What Cosham did*, Morjune said, *let Cosham answer. And I don't just mean what they did to me. I mean the handing over of Geoffrey Carne to them that killed him, the driving out of Willem Turling, all that they've ever done out of fear or hate or cruel thoughtlessness. But I should like to let them choose their own penance. The pain that matters is the pain that's willed, not the one that's laid on like a yoke.*

Anna thought on this a while, and at last let go of the rope. "Good enough," she said heavily. And then to the crowd: "Do you hear, all of you? Your healer is still plying her trade. Still trying to make you well, where you're sick. If it were up to me, my physic would be to bleed you. But this dead girl just brought my brother back from the rim of the grave, so God forbid I gainsay her." She leaned in close to speak in Makepeace's ear, gripping his head in her wide, strong hand to tilt it up. "As for you, goodman cunt, you owe your life to the girl you killed. If you want to keep it, you were best stay a long ways off from me."

She walked away. Makepeace knelt with his head bowed while Parson Lebone freed his neck from the noose. Then his wife and two of their daughters led him away. His face was a dark mask, plastered with the mud of the street, but I could see the tracks that his tears had carved in it.

Morjune came and stood by me. *God bye you, Willem Turling*, she said softly.

"God bye you, Morjune Scour," I answered her. "I think I remember pulling your hair when we were younger, and you laying open my head with a slate in righteous vengeance. When were you wont to be so wise, and so forbearing?"

Since I died, I suppose.

I asked no more, for I knew well enough what she meant. Things do look somewhat different when you look at life from a point that's beyond its further end.

XXX

In which Cain Caradoc makes ready for battle

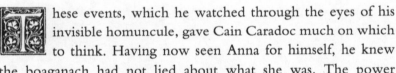hese events, which he watched through the eyes of his invisible homuncule, gave Cain Caradoc much on which to think. Having now seen Anna for himself, he knew the boaganach had not lied about what she was. The power seething in her was impossible to ignore. She must be a titan of her own kind, a queen, in whose blood the speechless energy of the change ran pure and strong. Such creatures were dangerous indeed, the source of their power primal and unknowable, but the boaganach had told him a way to hobble this one so she could not challenge him.

The ghost, Caradoc decided, was no threat at all. In life she had been no more than a hedge witch, with some natural talent but no training in the lore and practice of high magic. Now, being dead, she was even less than that. He did not need to be concerned there.

Out of the three of us he was the most intrigued by me. The boaganach had said I was a revenant, but there must be more at work here than that. I bore a human face but the haphazardness of my lumpen body, with the bones sticking out of it this way and that, gave him to wonder what I had been in life. A man under a

216

curse, perhaps? A victim of some hideous torture? Or it might be that I had died by falling down a mountain and had been shovelled into the grave in gobbets.

Then he heard Morjune speak my name – out loud in front of the villagers and a second time more softly when the two of us spoke alone. Turling? Had he misheard? No, there it was again. Turling. Whence and why did he know that name? It was not as if he had had much to do with the fief at large. He barely left the castle.

It came to him at last. Night, in the woods, when he still lived in his spell-charmed house. A peasant couple on their knees, kissing his hands. Yes, there it was. *I am Jon Turling of Cosham, and this my wife.*

And the son for whom they had entreated him was named Willem. Absurd and implausible though it seemed, the brutish monstrosity with the mismatched limbs and stoop-shouldered gait was a thing he himself had made by means of his art. Which meant, of course, that he had taken a tithing of the boy's soul to incorporate into his own being.

The discovery was both welcome and exquisitely amusing. So far from being a menace to him, this ungainly thing could be recruited in an instant to Caradoc's own cause. He could command the monster simply by unwinding the sliver of Willem Turling's spirit from his own soul and fashioning it into a new spell. True, he would lose so much of his prolonged life as the boy's spirit had granted him, but given the immense reservoir of magical power he was about to conquer and possess, the expenditure seemed a trivial thing indeed.

This left only the bear-man, whom he had not yet seen. Again, the boaganach had told him how to proceed here. All that was needful was a little of the man's blood.

This proved to be a very simple thing to obtain. The homuncule followed Morjune and me when we went back to Theakston's barn to see how Kel was faring. We had thought to find Anna at his side, but she was sitting some distance away on one of the farm's boundary stones. She was guarding the barn's door, but also sitting alone with her thoughts as she pondered on what had just passed.

The homuncule spied on us from a roof beam as Morjune once more tended to her patient and I brought water for him to drink. So the bear-man had taken hurt during the fight on the road! Caradoc was pleased to discover it, not out of pure despite but because it fitted well with his purposes. Choosing a moment when our eyes were elsewhere he had the little winged man swoop down from the beam, snatch up a piece of straw and fly back up again. Blood from Kel's wound had fallen on the straw and dried there, dyeing it black. That would give the sorcerer wherewith to work.

Caradoc felt his errand was done, but he was wary of over-looking some detail that would vex him later. He had the homuncule fly into every house in the village, into the barns and outhouses, into the kirk and the attached rectory. Even then he did not bring it directly back to the castle but made it fly in widening spirals outwards from Cosham in case there was some encampment in the fields or commons that he had missed. He had not forgotten that the boaganach had spoken ambivalently of there being more foes than three to be counted. Well, the ghost-witch made up the tally to four, but he could not get beyond that. Belike, he told himself, if there were others they were only men of the village who had joined the lists because their own children were threatened.

It did not matter. He would outfit his men-at-arms with such weapons as would be unanswerable, even if they faced a force three times greater than their own. He would finish this – for his own satisfaction as much as anything else. Even now, he knew, he could change his mind. It would surely be easier to procure what he needed elsewhere. But it would irk him past reason to remember afterwards that his will had been checked. No, Cosham's children would be his. And Cosham would be ash.

Even before the homuncule returned with its precious cargo, Caradoc was assembling his raiding party. There would be no half measures this time: he would fall upon the village like an avalanche.

After all, once he had succeeded in his goal he would have no need of men-at-arms or servants of any kind. All the created world would bend itself to answer his smallest whim.

Through Baron Horvath he gave orders. All the men of the garrison should arm and ready themselves at once, and form up in the bailey yard in marching order. The men-at-arms made haste to obey, though they evinced no great enthusiasm. Fisher had been tight-lipped about the fight on the Cosham road, but any fool could see that twelve men had set forth and only one had come limping back. They were not cowards, but those numbers preyed on their minds a little.

There was another problem with the castle's cohort, which is perhaps worth mentioning. It was not one cohort, but two, the one being the brigands who had been with Horvath in the forest and the other the soldiers who had defected from Robert Carne's household after his death. The two stood side by side when their duties called them to it, but they ate and slept, diced and gossiped apart.

Fisher was of the forest faction, which meant that the castle veterans did not like or trust him much. He knew this, and did not relish the thought of commanding them in an action. Withal, his recent travails on the Cosham road weighed grievously on his mind. When the baron summoned him to the longhouse he went with dragging steps.

"The men stand ready, lordship," he said, fist clasped to his chest in a martial salute.

"Ready for what, though?" the poppet baron demanded.

Fisher did his best to show a steely resolve. "For anything, lordship. They'll go where'er you lead them, though it be to the gates of Hell itself."

"Well it's not so far as that by half," the baron said. "We're only riding to Cosham."

Again to Cosham! Fisher's heart sank. But it rose again somewhat when the baron summoned his sorcerer with an imperious snap of his fingers. "You'll be under my command this time," he assured

219

the guard captain. "And you'll be better prepared. Cain Caradoc, make sure that my captain has magical aids that will ensure his victory."

Caradoc bowed deeply, with a great show of servility. By now he had received his homuncule home and made his own preparations, which he was only too anxious to put in train. "Of course, good my lord," he said. "It is my privilege to serve."

"See to it then," the baron barked. He turned on his heel and left the two of them alone, freeing Caradoc to act on his own behalf rather than through his proxy.

"Be of good cheer, captain," he said to Fisher. "I'll give you more than you could possibly need. See what is here."

He gestured to the table before him, which was all bare save for three things: a torc, an arrow and a short-sword in a richly ornamented sheath. Fisher was impressed by the first and third of these. He could not help thinking about the price they might fetch if he were to defect from the baron's service and head south for London. About the arrow he had no feelings at all, being no archer.

Caradoc picked up the torc first. It was made of bronze plates, each about the size of a man's thumb, and was of the finicky Norman type that closed with a tenon clasp. It was good workmanship but Fisher did not like it overmuch.

"This is for you to wear," Caradoc said. He placed the torc around Fisher's throat. With the click of the clasp's closing the guard captain experienced an extraordinary sensation, as though a blast of wind had blown all through him, leaving him chilled but roused to full alertness. His skin prickled.

"Has it . . ." His mouth had filled with saliva. He swallowed it again with difficulty. "Has it some magical power, sieur?"

"It has." Caradoc inclined his head. "At time of need my magic will act through it, to such effect as will gravel your enemies and bring them to despair."

"I . . . I thank you for it, sieur, with all my heart!" Fisher stammered.

"You will carry, besides, this sword," Caradoc continued. "I made

220

it for the baron, but he has graciously ceded it to you for the duration of this fight. It is as sharp as Hell's reproach. Do you but break a foeman's skin with it, and he will die as surely as if you had struck him to the heart."

He handed over the sword, which Fisher buckled straightway around his waist. He was well pleased withal, but also somewhat puzzled. "I . . . I thought the baron said he would lead us," he ventured.

"And so he will," Caradoc conceded gravely. "But he has singled you out, guard captain, for a special mission of great import. You remember why it is we're marching against Cosham?"

"The children."

"Aye, just so. To claim the children. And it may be the villagers will try by some desperate wile to keep them from us. If they should, you – you and none other, guard captain – will be our riposte to them."

This flattery served its purpose. Fisher puffed up with pride, thinking himself a fine fellow indeed. Still, there was one question he could not forbear from asking. "What if the monsters come again against us?"

Caradoc smiled. "You need not worry about them," he said. "They will be well taken care of. The great bear I will hobble myself, with a charm that I have already in train. For the other one, the monster with the claws and teeth and scales, you will have this." He picked up the arrow and held it out for Fisher to take.

Fisher turned it over in his hands. As with the torc, he felt the power hidden within it and knew it for a thing of sorcery. "What will it do?" he asked.

"Give it to your best archer. Have him keep it strung and ready as you come into the village. If that monster comes against you he should let fly. As with the sword, it matters not a whit where it strikes. The beast will take such hurt as will never mend."

Fisher was feeling more heartened with every moment. "How for the third?" he asked eagerly. "The one that burrowed up from under the road and toppled me in the dirt? What will become of him?"

"That one will fight with might and main," Caradoc said. "But he will fight for you, not against you." He laughed at the expression of amazement on the captain's face. "Do not ask me how, or why. But do not fear him. When the time comes he will be added to your number."

He went on to explain to the captain the orders that would apply to him alone. He would be Caradoc's sheet anchor in case all his other plans and stratagems were countered. It was hard to justify the expending of so much effort on a ploy that would almost certainly not be needed, but Caradoc could not put out of mind those others of which the boaganach had spoken. Suppose there were more besides the ghost of a dead witch? It was better to be sure.

This way it did not matter what champions Cosham could raise up. His victory was assured beyond any doubt.

XXXI

In which battle is joined

e had hoped to have longer. As it was, so many things that we had thought to do were omitted or left unfinished.

I say *we*, but as you may have guessed the most of our plans came from Kel, and while he was recovering from his wound he could do but little to put them into proof. Under Morjune's ministrations he healed more quickly than we could ever have believed, but still the time left to us was too short. We had a day and a night in which to rest ourselves: the morning of the next day brought the alarum.

We had removed from the Theakstons' barn to the village green. Anna wanted to take no more favours from the village and to have no more converse with its people than she could manage. We slept in our clothes on the grass, around a fire that Anna had set. It was comfortable enough and gave us this much of advantage, that we were close by the well when Peter sprang forth to tell us that the castle gates were thrown open and the whole of Horvath's company on the move. More than eighty men-at-arms, he said, and some thirty horse. "They've left the castle deserted. From the jakes to the gateposts there's nothing stirring."

"What of Caradoc?" I asked him.

"I did not see him. The baron leads them, and they march under his banner."

"A banner, is it? As if this were a battle they rode to, rather than a slaughter." Kel spat on the ground. "A fuck and a fart on them. They're cowards and lackwits all, and they'll weep for their hearts' despite when they see what waits them here. Once-Was-Willem, go have the parson ring the bell to bring everyone to their stations."

I ran to do it. Lebone was dismayed when he came to the rectory door at my knock. "So soon?" he said, blinking sleep out of his eyes. "We're not yet ready!"

"I'm sure there are many riding under Horvath's banner that feel the same," I told him. I meant to hearten him, but it was a foolish thing to say. The thought of that great host marching against us was not welcome to either of us.

He went into the kirk to ring the bell, and I hastened back to where Kel and Anna were standing now in the middle of the street. Morjune was with them, her fists clenched and her face a mask of fury.

"You'll fight for Cosham?" I asked her, all astonished. "Even after Cosham killed you."

I'll fight against them that would harm children, she said. *Whoever they answer to, and whatever colours they come in.*

There was a great bustle all around us of men and women running to their places. Though we had not managed to set all of the ambushes we planned, we had at least found ways that the villagers could be active in their own defence. I hoped that none would die as a result, but the hammer that was about to fall on Cosham was of so great a size, it was hard to imagine that it would spare any.

I have said that Cosham had but the one street, but that is not altogether true. There was the main street, which had an elbow halfway along its length, so you could if you wished to see it as two streets meeting. There were dwellings on both sides of the street all the way to the elbow, but few thereafter for that was

224

where the street fronted the green which was mostly open. At the furthest end, beyond the turning point, was the kirk with its rectory, a few of the yardlanders' houses and then common land beyond.

We had placed ourselves at the elbow, facing east, which was where the castle stood and whence the raiders must come.

And now here they were. Not the horsemen, who I thought must surely come first, but a line of men-at-arms with pikes and behind them a second line with bows. Perhaps a dozen of each. More were coming on behind them, but they all stopped when they reached the first houses.

The baron, mounted on a grey charger, picked his way through them and they parted to let him by. He carried his own banner, whose colours were dazzlingly bright – though not so bright as his armour, to which Cain Caradoc's spellcraft still gave a golden gleam that all but blinded those who gazed upon it.

"Men and women of Cosham," Horvath called. "I am your lord, recognised and anointed by your king, and yet you have shown me cursedness and defiance. You have ignored my edicts, scanted my honour and murdered my soldiery. Come out of your houses now. Kneel down side by side in the dirt and beg my forgiveness. Your children as you know are forfeit, but you may live to bring forth more if you show contrite hearts today. Entreat my mercy and it may yet be yours."

There was something wrong with his voice. It had an echo to it, as though it sounded in a cave. It chilled me, and I did not believe for a single heartbeat that his mercy was to be had. It seemed nobody else did either, for there was no answer.

"Enough of this," Anna muttered. "We can't close the trap if they come not by us."

"They're waiting for something," Kel said. "Belike their riders have gone the long way about and mean to surprise us, coming across the fields. Let's see if we can give them a little encouragement."

He dropped his breeks, took his pizzle in his hand and pissed. He did it without heat or haste. When he was finished, he gave

225

the pizzle a shake and tucked it away again. "That's for your mercy, Baron Cutpurse!" he shouted down the length of the street. "And that's for the men we killed. Not a one of you is worth more than my piss, and the earth's burden is all the lighter for the dozen we tore asunder."

"Marry, look at you!" Anna bellowed, tipping the scales a little further. "You're all fucking rabbits. A fart would knock you flat. Does Pennick breed a man that dares to cope me?"

"Pennick's men will blight and scotch you!" a man shouted back. A cheer went up from the host behind him.

Anna bent down and picked up a rock that was lying in the road. It was about the size of a man's head, covered in moss and caked earth. She hefted it in her hand, feeling the weight of it and at the same time measuring the distance – which was twice a hundred strides.

Her arm writhed suddenly with ropes of muscle that wrapped it around and about. Her upper body bulged.

The arm shot forward, so quick that it rent the air and made a sound like a soft thunderclap. The rock sped like any cannonball. It landed in the chest of the man that had answered her. He folded around it, all the bones in his upper body shattered in an instant. He fell without even a cry.

That was enough at last. The pikemen did not wait for their commander's order, but with a roar began to run down the street towards us. Behind them the archers drew back their bowstrings and loosed their first shafts. For better or worse, battle was joined.

The pikemen ran straightway into the first of Kel's ambuscades. The ground gave way beneath them and they plunged down into the pits we had dug, where sharpened stakes gave them pain and insult and in some cases a sudden quittance.

Then from the houses on either side the men and women of Cosham let fly with rocks and stones, or skimmed the slates that Anna had made them gather and sharpen to a fine edge. Here and there a man-at-arms stumbled and fell. Few if any of the wounds they took were fatal, but being trampled by their comrades as they came on at a headlong rush was another matter. Some were pushed face-down into the mud and stifled. Some had their necks or backs broken and did not rise from where they had fallen.

We ran to meet them, through a snickering rain of arrows. Anna went before Kel to shield him since her flesh, like mine, did not easily take hurt. Morjune was faster than any of us though, and reached the oncoming soldiery first.

Her flames engulfed them. They did no harm at all, but when you put your hand into a fire there is always a moment of shock and numbness before the pain announces itself. The oncoming wall faltered and broke as the men-at-arms flinched from the hurt they thought must come.

In that moment we were upon them and among them. Anna was a wall of teeth and claws that left dead and broken men behind her. Kel wielded an axe in each hand, his heavy blows breaking through armour all the way to flesh, and then through flesh to bone.

I carried no weapon, for I had no skill with any, but I set to with my fists and worked what harm I could. Some of the men I struck fell and did not rise again – and some of their fellows wasted their time in hewing at me, which availed them nothing, rather than attacking my friends.

But for all this we were not faring as well as we needed to if we were to win the day. Not all the men-at-arms were engaged with us. Some had broken off to kick down the doors of the houses on either side of the street. They were going inside to search for the children and deal harshly with the stone-throwers. We could not pull away from the fray in the middle of the street to stop them – and at any moment our foes would break past us and surround us. We would be in a desperate case if they did.

Up to this moment Kel had been fighting as a man – mostly so he could call out orders to the villagers. Now he gathered his will and began to take himself into his change.

I say *began*, because he did not finish it.

XXXII

Of the nail and the arrow

ou may have been wondering this while where Cain Caradoc was as all of Cosham was overwhelmed with blood and wrack. The answer is that he was in two places at once.

His body remained in the bailey yard at Pennick. He knelt on straw and damp earth with his head bowed and his eyes closed. His mind, meanwhile, was somewhere else entirely. He was watching the battle through the eyes of his winged homuncule which was perched on the thatched roof of Matthew Theakston's house. He needed to be close enough to the unfolding skirmish to see Baron Horvath and control his movements. Also, he wished to be ready to intervene with his prepared enchantments as they were required.

That time was now come, he decided. It was not that his soldiers were faring badly – far from it – but that he did not trust them to carry this home without his help. So what to do first? He surveyed the field and considered his options.

The ghost-witch was trying to harry his men-at-arms with her foxfire, but they had learned by now that it could not hurt them and they paid her no heed at all. Neither did he.

The *ulfeðnar* woman was fighting fiercely, but there was nothing to be done there until his horsemen arrived. They had gone the long way about so that they could surprise Cosham's defenders from behind, charging across the commons onto the village green. They would bring the magic arrow with them when they arrived, and − so long as the archer did not miss his mark − that would take the woman straightway out of the fight.

It must be either the revenant or the bear-man then. Both were in the thick of the fray, but the one was fighting with twin axes and the other with his bare hands. Moreover, as he watched, the bear-man began to change, his upper body bulging with sinew and quickening with golden fur.

Clutched in Caradoc's left hand was an iron nail, onto which the shape of the rune *gyfu* had been scratched − a simple cross like a mark in a tax-collector's ledger. In his right hand was a hammer. On the ground at his feet lay the wisp of straw that was discoloured with Kel's blood.

Caradoc drove the nail through the straw with a single tap of the hammer. "Kel Kjetilson," he intoned. "*In imagine hominis manere. Ursus noli. Bestia noli. Quodcumque esse noli, nisi humanum.*"

On the street in Cosham village Kel was then full in the middle of his transformation. He staggered and almost fell, haled back into his man's shape as suddenly and violently as if he had been thrown from a rearing horse.

One of Horvath's men-at-arms, seeing Kel's sudden confusion, ran at him with his sword raised. Dazed as he was, Kel stepped aside from the man's wild thrust, brained him with the flat of his axe and then leaned down to finish him with a second blow to the chest. He did all this with a deep frown on his face, as if he were trying to remember why he had come there.

I cried out to him over the heads of a dozen men that stood between us. "Kel, what's wrong? You must change now, and lend your full weight to this!"

He spared me one fearful, furious glance and shook his head.

I opened my mouth to speak again, but whatever I said the words would have been wasted, for at that moment a thunderous

229

roar sounded from behind our backs. I turned my head to see Baron Horvath's horsemen charging across the green at full gallop to strike us from the rear.

Against mounted men with swords and lances we would fare very ill indeed. Kel and I would be trampled in a second. Only Anna could hope to oppose them, and she moved now to place herself between the oncoming knights and the rest of the defenders. She spread herself outwards and upwards, assuming a towering shape full of fanged mouths and clawed limbs that struck terror into every wight's heart that was there.

But by the same token she made herself the very easiest of targets. An arrow from the front rank of the oncoming knights struck her in the shoulder. She was already feathered with a dozen shafts and they did not seem to have slowed her, but this one was different.

This one shone yellow-white like the sun at noon-day, and it sang – a single high note, like the ringing in your ears when you've taken a buffet to the head, only it was a hundred times louder. Loud enough that Anna's scream, as she threw back her head and gaped her many mouths, could not be heard at all.

She convulsed in agony. She fell backwards, and as she fell a great wave seemed to pass through her exactly as waves pass through the waters of the sea. Her flesh rippled and reshaped itself. Her body first sagged towards the ground and then ballooned outwards. Fresh faces budded on her back and shoulders as she bowed down, and all of them were agape in expressions of torment and distress.

The limbs on which she had been running either shrivelled and shrank or else retracted themselves entirely into her body. All her complex, shifting shapes resolved themselves into one heaving mass from which a single tail or tentacle protruded, elongated and undulating like a snake. This tail all but levelled the nearest houses in its thrashing. The rest of her lay grovelling along the ground.

Still she was trying to remake herself: new limbs of many different shapes lunged ever and again from her flesh to claw the air, but they quickly dissolved and sank back into the central mass. The

230

singing arrow had bitten deeply into her mind, and though it could not kill her it was stealing her sense of herself. Soon she would be nothing but random flesh, her spark of consciousness extinguished beyond rekindling.

Here and there behind her, flames – hot ones, not cold and hurtless ones – blossomed where the men-at-arms had put some of the houses to the torch after finding no children there. Their work was far along and speeding well.

Caradoc, still seeing all and directing all, was well pleased. He turned his attention now to me. He saw me at the rear of the fray, swinging and twisting as if in some frenzied dance. He saw the felled fighters at my feet – not so much as a quarter of Kel's tally, to say nothing of Anna's. He saw swords carve and furrow me again and again, and though my jellied flesh strove ever to remake itself, it trailed now in tatters from my trunk and from my limbs. One of my arms hung limp from my shoulder, held to the rest of me by the thinnest thread of tissue. I had been struck so many times in the face that there was but little face left. Yet blinded and hobbled I fought on, as how could I not?

Ah yes, Caradoc thought. The thing that had been Willem Turling. It was barely standing, but it stood in the path of the advancing horsemen. Who knew but that it might be able to do some mischief yet?

He readied another of the spells he had prepared – not the last, but almost the last. He spoke my name, and a word of binding that would make me his willing slave.

XXXIII

In which four become five, and then six, but all is not enough

Even before the horsemen came into view I could see that we had lost. We might hold our own against such a great host for a little while, but we could not pin them in place while we fought them. Already they were spreading out to pillage the huts and longhouses in search of Cosham's children. I could tell where they had already been by the smoke and flames that were rising from the buildings on both sides of us.

Then the arrow hit Anna and her body began to spasm and dissolve. She was still a danger to the men-at-arms nearest to her, but only *per accidens* as her great mass twisted and thrashed. She seemed to have no knowledge of where she was and no control over her body's movements.

Kel had not stopped fighting. Surrounded by foes, he swung his two axes with a will. If Cain Caradoc had thought that barring him from his beast shape would leave him helpless, he had been greatly mistaken. A battle fury had overcome him to the point where he had become a bare-sark, heedless of his own safety and indeed of anything besides the struggle itself. He would not stop or slow until he died.

But for all he could do, and the little I might manage, we had lost in an instant our strongest fighter. Without Anna I could not see a way we could prevail. Hell was gaping wide to claim us, each and all.

That thought brought me of a sudden to a truth that now in calmer consideration seems all but obvious. If Hell gaped wide, what point in trying to avoid it? There might be more to be said for embracing it.

I took a step back, and then another. I dropped my arms to my sides.

Walk through her gate, the rhyme said. Or speak her name, or pluck her flower. Well, I was far away from gate and flower, so the middle one of those three would have to do.

"Jill," I said. "Unsung Jill. Do you hear me?"

I could not hear my own voice over the pelting, screaming chaos of the fight, but I heard hers when she answered me – for though her voice was soft, she spoke from right beside my ear.

"I'm older than mountains, child, but not so old that my ears have failed me. I hear you well enough. Say what you would."

"Why, I'd look into your blood-red eye," I said. "If so be your offer stands and you will fight for us. For us and for Cosham."

"You know what it means, to meet my gaze?"

"Yes." I shaped the word with my lips but could barely speak it. The fear that filled me then was greater than anything I had ever felt on either side of the grave.

"Then turn," Unsung Jill said. "And behold."

I turned to find her standing right at my back. I cannot say what I expected to see. An old woman, haply, for her voice was a beldam's voice with a dry crack running through it. But Jill was a thing outside of nature, and her body was no more a woman's body than mine was a boy's. It was a kind of greyness like a skein of cloth, that reached from the ground to a height that was taller than the tallest man. The greyness deepened to black when you looked at it, and when you looked away again the black would not easily leave your eyes. It was as though she wore a dress made all of darkness – the darkness at the bottom of a well or in the depths

233

of a cave, that confounds us with phantoms of shape and movement. Two bone-white arms hung to either side of that shapeless smudge of dark, and a bone-white head hung above it. The head was long and narrow, her mouth a ragged hole with no lips, teeth or tongue that could be seen. It did not seem to move as she spoke. "Be bold now," she growled. "Be as good as your word."

Her eyes! One was green, and as bright as any lanthorn. The other, the red one, seemed to suck light into itself. It was a hole in the world, and to look into it was to fall from the world into another place.

Almost, I failed to do it. My muscles rebelled against me, trying to make me flinch and turn aside. Unsung Jill bent from the waist until her face was on a level with my own. The red eye grew large in front of me, wider than the door of a barn and thirstier than the sea. It fastened on me. It held me.

It took me.

In the very moment that Cain Caradoc spoke my name and cast his spell against me, I was gone. Unsung Jill stood in my place. She straightened again, blinked once – with her green eye, for the red one never closed at all – and strode into the fray.

I will tell you what became of me, but I will tell it in its place. I fell through darkness to a place of darkness absolute. I made the journey none can make more than once, to the bonfire of souls where it's said that the Satan, the adversary and accuser of the world, rules alone.

A terrible fate, you might think. But had I stayed where I was, Cain Caradoc's spell would have pierced my soul and abstracted me from myself. I would have become his slave, incapable ever after of forming thoughts or plans of my own. Evading that fate was worth a great deal of torment, though perhaps not an eternity of it. Eternity is a very long time.

At all events, I was gone now from Cosham and from every other corner of the earth. I would not stand on solid ground again for a very long time indeed – a time so long it cannot be counted in mortal years.

But I had left my proxy behind me, and now she made her presence felt. Unsung Jill walked between Horvath's soldiers, who fell to the ground though she did not seem to touch them. When she passed Anna she reached out and tapped with the tip of her bony finger the shaft of the arrow that stood just proud of Anna's heaving flesh. The shaft crumbled to dust and the changer queen awoke once more to her own self.

Nothing could stand in Jill's way. She strode on until she came at last to Baron Horvath, his brilliant banner in his hand, exhorting his men-at-arms from the end of the street with burning buildings all around him.

She took him from his horse and for all his golden armour and brilliant banner she folded him like a garment. It was easy to do, since there was nothing inside him. Hollowed out by Cain Caradoc's magic, he was naught but skin. Jill raised her arms high and brandished him as he had brandished his own coat of arms. She tore away his breastplate and flung him to the ground, all torn and tattered and broken open to show the emptiness inside him. She revealed him for what he was, a sad and spent seeming rather than a man.

The soldiers of Pennick cried out in wonder and horror. These men were not cowards, for all that they had come here to make a prey of children. They had found the courage to go against monsters, after all. But to find out that their commander was a monster too, or at least no living man, took the heart out of them. What was the worse for them, the arrow being gone from her shoulder, Anna had now revived from Caradoc's spell and risen again in all her terrible glory. The men-at-arms would fain have fled, but they could not for they were caught between the changers on the one hand and Unsung Jill on the other, with nothing but spiring flames in between. There was nothing for it but to finish what they had begun and make themselves a way out of Cosham village by force of arms.

Captain Fisher helped them to rally. Though he had seen his master fall he knew he was nonetheless girded strong with magical

235

protections. He led a charge down the street with his riders behind him, thinking to put an end to all the villagers' resistance at once. He came against Kel, who was fending off two fighters already. With a wild swing of his sword, the captain struck one of Kel's axes from his grasp, then turned about and came back for another pass. Kel, being caught off-balance and still pressed on other fronts, could offer no defence. He only dropped low under Fisher's sword, which by purest chance as the captain thrust took one of his own soldiers with a nick in the cheek. The man fell as if he had been struck a mortal blow – which indeed he had, since any stroke from that blade was fatal. He was dead before ever he hit the ground.

Now it was Kel and Anna who were trapped, between the riders and the foot soldiers – but Cain Caradoc, still spying through the eyes of the homuncule, had noticed a curious thing. The villagers who had flung rocks and slates at the men-at-arms erewhile had retreated from their homes when they were put to the torch, but they had not joined the fight in the street. Instead they had fallen back to the kirk. They stood in a ragged line in front of it, armed now with pitchforks and mattocks and the occasional sword or pike snatched from a dead soldier's hand. The children had not been in any of the houses this while, which was why the searchers had not found them. They were in the kirk!

Fisher was turning for yet another essay against Kel, but the homuncule flew down from its eyrie and alighted on his shoulder. "Stay, man," it hissed in the captain's ear. "Leave the common soldiery to finish this fight. Go you to the kirk now. Pick a way through yonder rabble and see for me what is inside."

Fisher knew that voice. Hearing it now, issuing as it seemed from the empty air, gave him to shudder – but he did not dare to disobey. He realised in that moment how the baron had continued to issue orders despite being all hollow like the inside of a drum, and knew for a certainty who his real master was. He wheeled his horse about without a word to the men who had been following him, and headed straight for the kirk's door.

Anna and Kel were now hard beset, but Morjune and Jill came

236

both to their rescue. Morjune threw up gouts of flame in front of the riders, whose horses reared and bolted at the fearsome sight. Back and forth she went, weaving knots and arabesques of fire, forcing the riders ever and again to shy away.

Jill went the other way. Where Morjune brought fire, she reached for water. She threw up an arm and beckoned imperiously at the sky. The dark clouds overhead obeyed her hest at once, letting fall a driving, drenching rain.

She meant the storm as an invitation, and it was accepted at once. Out of the well in the middle of the green a waterspout rose to meet the rain. Forth from it came a slender figure that sprinted from raindrop to raindrop, his feet never touching the ground.

Peter Floodfoot was the shepherd of the tempest, commanding both its downpouring waters and the upwelling waters of Erren that were gouting from the well. They came together like a braided rope, a moving torrent that slapped the horsemen out of their saddles and threw them to the ground. They put out the burning houses, too, but Morjune's ghost-flames were not quenched.

Woe to the fighters! Seeing that all was lost they tried to rally and retreat in good order, but with the sluices of Heaven all opened they could not see where they were going. They ran onto Anna's claws or into Jill's clammy grasp. They were unseamed by Kel's remaining axe or drowned in the mud under Peter's heel. Even gentle Morjune played her part, using her fires to pen the soldiers in and steer their feet towards her comrades. There were few indeed of Pennick's meinie who survived that day's work.

But there was one not yet accounted for. Captain Fisher had by this time reached the kirk. He climbed down from his horse and approached the armed peasantry without haste.

"Best to stand aside and let me in," he said, like the wolf in the old tale. "Who copes me dies."

The villagers of Cosham did not hesitate. Seeing that this was only one man that was come against them they rushed at him with their makeshift weapons to do violent execution.

237

They were outmatched. Fisher was a seasoned fighter, and withal he wielded a sword freighted with powerful magics. He used it with cold and ruthless precision: men and women both fell dead as soon as it touched them.

But the villagers were fighting for their children, and they knew they were the last and utmost line of defence. They flung themselves on the captain, not to strike at him now but to pin him in place and keep him from entering the kirk. Cain Caradoc, through the homuncule still a-squat on Fisher's shoulder, saw the danger. If Fisher could not swing his sword he would be helpless. That would not do.

With a word of power, spoken through the homuncule's lips, the sorcerer caused the sword to shatter. Splinters of it flew in all directions, and where they hit they killed. Five died in the space of a breath, including Matthew Theakston, even though the wound he took, to the ball of his thumb, was almost too small to leave a scratch.

Out of the carnage Fisher came walking with the arrogance of a king. The survivors drew back and dared not touch him – though if they but knew it he had no more weapons about him and could not have opposed them.

He flung open the doors of the kirk and boldly stepped inside. Huddled in the pews were all the children of Cosham, with none left to guard them save Parson Lebone and Alan the sexton. Both men ran forward to do what good they could, but Cain Caradoc had all he wanted now. The homuncule spoke again, a single shrill syllable.

There was a spell within the torc around Fisher's throat just as there had been within the sword he held. It was a spell of trans-portation, and that little word woke it. The magic went out from Fisher in a great wave, hit the walls of the kirk and rebounded, meeting itself as it both came and went at once. It touched the children where they hid under the benches as their parents and their priest had told them to do. It sank into their being.

Then in a great gusting pulse of power they were gone.

The backwash from so strong and sudden a spell went back to the torc with a snap like the cracking of a whip. It broke Fisher's neck. He sank to his knees, his eyes wide with shock and dismay. He was the last man of Pennick to die that day: out of the whole garrison, the only survivors were a few that had managed to flee through the half-ruined houses after Peter's flood had extinguished the flames and made good their escape across the fields.

But it did not matter. The defenders of Cosham had failed at the last, and Cain Caradoc's triumph was complete.

XXXIV

Which concerns Hell, and my going there

ell was a very long way down. I admit this was somewhat known already, but it seemed to me that I fell for hour after hour, day after day. I had not thought there was anywhere that sat so low.

What I fell through and what I fell towards were alike nothing. It was not that it was too dark to see, but that nothing was there to be seen – only a greyness like the greyness of Unsung Jill's dress (unless she wore no dress, and the greyness was all her substance).

There was a bitter wind that plucked at me, then buffeted me, and at last tore at me with fingers of ice. It took my breath from out of my mouth, but I had not had very much use for breath since I came out of the ground so that was scarcely a hardship.

I have said it felt like days, but that is not the whole truth of it. It was long enough that I forgot to count the time. It was long enough that I began to forget who I was, and where I was come from. That was frightening, and I did my best to rehearse these matters, speaking them over and over in my mind and mouthing the words though I had no breath with which to speak them.

It was long enough that despite the wind's ill-use of me I drifted at last into a fitful doze. In fact I slept more than once, waking each time with bleared eyes and puddled thoughts to find that nothing had changed. Perhaps, I thought, I had been mistaken all this while: perhaps Hell was not a place where you could dwell but only this endless hurtling fall. Satan might be plummeting still, for aught I knew, an unfathomable distance below me.

I was wrong about that. My fall did end, though I cannot tell you when or how. I was roused from one of my unrestful stupors by the unfamiliar sensation of stillness. I had reached landfall, as it were, in my sleep. I opened my eyes, gratitude and relief surging within me.

They died again at once when I took in my surroundings.

I wish I could describe to you what I saw – and heard, smelled, tasted, felt – but I cannot. I can tell you that there were mountains piled on mountains, and that would be true. That there were trees, or things that grew out of the ground like trees, though their substance was not wood alone but stone and metal, flesh and air, sorrow and winter fog; that there were stars burning in a firmament over my head, and also from within the mountains and the trees and up from under them; that the ground on which I lay was not ground but a sad song about lost love, and at the same time a skein of scorpions' tails except that the tails were cast in bronze and wreathed about with jagged sheets of cold lightning that whispered in unearthly tongues where my shoulders touched them. All these things would be true, but all do not come close – not so close as a thousand leagues – to describing the strangeness of the place.

I thought I had gone mad. Every sensation perceptible to a mortal mind assailed me all at once. I speak of the ground, as if the ground were a thing distinct from the other things that were there, but it was not. Nothing was its own self but rather all things were merged together in ways my eyes could not explain to my mind nor my mind interpret.

I lay there – or stood there, since up and down and round about were in no wise discernible – for a very long time, frozen in place by my own incomprehension. I had thought that Hell might be an endless fall, but it seemed that it was rather an endless everything.

"Hail to thee, friend," said a voice that seemed at the same time to speak from right beside me and from a great distance. I turned (I think I turned) and when I beheld the speaker I was filled with even greater wonder and confusion. It had four faces, only two of which were human (one of a man and the other of a woman), three pairs of wings, and a great many limbs of different kinds and sizes. Wheeling bands encircled its body, out of which a thousand eyes stared at me all at once. I only ever knew one wight that was so strange and so several.

"Anna!" I cried. "How are you come here?"

"You mistake me," said the creature. "I am Zerachiel, of the Elohim. I called you friend because of what you carry." The creature extended an arm. The limb had more joints to it than a human arm is wont to have, but there was a human hand at the end of it. A finger unfolded from the hand to point at the bone-carved flute that hung at my neck on its hempen cord. "This is the *relictum summum beatum*, shaped from the bone of my sister-brother Yaldabaoth. It would not abide you if you were not worthy."

"I . . . I entreat your pardon," I stammered. "I took you for one that I knew."

"Others have said that to me. It seems I have features of a very common stamp."

I was very far from agreeing, but my strange new acquaintance did not appear to be making a joke. Their faces – I will say they, so as not in error to say he or she – were solemn. "My friend is a changer," I said, by way of explaining my mistake.

"Ah! One of the Nephilim, you mean."

"I do not think so. She has a body that partakes of many bodies, and changes as she moves."

"That is Nephilim. Sundry of my kindred lay with the daughters of Eve, in times past, and against all expectation the unions were sometimes fruitful. Your friend is of our blood, but the blood has been diluted by the admixture of time – time being a thing we Elohim know not. I take it then that you are come from Earth. Do things go well there? Are mortal beings happy with their lot?" The creature's human faces smiled. Their other faces changed from lion to snake to lamb to things whose names I did not know.

I picked my words with care. I had heard in one of Parson Lebone's sermons that angels had six wings, and Zerachiel sounded like an angel's name. If this was an angel that was addressing me I did not wish to insult them. "Some of them are happy, certes," I said. "Or at least for some of the time. None are happy always."

"No? Why not?"

"There are things that vex or distress them. Sickness. Hunger. War. Loss and hurt of many kinds."

"How fascinating! But still, to experience the joys of sensation. Existence. Thought. Feeling. Do they not grow like flowers? Do they not dance like fountains? We have gone to some trouble, and we continue to labour. It would be good to know that the great feast and plenitude we have laid on is appreciated."

"Forgive me," I said again. "Can you tell me who and what you are? And if it please you, what this place might be? It is very strange to me! I was told I was coming into Hell, but I had thought Hell was a place made up all of one self thing, which is fire. Or else torment. But this place seems compounded of more things than I can tell."

"Oh this is Hell, to be sure," the creature assured me. "But as to what Hell is, I believe there are many mistaken beliefs on that head. Since you are already come, and since you bear that blessed token, I would be happy for its owner's sake to show you what we do here. I am, as I have already said, Zerachiel of the Host." The creature shifted their great, uneven bulk in a way that was suggestive of a bow. "If it please you, how are you called?"

I inclined my head. "My name is Once-Was-Willem, sieur," I said. I did not ask whose token it was I carried. Since Zerachiel seemed to set such store by the bone-flute, I was ashamed to admit that I had only found it by the way.

"Well met, Once-Was-Willem," they said, throwing wide all

243

their varied limbs. "Come now, and see what Hell is. Only fear no torment, for we have none. Our work is other."

The angel – for I was sure now it could be nothing else – moved away. I tried to follow but did not at first succeed. My legs made the motions of walking, but this did not advance me as it would have done on Earth. I called out to my guide. "Zerachiel, I cannot move!"

The angel turned. "It is best to look at the ground before you," they told me, "and hold in your thoughts some feature of it. Its colour, perhaps, or else the timbre of its voice or the wake of its history. Meditate on that thing as you walk, and it will be as a clew or thread for you to follow. It will be hard at first, since you are come here in the flesh rather than the spirit. Flesh has little lease in this place. But you'll learn the trick of it quickly enough."

I was uncertain how to follow these instructions but I did my best. I stared at the space through which I must move, be it under me or over me or around me, and did my best to inscribe what I saw in my mind. It was as though I was trying to fix my eye on a single bubble in a stream's spate, that breeds a thousand thousand bubbles every instant. It seemed impossible that it could achieve anything, but this time when I took a step I found that I did indeed move – if not forward then at least a little closer to the angel.

"Very good," Zerachiel said. They went on again and I did my best to follow them. The results of my efforts were uneven. Sometimes a single step took me a great way, while at other times I seemed almost to walk in place. But the angel's words were proved correct. I began to puzzle out the way of it, and though my motions must have looked foolish and awkward I managed to catch up with my guide and then to keep pace with them.

I was still all but dumbstruck with wonder at the nature of this place, which defied my mind to compass or comprehend it. I will not try again to describe what is indescribable, but I was aware now of a sound, a kind of music almost unbearably sweet, that resounded in the air all around us. "Is Hell a part of Heaven then?" I ventured to ask.

"Why would you think so?"

"Only that there's such beauty and strangeness here, where I'd thought to find only cruelty and misery."

A movement passed through the angel's many limbs. It might have been a kind of shrug. "We did not make a Heaven," they said. "Heaven is only a pleasant fable. Most of what you see around you here is only what we had left over when we were done."

"Done? Done with what?"

"With the making of the world."

We were come now to a kind of break or gap in the immensity, as sharp as a cliff-edge. At its rim stood more angels, or at least more beings that shared Zerachiel's form and – if I may speak so about a being so varied and inconstant – their features. There were more of them than I could count, but that does not mean they were a great multitude. They may have been few or many, but howsoever great or small the total might have been my mind could not hold it. When I looked at any one of them it straightway filled my sight so I forgot all the others, though I knew they were still there.

The sound I had heard erewhile was louder now. I realised with awe that the angels were singing. Each one had some of its many faces uplifted, mouths open wide, and although each sang many different notes at once, the harmony was perfect. Zerachiel was singing too, and had grown or put forth three more human faces in order to do it. They had come to a halt, but they urged me forward with a wave of their hand.

Full of hungry curiosity, I went to the very edge of that abyss. A long way below me ran a rushing torrent, but it was not water. It could not be, for water (my friend Peter aside) does not have a face, and this torrent was made of nothing else but faces.

They were the visages of women and men, children, animals and birds of all kinds. In between them were specks and dots of colour that I thought must be the faces of lesser creatures, insects

245

perhaps, that were of too small a size for me to make out clearly at such a remove. Though for the most part they flowed like a river, some few here and there moved more slowly than the main of the flood as if they had been caught in some eddy or standing current. Some of them looked up as they passed by us, at the angels standing round and at the vastness of this world below the world. One or two of them looked into my eyes. I felt myself held by their gaze: deep emotions stirred within me, as if these were old friends whose names and faces I had until this moment forgotten.

"I don't understand," I said. My voice sounded harsh and vile in my own ears next to those angelic harmonies. Tears were coursing down my cheeks, but I could not have said why I cried.

"It is the river," Zerachiel said.

"But why?" It was a kind of surrender, that bald and unavailing word. I realised I did not know enough even to ask the right questions. All I could do was stand with my cupped hands out like a beggar.

"Look around you, Once-Was-Willem. Do you not see how this place is made up of mismatched orts and fragments? Of left-overs and imperfect echoes? Why do you think this is so?"

"I cannot say."

"It is because we did not build perfectly. When we Elohim made the world, we had no pattern to follow. Nobody had ever done such a thing before. That the world still stands at all is tribute to our vision and the skill of our hands. But we were not perfect. How could we be? We made what we thought we would need, but we could only guess. Sometimes we made too much of a thing, or crafted it to the wrong shape or sense. We built Hell to be a storehouse for the things we had fashioned but could not use. A place to hide our mistakes.

"But in some ways our biggest mistake was you."

"Me?" I was greatly cast down. But the angel's next words reassured me.

"I do not mean you alone. I mean humanity. More specifically I mean your bodies and your souls. We applied all our skill and

246

care to their fashioning, but still the two would not laminate. Try though we might we could not find a way to keep spirit pent within flesh for more than a hundred years or so. Oftentimes it was much less than that. Body would fail and soul would fall free of it, unhoused and helpless. Neither could be made to last.

"It was calamity! Calamity of calamities! This had been the point of our work, the purpose and the pinnacle. What was a world without beings of sense to perceive it and love it? We had not squandered our might and our birthright to make a sculpture."

"Are they . . ." I pointed down at the torrent that passed unceasingly below us, the eyes that held us in place with their speechless contemplation. "Are those souls that are flowing past us here?"

Some of Zerachiel's mouths – the ones that were not singing – smiled. "You are perceptive. They are seldom to be seen in this pure state, but that is what they are indeed. This was how we solved our great dilemma, or at least made shift to work around it. We took the two ends of creation, the moments of ontogenesis and thanatos, birth and death, and we joined them together like the clasp of a belt. This river, which the ancients called Lethe, is the gate through which each soul passes between its death and its rebirth. At the one end of it the souls of the dead fall in and are carried away. The other end debouches once more into the living realm, providing a steady flow of new souls to be sealed in flesh and given breath again.

"The river is thus the source and guarantor of life's continuance. Of all the wonders we have made – and they are numberless – this one is the greatest of all. It underpins all else and makes it possible, by collecting up the life that would else have drained from the world for ever and channelling it back to be used again."

A look of sorrow passed suddenly across all Zerachiel's faces. One by one their mouths ceased to sing. "But it cost us dear," they said heavily. "The river flows because we Elohim sing it onwards. But it only exists at all because seven of us gave up their very being to make it and fix it in place."

"They're dead?" I said.

247

"They cannot die. But they are sequestered from us for ever. Six of them you see below you. They dissolved themselves down into their essence to become the river that carries the souls of humankind. The seventh, great Yaldabaoth, has taken on alone the work of all the others. He lies in his own tomb and dreams the world, to keep it from ending."

I could not keep from exclaiming aloud, "Six to keep the living alive, and only one for all the rest of the world!"

"Of course. How should it be otherwise? The world is like unto the setting for a jewel, Once-Was-Willem. The living are the jewel. All that we do is for their sake. Your sake, I should say."

I went down on my knees. I would have done it before, but my control of my body's movements in this place was still far from perfect. "Angel!" I cried. "Zerachiel! I do not know why this vision was bestowed on me. I have done nothing in my life – in either of my lives – to deserve it. I thank you with all my heart for expounding it to me. To have seen you at your labours and heard your wondrous song is such a blessing as I could not have imagined. But unworthy as I am, I have a further boon to ask."

"What is it?" Zerachiel asked.

I screwed up my courage. When I had spoken Jill's name I had thought my life was ended. But finding now that Hell was not a prison house, I had begun to hope that I might yet escape it and rejoin – if it were not already too late – the fight I had sworn to undertake.

"My coming here," I told the angel, "although I chose it freely, was in many ways untimely. And since you tell me this river leads back to the world of the living, will you give me leave to dive into it and be carried home? There is a task of some urgency that I have undertaken, and I wish beyond all things to finish it."

Zerachiel unfolded their wings, which were of so great an extent that they formed a kind of tabernacle around us. I did not know what the gesture meant. It was as though they were about to utter a great secret and wished to keep it sealed between the two of us. Or perhaps they meant only to keep me from the course I had just described. "Certainly you may enter the river, Once-Was-Willem," they said. "It is your birthright. You came here by way of the Witness's eye, I imagine? All those who have come to us in that way have left us by jumping into the river, though some stayed longer than others before choosing it. But you should know that it will not take you where you wish to go."

The words, so categorically spoken, dismayed me. "But the river goes from death back into life, you said!"

"And so it does. But it flows always in one direction, which is forward. Forward in time, the necessary element for all life. It cannot be made to run back on itself. That is as if you were to ask for the ages of man to be unravelled and the garden of the dawn replanted. To enter Hell, Once-Was-Willem, is to become part of the mechanism of eternity. We Elohim stand outside of time, and tend it. We bide in our stations, in our service, until the hours and the years shall run no more. You might stay here if you wish, and learn our song – though you cannot sing it, for you have but the one mouth. But if you should leave by giving your body to the river and surrendering yourself to its flow, you will be born again into a new life, not returned to the one you formerly knew. That is what all who have come here before you have done, whether late or soon."

These words brought me close to despair. "But my wish – my need, I should say – is to take up my life again where I left off! Could I not climb back up through the void above us then, to the place whence I fell?"

Zerachiel shook most of their heads. "That is impossible. Where would you place your hands, and your feet? The void has no edges."

"But you – you have wings. Could you not take me?"

"By no means. Even for one such as myself the journey would be many years long. I may not leave my place for such a span."

"And is there no other way?"

All Zerachiel's many eyes in all their many faces and in the glowing bands that englobed them closed at once.

"Angel," I persisted, "I beg you as my only friend in this place. Is there no other way I could go?"

Zerachiel only laid some of their fingers across some of their lips, bidding me to silence. Their eyes were still closed and their heads all bowed. Some of the other Elohim were now moving up to join us. They stood around us in a circle but they did not offer greeting or comment, nor did they ever leave off their song. All seemed to be waiting on Zerachiel to speak again.

"There is another way," Zerachiel said at last. "Or there may be. I know not. It has not been done before."

"It should not be done now," two of the other angels said. They spoke at once, the same words at the same moment, as if they had practised it. Their human faces were stern, their other faces all averted. "What if the world should end?"

"My thoughts exactly," Zerachiel agreed. "What if that is why he is come? What if the world's end threatens, as it has before, and he is the one that must mend it?"

"Why would you think so?" the two demanded. And then to me, "Is that your purpose?"

"My purpose is to save the children of Cosham village," I said. I might have lied if I had thought it would help me, but I understood almost nothing of what was passing here.

One of Zerachiel's faces turned to me while the others all still met the stern gaze of its kindred. "Lend me the token," they said. "For a moment only. You have my word it will be returned to you."

I lifted the cord over my head and placed the bone-flute into Zerachiel's outstretched hands. They raised it to each of their faces in turn. Ever and again they closed their eyes and pressed the instrument to the forehead of each face, mouthing a word I could not hear. Then they held it aloft for the others to see.

"We know what it is," declared the two who spoke as one. "But how did he come by it?"

"It was never mine to own," I admitted. "I only found it, washed up on the bank of Erren river close to where I live. I thought I might learn to play it, but I could not coax a sound from it."

"Of course you could not!" said the two in tones of stern affront. "What are you, child of clay, to attempt such a thing?"

"Souls of my soul," Zerachiel chided them, "you listen but you do not hear. He told you that he found the token. He believes it was only chance that put it into his hands. But the *relictum summum beatum* is not answerable to chance. It knows its purpose, and its place. If it came to Once-Was-Willem, it was because he was the one best placed to bring it to where it was needed. I believe that more depends upon his striving than any of us can know. And I believe we must help him, if only to point him in the right direction."

The two who spoke as one looked grave and shook their heads. I was sure they would offer more argument, but they did not. They sang instead, and one by one the others joined them. It was a very different song from the one they had sung before. It was an ululation, a wailing cry that rose and fell, taken up and then sustained by human throats and animal throats alike.

When at least they fell silent, the two nodded their heads. "We accept your argument, Zerachiel," they said. "If you are wrong, this mortal child will abide it dearly. But if he chooses to attempt it, we will not raise exception."

I turned to Zerachiel, desperate to understand at least some of what was happening. "If I choose to attempt what?" I asked.

They proffered me a sad smile from three faces that were all of children and all new-come, or at least I had not seen them before. "To walk upstream, along the river's bed. The river's force is great, Once-Was-Willem. A naked soul once entered into it cannot fight its current. It must perforce be carried onward to its rebirth. But you are not a naked soul. You have a body. It may be that you will have the strength and weight and will to set your face against the stream and walk upwards."

"And this will help me?"

"It might. I have good hope. You must understand, our sibling Yaldabaoth was very wise. The wisest of us all, and the strongest. As they dream the world they dream its every moment all at once – its presents, its pasts and its futures. If an error occurs, if the

251

world wobbles and slows or else is in danger of coming to harm, they dream the one that can mend it. Things have gone badly in the past, but always the mender has come in time. Your being here now makes me believe the same thing is happening again. I do not know if you yourself are the mender — I think not, for you are very small and very weak — but I am convinced you have a part yet to play."

They gestured towards the rushing flood before us. "I have said that the river moves forward in time. To say so was to simplify a thing that is not simple at all. Time, in the sense of a progression of hours, days, months, years and so on, exists only because the river's current creates and defines it. If you were to go against the current — if you had the strength of spirit and sinew to achieve such a thing — you would move backwards through the hours and days of your own existence."

"That is not certain," said the two who spoke as one.

"No," Zerachiel said. "It is not certain. Possibly life itself is an effect, a consequence of the forward flow, in which case you would cease at once and be gone from the skein. Or the current may fight you, break you in pieces and sweep the pieces away. There are many imponderables here. But I am hopeful."

"We are not," said the two. "But we see no other possibility beyond what you have outlined."

"Then I will do it," I said.

Zerachiel nodded. "May providence be with you," they said, putting the bone-flute again around my neck.

"Thank you, angels," I said, "for your counsel. Thank you also for being the keepers and guardians of human life. I am honoured beyond any measure to have met you — and you, Zerachiel, most of all. Farewell."

I moved towards the river and made to descend the bank. It looked precipitous, and I saw few if any handholds in that strange and variegated surface.

"Let me help you," Zerachiel said. They extended a hand and I took it, thinking that the angel would lower me gradually towards

252

the river's brim. Instead they pulled me towards themselves, gripped me in a great many of their limbs and raised me high over their head.

"The current is strongest at the edges," they said. "You will fare better at the centre." And with those words they flung me, high and far.

XXXV

Which treats of what passed in my absence

hen the battle was done and Anna had returned once more to her human shape, she led the others to the kirk to see how the defenders there had fared. I mean that she led her brother and Morjune. Peter had vanished back to the well even before the rain Jill had summoned slackened off, while Jill herself stood back as if she was mindful of the terror her fearful presence would provoke. Or perhaps it was only that she waited to see what would come next. She was still bound by the bargain she had made with me, to keep Cosham's children from coming to harm, but it was not clear what that bargain would next entail.

At the kirk door the parson all in tears relayed the unhappy news. "They are gone! All of them are gone! There came a man, on a charger, and . . . and he killed so many. We tried to stop him, but he came among the children and he took them! By magic, it must have been, for they vanished all in an instant. The man fell. He lies dead inside, but . . . but . . ."

He could say no more. He only gestured at the bodies of men and women sprawled all across the steps, the empty kirk, the weeping survivors.

"It was magic indeed," Kel said. "Cain Caradoc is a wily bastard.

The slightest of his plots has other plots within it, as if an egg should hatch out into another egg. But we know where the children have been taken."

"Do we?" Anna asked. "How so?"

Kel shrugged. "The soldiers came to bring them to the castle, did they not? If that was Caradoc's goal to begin with, it's not likely he would have changed it. We know now that the baron was Caradoc's creature all along. If the castle was ever under Horvath's rule it was not for long. The wizard holds sway there now – and whatever plans he has for the children, that is where they will unfold."

Anna nodded slowly as she thought this through. "Belike," she agreed at last. "Then that's where we must go. But first we must find out what has become of Once-Was-Willem."

She turned back to the parson. "All is not yet lost," she said. "Console these people as best you can. We go now to see what can be done."

"Then we will come too," a young man said. It was Rafe Theakston, one of Betheli's brothers. Rich and Simon stood at his either hand. All three had taken hurt in the fight but were still standing and were of undaunted courage. Their mother came now to join them, clutching a bloodied paring knife in her hand. "Let us fight with you," she said. "Pennick took my daughter, and now it has taken my husband. I'll carve my quittance out of that wizard's flesh."

By ones and twos the rest of the villagers approached, boldly or timidly, in rage or hate or hope, to offer their hands and hearts to the storming of the castle. Fully a third had perished in the fighting, and many of the vanished children – though they had no way of knowing it – were already orphans. Anna was still not inclined to look on the men and women of Cosham kindly, but the courage they had shown and the losses they had sustained somewhat tempered her despite. She saw too that they were sincere in their wish to help, and she did not find it in herself to refuse them. She only bade them wait on her command and went to speak with Unsung Jill.

255

She did so very warily, shielding her eyes with her hand and making sure she looked mostly at the ground at Jill's feet. She knew the danger she was in, even though she had seen Jill join the fight on their side.

"So please you, beldam," she said, "we're grateful for the help you gave us just now, but may I ask how you come to be here? And what became of our friend Once-Was-Willem? It seemed to me that one moment he was there, then the next you stood in his place."

"And so it was," Jill said, her voice as hard and sharp as a knife against a strop. "He summoned me and we made a bargain. I am to lend you my aid until the children of Cosham are saved from their present peril."

Anna considered. "But where is Once-Was-Willem now?" she asked.

"In Hell."

So startled was Anna at these words that she forgot herself and almost looked Jill in the face. "In Hell?" she echoed. "You mean he's dead?"

"I mean what I have said. He is in Hell. He agreed to go there as part of our bargain."

"That was a hard bargain indeed, beldam! And how long must he bide there?"

"I never knew any to return. Hell is not the jakes of an inn, that all may come and go from as they list. Hell is Hell."

Greatly dismayed, Anna returned to Kel and Morjune and told them the news. They sorrowed in their turn, thinking me lost for ever. "It was a good bargain, even so," Kel said. "I mean for us, not for Once-Was-Willem. The hag made all the difference in the fight."

Except that we lost in any case, Morjune reminded him. *Poor Willem! I do not think he will thrive in Hell.*

"Not many do," Anna said sourly. "I grieve for Once-Was-Willem. We would none of us be in this broil if it were not for him, though Kel is right that he was no great fighter. We should carry on and finish this, and let that be our remembrance of him."

256

Kel and Morjune agreed. They went to tell Peter what had befallen, and to bid him go before them to the castle and spy out where the children were taken. Peter was greatly dismayed, both by the news of the children's abduction and by what he heard of my fate.

"I saw him vanish from the street," he said, "with Unsung Jill right beside him. How can we trust her, knowing what she did? Should we not send her away?"

"I'm not even sure how we might do that if we wished to," Kel said. "And as things lie with us now, her help might be needful. Peter, will it please you return to Pennick and see if—"

But Peter did not allow him to finish. "Hold!" he said, throwing up his hands like one who would pray but could not find the words. "Oh, hold hard!" And then with a wordless cry he dissolved into water drops, falling back down the well as a fine rain.

Kel ran to the well's coping and looked down. There was no sign of Peter there. "Peter!" Kel called out. "Peter Floodfoot!" But no answer came.

Kel turned to his sister, angry and confused. "Why did he not stay and hear me out? He must know the fight is not yet over."

"Perhaps he has no more stomach for it," Anna said. "He was ever given to gentleness. And he only came in the first place for friendship's sake."

"He might have stayed for the same reason." Kel could not hide his frustration, but he said no more. Rejoining the villagers, they set off in a ragged column towards the castle. Jill went at their head so that none would run the risk of looking into her face. Behind her went Anna, Kel and Morjune. The villagers came last and kept as much distance as they could between themselves and the beldam, whose presence frighted them more than the enemy they went to face.

257

XXXVI

In which, despite our striving, the children come at last to the castle

he air thickened and cleared again. Into the bailey yard which otherwise stood empty the children came sprawling and tumbling, deposited ungently by the workings of Cain Caradoc's spell. They sat up and looked around them, some whimpering in terror while others were stoically silent. My cousins, Arran and Luce, were among the latter. They hugged each other for comfort but uttered no plaint or sob.

And now here came Cain Caradoc himself, walking to meet them. "Welcome, little ones," he called out happily. "Welcome to Pennick. And please, do not weep. This is a gladsome day, and you should rejoice to be a part of it. Come with me now, and speak no word. Be good, obedient boys and girls, and I promise you your suffering will be short."

Arran and Luce exchanged a glance. They did not much like the sound of this, and they had no intention of being obedient. "He's in a great hurry," Luce whispered to Arran.

"That he is," Arran agreed. "He's afraid that Willem and his friends will come."

"So the longer we make him tarry, the better." Luce stood up and threw out her arms. "Caradoc!" she shouted. "Great Caradoc! Let us behold you!"

"Let us praise you!" Arran cried, scrambling to his feet beside her. "Is it not meet we praise you, that has triumphed over ghosts and striding dead, changers and witches and boggarts and all?"

Cain Caradoc was taken aback. After his experience with Betheli he was expecting only defiance and rebelliousness from Cosham's children. The last thing he had looked for was adulation. But underneath his astonishment, which was great, was a tickle of pleasure.

Ever since he came to Pennick he had been obliged to pretend subservience to Maglan Horvath, and it had grated on his spirit. He was not wont to hide his greatness. Now here, of a sudden, were two that seemed to have seen it despite its being hidden, and who wished to testify to it.

"You are kind," he said, bowing in mock civility. "And yes, I did those things. But my true triumph is yet to come. Follow me, and bring your fellows. We have great work to do."

"But can we sing your worship first?" Luce asked.

"My worship?" Caradoc repeated. "What is that? What do you mean?"

Luce did not explain, but broke at once into song. What she sang was *Lucis Largitor Splendide*, but in the English tongue. Parson Lebone had made the translation himself and taught it to his congregation. "As if the sun had second birth, brighter by far than sun of Earth! You draw our hearts as flowers turn, when the sun's orb on high doth burn!" and a great deal more besides. Obviously it was of God she sang, but Caradoc did not know this. He had never encountered either the words or the tune, both being of the parson's devising.

Oh, he knew he was being flattered. But the experience brought him such pleasure that he did not mind. He stood with his arms clasped behind his back while Luce made her way through all seven verses of St Hilary's hymn. When she was done he applauded her heartily. "Wonderful," he said. "You sing like an angel, child. And you will walk at my side ahead of all the rest. Come. This interlude has been delightful, but I can afford no more delay."

Luce made a great show of bashfulness, and drew out the business of approaching Cain Caradoc as far as she dared. At last, his patience running out, he seized her by the arm and led her towards the steps of the mound. "Come," he called. "Follow me. Any that tarry will suffer for it."

Luce was hauled along whether she would or not. The other children were loath to follow but did not dare to disobey. They went with dragging steps. Last of all came Arran, who had used the time while Luce sang to load his pockets with stones from around the base of the bailey's well.

As they all walked in a straggling line up the steps to the top of the mound, he kicked off his shoe to make a marker, then let the stones fall one by one after it. It was the only thing he could think of to do. At least if any came from Cosham they might see the line of stones and guess where he and the others had been taken.

At the top of the mound Caradoc paused and considered. Arran and Luce had been correct in their guess: he was troubled by the thought that those who had opposed him in the village might come against him now when he stood at last on the brink of success. The spell of the cornerstone was still strong, and should hold, but he did not wish to lean too hard on *should*. And he had another trick yet to play.

It had aggravated him when I had disappeared during the fight in the village before his spell could strike me. But it meant the spell was not expended. The tithing of my soul that should have given him power over me was still his to use. And he had thought of another use for it.

At the door of the keep and at Caradoc's right hand stood Drede Ich Nawhit. The dire and piteous creature had not moved from that place since the day of its birth and death many months before. The wizard touched his fingers' tips to the strange knight's face,

260

where its eyes should have been. He let the tithing of my soul flow from him into Drede Ich Nawhit. Drede Ich Nawhit stirred at once. It tilted its neck back, then flexed it one way and another, as if it had taken a cramp from standing still for so long.

Cain Caradoc was filled with delight. It displeased him when any of his labour went to waste, and this allowed him to redeem two errors at once. He gave Drede Ich Nawhit his instructions. "Defend this gateway. After me and these children, let none pass through it, or come inside the keep by any other way. Kill them that try. Never relent."

Without another word he passed on. The children shrank back from the mound's grim guardian, but it had been told to ignore them and it offered them no harm. On into the half-built shell of the keep they went, and then down through the trapdoor into the mound.

All was at last in place for Cain Caradoc's ascension, and for the sacrifices which it demanded.

XXXVII

Which tells of my journeying too far and too wide

here was no splash when I entered the river. I sank straightway into its depths, which were neither warm nor cold, light nor dark. I had braced myself for its turbulence, but the current – and the danger – were not as Zerachiel had described them.

All around me a myriad souls rushed by, which was easy enough to bear. But they rushed *through* me too, and that was harder. Every impact tore from me for the smallest portion of a moment the sense of who and where I was, as the great gathered whole of someone else's thoughts and feelings collided with mine. I was remembering lives I had never lived, sorrows and joys that had never been mine. The current itself was not so strong, but with each step I was on the verge of surrendering to it because I had forgot why I was fighting it in the first place.

I tried to find a rhythm, thinking that it would make my progress easier, but the riverbed was uneven. I stumbled ever and again, and with each false step the current threatened to pluck me away into the sundering flood.

On an impulse I clutched the bone-flute. As soon as my fingers closed over it my head seemed to clear a little. The buffeting of other lives and memories, names and faces, thoughts and emotions did not slacken, but perhaps they hit with less force than before. I was able to hold them at bay by reciting my own name and reminding myself to move forward. Since it was not water I waded through, I found I could speak the words out loud. "On, Once-Was-Willem. On. On. On."

I do not know how long I walked. I do not even know if the question has any meaning. Years and leagues are not measured on the same yardstick. I realised too late that I should have asked the angel for some guidance on how far I should go. It had seemed long when I fell down through the void into Hell, but there was no way of holding this journey up against that one. All I could do was to choose my moment and hope for the best.

That was what I did. But when I tried to direct my steps towards the river's edge I found myself rebuffed by the stronger current there. Still growling my own name, still assailed by the lives of countless others, I staggered on until I felt the gradient under my feet shift. Then I dropped down onto all fours and crawled forward blindly, eyes tight shut, until all at once a brilliant light and a heavy heat fell upon me, as if I had strayed too close to a fire.

I fell down straightway, and lay for a long time on what felt like dried and rutted mud, breathing in scents of earth and flowers and cut grass. When at last I rolled over onto my back and opened my eyes, the first thing I saw was the sun, hanging high in the heavens. I was lying in the bed of a road, as I had suspected. Crickets were singing loudly in the grass on either side of me. One of them jumped onto the back of my hand as if to greet me, and then at once away again.

There was nothing to tell me where I was, or when. The fight in Cosham had taken place on a cold winter's day, with clouds hanging in the sky as dark as ripe bruises. I needs must be a long way from there, but in what direction? Had I arrived too early or too late? What place was this?

Voices drifted towards me from further along the road. Quickly I crawled into the undergrowth to hide myself.

263

Two women walked by me on the road. Both were dressed in much the same garb as the villagers of Cosham were wont to wear, except that their faces and arms were burned brown by the sun and one wore her hair bound up in an orange kerchief in a fashion I had never seen.

That one spoke to the other such words as I never yet heard and could not make out clearly. The other shook her head as if in a show of sorrow – though she smiled at the same time. "*No'm meravilh!*" she said, or something like. "*J'a tant de dépit dan mon cors quant il me fa ca.*"

"*T'as razon,*" said the first. "*T'a tes dezavinens, que diable!*"

Both women went their ways, still laughing and talking each to other.

I stood up at last, when I was sure they were gone, and followed along behind them – not because I desired their company, but because I thought they must be going to their village and if I did the same I might get some sense of where I was.

I was not wrong about that, but their village when I saw it from the top of a hill was a great surprise to me. It had some huts of wood that would not have looked out of place in Cosham, but most of the buildings had walls of what looked to me like stone, save that no stone was ever so white. The whole place was the colour of fresh-fallen snow, or bleached bone. And if the houses were of too light a colour the people were too dark, as if that bright and blazing sun hung ever in the sky here and in the course of years had slowly roasted them.

By this time I knew I was not in England. The flowers by the roadside were as strange to me as the peasant girls' words had been, and I had seen a bird sitting in a tree that was like a magpie save that its head was as red as blood and there were flashes of brilliant blue all along its wings. The river had brought me out a very long way from home. All I could do now was to find my way back as quickly as possible and pray that I had not missed my mark by too wide a margin.

And that was what I did.

I will forbear to tell you of the journey. It was long. It would have been long even for someone who spoke the language of that place and knew the roads. For me, a stranger who could not ask the way nor even take the risk of being seen too closely, it was all but never-ending. I stole a bolt of cloth from an inn-yard and made myself a kind of cloak from it. Under that cover I would approach strangers on the road and repeat the word "England" until they either ran away or pointed me in a direction. Sometimes – not always – it was the right direction.

Many months passed in this way. I walked and walked and walked, mostly at night, always alone. Whenever I came to a river I followed its bank until I found a bridge. When I came at last to a great flood I walked until I found a port. And then another. And then a third. At last when I said "England", someone pointed to a boat. I crept onboard in the dark of night and hid myself.

In my home country at last I set myself to walking again. I needed a new word now. I thought "Cosham" might do, but for a long time I met nobody who had ever heard of it. I found my way instead to London, without meaning or wanting to – London being a place that took in wayfarers through some magic that bent all roads towards itself.

In London I heard the death of the outlaw Geoffrey de Mandeville being cried, which was the first time I had any idea of the date. I remembered Kel talking about de Mandeville one night on the mountain when we sat and watched the moon together. Kel had been sad that the man died as he did – killed by accident in a foolish quarrel, and excommunicated to boot so he would not get honourable burial. Like Maglan Horvath, de Mandeville had fought for Empress Matilda and then turned outlaw, but he had done it a long way south of Pennick, in the fens of Cambridge.

So now I knew I was not too late. Though the river had brought me out in the wrong place, it had disgorged me into a time before my descent into Hell. The day of the fight in Cosham stood yet more than a month away. Surely I could walk from London to Trent in that time, if I dallied not along the road.

But fate seemed now to have set itself against me. There were fresh rebellions in the north, mostly around Chester, and the roads were full of King Stephen's armies hurrying to answer them. I was forced to travel by hedgerows and by-ways, losing time in their meandering turns and sometimes being forced to go back on myself when the track ran out. I was not sure of the days, for my parents never taught me to count past yan-tan-tethera, but I knew that my time was fast running out.

In hope of making better speed I left the roads and tried to chart a course that might be more direct, cutting through forests and over hills. It was a poor decision. Any time I gained from the straightness of the path I lost again through all the times I mistook my way.

One day as I was crossing a stretch of moorland, a thick fog came down on me so suddenly it was like the drawing of a curtain. I should have stopped and waited for the way ahead of me to become clear again, but I was too desperate and too stubborn. I strode on, though I could not see the hand at the end of my arm, determined to lose no more time. Stumbling into every ditch, sent sprawling by every loose stone or pothole, I went from walking to crawling, feeling my way where I could not see it.

So I came at last into the shallows of a river that blocked my way. What is this? I thought. It cannot be Trent, for I'm a day away at least from those reaches. One of Trent's tributaries then, though it was too wide to be the Soar and too deep for Blithe Water.

The fog was lifting at last. Up ahead of me was a mountain slope whose shape I thought I knew – though I was used to seeing it from the other side. A feeling grew in me, a recognition that came as much through my heart as through my eyes.

Erren. I was knee-deep in the waters of Erren. I cried out loud, and then I laughed. In the access of my joy I plunged my hands into the water and then flung them into the air, letting the spray shower down on me and around me. It was like a second baptism, the sacredness coming not from any god or saint but from the simple fact of homecoming.

"Oh let me not be too late!" I cried. "Let me be come in time!"

Knowing now where I was, I knew also that I had once more lost my way and veered too far into the west. I turned to follow the bank of the river instead. There were bramble thickets that had stood since English kings spoke English rather than French, but I walked through even the thickest of them without slowing. If my flesh was torn it would quickly mend, and I did not mind the pain or even feel it — not when I was so close to my journey's end.

Closer than I knew, in fact. For soon the water began to bubble and froth as if it was all a-boil. A waterspout sprang forth, and shaped itself into a face and form I knew well.

"Once-Was-Willem!" Peter cried out. "How come you here? I saw you vanish from the street in Cosham but minutes agone. And Kel Kjetilson said you were sent to Hell!"

My heart leapt at his words. Minutes ago, he said. Then in spite of all my journeying and my wandering by the way I was come back to the same day and the same hour in which I had left! It was almost as if the river of souls had known where to send me, and had balanced time against distance in such a way as to make the whole sum come out right.

"I was," I said. "I was in Hell for a little while, and then in other places. Oh, it's good to see you again, madcap boy! And I'd embrace you if I could, since I'm drenched already. But I must not stay. I'm yet three leagues or more from Cosham, and there's no time to tarry!"

"The children are in Cosham no longer," Peter said. "The wizard took them. We think they must be in Pennick by now."

That bitter news hit me like a blow. Not only was Pennick further still, but in spite of all our efforts the children we had thought to protect had fallen into the hands of our enemy. "Tell Kel and Anna I'm coming!" I cried, and set off at a run.

Peter kept pace with me effortlessly, dancing over the water like a skipped stone. "Stay, Once-Was-Willem!" he called. "Tell me this.

267

Since you came out of the grave, are you still in the habit of breathing?"

"When I remember to," I said, slowing. "But it doesn't seem to vex me when I forget. Peter, we must make haste! Time is against us."

"Aye, but there is a nearer way. You have only to jump."

"To jump?" I echoed him. "Into your flood?"

"Into my flood, and into my safekeeping. I'll bring you to Pennick by the quickest road."

"Truly?" I asked him, for I found it hard to credit.

"Truly. If you love me, do it."

And since I loved him dearly, I did. I had tried to have little to do with rivers since my time in the river of souls, but this was different. This river – every drop of it, from bank to bed and back again – was my friend. And my friend was more powerful than I had ever dreamed.

Peter rose in spate. He gathered me in his arms, drew me down and bore me on, covering those leagues in a hurtling rush. His embrace was fierce. Had I been any mortal man I should have been drowned by the swell or dashed in pieces on the rocks. But I was something else, and for once I was nothing but glad of it.

XXXVIII

In which the seven come at last together, though they do not yet know it

hen my friends arrived at Pennick they found the castle gates closed against them, but with no defenders to be seen. Anna did not slow. She transformed into a shape out of nightmare, with a great many legs that were like spiders' legs except that they ended in long-fingered hands like those of salamanders. She scaled the wall in a few seconds, climbed down inside the fortress and unbarred the gate for the others.

Morjune, to whom the gate had never been a barrier in the first place, had already gone ahead to scout. She returned now to say that there were no men-at-arms at all in the bailey yard. A scattering of servants had barricaded themselves in one of the longhouses, she said, but they could safely be ignored. Of the stolen children she had seen no sign.

"Look there," Kel said, pointing to the well in the bailey yard's centre. He had seen Arran's shoe where he had kicked it off, and now drawing close he saw the line of stones that led from it. "At least one of those children has their wits about them. This is a trail they've left for us."

"And it goes up there," Anna said, pointing to the steps and the half-finished stone keep that stood atop it.

Hearing this, Rafe Theakston did not hesitate but ran to the steps and began to ascend the mound. His brothers followed him, and the rest of the villagers came close behind. They could see that the keep was as yet no real fortification. It had no door, and one of its round towers was but a single layer of stones. If their lost children were within the villagers meant to find them and bring them home, let the wizard do what he would.

Kel followed more slowly, as did Jill, but Anna raced up the side of the mound and outpaced them quickly. She would have been first through the gateway, which gaped open before her, but as soon as she hit it her storm of flesh flattened, buckled and sprawled. It was as if she had run headlong into a solid wall: in fact it was the spell of the cornerstone, as strong as ever.

The villagers threw themselves at that open gate, or tried to step over the wall in the places where it did not yet come up to their calves. All came up against the same sightless barricade, and all were stopped dead. They could not go an inch further.

"Another spell!" Kel exclaimed, after trying both his hands and his axe against it.

"Aye," Morjune said. "But this one is singing."

"What do you mean?" Anna asked. But Morjune did not answer. Drifting in the air like thistledown she crossed to the cornerstone and knelt down beside it.

Anna made to follow, but Jill's icy hand clamped down on her shoulder and stayed her. The beldam pointed wordlessly through the gateway's arch. The keep had not been left entirely without defence after all. A single figure was walking towards them from among the abandoned piles of stone and half-finished walls.

It was shaped like a man, but it had no face. It carried no weapons neither, save that its right arm was a sword and its left arm a mace. This was Drede Ich Nawhit, given new life through a little admixture of my stolen spirit.

"How came this thing to be inside the keep, if the wizard's spell stops all from coming by it?" Kel demanded.

"It stops those who are the wizard's foes," Jill intoned. "It will not stop him. Defend yourself, changer."

And indeed, at that very moment, Drede Ich Nawhit stepped across the invisible barricade from its further side and was among them. Kel stepped into its path and was the first to front it. It swung with great force and speed but indifferent aim. Stepping aside from the blow, Kel struck it full on the shoulder with his axe. Drede Ich Nawhit's pauldron rang like a bell, but the axe glanced hurtlessly off and Kel all but lost his balance as his foe failed to move so much as an inch. The following swing from Drede Ich Nawhit's mace would have brained him if he had not by reflex ducked aside.

Drede Ich Nawhit came on, swinging with its left and right arms in turn, untroubled by any ripostes that Kel made. When Anna charged in from the side, thinking to topple it, it stood its ground. Its feet seemed anchored in the roots of the earth, and though Anna clawed and pummelled its whorled brown armour with myriad limbs, it barely seemed to notice.

Turning in an instant to face this new challenge, Drede Ich Nawhit gave Anna such a storm of fearful blows with mace and sword alike that she was driven back. It bore her before it, to the edge of the mound and over. She tumbled down heels over head and could find no purchase until she reached the bottom.

Now Drede Ich Nawhit turned on the villagers, who backed away from those terrible weapons and their yet more terrible bearer. When the thing pursued, Unsung Jill stepped in the way. She leaned in close, her baleful red eye opened wide. Drede Ich Nawhit did not seem troubled. It had not an entire soul within it but only a tithing, and perhaps a tithing cannot be sent to Hell without the rest of it. Drede Ich Nawhit struck back at Jill, and its sword stuck fast in the shapelessness of her grey gown. It essayed to tug the sword free, but could not.

This was the moment when I returned, bursting up out of the well in the bailey below on a jet of water that had carried me, like a straw in a mill-race, across many miles. It might have looked

271

impressive had I not at once fallen back again, flailing and tumbling, to land on the flags with an impact that drove my bones out through my jellied flesh.

I was scarcely noticed. Kel was raining blows on Drede Ich Nawhit's back and shoulders, but aside from raising a din like that of a blacksmith's forge he was having no effect. Drede Ich Nawhit, for its part, was trying to tug its sword free from the clinging shroud that was Jill's body.

At the foot of the mound, Anna drew in most of her limbs apart from two long arms overlaid with thick bands of corded muscle. With these she took hold of a great slab of grey stone and hurled it. For all her strength it seemed the throw would fall short as the massive block turned lazily end over end. But she had judged well. The missile hit Drede Ich Nawhit from the side and kept on going, carrying it through the gateway from which it had but recently emerged.

That gave our friends some respite, but they could not press their advantage. The spell of the gateway still resisted them, so Drede Ich Nawhit was now gone beyond their reach.

"A storm!" Peter cried out, towering over the well in a fountaining spume. "Jill, send me a storm!"

Unsung Jill looked up at the sky and made a peremptory gesture. The clouds opened again and another deluge began, even stronger and more sudden than that which had fallen on Cosham.

Peter and I ran together up the side of the mound. At least, we started together. But Peter soon outpaced me, and reached the gateway just as Drede Ich Nawhit strode through it again. As the two clashed, Peter lost all semblance of his human shape. He became a sort of vortex of water, a whirlpool in the air, centred on Drede Ich Nawhit's head and shoulders. He was trying to find a way between the plates of the creature's armour so he could drown it. But it did not seem that he was succeeding. Either the armour had no seams or Drede Ich Nawhit did not need to breathe.

Now here were Kel and Anna come again into the fray, the one with his axe and the other with her claws, what time Jill turned

272

her attention to the gateway and tried with all her might to push through it. I had reached the top of the mound now and added myself to the effort, seizing hold of Drede Ich Nawhit's mace-hand so that it could not dash out Kel's brains. I lasted for perhaps two heartbeats before a shrug of its arm laid me on the ground.

Morjune, meanwhile, had stepped away from all this broil into the cornerstone. The shield spell, that to us was as solid as a wall, felt to her as she slid through it only like an unpleasant prickling.

You might say that the rest of us – save perhaps for Jill, who still pressed hard against the gateway's empty air – had lost sight of our true purpose. We struggled against Drede Ich Nawhit because it seemed to bar our path, but defeating it would by no means win us ingress. The more important barrier was the shield spell, and it was to the spell's main ingredient that Morjune now introduced herself.

How now, Betheli Theakston, she said. *When I heard you had been invited to the castle I had not thought to find you in such strait lodgings. Let us see how we can go about to set you free.*

She would need to be quick. A hundred strides below us all, Cain Caradoc had reached the bottom of the stairs that wound down inside the mound and was now leading the children across the great cavern to the thing he had once taken for a table. He had learned his error soon enough – but now he felt that the topmost bone of Yaldabaoth's spine would do very well indeed for an altar.

XXXIX

In which Anna claims her birthright

ow many grains of sand make a hill?

My father had asked me that question when I was a child, both to tease and to enlighten me. The riddle is expounded thus. Take one grain of sand away from a hill, and you will not change it. Take another. One grain of sand can never make the difference, so your hill remains as high as ever. Proceed in the same way: remove a grain, and then a grain, and then a grain. What you take away each time is too small to matter, so the hill is safe. But when you take away the final grain, it's gone. At some point in your labours it stopped being a hill, and then it stopped being anything at all. But when did that happen?

I ask this now because in the battle we fought at Pennick Keep it was a matter not of children's riddles but of desperate struggle. Cain Caradoc was mighty, to be sure. We champions who had chosen to go against him were mighty too, but it seemed we were not mighty enough to prevail.

And yet we had one thing yet to hang a hope on. It was a thing we reckoned not, a thing that was like grains of sand, uncounted and small enough to overlook – and to our shame we *had* overlooked them. But then, so had our enemy.

Cain Caradoc scooped up the first of the children in his arms and laid her on his blasphemous altar. It was my cousin Luce he chose, no doubt because she had been so loud before and had insisted on his attention. For better or worse she had it now.

Drawing his dagger from its sheath, Caradoc began to speak the spells that would empower it. Intoning the while, he raised the dagger high in his left hand. With the right he gripped Luce's throat to keep her in place.

Yet as he drew his spell-weave tight around the blade, his concentration suddenly faltered and he stumbled in his recitation. The requisite line was *quomodo haec anima intus inclusa*, but the words skittered away like cockroaches before a candle. Something was pressing on his mind, a throb of pain that seemed many-fingered and pervasive.

I have told you before, I think, that sorcerers remain bound to the spells they make. So it was here. A long way above the cavern and its altar, on the crest of the mound, the villagers of Cosham were pushing with all their might against the invisible wall that Caradoc had placed there. Our Unsung Jill was pushing too, in the very centre of the gateway's arch, but I think in this case – being much more spirit than flesh – she did not add so much to the enterprise. However that may be, the ceaseless press of so many bodies against his spell wall was like a band of iron clamped across Caradoc's forehead. The pain of it scattered his thoughts.

Enraged to be so interrupted, he did his best to collect them again. But Luce had seen his hesitation and judged the moment right for further rebellion. While Caradoc was glaring up at the chamber's ceiling she drew her legs up to her chest. Then when he turned again to bespeak the dagger she kicked out with as much strength as she could bring. She had hoped to catch the wizard in the side of the head, but her reach did not extend so far. She did, though, strike the dagger from out of his hand.

Caradoc's fury spilled over. He gave Luce a ringing slap across the face. The force of the blow was enough to make the back of her head hit the slab of bleached bone on which she lay. Stunned, she could resist no more. But Arran had been striving all this time against the spell of immobility the sorcerer had cast on him. His arms seemed fixed to his sides, but the spell had allowed him to walk before and though it barred him from running away, it still left his legs free to move. When Caradoc bent to retrieve the dagger, the boy kicked it away across the floor.

At once Caradoc drew his spell-wave tighter, freezing Arran and all the others into complete immobility, but he was obliged now to search for the dagger where it had fallen and fetch it back again. It was not so much, you might think, but in this wise the children bought precious seconds, hoping that their rescuers were on the way and the delay might make some difference.

At that moment the hope seemed all forlorn. The spell of the cornerstone still barred our way and Drede Ich Nawhit was climbing to its feet, undaunted by the massive stone block Anna had hurled at it. We could not see a way past either.

But in the cornerstone, Morjune and Betheli were still closeted together, and Morjune was doing what she did best. Both with her magic and with her gentle words she was calming Betheli's tormented spirit and healing the harm her sojourn in the stone had done to her. *You'll be alone no longer*, she promised the girl. *Even if we fail today, I'll not leave you.*

I have not been altogether alone, Betheli said. *I made stories to comfort myself, and the stories became a kind of world I lived in.* Her voice was so thin and so soft Morjune could barely hear her, but it grew stronger as she revived. *Then a goblin came and told me there were spells in here with me, and I set about to find them. So I'm rather too cramped than too lonely. Morjune, if your friends would only free me from this stone, I could do such things!*

They cannot come at the stone because of the spells. You must strive to free yourself, Betheli. I can give you strength and sinew, but the effort must be yours!

Outside, before the empty gateway, I bethought me at last of what I had learned in Hell, and prayed it was not too late to put it in proof. "Kel," I cried, "do you and Jill cope yonder knight.

276

And Peter, let none come by us, for I must talk with Anna or we fail entirely."

Anna was then climbing back up the side of the mound, sprouting spikes and claws and scorpion tails as she came. I met her in the way and would not let her pass.

"There's no time for talk, Once-Was-Willem," she said. "Stand aside now and let me be about!"

"It will do no good, Anna," I said. "But I think this might." I held out the bone-flute for her to take.

She stared at it in consternation. "What have I to do with such a kickshaw?" she asked me.

"It's no kickshaw. It's a thing made from an angel's bone, and fashioned by an angel. A thing that angels used to make the world. But only one who's of their lineage can play it."

"Then why give it to me?" She made to go around me but I scrambled to stay in front of her. "Once-Was-Willem, let me by!" she cried, enraged.

"The angels are such things as you are, Anna!" I told her. "You have their blood. They know of you – of those like you – and call you Nephilim. And they said this flute had the power to make and mar and mend. But look, it has three mouthpieces and three sets of stops. There's none but you has enough mouths and hands to play it!"

There came a crash from above us, and a bellowed curse from Kel, but I dared not look around to see what was towards.

"I've no more music in me than a piss-pot has wine!" Anna shouted. "This is madness!"

"Try it, at least," I said. "Anna, I beg you!"

She had already reached out with two huge arms to lift me and set me aside. Before she could, Unsung Jill rose up of a sudden between us. We did not see her come. Between one breath and the next she was there, and Anna was obliged to turn her head away so as not to look Jill in the eye.

"I saw the one that played that instrument last," she said, her dead voice almost too soft to hear. "He had somewhat of your

277

complexion. You should listen to the boy. Certes if you do not, we go no further."

She looked behind her as she said it, and I followed her glance. Before the gateway Kel was down on his knees, fending with his upraised axe blow after blow from Drede Ich Nawhit's sword and mace. He struck no blows of his own: it was all he could do to ward off the unrelenting attack. Peter was trying to keep Drede Ich Nawhit off balance by shepherding the tempest against him, buffeting him with arrows of rain and fists of wind, but Drede Ich Nawhit paid him little heed.

Jill was gone from our side, as suddenly as she had come, and up on the crest of the mound again. She draped herself over Drede Ich Nawhit like a shroud, slowing his movements as she had done before. Kel was able to scramble to his feet and resume the fight, though his blows still had no effect save to strike sparks off that fearsome armour.

"Please, Anna!" I said again.

Anna drew a deep breath. She looked up at last, her eyes wide and fearful. "I have no cunning for it," she said. But she reached out and took the flute from my hands.

Since it had three mouthpieces, she grew herself two more faces to put to them. My mouth fell open in wonder when I saw them: she looked more than ever like the angels I had met in Hell.

Anna's three faces leaned in closer to each other. She touched the flute to all her lips at once. For a moment no sound came, and I thought I had been wrong after all. But then a skirling note broke upon the air, in much the way day is said to break. I can find no better way to tell it, for it seemed to me that I could see the music as well as hear it.

Except that it was not music yet. It was three separate skeins of sound that wound through the air like banners. They were so slender, and so beautiful! They seemed to thread themselves between the raindrops, as if even water was of too coarse a substance to touch them. Above us the fight still raged, but here on the side of the hill it seemed now to be a world away.

278

Tears fell from Anna's eyes as she played, not of salt water but of blood. She staggered and almost fell as her vast body rippled like the sail of a ship in a strong wind. I had not known what I was asking her. She had angels' blood, yes, but only through her mother. The human half of her must now contend with the raw power of creation that birthed the sun and stars, the souls of men and beasts, the green earth and the fathomless firmament.

XL

And now all things are come to a poise

nd now all things were come to a poise.

In the cornerstone, Betheli Theakston strove with all her might to break free from the bonds Cain Caradoc had laid upon her. Morjune the witch added her own powers to this effort, using her magics both to strengthen Betheli's resolve and to tear at the weave of the wizard's spells. But those spells were strong indeed: though the two ghosts made some headway, it was slow and gruelling work.

Around the unfinished keep the villagers still threw themselves against its invisible walls, to even less avail.

Drede Ich Nawhit tossed back its head, shrugging off Unsung Jill's grip as if she had never been there. With a swing of its sword it shattered Kel's axe, turning the blade at the end of its arc for a sudden, deadly repass.

And under the mound, Cain Caradoc spoke the last word of his spell. Ensorcelled into stillness, Luce had ceased to struggle. She could only watch as the sorcerer raised up the dagger with a self-conscious flourish. Her brother watched too, as did all the other children, unable to lift a finger to intercede, seeing their own fate play out in front of their faces.

It was then that the flute's three notes combined into a single sound of all but unbearable sweetness. Anna felt the air all around her open itself out like the cupboards and drawers in some vast storehouse. We are wont to speak of music in terms of keys, but never did key unlock so vast a treasure.

The flute was a tool designed to assist in the making of the world. And since the world is not one thing but many things, the flute must likewise be many things laced and layered into one. In the music's echoing note it now unfolded and showed itself in all its hugeness and complexity – but to Anna alone.

The moment stretched. All things were stilled, waiting on her leisure. The very raindrops paused in their descent until such time as she gave them leave to fall.

Anna's wonder was so great she almost broke off from her playing, but she knew it was only the music and nothing else that gave her this reprieve. She opened more mouths – one, two, three – and sucked in breath to fill her lungs ever and anon as they emptied so she could maintain the note. She played a *bourdon*, a drone, the while her spirit ranged through the ethereal implements the bone-flute now displayed to her.

I cannot describe the tools the angels use. I did not see them, and am not like to do so. They were not made of the same stuff the world is made from, or of anything a human hand or human mind could grasp. They were strange beyond measure, and yet they had been fashioned with such skill that to look upon them was to feel their several purposes pressing all at once upon your understanding.

The effect was dizzying. Anna could not sort what she needed from what she did not, what was great from what was small, what was fine and delicate from what was blunt and mighty. But some of the tools came more readily to hand than others: it is oftentimes hard to make and to mend, but marring takes no great skill at all. *Very well*, Anna thought. *Very well indeed. I will go about to mar, then!*

She marred Cain Caradoc's magics, sending forth from the flute a skirling shriek as harsh as the crack of a whip. It tore through

281

the air, poorly aimed but terrifically potent. It hit Drede Ich Nawhit, who stood full in its path. The spells that had made it – and there were many – began at once to unravel. The armour that covered it from head to foot shrivelled and boiled away like snow thrown on a griddle. Kel did not know what was happening, but he saw that his enemy, invincible up to then, was now exposed. He took the head of his shattered axe in his two hands and thrust it forward, burying it deep in Drede Ich Nawhit's chest.

Or rather in my chest, for Drede Ich Nawhit was no more than a shell animated by the piece of my spirit that Cain Caradoc had taken from me. It felt as though my heart had exploded. I opened my mouth to scream, but my breath went out of me too quickly. I fell without a sound.

And still the music went on. It tried to enter the keep and the mound below it, where Caradoc was weaving magic even then. Finding the shield spell in its path it swerved aside, feeling its way along the edges of that barrier until it came at last to the spell's source.

It focused on the cornerstone. The high, shrieking note ranged all across the outer surface of the stone until it cracked across – and a moment later shivered into a thousand pieces.

Betheli, suddenly free, sped at once towards the man she hated, led unerringly down and inward by the magic that had previously bound her. Morjune stayed at her side, pouring strength and fire and will into her as she went.

In the chamber below the mound, Cain Caradoc's hand, stayed for a few moments when the flute first sounded and time unwound itself, now descended in a rush towards Luce's heart.

It did not touch her. The blade broke in Caradoc's hand, so suddenly that his hand, continuing on, gashed itself against the jagged edge of it. He cried out in pain and rage – and then in stupefaction as he saw what stood between him and the girl that should have been his prey. Two ghosts, girls themselves, with their arms thrown wide. Between their outstretched fingers glittered what was left of his own shield spell.

On that day of wonders, this little wonder went almost unnoticed. Betheli had salvaged a little of the shield from the flute's wave of unmaking and brought it with her to frustrate Caradoc's will at the last.

He struck at her again and again. Blood from his torn hand smeared the shield's invisible surface, but he could not break through. His will had been usurped – by the girl that same hand had slain.

Great though his shock and chagrin was, worse came quickly at its heels. He felt his sinews weaken and his heart skip. Staring at his bleeding hand, which still clutched the hilt of the shattered knife, he saw his flesh bleach and sag and blossom with liver spots. The flute's note, echoing on, was now assailing the magics that sustained his body. He had lived on far beyond the span promised to humankind by turning the souls of children into fuel to stoke the furnace of his power. But the furnace guttered now, and the withering years long held at bay by its heat came all in a rush to claim him.

Up above, on the mound, the invisible wall that had held back the clamouring villagers was of a sudden no longer there. They rushed – those that fell not on their faces – headlong into the keep, but of course they found it empty and their enemy nowhere to be found.

Unsung Jill passed through them like a cold wind. She knew full well what the mound was and she had a better sense than any of us what Caradoc purposed to do there. She found the trapdoor and prepared to set her will against it, but the wave of Anna's music passed her by and dispelled at once the magical wards that protected it. Jill tore the trap from its hinges and flung it away, then was gone from sight in an instant.

I do not say: from *my* sight. I saw none of this. I had fallen to my knees on the side of the mound, and then forward onto my face. I was dying again, or felt I was, as the lifeblood poured from what was left of Drede Ich Nawhit's body. My spirit being a part of that sad and fearful creature, it seemed we must perforce share a single death.

But the others saw where Jill went, and Kel followed straight after her. Peter lingered behind, for there was enough of a roof on the keep to fend off the rain and he could not go where it was dry.

Down in the chamber, feeling his strength pouring out of him like flour from a burst sack, Cain Caradoc saw the moment of his glory and fulfilment pass away from him, and made a desperate choice. It might kill him, but since he was dying already he had little to lose. And the prophecy had promised him that his project would succeed. He would achieve his goals and become immortal. It was intolerable that he should come so close and yet fail.

Gathering what was left of his might and his magic, he reached out, as he had done the first time ever he stood in that chamber, and joined his spirit directly with that of Yaldabaoth the sleeper. The first time he had done this he had felt like a leaf in a torrent, buffeted and beaten down by the Elohim's almost limitless power. This time at least he knew what to expect and was able to brace himself.

The trick, he realised, was to *use* the power as quickly as it came. The torrent hit him all alike, but he sent it onwards. He threw it against the skein of Anna's music with reckless force and in reckless abundance. Up on the mound Anna was checked. The bone-flute shattered in her hands as the great wave hit her with all the force of an earthquake. For all her might and mass, she was thrown backwards through the air like a rag doll. She landed hard and did not move.

Cain Caradoc was now experiencing what Anna herself had felt erewhile. As before, something of the Elohim's thoughts and perceptions came along with its power. Time and space and all possible and conceivable things reconfigured themselves around him – took him as their centre, arrayed themselves before him like vassals before their king. He felt himself rise up, though he did not move at all. He rose towards a spiritual height, a height that could only be called omnipotence. Perhaps it fell just a little way short of that eminence which is God's alone, but certes it

284

was high enough. Cain Caradoc laughed incredulously, his eyes wide with wonder.

Before those wide eyes, in that same instant, rose Unsung Jill. She stared into the sorcerer's face, and he stared back – into her green gaze, and her red gaze.

The ruin that took him was one that had been prepared for him at the very dawn of time, when Yaldabaoth first dreamed the world. Kel came sprinting down the stairs into the chamber a few moments later, but still he came too late to see what passed. Cain Caradoc was gone from the world. Nothing remained of him but a sulphurous smell and the echo of a scream.

XLI

In which Cain Caradoc achieves his dearest wish

nce more I am come to a thing I cannot well describe. It was a strange wonder, and I did not see it with my own eyes. I can only tell you what Luce saw, for she told it later, and what Unsung Jill revealed later still to the ears of the seven alone.

To take Luce's account first, she said that after meeting the gaze of "the tall and terrible woman" the sorcerer seemed to draw in on himself. He became thinner, as if he were being stretched on a rack. His face, the while she could still see it, was full of fear and dismay, but she did not see it for long. In the space of three breaths, or perhaps four, Caradoc was pulled out so tight and so slender that it seemed he became a kind of rope or yarn, and then the finest of threads, and by and by too thin to see at all. "I don't think he'd gone, though," Luce told her listeners. "Or not all of him. He was screaming, you see. And all the while he was getting thinner and thinner the scream was getting higher and higher, but when I stopped seeing him I could still hear the scream – the way you can hear bats when they fly over you at night and it's so high a sound it's almost not a sound at all. He went on screaming like that for a very long time. He was still screaming when we went up out of the cave, and when we left the castle. I think he might be screaming yet."

What Jill said was this: Cain Caradoc looked into her red eye. Hell took hold on him, and he fell. But at the same time, being anchored in Yaldabaoth who was fixed and immovable, he stayed where he was. "He has no say in which of those things he obeys. He obeys both. He falls, and he stands. And as Once-Was-Willem can attest, he falls and stands not in time but in eternity. The stretching out and sundering of his soul will never be accomplished, for to finish either one would exclude and efface the other."

"Is he alive," Anna asked, "or is he dead? Just tell me that."

"The question has no meaningful answer, Anna Kjetil's daughter. It is as if a man should stand hidden behind a curtain, and you should thrust a sword through the cloth in the place where you think he is most likely to be. Is he alive, or is he dead? Until you draw back the curtain you cannot know. And in this instance the curtain stands forever out of your reach."

For my part I think this: Cain Caradoc sought immortality and the prophecy promised him he would find it. I believe he lives still, plummeting through the endlessness of the abyss while at the same time he is pent within the dreaming skull of Yaldabaoth. Moreover, I believe it was for this purpose and this purpose alone that Unsung Jill was given her Hell-gaze in the first place. The Elohim see all time as clearly as you can see the lines on your own hand. Yaldabaoth, before he sank into his dreams which are our world, saw Cain Caradoc's approach across the centuries and forestalled him by putting Jill in his way.

Or as it might be, by putting all seven of us in his way. I do not deceive myself that only Jill out of all of us was the angel's unwitting instrument. I think we all were, even Anna who was his living kin.

At least, I think this was so up to the moment when Cain Caradoc fell. That after all was the end towards which the Elohim must have been working – and not because the children's lives were in danger but because the world was. If Caradoc had stolen

Yaldabaoth's power it is unlikely that he would have made a good steward for the world he thus inherited.

But howsoever we were conscripted into the sleeper's cause, once the threat was dealt with and he was safe again in his slumbers, providence no longer had a plan for us. We were free again to go our ways, to be and do what we wished. Those of us already dead were somewhat circumscribed in their choices, to be sure, but such as they were we were free to make them.

Anna lay at the foot of the mound, hurt unto death. Cain Caradoc's final sally had torn and savaged her within and without, breaking her bones and bursting her innards. The remains of the flute lay in orts and fragments all around her in the dirt of the bailey yard, onto which her blood was gouting from many wounds.

Through bleared and failing eyes Anna saw me, or what was left of me, lying close beside her. When Kel's axe buried itself in Drede Ich Nawhit's chest, the little paring of me that had animated it took most of the hurt and communicated it straightway to me. I do not pretend to understand how such things work, but that paring seemed in some way to be inwoven with the spell that had haled me up from my grave. I was not dying, being already dead, but I was returning to the state in which the spell had first found me. I was becoming a broth of liquid flesh and a scatter of bones.

The bones, Anna told me later, were what gave her to see what must be done.

I had told her she was of the lineage of angels, and she had seen the proof of it when the bone-flute obeyed her will. And the bone-flute derived its power from its maker, having been fashioned by him out of his own substance to shape the world. The music it played was a magic a thousand times purer than any spell Cain Caradoc had ever scraped together.

In the normal course of things, the bones of angels are hard to come by. But Anna was herself of the lineage of angels, so it might be that she already had within her own person what was needful. At any rate she saw no harm in trying. She opened her many mouths and began to hum – the self-same notes Yaldabaoth's flute had made when she bent herself to play it.

She had but little breath to do it, and she did it through the bitter taste of her own blood. She was using up the last of her strength, with only the smallest inkling, the barest hope of what might come of it.

As before, the notes stayed for a few moments entirely separate and distinct. Then they twisted themselves together into one sound, and her naked will once more met the naked world.

She began with herself, since all else depended on her surviving. She knitted her bones back together, sealed her wounds shut, and restored to their wonted shape and function all the parts of her that had been hurt.

Then she did the same for me. She might have done what Cain Caradoc's spell had failed to do and made me boy again, but she only took me back to what she thought of as my true self, which was the monster she had met on the mountain.

Anna did not stop there. She opened more mouths, both to breathe and to sing. Three voices became six, a dozen, a hundred, a chorus whose unearthly harmonies filled not just the air but everything there was. When the music reached Morjune and Betheli down in the cavern they felt themselves for a moment startlingly heavy, as if leaden weights had been appended to their limbs. When the feeling passed they found that they were no longer unhoused spirits but living girls.

When the tune reached Jill she paused like one entranced, and a single tear rolled down her cheek. The tear was red, and it carried away the mote of Hell that had stuck fast in her eye so long ago.

Anna would have gone on for ever, letting her music run on through earth and air and the thoughts of men, setting right all things that were awry. But she remembered the words that Morjune Scour had said to her once on Cosham green, when she made to hang Jem Makepeace: *the pain that matters is the pain that's willed.* And if that's true of a penance then how much more true must it be of a blessing? She could mend the whole world, but only by changing the hearts of them that lived in it, overwriting their will with her own. It would not do. They must find their own way to happiness, or to whatever other end they chose. She would not make them her contented slaves.

XLII

The end of the seven

I am all but done.

The children were brought home to Cosham. At their head came Betheli Theakston, carried on the shoulders of her three brothers. In truth she felt strong enough to run the whole distance, but she did not wish to take away from their triumph.

Morjune Scour was not in their number, though. By this time the children had told the story of how she and Betheli came at the last moment to save them, and there is no doubt she would have been welcome, but she was chary of placing herself again in the power of the people who had killed her once before. When they looked for her – and I assure you they searched with great diligence – she was nowhere to be found.

Morjune had said that penance must be willingly undertaken. The villagers of Cosham, urged onto it by Parson Lebone, set about to make such amends to their murdered healer as they could. They cleaned her cottage inside and out, replaced the broken furniture with the best of their own, took away the shutters from the windows and put fresh thatch on the roof. It was as if they were building a pretty box for swallows to nest in. But the nest remained empty.

Some days later the seven of us met on the slopes of the mountain.

291

It was not a chance meeting. Anna had sought out every one of us and made us promise in the most earnest terms that we would come. When we were all gathered, and seated at our ease around a fire she had made, she told us why: it was to say goodbye.

"Having learned for the first time what I am," she said, "I feel I need to meet my aunts and uncles and aunt-uncles and see what kind of a family has been wished upon me."

Betheli clapped her hand to her mouth in shock. "You're going to Hell?" she exclaimed. "Like Willem did?"

"She is," Kel said. "And I'm going with her. Anna followed me into the lists of war. Family reunions are only a little worse."

"And since I know from Once-Was-Willem that the going is easier than the coming back," Anna went on, "I wanted to see you all one last time. We fought together, we seven, and it was a hard fight. I love you all for the sake of what we shared. And if I can do you any service before I leave, be it to hale the sun out of the sky or make the stars to spell out your names, say it now."

For a long time nobody said anything at all. It seemed we were full of feelings that could not easily be unpacked in words.

"I would have asked you to heal my sickness," Betheli ventured at last, "only I know you did it without me asking – for before I died I was mostly too weak to stand, and now I can outrun any of my three brothers. You've given me so much already, Anna, I'd be shent to ask for more."

"And I," said Unsung Jill, in her voice of knife on whetstone. "Two gifts you've given me, changer. You took the red mote from out of my eye, which was much. But now you say you love me, and I think that may be more – for I was ever hated and I hated all in my turn. Love is not something I looked to have. Like the girl, I have no further boon to beg."

"There's nothing I need either," Peter Floodfoot said. "Only good friends and good tales – and now I have a fullness of both."

Morjune laughed. "It falls to me to be selfish then," she said, hanging her head in a semblance of shame. "I have a favour to ask, and it's not a small one."

"At last!" Anna said. "Go to, Mistress Scour. What would you of me?"

"I'd like you to finish the work that was started at Pennick."

Anna could not hide her surprise. "Rebuild the castle? Why?"

This time Morjune's blush was real. "Not all of the castle. Just the keep. I stayed up there when everyone went away and I've been living there since. I like the view, and the sweetness of the air. I don't mind if you make it smaller than it was, Anna. It's only that I'd like to have a place to bide – and since I love these lands I'd as lief not remove too far from them.

"Parson Lebone when he found me at last begged me to come back to Cosham. He said I'd be honoured there, and given every comfort. My own house back. My old employment. A yearling share of flour and potatoes. But I find I can't look on that prospect with any joy. My neighbours would be those that burned me, and though they've asked my pardon and I've given it I fear I'd find little ease in their company. Pennick Keep would suit me better. I could still go into the village if I was needed to work a healing. In fact I could serve all the villages of the fief. But if they had a mind to burn me again I'd have my own fortress to fall back on."

"Would you want all the keep to yourself?" I asked her. "Or could you bear to share it?"

Morjune gave me a smile as warm as the sun at noon-day. "The next thing I meant to do was invite you, Once-Was-Willem," she said. "All of you, I mean. There'd be room enough for everyone to come whenever they wanted to. Peter, you could live in the well – or if that was too strait for you, still you could visit as often as you liked. And if the seven were ever needed again, the keep would be a place where people could come and find us, and ask for our help." She ran out of words, and cast her gaze somewhat nervously at Anna. "Such was my thinking, at all events. But . . . if it's too much . . ."

"It's not," said Anna, leaning over to kiss Morjune on her cheek. "It's the best plan I ever heard. And it has this merit too, that Kel and I will be able to find you when we return from Hell. It will

293

be good to know that we've somewhere to rest among friendly faces. That thought will give us great cheer, especially if the road turns out to be long."

Morjune clapped her hands together. "You'll do it, then?" she asked.

"I'll undertake it before ever we rise from this fireside." Anna turned to me. "But that leaves one more," she said. "Once-Was-Willem, is there aught you'd ask of me? I could bring you back to what you were before your death, if that's a thing you'd like."

I shook my head. "It's not, Anna," I said. "I could not imagine swapping this second life for that first one. I'm too much monster now to be happy as a boy again. And who would trade a place in the seven for a plot of land in Cosham village?"

Anna sighed. "Nothing, then? It's no easy thing, this gift-giving. I know now why the three kings in the story did such a poor job of it."

"No," I said, "there is one thing."

XLIII

ive me this, I said.

Teach me how to read and how to write. Instruct me in my letters, both to know them when I see them and to copy them in good form.

Give me pen and ink and parchment, and enough of space and leisure to set down what we did at Cosham and at Pennick. Grant me the skill to part the mists of time and to peer into other people's hearts, not for ever but for so long as it takes for me to verify every detail and to make sure I do not mistake me even in the smallest particular.

I will call it *The Story of the Seven*, and when it's done I will give it to Parson Lebone to keep with all his other books in Cosham kirk. But he will only hold it in trust for the children of the village, and if any ask he must read it aloud to them. Even if he has a sermon to write or a mass to deliver he must straightway take down the book and recite it from first to last, for the telling of it belongs to those children as much as it does to us.

And perhaps, in the fullness of time, copies might be made by a scribe of trusted probity to be distributed to other villages in fiefdoms far distant from Pennick. It might even be transcribed into foreign tongues and sent to nations whose names and customs

I know not. For there are many besides the children of Cosham who bide the cruelty and arbitrary will of those with great power and meagre conscience. It is not unlikely that there will come a time and a confluence of events where we seven might usefully offer our service.

Our lives are stories when we live them, and they are stories again when they are remembered. Let any broach this tale and lo, at once we take our places once more just as we did the first time. We find each other again. We fight again, and suffer, and prevail.

If you need us, the last line will say, come and find us.

About the author

M. R. Carey has been making up stories for most of his life. His novel *The Girl With All the Gifts* has sold over a million copies and became a major motion picture, based on his own BAFTA Award-nominated screenplay. Under the name Mike Carey he has written for both DC and Marvel, including critically acclaimed runs on *Lucifer*, *Hellblazer* and *X-Men*. His creator-owned books regularly appear in the *New York Times* bestseller list. He also has several previous novels including the Felix Castor series (written as Mike Carey), two radio plays and a number of TV and movie screenplays to his credit.

Fine out more about M. R. Carey and other Orbit authors by registering for the free monthly newsletter at orbit-books.co.uk.

Help us make the next generation of readers

We – both author and publisher – hope you enjoyed this book.
We believe that you can become a reader at any time in your life,
but we'd love your help to give the next generation a head start.

Did you know that 9% of children don't have a book of their
own in their home, rising to 12% in disadvantaged families*?
We'd like to try to change that by asking you to consider the role
you could play in helping to build readers of the future.

We'd love you to think of sharing, borrowing, reading, buying or talking
about a book with a child in your life and spreading the love of reading.
We want to make sure the next generation continue to have access
to books, wherever they come from.

And if you would like to consider donating to charities that help
fund literacy projects, find out more at www.literacytrust.org.uk
and www.booktrust.org.uk.

Thank you.

 hachette
CHILDREN'S GROUP

little, brown
BOOK GROUP

*As reported by the National Literacy Trust